THE
BURIED
PYRAMID

TOR BOOKS BY JANE LINDSKOLD

Through Wolf's Eyes
Wolf's Head, Wolf's Heart
The Dragon of Despair
The Buried Pyramid

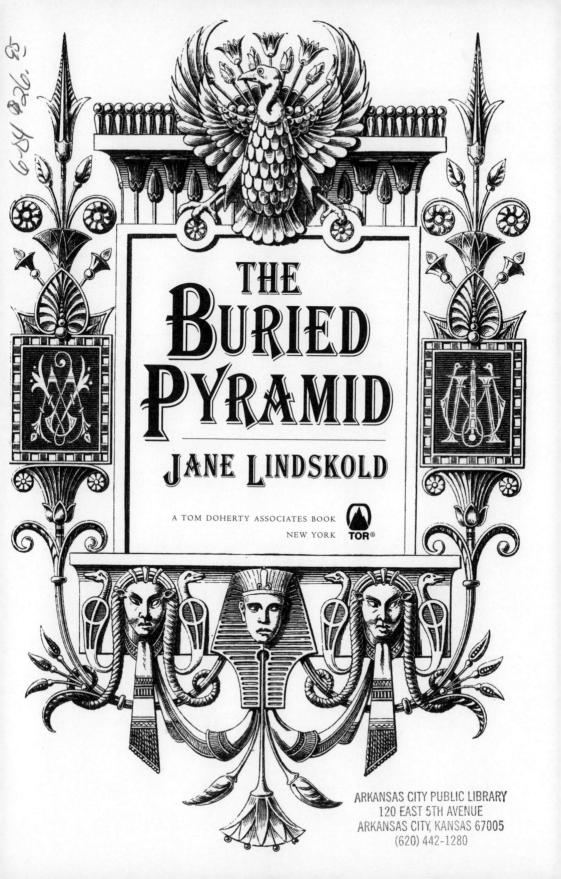

THE
BURIED
PYRAMID

JANE LINDSKOLD

A TOM DOHERTY ASSOCIATES BOOK

NEW YORK

THE BURIED PYRAMID

Copyright © 2004 by Jane Lindskold

Book design by Milenda Nan Ok Lee

Interior illustrations by Edward Murr

Edited by Teresa Nielsen Hayden

This book is printed on acid-free paper.

A Tor Book
Published by Tom Doherty Associates, LLC
175 Fifth Avenue
New York, NY 10010

www.tor.com

Tor® is a registered trademark of Tom Doherty Associates, LLC.

Library of Congress Cataloging-in-Publication Data

Lindskold, Jane M.
    The buried pyramid / Jane Lindskold.—1st ed.
      p. cm.
    "A Tom Doherty Associates book."
    ISBN 0-765-30260-8
    EAN 978-0765-30260-1
    1. Excavations (Archaeology)—Fiction. 2. Americans—Egypt—Fiction. 3. British—Egypt—Fiction.
4. Archaeologists—Fiction. 5. Egyptologists—Fiction. 6. Conspiracies—Fiction. 7. Young women—Fiction.
8. Pyramids—Fiction. 9. Egypt—Fiction. I. Title.

PS3562.I51248B87 2004
813'.54—dc22

                                      2003071133

First Edition: May 2004

Printed in the United States of America

0 9 8 7 6 5 4 3 2 1

For Jim, my favorite archeologist:
Indiana Jones could only hope to be as exciting as you are.

And . . .

For Kay McCauley:
Thanks for believing.

ACKNOWLEDGMENTS

I'd like to extend my thanks to a few of the many people who made their resources and knowledge available to me while I worked on this novel. My husband, Jim Moore, offered advice on weaponry, as well as his usual irreplaceable assistance as first reader and sounding board. Pati (P. G.) Nagel shared information about period steamboats and attire. John Miller and Gail Gerstner Miller loaned me period travel material and works on Egyptian magic. The staff at the Taylor Ranch Branch of the Albuquerque Public Library provided assistance tracking down works I wouldn't have been able to find otherwise.

Yvonne Coats and Sally Gwylan both read earlier drafts of the novel and offered some cogent comments. My editor, Teresa Nielsen Hayden, offered numerous comments and an ear for period diction.

A special service was provided by the folks at Tekno Books, who gave me an excuse to investigate the background of this novel in "Beneath the Eye of the Hawk," which appears here in slightly altered form following its debut in *Pharaoh Fantastic*, edited by Martin H. Greenberg and Brittany A. Koren.

Profound thanks go to my agent, Kay McCauley, who wouldn't give up on this project, even when I might have done so. Thanks, Kay. You're a trump.

For those of you who are interested in this book or other of my projects, I can be contacted through my Web site at janelindskold.com.

CONTENTS

THE BURIED PYRAMID

Beneath the Eye of the Hawk

TWISTING AROUND on his galloping camel and glimpsing the pursuing Bedouin resolving into form within the dust cloud stirred to life by their own pounding mounts, Neville Hawthorne spared precious breath to curse the day Alphonse Liebermann had come to Egypt.

"Alphonse Liebermann is a cousin of Prince Albert," Colonel Reginald Sedgewick explained to the tall, broad-shouldered man standing in front of his desk. "A German, of course. Something of an archeologist and theologian."

Colonel Sedgewick smiled rather deprecatingly.

"Or rather I should say Herr Liebermann fancies himself an archeologist and theologian. If my reports are correct, he is a hobbyist more than anything else."

Neville Hawthorne, captain in Her Majesty Queen Victoria's army and currently assigned to the diplomatic presence in Egypt, didn't permit his lips to twitch in even the faintest of smiles. He knew such wouldn't be appreciated.

Colonel Sedgewick—in civilian life a lord and knight—might feel free to comment on the foibles of his social betters, but Lord Reginald Sedgewick did not think his junior officers—at least those without honor or title—should share that privilege.

Indeed, there were times, Neville mused, that Sedgewick probably thought that those without appropriate social rank and fortune shouldn't be permitted to hold officer's commissions. However, snob or not, Sedgewick recognized talent and ability. It was for both of these qualities that he had summoned Captain Hawthorne to him.

"As a courtesy to our queen's German relations, I'm assigning you to be a nursemaid to Herr Liebermann. Won't call it that, of course. Aide. Bodyguard and translator. Liebermann will need the latter. Understand he doesn't have much in the way of Arabic, though he's fairly fluent in French."

Neville Hawthorne nodded, hiding his sudden interest behind a properly impassive face. Fluency in French was not only useful but necessary in some circles of Egyptian society. France, like England, had numerous interests in Egypt. Indeed, despite—or in some cases because of—the reforms instituted by Muhammad Ali and continued with more or less enthusiasm by his heirs, French remained an important language in both Egyptian society and government.

What tantalized Captain Hawthorne was that his commander had singled out Arabic from the slew of languages spoken in modern Egypt—Armenian, Greek, Coptic, and Turkish, in addition to English and French.

Most Europeans didn't have much Arabic. Nor did they need it. Even if this cousin of Prince Albert's was interested in archeology and theology, he could research to his heart's content without ever speaking a word to the Arab population. Indeed, the majority of archeological matters were still administered by the French.

"Then Herr Liebermann wishes to travel outside of the usual areas, sir?" Neville asked.

Colonel Sedgewick nodded, his eyes narrowing appreciatively as he reconstructed the course of deductive reasoning through which his subordinate had reached this conclusion.

"That's right," he said, glancing down at a letter on his desk. "Says here that Herr Liebermann wants to do some desert exploration. That's why he needs you to ease the way for him. Wouldn't be necessary if he were staying on the usual tourist routes."

"Very good, sir," Hawthorne replied. "When do I meet Herr Liebermann?"

"He arrives in Cairo two days from today."

A stack of papers, including Liebermann's original letter, was pushed across the desk, and Neville gathered them up. He was careful to not so much as glance at the documents until his commander had finished speaking.

"To enable you to be at Herr Liebermann's disposal at all hours, you're to put up at whatever hotel he chooses. If he has no preference, use Shepheard's. My clerk will have expense vouchers for you. Make reservations, just in case."

"And my staff, sir?"

Colonel Sedgewick looked momentarily irritated, obviously thinking that Captain Hawthorne should be thanking him for his generosity. Then he reconsidered.

"Yes. I suppose if Prince Albert's cousin wants to go out in the desert, you'll need help. You can hire natives to handle the baggage and camels, but I'll give you a sergeant to wrangle the lot. Any preferences?"

"Sergeant Bryce, sir. Edward Bryce. He knows Egypt well, speaks Arabic, and has a way with the natives."

"Bryce . . ."

Sedgewick frowned. Captain Hawthorne held his breath.

"Wasn't Bryce just brought up for something?"

"Disorderly conduct, sir," Neville replied stiffly. "Drinking. Brawling."

Whatever Reginald Sedgewick's snobbery regarding the proper social class from which commissioned officers should be drawn, he was also a seasoned veteran and no great advocate of the stricter discipline some of his colleagues tried to enforce off the field.

He snorted.

"Disrespect to officers?"

"No, sir. Bryce took exception to how a lady was being treated. Got into a fight."

"Did he win?"

"Yes, sir, but he'd had a bit too much, got rather battered, and consequently was late getting back to quarters. His uniform was wrecked. Officer on duty wrote him up."

Colonel Sedgewick shook his head in disbelief.

"You can have Bryce. If anyone protests that he's being rewarded with soft duty for unbecoming behavior, send them to me. I'll tell them a few hard truths about just how soft a bed of desert sand actually is."

Alphonse Liebermann proved to be short, wiry, and somewhere into his fifth decade. Bald as an egg, he sported the most magnificent eyebrows Neville had ever seen— bushy, even sweeping grey specimens that leapt to punctuate their owner's every exclamation. They completely intimidated the German's perfectly unexceptional mustache and, indeed, made it hard for one to remember that he had any other features at all.

Liebermann was accompanied by one servant: Derek Schmidt, a tall, thin man with bristle-cut greying hair. Schmidt possessed a soldier's erect posture and a distinct limp that showed why he was no longer in active service. He had taken charge of the baggage with such efficiency that Neville had been unsurprised to learn later that Schmidt had begun his career in the Prussian equivalent of the quartermaster corps.

"I have a secret, Neville," Alphonse Liebermann confided several days after their initial meeting. He kept his voice low, and his English was so heavily accented that the phrase sounded rather like "I haff'a secret."

Neville Hawthorne nodded, not certain how to respond to this strange confidence. However, he liked the little man—who had insisted immediately they place themselves on a first name basis—so he replied encouragingly,

"I'm not at all surprised, Alphonse."

Neville had not needed to be a great genius to figure this out. In the first few days since he'd arrived in Egypt, Herr Liebermann's actions had been focused and purposeful. He had avoided all the usual tourist attractions—although he had looked longingly toward where the Pyramids at Gizeh created a magnificent backdrop for the modern city.

When Neville had offered to arrange for Alphonse to take a tour, the German had shaken his head determinedly.

"No. That will not be necessary. I have seen the Great Pyramids before. I have more important tasks to perform than visiting them again."

His tone had held portents of grand deeds to come, and Neville was reminded of it now as Alphonse continued speaking.

"I am preparing to make," Alphonse said, "a discovery that will set my name in the pantheon of archeology, alongside Winckelmann, Belzoni, and Lepsius. I have finished my preparations here in Cairo. You have our tickets?"

"I do," Neville said. "Tickets for a steamer to Luxor. From there we will change to a dahabeeyah. Sergeant Bryce has gone ahead to make arrangements for camels and a few native servants."

"Very good." Alphonse returned to his prior topic of conversation. "Neville, mine will be a landmark discovery. It will make a turnover of archeology, reveal things about not only the days of the pharaohs, but about our entire conception of reality—about the relationship of gods to men."

Neville nodded, trying to match Liebermann's serious intensity. It was difficult. This crazed German seemed so like something out of a stage play that bouncy music hall tunes kept playing across Neville's inner ear.

For a fleeting moment Neville wondered how Prince Albert's family actually felt about this cousin. Perhaps Alphonse was an embarrassment. Perhaps he was supposed to get lost in the desert. Maybe that was why Neville had been picked for this honorable duty rather than one of Lord Sedgewick's more socially advantaged cronies.

Alphonse lowered his voice still further, "When we are away from Cairo, then I will confide in you what—and who—we are seeking. For now, I do not wish attention drawn to us. Would it be too much trouble for you and Sergeant Bryce to wear civilian clothing?"

Neville cocked an eyebrow, but forbore requesting clarification.

"It will be no problem at all."

On their first evening aboard the steamer, Alphonse invited Neville to his cabin for brandy and cigars.

Although the weather on deck was pleasant, and several of the young ladies taking the cruise were not nearly as snobbish as Colonel Sedgewick, Neville reported to the German's spacious stateroom. He was unsurprised to find Alphonse poring over a sheaf of closely written pages.

"Captain Hawthorne," Alphonse said with more formality than he had shown since his arrival, "please, be seated. My great thanks for your coming to me. I have given Schmidt the evening off so we may speak in confidence."

Neville nodded, accepted the brandy offered, declined a cigar, and leaned back in the well-upholstered chair Alphonse indicated. He'd had a heavy dinner, and the rhythmic thumping of the ship's engines threatened to put him to sleep.

"In Cairo, I told you I had a secret," Alphonse began. "Now I will reveal this secret to you. You will become the second European alive—or so I believe—to know a great mystery."

"I am honored," Neville said and hoped that his suppressed laughter would be taken for British stuffiness.

"Very good."

Alphonse swirled the brandy in his snifter and settled himself more deeply into his chair. Although he kept his notes spread near, he never once consulted them. Clearly this was a tale he knew by heart.

"Some years ago," Alphonse said, "when I am doing research into the historicity of Moses, I hear an amazing tale from a Bedouin rug merchant."

"Wait," Neville said, raising an inquiring finger. "I thought you didn't speak Arabic."

"I do not," Alphonse said cheerfully, "but this merchant spoke French. Now, I must tell you that I do not think I was meant to hear this tale. The Bedouin was very old, and when I asked him about Moses, calling him 'the Lawgiver,' the Arab began to speak of another lawgiver, one from long ago. His lawgiver was a pharaoh named Neferankhotep. This name means 'Gift of a Beautiful Life.'"

Or "complete" or "perfect," Neville thought. He didn't read hieroglyphs, but he had worked his way through some of the modern commentaries and found the material fascinating.

"Now, even in ancient times," Alphonse continued, "Egypt possessed an excellent legal system, one that—in theory—protected the commoner on equal terms with the highest noble."

Alphonse grimaced, those amazing eyebrows lowering then rising once more.

"But, Neville, we know that theory and practice are very different. In practice, those with title and property are treated far better than the peasants who have little or nothing."

"True enough," Neville replied a trace sourly, "even today."

Alphonse's gaze was so penetrating and sympathetic that Neville was embarrassed at his own petty grievances.

"But not when Neferankhotep reigned," Alphonse went on, waggling an admonishing finger. "When this good pharaoh reigned there was perfect justice, such perfect justice that all his people loved him. They wished that his mortuary complex would be finer than any pharaoh had ever known. The good Neferankhotep would not have this.

"He indicated an outlying valley, far from the fertile lands and said, 'Give me only a simple rock tomb, make my shabti figures from clay, my amulets from common stones. If these charms and honors are enough to serve my people in the afterlife, then they will be sufficient for me.'"

Guess we won't make our fortunes in gold and precious stones, then, Neville thought and poured himself a touch more brandy.

Alphonse's voice fell into a sing-song, storytelling mode in which his German accent became oddly, pervasively musical.

"Eventually, Neferankhotep's life upon the earth ended. The mortuary priests immediately began the arduous process of embalming the pharaoh's mortal remains. On the very day that they began their work, a terrible sandstorm arose in the humble valley wherein the pharaoh had requested he be entombed. Watchers claimed that they could see towering forms moving purposefully within the clouds of sand and grit. The sandstorm raged with unabated fury until the very day that Neferankhotep's body was ready for burial. Then, as the last seal was set upon his sarcophagus, the storm vanished.

"Within the once barren valley stood the most magnificent pyramid that anyone had ever seen, complete with a complex of temples, chapels, and long avenues of guardian beasts. The decorations on the buildings and on the sarcophagus that awaited the pharaoh's mummy were of gold, silver, electrum, and precious stones, more and richer than had ever been seen before. Magnificent alabaster statues, one representing each of the myriad gods and goddesses of ancient Egypt, stood silent watch over the compound.

"The message from the gods was clear. Therefore, here in this complex crafted by the hands of his sibling gods who loved him, Neferankhotep was entombed. A community of priests was established to watch over the pharaoh's sacred person and to offer sacrifices at the appropriate times.

"All proceeded in honor and grace for many years, then thieves—some say greedy or jealous priests—attempted to loot Neferankhotep's pyramid. They did not manage more than to cross the threshold. As they made their nefarious intent clear, an enormous sandstorm arose from nowhere, although elsewhere the day remained still and clear. For seven days and seven nights the storm raged, a red glow as of divine fury at its heart. When it died away, the entire compound had vanished.

"What remained was an empty valley. Towering statues of the greatest Egyptian gods, armed as for war, stood at the four cardinal points. A warning against future desecration was deeply etched into the cliffs surrounding the valley. From that day forth, the Valley of Dust—for so it came to be called—has been a shunned and sacred place, although rumor says that there are those who, to this day, are sworn to protect its treasures."

Herr Liebermann concluded by bowing his head in a manner that would have seemed affected had it not been clear that he was deeply moved by what he had just related. Neville didn't want to admit the truth, not even to himself, but he too had been swept up in the tale.

Therefore, Neville forced himself to sound casual as he asked, "So, can I take it that you have a line on this Valley of Dust?"

"I believe I do," Alphonse said dryly. "Would you bear with me through another tale?"

Neville reached for the brandy and poured himself a touch. "I would listen in fascination," he said.

Alphonse accepted the unspoken apology, swirled his own brandy once more, and began.

"The tale of Neferankhotep was very interesting to me, even more so when I realized that I was apparently alone in having heard it. True, archeologists have not translated all the texts, even from those tombs and temples they have found, but it seemed to me that I had come across something wonderful and unique. I began to research the sources of the tale, actively soliciting traveler's accounts and legends, looking for any hint that might lead me to Neferankhotep and the Valley of Dust. For a long time, I met with little success.

"Then one day a tightly wrapped package was left for me at my hotel. All the concierge could tell me was that it had been left by a woman, a desert Arab, or so he thought. He said she had asked in very bad French if this was where the German gentleman who was collecting legends was staying. When the concierge had confirmed this, she insisted on leaving the package. The concierge thought she seemed nervous. We were both surprised that she had left no way to contact her, for surely she expected payment.

"I thought about seeking the woman, but how to tell one woman from so many? I decided that she would return in her own time, perhaps after I had an opportunity to inspect her offering and would be more prepared to pay her. Perhaps her menfolk didn't know she had come to me. Perhaps she wanted to keep the money for herself. So relieved of anxiety on that point, I retired to my room and unwrapped the package."

Alphonse placed his hand on a slim volume bound in faded and cracking leather.

"The package contained this journal, written by an explorer who calls himself Chad Spice. Much of the contents are of little interest—at least from an archeological standpoint, though as an account of a wandering life it holds some amusement value. Let me read to you directly from the salient portions."

Neville nodded, fighting an impulse to lean forward like a child anticipating a treat.

"Please do."

Again the German's voice shifted, this time becoming not so much sing-song as clipped and terse.

I was a fool beyond mortal knowing when I attempted to win the favor of Sheik Azul's daughter. In the dark of night, warning came to me that the sheik would have my life. I stole a horse and fled. At the rising of the sun, I saw that I had compounded my crimes. The horse I had chosen at random in the darkness proved to be the second favorite among the sheik's mares.

Terrified, I fled and with God's help managed to elude my pursuers. Yet I feared their wrath would follow me even into neighboring villages, and so I turned my course into the desert, for Sheik Azul rules a riverside town. In this way I thought I might bypass him and his allies. In the desert I came into an area where cliffs and broken ground barred me from returning on a straight line to the river. Thus I was forced to push deeper and deeper into the sandy wastes.

After some days, the lovely mare I had stolen died from the harsh conditions. Without her blood to sustain me, I nearly perished from lack of water and the punishing force of the sun. On what surely would have been my final day on Earth, I glimpsed a towering rock jutting solitary from the sand. Spending my fading strength mercilessly, I stumbled into its shade and there slept until the cool of the night.

When I awoke, my tongue had swollen to fill my mouth. My eyes and lips were encrusted with sand. Maddeningly, I imagined I heard the musical trickle of falling water. Staggering to my feet—though I believed myself insane—I followed the sound. Moving as in dream or delirium, I descended the slope until I came upon a tiny spring welling from the rock. I drank my fill and slept, waking only to drink again. When dawn came I saw I had come to an oasis populated only by goats and lizards.

I stayed in this oasis while I regained my strength. As my senses returned to me, I realized that I had stumbled into what must have been a holy place to the people of this land. Four gigantic statues—one of which had been the "rock" under which I had first sheltered from the sun—flanked the gentle vale, and picture writing, marvelously fresh, adorned the rocks.

Although the sun's passage made clear which way east (and the Nile) must be, I feared to depart the oasis. Yet as I grew stronger I became both restless and fearful. Goats are not common in the heart of the desert. Who had put them here? When might the goats' owners return?

One exceptionally clear day, I saw to the south and east a shape like unto the head of a monstrous hawk crested in green. Further study revealed it to be a vast rock. The greenery seemed to promise water, so I resolved to make this Hawk Rock my new goal.

After killing several goats—for they were as tame as pets and offered no struggle—and making bags for water from their innards, a rough cap for my head and slippers for my feet from their hides, I ventured across the sands to the Hawk Rock. The distance was greater than I had imagined, but once there I again found water and so recovered my strength. While I recuperated, I noticed inscriptions like unto those I had seen at the oasis. From the Hawk Rock I made my final push to the Nile.

Worn and near mad, I stumbled at last from the sandy wastes. Joyfully, I plunged my head into the silty waters. The natives of that place looked at me as if I were insane. I fear I did not help myself to gain their regard, for as soon as I recovered enough to stand, I stood and saluted the Hawk Rock and, invisible beyond it, the Oasis of Statues that had saved my life.

Alphonse closed the journal.

"Chad Spice records that as soon as he recovered from his ordeal—and the villagers treated him with the kindness that all Muslims are enjoined to offer beggars and madmen—he made his way to Luxor. There he found European allies who, hearing of his ordeals, took pity on him. Initially, Spice relaxed, but then he began to feel uneasy—as if he were being watched. At this point, he decided to depart for Cairo. As far as I can tell, Chad Spice never arrived. If he did, then he lost this journal along the way."

Neville frowned. "You mean his account ends?"

"That is correct, my friend. The last entry tells that he has signed as deck hand on some vessel and planned to depart the next morning. He was in high spirits."

"Odd."

"Very." Alphonse put the journal aside. "However, what happened to Chad Spice does not interest me. What does interest me is this Oasis of Statues he describes. It could well be the Valley of Dust. It is isolated from the usual burial grounds—as Neferankhotep wished to be. It is guarded by four statues, as legend says the Valley of Dust was guarded."

Neville couldn't quite accept this leap in reasoning. Egypt was riddled with burial grounds, temples, and other ruins. He sought for something encouraging to say.

"Even if it isn't the Valley of Dust, Alphonse, you certainly seem to be onto something. Are we hoping to find this Hawk Rock? Spice's journal seems to indicate that it can be seen from the banks of the Nile, and it must be in the vicinity of Luxor if he went there as soon as he recovered his strength."

Alphonse's eyebrows shot up. He looked both amused and smug.

"Neville, I have already located the Hawk Rock—at least I believe I have. Using Luxor as a starting point, I have spent the last two winters traveling up and down the Nile shores, venturing into the fringes of the desert. Last winter, using the most powerful telescope I could transport with me, I sighted a feature that could well be the Hawk Rock. Summer was too close to wisely venture into the desert, but now . . ."

Neville Hawthorne raised his snifter in a toast.

"To the Hawk Rock!"

"I had a devil of a time getting camels," Eddie Bryce reported. "Seems like everyone had promised their beasts to someone else. Finally managed by catching up with a dealer before he reached Luxor. Camels and drivers will be waiting for us when we get off the boat."

Lean and sun-browned, handsome in a rough and ready way, Edward Bryce did not seem old enough to have fifteen years of honorable—if not always distinguished—service behind him. However, at age eight Eddie had run away to become a drummer boy, thus escaping a life of drudgery as a younger son in the great brood of a Sussex farmer.

In those fifteen years, Eddie had seen much of the British Empire. Early on he had discovered a liking for both languages and people. The first interest had thrown him and Neville together. Then Neville had learned that though Eddie spoke over a dozen languages quite well, he could hardly read, even in his mother tongue. Neville's determination to teach Eddie to read—over the younger man's initial protests—had cemented the friendship.

"The *reis*," Eddie continued, using the Arab term for a ship's captain, "says he is prepared to sail whenever Herr Liebermann is ready."

"Tell the *reis* tomorrow morning," Neville replied. "Herr Liebermann is impatient to be off."

The voyage up the Nile was—except for crocodiles and hippopotami in the waters, and aggressive merchant *fellahin* along the shores—uneventful, restful, and lovely.

Neville drowsed beneath the on-deck canopy and engaged in long discussions about archeology with Alphonse. The four Europeans played whist almost every night. After hearing about the fight in which Eddie had acquired the bruises that, though faded, were still greenly visible, Alphonse took a liking to the sergeant.

"You are a knight errant," Alphonse announced, greatly amused. "Like Parsifal or, since you are English, maybe Galahad, yes?"

Bryce, who was about as far from a virgin knight as was possible, grinned, but he didn't disabuse the German of his illusions.

Camels and drovers were indeed waiting for them at the appointed spot, but Neville could tell from the storm cloud that settled over Eddie's features as the dahabeeyah came into shore that something wasn't right.

"Problem?"

"Too few camels. Looks like about half—and the worst half—of what I ordered. Can't tell about drovers."

Neville frowned.

"Find out. I'll keep Herr Liebermann busy unloading gear."

"Right, Captain."

Later, Neville headed to where Alphonse and Derek were checking items off a list.

"Bad news, Alphonse," Neville reported bluntly. "Seems that we have about half the camels for which Eddie contracted. The man who stayed—along with his son and daughter—claims that his partner left after the local sheik started telling stories about some curse out in the desert."

"How many camels do we have?" Alphonse asked.

"Seven," Neville replied. "Solid beasts. I'll say that for them. All are trained to take either riders or gear."

"Seven is enough," Alphonse said. "My gear is not so much. This will make carrying out artifacts difficult, but then we have no assurance we will find any. If you are willing, Captain Hawthorne, I will still go on."

"Your gear may not be 'so much,'" Neville reminded him, "but we'll still need additional camels to carry water and fodder."

"But there is water at the Hawk Rock!" Alphonse protested.

"So that old journal said," Neville replied. "Things might have changed. That might not even be the right rock. No sane man goes into the desert without water."

Alphonse nodded, then turned to his assistant.

"Derek, how we may repack? You are a very magician at this."

Schmidt looked thoughtful. "I'll have a word with the drovers, sir. See just what weights the camels will carry and repack accordingly."

Neville surrendered.

"Sergeant Bryce is with the drovers," he said to Derek. "Ask him to translate for you."

Dawn was barely pinking the horizon when they set out. In addition to the four Europeans, their party had been augmented by three Bedouin: Ali, Ali's son, Ishmael, and Ali's daughter, Miriam. Miriam rode the camel which carried the water, riding lightly despite her enshrouding robes.

"She weighs hardly more than a feather," Eddie confided to Neville, his eyes bright with interest as he glanced back at the graceful figure. "She's the reason her father stayed when his partner left."

"I suppose," Neville said, thinking of his own sister, "Ali needs a dowry if he wants a good marriage for her."

"I don't know about that," Eddie said, "but from what I overheard, Miriam's got more pluck and character than the men. She won't run off from nothing. Won't let them run off neither."

———————

It would turn out that Eddie was wrong about this, but when the time came, no one blamed Miriam at all.

As Chad Spice's journal had noted, distances across the open, featureless desert were very hard to judge. After one day's steady travel the only reason Neville felt certain they hadn't been marching in place was that the village along the Nile had diminished into tiny shapes that vanished from sight as the ground over which they traveled became more and more uneven.

By end of the second day's travel, however, Neville began to entertain a quiet certainty that Alphonse Liebermann had been correct in his assumption that the distant shape he had glimpsed from the Nile was the Hawk Rock. By the end of the third day's march, Neville—and everyone else—was certain.

They began their marches at dawn and continued until the heat of the sun became unbearable. Then they would pitch pavilions, rest until the heat began to lose intensity, and resume. Had their goal been larger or more certain, they might have navigated by the stars at night. As it was, even the eager Alphonse preferred to have their goal visible before them. Then, too, pitching tents and tending to camels by starlight were tasks that none of them cared to undertake.

On the night following the third day's march, Neville had wandered a short distance from the camp, seeking peace and quiet to cool his mind as the darkness cooled his body. No one would ever say that Alphonse Liebermann was a dull traveling companion, but his intensity scorched nearly as much as did the sun.

Neville rapidly became aware that he was not the only person out in the darkness. Three voices, speaking Arabic, caught his ear. Within a few phrases, Neville recognized the voices of their camel wranglers: Ali, Ishmael, and Miriam.

Miriam's voice, more high-pitched than those of her brother and father, carried clearly.

"Allah will keep us safe. Have you forgotten the creed? There is no God but Allah! How can you fear these ancient curses? They are the credulous beliefs of credulous people."

Ali replied, "But my brother, your uncle said . . ."

"Uncle is more than half pagan!" Miriam nearly spat the words. "I thought you were wiser than he."

She certainly does have her share of pluck, Neville thought, remembering Eddie Bryce's description with amusement. *I wonder if Eddie realizes just how much.*

It hadn't escaped Neville just how frequently his sergeant found excuses to exchange a few words with the girl. Bedouin tribes varied greatly in how much liberty they gave their women—and a camel merchant like Ali might be forced to give his daughter much more freedom than would a wealthy man who could afford a fully isolated harem.

Nor had Neville missed how often Miriam's dark eyes—all of her face that could be seen over her modest veil—followed Eddie as he went about his duties. Doubtless Ali had noticed as well, but it was becoming apparent that Miriam was more than a match for her father. Clearly as long as she did nothing untoward, Ali would avoid scolding her.

"Besides," Neville heard Miriam continue scornfully, "would you have us flee on foot into the desert? The English will not lightly let you take the camels."

Ali muttered something that Neville did not catch, and Miriam's reply did nothing to clarify the matter for him.

"Are they, then?" she said, and Neville could imagine the toss of her head. "Well, then, run if you are afraid of a big rock. I am not."

"You will obey your father!" Ali growled.

Neville decided that, unless he wanted to have a mutiny on his hands he'd better interrupt this disturbing conversation.

He cupped his hands and called out in English: "I say! Ali! Ishmael! Where have you gotten to, damn it?"

He repeated the same, leaving out the emphasis, in Arabic.

He heard a muttered exclamation, then Ali called out in a mixture of Arabic and English:

"We are here. We were only praying."

The three returned to the camp soon after, and Neville saw no reason to make an issue of their absence, but over the evening card game he warned his companions about the possibility of mutiny.

"I don't think Miriam is at all for it," Neville concluded, "but both the men are frightened of the Hawk Rock. Frightened men do foolish things—but I don't think they'll attack us. Sneaking off in the night with as many of the supplies as possible seems more likely."

Eddie suggested a rotation that would "accidentally" keep their camels and gear under watch at all times. Neville agreed, and when Eddie volunteered to watch, suggested instead that rather than anything overt they begin with Derek Schmidt dossing down near the camels.

"I shall complain about you people's snoring," Derek agreed with a wry grin, "if anyone asks, and perhaps even if they do not."

These arrangements must have been satisfactory, for dawn found their company and their gear intact. By the following night they knew they would reach the Hawk Rock mid-morning the next day.

The Europeans remained alert that night, but when Eddie rose shortly before dawn, Ali and Ishmael were gone. They had taken nothing but their own gear, some food, and water. The camels—and Miriam—remained.

"They are cowards," the girl said. "They fear this rock so much that they abandon me and even the camels."

"How," Neville asked, "will your father and brother survive a four-day journey across the desert? Four days, that is, by camel. It'll take more time on foot."

Miriam paused rather longer than Neville thought necessary before answering.

"They are Bedouin!" she replied proudly. "Not soft Europeans. They will have no difficulty."

Neville didn't doubt that the Arabs were tougher than he was, but he'd seen how ready both Ali and Ishmael had been for the afternoon's rests. He kept his suspicions to himself.

"Miriam," he asked gently, "do you want to follow your father, or go on with us?"

"I go with you," Miriam replied without a pause. "I am not a coward to be afraid of a big rock, and you are men of honor."

"Thank you for your trust," Neville said. When Miriam returned to her tent he added in a soft voice to Eddie, "Make certain we live up to that trust. Do you understand me, Sergeant?"

"I do indeed, Captain Hawthorne," Eddie replied crisply, but the light that had entered his eyes when he discovered that Miriam had not fled didn't diminish in the least.

The defection of Ali and Ishmael did not change Alphonse's plans. He put himself on point when they departed and insisted Neville ride at his side. This close, the rock no longer resembled a hawk. The lines that had seemed to define wings and other features were revealed as crags, cuts, and the work of erosion.

"You and I, Neville, will look for any paths or trails," Alphonse said happily, "and for the water of which Chad Spice wrote."

Neville nodded, though his choice would have been to ride along the group's flank, watching for any signs of trouble. He'd moved Miriam to the center of the group, Eddie to the rear. Both Derek and Eddie had been cautioned to keep alert for anything out of the ordinary, but he feared that Eddie had eyes for nothing but the pert little Arab girl perched atop her camel.

She's hardly more than a heap of cloth, Neville thought, *but Eddie's transformed her into a princess.*

As they came closer to the rock, Alphonse spotted a steep trail that led toward the top. Despite Alphonse's eagerness to begin exploring at once, Neville insisted on circumnavigating the rock before taking any other action. They found no evidence of any other human presence, but Neville noted several places where the rock could be climbed if the climber possessed sufficient patience and rope. Ample animal tracks—from small jerboa to what looked suspiciously like jackal—raised hopes that water was still available.

Alphonse's trail proved to be too steep for the camels, but a small, sheltered box canyon tucked in the hollow of the hawk's eastern "wing" provided an ideal place to pitch camp.

Neville assigned this task to Derek and Miriam, insisting that Eddie take a rifle and stand watch near the canyon's opening.

"But Miriam can't understand either German or English!" Eddie protested.

"Derek can make his needs clear with signs," Neville replied. Then he lowered his voice, "Get a hold of yourself, man! She's a Bedouin. You have no idea what she looks like under all that cloth, and I'm not at all convinced that her menfolk have abandoned us. Their best survival strategy would be to follow us, get hold of our gear, and leave us stranded."

Eddie nodded, a trace of stubbornness still in his eyes.

"Think of what you're doing as keeping Miriam safe, if you must," Neville offered. "Do you think her father will believe we left her unmolested? Unless this entire thing is her plan . . ."

He bit his lower lip thoughtfully.

"Never!" Eddie said and stalked off to his post.

Great, Neville thought. *I wonder just how much Alphonse is to blame for this? Him and his damn Parsifal!*

Slinging a rifle across his back, and checking the load in his pistol, Neville went to escort Alphonse up the trail. Both men carried axes in case there was heavier vegetation above.

"Surely you do not think you will need a rifle," Alphonse asked, his eyebrows taking flight in surprise. "A bucket perhaps. I have put a collapsible one in my pack."

"Hunting," Neville said shortly. He and Alphonse had already debated the need for the party to carry more weapons. "Where there is water, there may be game."

Alphonse nodded approvingly, and without further discussion they began their climb. The steepness of the trail was the least of their difficulties. The sandy soil proved to be permeated with small pebbles that rolled underfoot, so that each step must be carefully tested. The occasional rocky stretches, though more challenging to climb, at least provided reliable footing.

Eventually, the trail spread out into a more or less level area, sheltered on all sides by rocky outcroppings, the highest of which, facing to the south, must be the head of the "hawk." The entirety of this upper canyon was lightly covered in bristly vegetation. Some of the shrubs clustered along the edges were as much as waist high. Ferocious-looking thorns testified how they had reached that height in such a barren region.

"Good fodder for the camels at least," Neville said, poking a narrow-leafed bush with the butt of his rifle. "Now let's see if we can find water. Check where the vegetation is thickest."

Alphonse nodded absently. He hadn't heard a word.

"This is the place," he announced rapturously. "It must be. I can feel it. Somewhere Chad Spice wrote, there was an inscription . . ."

Neville sighed. Clearly necessities like water and food took second place to archeological finds on the German's list of priorities. However, the canyon wasn't terribly large. Unless trouble came down from the rocks, he could cover the area with his rifle.

"Keep an eye out for snakes . . . and scorpions," was all he said, but he was thinking about human vipers, not natural ones.

Neville easily located the spring welling up along the eastern edge of the canyon. He was beginning to hack away the shrubs that crowded around it when Alphonse cried out.

"I have found it!" he said, executing an impromptu dance of victory.

"Ye gods, man!" Neville exclaimed. "I thought you'd been bitten by a cobra."

"It is here," Alphonse said, pointing to the southern wall of the canyon. "Incised into the side of a rock."

He knelt and started brushing at something with his sleeve. Despite his own responsibilities, Neville crossed to examine the German's find.

"It looks like an obelisk," Neville offered a moment later, "fallen on its side. I bet it was erected where the taller rocks would protect it from the weather."

"I agree," Alphonse said, bending closer to inspect the writing. "Hieratic, rather than hieroglyphic, I would guess New Kingdom period."

"That's a good deal later than I imagined your Neferankhotep," Neville said, frowning.

"True."

Undaunted, Alphonse rummaged in his pack until he came up with a rolled sheet of paper and a chunk of drawing charcoal.

"I will make a rubbing," he announced, "so that I may make my translation in the camp. Derek will assist me."

Neville wasn't surprised to learn that Alphonse's servant possessed the training to assist his master with this task. He was coming to respect Derek's competence as a matter of course.

"Very well," Neville replied. "I will finish freeing up the spring. Judging from the steepness of the path, I rather hope we can lower water directly to the camp rather than carrying it down the trail."

By that evening, Alphonse and Derek had worked out a rough translation of the inscription. As Alphonse read it to the assembled company, his measured cadence was accented with theatrical flourishes of his eyebrows:

Remember that Anubis will bring you before Osiris.

Remember that your heart and your soul will be weighed against Maat.

Remember that the monster Ammit waits to devour the wicked.

The son and the self flies as the Nile and the boat.

The mother and the wife follow as the Nile and the boat.

Under the watching Eye of the Hawk, the homecoming is joyous.

"Nice," Eddie said judicially when Alphonse concluded, "but what does it mean?"

Alphonse replied happily, "The first three lines are traditional warnings or cautions, but the latter portion is not so clear."

Neville tilted the page Alphonse had handed around for inspection so he could read it more clearly in the firelight.

"I wonder," he said slowly, "if the boat mentioned here isn't an actual boat. Didn't the ancient Egyptians envision the sun as a boat? A boat on which a bunch of gods sailed?"

"Sometimes," Alphonse replied. "Another common image was of a flaming ball being rolled by a dung beetle—this is one reason the scarab beetle was sacred and used for amulets."

"Slow down," Neville insisted. "Sometimes too much knowledge is counterproductive. What's caught my eye is the way these people go 'as' the Nile and the boat. If the boat was a usual type of vessel, why 'fly'? I assume you didn't employ poetic license in your choice of words?"

"I did not," Alphonse said stiffly.

"I didn't think you would," Neville replied soothingly. "Now, here we have an inscription dating from a lot later than the legend you're tracking down, right?"

Alphonse nodded, still frowning.

"What if it offers some sort of directions?" Neville continued, excited by the picture that was building in his mind. "Directions written down later, for those who might have forgotten the way to the Valley of Dust but who might need to go there to make offerings? If the boat is the boat of the sun, then it travels from east to west. The Nile travels south to north—contrary to just about every river I know. It's stretching some, but what if traveling as the Nile and the boat is traveling northwest?"

Alphonse's frown was replaced with a grin.

"If this is so," he said, "then the reference to a homecoming makes sense. It is a coming to the Valley of Dust—the final home of Neferankhotep's mortal remains. And the Eye of the Hawk . . ."

"Confirms our guess," Neville interrupted, too enthused to remember his manners. "There are only a few directions from which this Hawk Rock would resemble a hawk. We came from southeast. The other angle that would provide the same general orientation is looking back at the rock from further to the northwest."

Eddie Bryce thumped him on the back.

"Maybe you're stretching, Captain," he said, "but it's a nice bit of work nevertheless. What do we do now?"

"Tomorrow," Alphonse said, "I will go atop the Hawk Rock and study the land to the northwest through my telescope. Perhaps I will see something. Even if I do not, I would wish to journey some distance in that direction to see if we can find evidence to confirm Neville's reasoning."

Derek interjected, "We may run short on provisions, sir."

"Nonsense!" Alphonse replied with an airy wave of his hand. "Captain Hawthorne has found both fresh water and camel fodder. With the departure of our guides, we have two more man's worth of provisions yet untouched. And the Valley of Dust was said to be populated with goats."

Neville didn't say anything about that last. He knew if he did Alphonse would merely point out that Chad Spice's journal had been correct on the matter of finding water at the Hawk Rock. Besides, if he was in the least honest with himself, he had to admit that he, too, was curious as to what they might find. Being part of a major archeological discovery could only do good things for his reputation, both within the Army and in wider circles as well.

"I think we would not be imprudent," Neville said, "to continue our journey at least a bit further northwest. Tomorrow morning while Alphonse makes his telescopic survey we will finish replenishing our water and cut fodder for the camels."

"Very good," Alphonse said, rubbing his hands briskly together. "Everything is perfectly in order."

Jackals barking in the small hours just before dawn were the first sign that everything was far from in order.

"That doesn't sound right," Eddie said to Neville, after the captain shook him awake. "Too many. Too scattered. I might believe it of a wolf pack, but jackals . . ."

"My thoughts exactly," Neville agreed. "I'm going to wake the others. I'll send Derek to help you ready the camels. Muffle the harness. We'll take the gear but leave the tents set up."

"Are we leaving?" Eddie asked, stomping into his boots.

"I want to get out of this canyon," Neville replied. " 'Box' seems too apt a description for it. Let's make certain the box doesn't turn into a coffin."

Neville woke Alphonse and Derek, warning them to keep both light and sound to a minimum. Then he crossed to the small tent Miriam occupied. He'd half-expected to find it empty, but the girl was waiting, dressed and alert.

"Those are not jackals," she said as soon as she saw him.

"I thought not," Neville replied. "This canyon is too closed in for my tastes."

"I understand," Miriam replied. "I will help with the camels."

"Good. Send Eddie Bryce to me. I want him on guard."

Since their gear had been ready for a morning departure, loading the camels didn't take long. The jackals' barking had nearly ceased, but Neville wasn't fooled into complacency. Earlier, whoever was out there must have been getting into position. Now they were probably waiting for better light.

By the time Derek reported that the camels were ready, Neville had made his plans. Open desert was hardly preferable to the box canyon, but it did offer a faint hope for escape.

"Form up," he told the others. "We'll get out and head east toward the Nile."

No one spoke. No one protested, though the glimpse Neville had of Alphonse's expression demonstrated more eloquently than any impassioned words that Neville would pay dearly if this proved a false alarm.

It isn't, though, Neville thought, and moved his camel forward.

Camels' feet are soft and made for traveling across sand. They are quiet, but not noiseless. Equally, though Neville's band carried no lights and the moon had set, the darkness was not absolute. Starlight is quite enough for eyes accustomed to its glow. Even so, Neville hoped they might get away with it.

But whoever it was who had raised the jackal's call in the darkness did not wait for daylight to attack. Perhaps someone noticed that, though the tents kept their places, the grumbling shapes of the camels were no longer picketed at the camp's fringe. Perhaps the attack had been planned for earlier in any case.

For whatever reason, before Neville and his band had traveled far from the Hawk Rock, a shrill cry of rage and disappointment pierced the clear desert air. Neville knew that their enemies would seek them to the east—for there was nothing but desert to the west. Speed, then, rather than deception was their only chance.

He thumped his camel and the creature reluctantly stretched out its limbs in an undulating run. The other camels followed suit without prompting. Indeed, the shrieks from where the Hawk Rock bulked behind them were prompting enough.

It's five days back to the Nile, Neville thought despairingly. *If they have camels or horses we're sunk. Maybe we should have fought it out back there.*

But he knew his small group wouldn't have had a chance. He and Eddie were in training, but Derek was disabled, and Alphonse didn't even carry a gun. Miriam would also be useless in a fight. Indeed, Neville expected that if he looked back he would see that her camel—and perhaps one of those bearing their supplies—would be gone. What better way for the Bedouin girl to win back her father's support?

Thus Neville was surprised out of all proportion when Miriam's camel drew alongside his own. The girl called out to him.

"Follow me, Captain Hawthorne. I know a place where, Allah willing, these superstitious dogs will not follow."

Neville did not permit Miriam to take the lead; she pressed her camel to the front. The beast—not the water carrier this time—lightly burdened by no other weight than her lithe form, took the lead easily.

And Neville followed. What else could he do? Miriam was offering some hope, slender though it might be. If her offer proved to be another trap—well, they were already into it up to their necks. Glancing back over his shoulder, he was certain he saw a fair-sized dust cloud occluding the stars and knew that at least some of their pursuers were mounted.

Miriam led them to an area where the desert was broken and rocky. A rise—nothing like the Hawk Rock but at least higher and more substantial than sand dunes—rose from the surrounding area. When they drew closer, Neville realized that the rock showed signs of having been carved and shaped. He was not surprised when Miriam drew her camel to a halt and announced:

"It is a necropolis of the old kings. My father and his brothers have come here to rob the dead, but they have never trusted the place. Their fear may slow them long enough for us to make a defense."

Neville saw the wisdom in her words. Unlike the box canyon, where they could be surrounded on all sides, here they could claim the high ground. His and Eddie's rifles were likely to have better range than what the Arabs carried—at least he hoped so. Even Derek and Alphonse might be able to be of some use—and he no longer felt a desire to dismiss Miriam out of hand.

"Can you use a rifle?" he asked her as they herded the camels within the most sheltered perimeter of rocks. Derek forced the beasts to kneel and efficiently began unloading the most necessary supplies.

"I can," Miriam said, "but I can do more than that."

Moving with a lithe grace that demonstrated more clearly than words that she had no fear of this city of the dead, Miriam showed Neville several openings into the tombs.

"We can shelter within," she said, "if needed."

Neville nodded.

"Eddie!" he called back to his sergeant. "I'm going to do some scouting."

"Right, Captain," came the jaunty reply. "The Bedouin have stopped just outside of rifle range. I borrowed the professor's binoculars and it looks like they're arguing."

Neville wasted neither breath nor time in reply. Lighting a candle, he ducked into the first opening. This led to a dead end, but the second opening led to a well-preserved chamber. He was about to penetrate more deeply when Miriam's voice came echoing down the corridors.

"Please, Captain Hawthorne, Eddie Bryce is calling. Someone has been hit!"

Neville was outside almost before the Arab girl finished speaking. Derek was wrapping a length of fabric around his employer's left forearm. Alphonse was pale and so shaken that even his eyebrows seemed to have lost their customary exuberance.

"Report, Sergeant!" Neville snapped, flinging himself down behind their makeshift bulwark and readying his rifle.

"Not all of them are scared of ghosts," Eddie replied, "but a whole lot more are scared of my rifle. Alphonse was clipped by a ricochet, not a direct hit."

"Where are they?"

"Pulled back out of range. We've got the drop on them, though, and a clear line of sight all around."

"Problem is," Neville replied, "you and I can't watch everywhere. If we are forced to start shooting . . ."

Eddie shrugged noncommittally. The matter wasn't worth spelling out.

"Please, sir," Derek said. He'd finished wrapping Alphonse's arm and was belly-crawling to join them. "I can watch."

"I can watch," Miriam said breathlessly in Arabic. She might not understand English, but Neville had already accepted that she was no fool. "And shoot."

Neville nodded. He shared out both rifles and sidearms, posted Derek and Miriam so that the group now possessed an overlapping field of vision in all directions, and felt completely hopeless. From what he could glimpse through Alphonse's binoculars the Arabs outnumbered them four or five to one.

Favoring his lacerated arm, Alphonse crept up beside Neville.

"Captain, this is a ruin, yes?"

Neville tried to manage a chuckle. "But not likely the Valley of Dust, I'm afraid."

"No. Not likely. However, I understand ruins where I do not understand warfare. With your permission, I shall continue the scouting you had undertaken."

"You have my permission," Neville said. "All I ask is that you make the rounds from time to time with fresh water. It's going to get damned hot out here."

"Of course!"

And it did get damn hot. The Arabs launched the occasional charge, but were driven back without much effort, occasionally dragging a wounded comrade. Sometime around noon, Miriam confirmed what Neville suspected.

"They can wait. Why risk shooting and harming the camels? A day or two is nothing, especially with water near."

Periodically, Alphonse made the rounds with water and food. Each time he gave Neville a report of his finds. The ruins were extensive, though thoroughly looted, at least where Alphonse had reached.

"But there is much the vandals did not take," he said. "Wood, broken furniture, cloth, even mummies destroyed beyond all recognition by those who stripped the amulets from within their wrappings."

Neville thought about this, and as the boat of the sun began to sink in the west, he came up with a plan.

———

"Wrap me so everything is covered," Neville ordered, "everything but my eyes and mouth—and don't restrict my movement."

"I still think," Alphonse said, ripping a sheet into long strips—the linen from the tombs that had inspired Neville was far too brittle—"that I should take your place. You are a better shot."

"But you are wounded, and I'm not going to risk anyone else in such a jackass plan."

"You're risking Miriam," Eddie grumbled.

"Miriam is risking herself," Neville countered.

To be honest, he didn't feel good about Miriam's addition to their plan, but he had felt he must accept her suggestion—no matter what danger to which it exposed her. Miriam's diversion meant his outlandish imposture would have a better chance of succeeding without getting him riddled with bullets.

Miriam's robes had been dishevelled, the fabric artfully streaked with blood harvested from a protesting camel. She was ignoring Eddie's displeasure—but Neville had no doubt she was aware of it, and flattered by his concern.

"Right," Neville said when his mummification had been completed a short time later. "Everyone knows what to do?"

Nods and a sullen "Yes, sir" from Eddie answered him.

"Start shooting."

Eddie and Alphonse aimed at a sandy patch and let loose a barrage.

"Now, Miriam," Neville commanded.

The girl let loose a piercing scream and bolted across the desert in the direction of the Arab camp. At the same moment, Derek released three of the camels. They'd guessed that the Arabs might shoot at a woman, but not if they risked hitting a valuable piece of livestock.

Neville pursued the fleeing girl. He moved fairly rapidly, but kept his gait stiff and motions jerky. He must follow close behind the girl, but not too close. Behind him, the shooting had ceased and their besieged camp was as silent as death.

He heard Miriam's wails and screams as she burst in among her countrymen. Despite himself, Neville held his breath. One word from her would destroy them in an instant.

"It came from the tombs," Miriam sobbed. "One of the old kings, avenging ancient wrongs. It tore the English to shreds and comes for us! Look!"

She screamed theatrically, collapsing into the arms of the nearest Arab—one who just happened to be among the Bedouin's best shots.

Neville moaned loudly and made a furious, throwing gesture in the direction of the nearest Arab. The man collapsed as if shot, not surprisingly, for he *had* been shot. Eddie Bryce had followed Neville, keeping to the shadows and trusting that misdirection and the fire-blinded eyes of the Arabs would keep him from discovery.

The Bedouins' reaction was all Neville could have desired. Those nearest to the fallen man leapt back, shunning the body. Neville gestured again and a second man fell.

The crack of the rifle was clearly audible, but no one paid attention. They were too busy scrabbling for the nearest mount or—more often—fleeing on foot into the desert. Derek had crept around and untied the horses and camels.

A few of the braver Arabs reached for brands from the fire, but an unearthly wail from the direction of the ruins froze even Neville's blood. The wail rose again, and Miriam shrieked:

"Another! Another! What demons have we unbound?"

That was more than even the coolest head could take. They hardly paid heed to the fact that the mummy had produced an artfully wrapped pistol and was adding to the death toll. Within minutes the enemy was scattered. Neville didn't plan to wait for the Arabs to get over their fear. His band could navigate by the stars and Alphonse was holding their camels ready.

Neville offered no protest when Eddie swung Miriam onto the saddle in front of him, only smiled.

When they were safely on a steamer bound for Cairo, Alphonse Liebermann explained that he no longer desired to search for the tomb of Neferankhotep.

"I have found a tomb now," he said, tenderly cradling his wounded arm. "A good one, if I choose to excavate. However, perhaps playing at pharaonic revenge has ruined me for archeology. It no longer seems so good to disturb the dead."

Neville nodded. "I understand."

Alphonse laid a hand on Neville's arm.

"I will be writing several letters when I return to Cairo: to the museum to register my find, to the Army and diplomatic corps to warn them of the restless Arabs in this part of the desert, and . . ."

He paused and smiled, his eyebrows dancing.

"And to praise a certain valiant Captain Hawthorne. I shall write my cousin, Albert, too. I think 'Sir Neville' would sound very fine indeed."

Neville had to agree.

The Arrival

IT COULDN'T have happened at a worse time, but Neville Hawthorne knew he had no one but himself to blame. He was the one who had stopped reading his letters. He was the one who had fled from grief into obsession. Now the consequences of that obsession were coming to roost, and he still had no idea how he was going to deal with them. At least he'd opened the letter in time.

Cold comfort indeed when one is standing at the dock, watching passengers file off the trans-Atlantic steamer, looking for a single young woman, not knowing if she will be recognizable. Neville thought he might recognize her. He had seen pictures, though the last one had been at least three years ago. Young women changed so much at that age.

Then, like the moment between shadow and sunlight, twenty years vanished, giving Neville his sister back to him as she had been when she had left for the United States with her new husband.

There stood a graceful figure, high-held head crowned with thick chestnut hair that defied a fashionable hat's attempt to tame it. There flashed the violet eyes beneath the shadow of the jet-trimmed brim. There in a tidy mourning black frock was the womanly form that had made Alice one of the acclaimed beauties of her debutante season.

Here again posed the loveliness that had stolen the heart of Pierre Benet—Pierre who had stolen Alice's heart in turn. When the senior Hawthornes would not consent to their daughter's marrying a penniless French physician, Alice had eloped with her Pierre. Soon thereafter the newlyweds had departed for the United States. Neville had not seen Alice since.

Recollection hit Neville as solidly as a physical blow. He would never again see Alice, not even if he made that long-postponed trip to the United States. A letter had arrived six months ago reporting that Alice and Pierre had died in a conflagration that had also destroyed their home. The fire had reportedly been set by savage Indians who had left nothing behind them but charred wood and the arrow-riddled body of the family dog.

The young woman who could not be Alice walked down the gangplank and made her way through the crowd, coming directly to Neville with perfect confidence. Clearly, she had recognized him.

"Jenny?" Neville said, and heard his own voice emerge hoarse and unfamiliar. "Little Jenny?"

"Uncle Neville," she replied, and her voice, sweet, but decidedly American in accent, broke the spell. "It's me, Jenny Benet."

She pronounced the surname English style, not the French "Ben-nay," but Neville heard traces of a French accent incongruously interwoven with the American. Jenny seemed about to say more, but she paused, studying him. Neville wondered what had caught her attention.

He had long ago recovered from the assault that had forced him to retire from the military, but the scars remained. Those on his head were mostly hidden by thick hair not unlike Jenny's own in color and luxuriance, but nothing would hide the ugly slash that began at the bridge of his nose and carried across his left cheek. Although in his mid-forties, Neville had taken care to remain active, and was not dissatisfied with his form. His father had gone to fat long before he reached this age. The limp remained, of course, and the slight unevenness of his shoulders, but these could not account for the strange expression spreading across Jenny's features.

"Uncle Neville," she said at last, "what's wrong?"

"You look," he managed to reply, giving only part of the truth, "so much like Alice. Those portraits your parents sent never did you credit."

Jenny grinned, a wide, open smile that nonetheless held traces of sorrow too fresh to be forgotten.

"I'm glad to hear you say it," she replied. "I always thought Mama was the prettiest lady I'd ever seen."

There was the trace of the French again, on the word "Mama," and hearing it Neville could imagine Pierre bending over his daughter's infant cradle: "Say Mama, little Genevieve. Say Papa."

Now that Neville could separate his niece from that momentary transformation into her mother, he could see something of Pierre in Jenny as well. These traits were less physical: a confidence he'd never seen in Alice until she'd defied everyone for her Pierre, an alert watchfulness that was a far cry from Alice's missish shyness, that disturbing tendency to assess her surroundings and make instant diagnosis. But then, except through her letters, Neville hadn't really known Alice these past twenty years. Maybe Jenny was like her mother in these ways too.

Neville would have been hard pressed to say what was more unsettling, this sudden onrush of memories, or what he knew he must confess in the near future. Neville settled for focusing on the immediate present, knowing even as he did so that he was delaying the inevitable.

"Are you tired, Jenny?" he asked. "I have a suite ready for you at my house, but if you are hungry we can send the luggage ahead, and stop for cakes and tea."

"Cakes and tea," Jenny replied promptly. "I'm too excited to sleep, and scared stiff that once I see a bed I'll drop off and miss my first day in England."

"Very well," Neville said with an amused smile.

Needless to say, they couldn't leave immediately. Jenny had left her traveling companions rather abruptly when she glimpsed Neville in the crowd on the dock. Now she had to return, make her apologies, introduce Neville, and all the rest. Happily, her companion—a married woman, coming to visit her brother and his wife—was eager to be away with them, so beyond making vague promises to call, there was no added impediment.

Neville thought this was a good thing. Given what he had to tell his niece, an audience would be rather awkward.

A few words to his footman, and arrangements were made for Jenny's luggage. Then Neville hailed a cab, and gave the address of a hotel whose tea room was very popular with locals and visitors alike. He thought it would be easier to tell Jenny what he must there, away from his house and its current uproar.

At least, he hoped it would be. Looking at Jenny, and noticing the lively curiosity with which she was regarding every aspect of London traffic, he wasn't at all certain.

————

Once they were seated in a private corner overlooking the room, with tea and iced cakes set before them, Neville felt he must begin his confession.

"Jenny," he began, but fate wasn't going to make this easy for him. There was a rustle of heavy silk skirts, and a throaty, melodious voice addressed him.

"Sir Neville, how delightful to see you. I thought you had already departed."

Without conscious volition, Neville rose to his feet.

"Lady Cheshire," he said, bowing over her hand. "May I present my ward, my late sister's daughter, Genevieve Benet? She has only just now arrived from Boston. Jenny, this is Lady Audrey Cheshire."

Lady Cheshire was a handsome woman in her late twenties. She wore her raven locks drawn up into a complicated arrangement that drew attention to her green eyes. The green of those eyes was echoed in the pale silk of her gown, a fashionably lace-trimmed creation in the French style, with a heavy bustle and a rather daring neckline.

Jenny made her curtsey as neatly as could be wished, but the quick glance she darted toward her uncle left Neville quite certain that she had not been so awed by this introduction that Lady Cheshire's reference to Neville's departure had escaped her.

"I am delighted to make your acquaintance, Miss Benet," Lady Cheshire said, apparently unaware of the undercurrents her words had stirred. "Or do you prefer 'Jenny'? Americans are so much more relaxed than we stuffy English."

Jenny gave an exquisitely noncommittal smile. "Whichever pleases you, Lady Cheshire."

Lady Cheshire raised one elegant eyebrow the slightest amount before turning to indicate the two people who waited politely in her wake. "May I introduce my own companions?" Lady Cheshire said. "Sir Neville, I believe you know Mrs. Syms. Miss Benet, Sarah Syms. Sarah, Miss Benet."

Sarah Syms had the horsey features so common in the English upper class. She was grey-haired and rather plain, with a wiry figure that suggested she kept herself active. This impression was borne out by how her pale blue eyes darted with lively interest between Neville and his niece.

"And Captain Robert Brentworth," Lady Cheshire continued.

Robert Brentworth was a well-built, muscular man who towered over everyone present. His skin was darkly tanned, making his deep blue eyes seem more vivid by contrast. Although his brown hair and mustache were a trifle too coarse to be fashionable, and his features were too regular to be striking, he radiated a vitality that made him undeniably attractive.

Jenny seemed to think so, for her gaze lingered on him for a moment before she glanced over to Lady Cheshire as if attempting to assess the pair's relationship.

Neville wasn't about to explain. Audrey Cheshire was the widow of Lord Ambrose Cheshire, a noted Egyptologist. Husband had been easily thirty years senior to wife, and so no one had been terribly surprised when he had predeceased her. Audrey had nursed her husband most devotedly during his final illness, but as soon as etiquette permitted her to put aside her widow's weeds, she had apparently put aside all memory of her husband as well.

Robert Brentworth had been an associate of Lord Cheshire's, but it was rumored that his devotion to his friend's widow had more to do with her copious personal charms—and possibly the fortune Ambrose had left her—than with any loyalty to Lord Cheshire's memory.

Though Neville had dared hope that Jenny's presence would stop Lady Cheshire's prying, he was disappointed.

"So when do you leave?" she asked archly.

"Within the week," he replied.

"That's very wise," she said. "Dear Ambrose always said that the weather was the greatest opponent for a venture such as you intend. I always found it difficult to believe how cold and snowy England was when we were abroad."

Neville managed a polite enough reply, but could feel his jaw hardening around the things he wanted to say. Perhaps Lady Cheshire detected his irritation, but perhaps she was only aware that she had forced her company on them as long as was polite.

"I must let you drink your tea before it cools," she said, as Captain Brentworth stepped forward to escort her on her way. "I was simply so surprised to still see you in England."

She turned to Jenny.

"Delighted to make your acquaintance, Miss Benet."

"The pleasure was entirely mine, Lady Cheshire," Jenny replied, and Neville was quite certain there was an ironical gleam in those violet eyes. "Mrs. Syms. Captain Brentworth."

They parted company with appropriate insincerities, and Neville managed a swallow of tea while Jenny settled her cumbersome skirts.

"Well, Uncle? You are going abroad?"

"I was about to tell you," he said rather stiffly.

She raised her rose-painted tea cup and sipped, neither helping nor hindering his explanation.

Neville found himself saying rather more than he had intended. "Your parents' deaths, that was the start. I had long meant to visit Alice in her new home, to see with my own eyes the life she described so vividly in her letters. As you know, I never made the journey. First, there were my responsibilities to the army. Then other things intervened. My parents had need of me; the weather was unfavorable; the political situation . . ."

He couldn't bring himself to mention his own recuperation from the injuries that had been inflicted upon him on that dark night, the events of which still haunted his nightmares. He told himself that Jenny had experienced enough suffering without his inflicting his own upon her vicariously, but he knew the truth was that he didn't want to dwell on those memories. The time when the doctors had nearly amputated his leg had perhaps been the worst, but there had been too many others nearly as bad.

Jenny's expression remained neutral. She refilled his cup, then her own, took an iced cake from the plate between them and waited.

"I resolved," Neville went on, "that I should not make the same mistake again, live to regret a promise unfulfilled. I began making arrangements for my return to Egypt."

"Egypt!" Jenny's exclamation held delight and surprise. "Oh, Uncle! When do we leave?"

Neville had not expected this. Indignation that he would leave her so soon after her arrival, anxiety for her own place in his absence, these he had considered, but not that a young lady ending one voyage would relish the prospect of another—and there was no doubt that Jenny relished the prospect of this one.

"I had not intended to take you with me," he began, cut to the quick when he saw the disappointment dim the deep violet of her eyes. "Jenny, I shall not remain in the cities. I know that Cairo has quite a well-established European community, but I would not be able to squire you about—even if I still knew anyone. It has been many years since I lived in Egypt."

"Cities?" Jenny replied. "I would like to see them. Cairo is Arab, of course, the Mother of Cities they call her, though I would rather see the pyramids and the sphinx. Alexandria has a more European pedigree than Cairo, and should be quite sophisticated. Yet Luxor that was Thebes of the ancient Egyptians, perhaps Abu Simbel, Karnak, Kom Ombo . . . Those are the places I yearn to see with my own eyes."

Neville blinked, and Jenny laughed, her momentary disappointment forgotten.

"Didn't you know that Mama used your letters to make me take an interest in geography? Your accounts of your travels, the trinkets you sent, the picture postcards, all made those places real and alive. I read tons about wherever you were. I was so sorry when you left the Egypt and returned to England."

So was I, Neville thought, but said nothing.

"I mean," Jenny went on, faltering slightly as if she had read his thoughts. "I mean, England was still exotic and Scotland sounded wonderful, but they weren't Egypt or India or Greece or wherever else."

Neville found his tongue.

"Alice did mention that she shared my letters with you," he said, "but I don't think I ever realized to what use she turned them—or what an avid student she had created."

"Now doesn't that beat all," Jenny said. "And here I am thinking that you know you're my greatest hero, right up there with Mr. Lincoln, who I do admire highly for what courage he had freeing the slaves and preserving the Union at such a terrible cost to himself. Mother must never have told you. She could be so very English, you know."

Neville realized that he'd been completely in error to ever equate his sister and her daughter. Alice would never have spoken this freely to a man she had just met—even an uncle whose letters she'd read for years. Indeed, Alice probably would have gotten all tongue-tied at the prospect of meeting one of her heroes. That was one of the reasons her romance with Pierre had caught everyone off guard, and why Father had thought that simply forbidding Alice to see Pierre would be enough. Neville had a feeling that forbidding Jenny to do something she desired would be about as useful as telling the sun not to shine.

"But, Jenny," he said as gently as he could, rather overwhelmed by his newly acquired status as hero, "I do not intend to stay in any of those cities. Doubtless I will pass through some of them, but I am not touring. I have . . . business to undertake."

"In the desert?" Jenny asked, and the glow in her eyes diminished not a whit. "I should like to see the Egyptian desert—camels, jackals, ruins of ancient temples. I think the Egyptian desert would be far more interesting than our American versions."

Neville was determined to nip this romanticism in the bud. "Camels are foul creatures—bad tempered and smelly. Jackals are not nearly as romantic as timber wolves, nasty scavengers that they are, and ruins are not at all what you might expect from the picture postcards."

Jenny dismissed this with a wave of her hand.

"Camels can't be worse than jack mules, and scavengers aren't nasty. They're useful. As for ruins, well, I've seen some that the old-time Indians left back home, and most of that's mud bricks, bits of stone tools, and busted pots. I liked that just fine, so I don't figure Egypt could disappoint."

Neville thought furiously, hunting for any way out other than bald refusal, a thing he already had reason to believe this pert American miss would find offensive.

"Jenny, my expedition is entirely male. It would not be proper for you to travel in such company."

Jenny shrugged. "I'm sure that where it will matter there will be some woman about, and I'll just attach myself to her if needed. If there's no one around to care, well, then, who will care?"

There was a certain logic to her argument, but Neville refused to be seduced.

"Currently, my expedition is very small—myself and two other men. Only one of those men is married, and so could be expected to understand a woman's needs and temperament. You ask a great deal of two bachelors."

Jenny didn't press the point, but Neville didn't think this was because she had resigned herself to remaining behind.

He had been planning on leaving Jenny because he had assumed she would want to remain in London. After all, there were the autumn and winter social seasons yet to come. She would be novelty enough to be invited to numerous balls and fetes—she might even land a good husband.

Still, if Jenny really wanted to accompany him, perhaps he could hire some army wife to assume the role of chaperon once he went into the field. Neville did feel rather bad about abandoning the girl so soon after her arrival, and this would ease his conscience and let him settle her where she could at least tour the museums and local ruins. A compromise might be best.

"Woolgathering, Uncle Neville?" Jenny asked, her tone amused. "I've asked three times. Who are the other members of your expedition?"

Neville could think of no reason not to answer.

"The only one traveling with me from England is Stephen David Holmboe, a linguist whose specialization is the ancient Egyptian language. In Egypt we will be met by Edward Bryce, a soldier with whom I once served. He has local contacts, and will be quartermaster for our group."

And military support, Neville thought. *No need to tell Jenny that, though, nor explain Eddie's peculiar lifestyle over there.*

"Linguist and specialist in the ancient Egyptian language," Jenny mused aloud. "And a quartermaster. And going away from the cities. That sounds like you're going treasure hunting."

"Not precisely," Neville replied frostily.

"I'm sorry," Jenny apologized quickly. "I've rubbed you raw. I forgot. Treasure hunting's not good form any more, is it? People don't hunt for treasure. They search for antiquities that will reveal to us knowledge about lost civilizations. Seems to me the thrill would be about the same."

Neville shook his head in mock chagrin.

"You're not responding like a proper young miss," he said. "Where are all the cries about snakes and spiders? Where are the warnings about the risks we shall be taking? Where the desire for iced drinks and the newest fashions?"

"Drowned at sea," Jenny answered promptly. "I heard enough chatter about fashion to make me ill. Half the women on board were fretting about whether their gowns were too provincial. The other half were already sure that their gowns were and were gloating over plans to visit the best shops as soon as they were ashore. I could tell you enough about bustles and the new debate over appropriate colors to make your head ache."

"No doubt," Neville agreed.

He noted that despite her efforts at self-control, Jenny had been forced to pat back a yawn.

"Come along, my dear," he said, helping her to rise. "We can talk more later. I can't have you falling asleep into your tea."

Jenny smiled sheepishly.

"Thought I could hold it back," she admitted, "but I'm bushed."

Neville settled with the shop, then handed Jenny into a cab. She fell asleep almost before the cab had rattled into traffic, her head drooping trustingly onto his shoulder as her mother's had twenty years before. The jet beads trimming the crown of her hat trembled with the motion of the cab, tickling Neville's cheek a little like tears.

Sir Neville's Secret

JENNY BENET awoke and didn't know where she was.

The bed in which she lay was canopied, and the sheets smelled of lavender, not the strong soap favored by the housekeeping staff at her boarding school. The carpets on the floor were richly-hued and of Persian design, the curtains heavy damask that shone sapphire in the pale sunlight. The furnishings were simple, but obviously of the best quality.

Then motion and a sense of something familiar caught her eye. Her trunks were ranked neatly along one wall, their lids open, and a plump woman whose name hovered at the edge of her memory was bending over the largest, unfolding items of clothing and putting them into an ornately carved wardrobe.

Jenny sat up and scrubbed at her eyes with the back of her hand, then glanced down and saw that she was wearing one of her own night dresses. With the sight, memory crystallized.

"Emily, isn't it?" she said.

The woman started, glancing around wildly, her hand fluttering in the vicinity of her ample bosom. Then her gaze rested on Jenny and she visibly relaxed. A warm smile lit her pleasant features, making them something far more interesting than pretty.

"You startled me, Miss, that you did! I'm sorry if I woke you, but I thought I could work without disturbing you."

Jenny looked at the amount of clothing hanging neatly in the wardrobe, and smiled.

"I'd say you did a good job, Emily. What time is it?"

Emily tilted her head to one side.

"Well, I'd guess around eight in the morning. Your uncle has had his breakfast and gone to call on some business associates. He said to tell you he'd be back for luncheon."

Jenny slid from beneath the covers and stretched, her feet buried in the comfortable plush of the carpet.

"I can't think when I've slept so late! Madame back in Boston would be lecturing me on sloth right enough."

"Now, I think you just might have needed the rest," Emily said comfortably. "That's what I think."

She looked Jenny up and down, tapping the dimple in her rounded chin with her forefinger.

"You'll be wanting a wash, if I mind you right. Would you like me to have a breakfast tray sent up for you along with the hot water?"

Jenny nodded. "That would be lovely."

"And your uncle asked if I'd stand as your lady's maid." Emily looked uncomfortable. "I said I'd try, but only if I could tell you that by rights I'm just a maid of all work."

Jenny laughed.

"Well, that's fine by me. I've never had a lady's maid. At school we laced each other up as needed. I figure I won't need much more here."

Emily relaxed visibly.

"Well, I can manage that much, I'm sure. Let me run down to the kitchen and ask Cook for a tray. I'll bring back the hot water with me."

Privacy had not been much available for Jenny either at boarding school or at home, so she found Emily's chattering company very welcome. In short time, she had learned that Hawthorne House maintained a relatively small staff: housekeeper, butler, cook, footman, Emily herself, and a boy to do the boots and other such chores.

This seemed like a rather large number of people to tend to the comfort of one man, but Emily rapidly made clear there could have been more. Sir Neville did without a valet. He didn't keep a driver or groom because his horses were stabled at a reliable livery establishment nearby, and he didn't keep a coach. Between them the housekeeper and cook handled the shopping, and the butler minded the wine cellar. The butler was also in charge of household accounts.

"The staff will even be smaller when Sir Neville goes abroad," Emily continued, returning to Jenny's unpacking. "The house is going to be closed, but for the butler and housekeeper to take care of immediate needs. Sir Neville has found places for everyone else, and now he's taking me and my man along with him."

Jenny recalled that the footman, Albert, or Bert as Emily preferred to call him, was Emily's husband of two years. They had no children, but Emily wasn't distressed.

"We're putting by for that day," she said, "and don't mind having a bit of time to do so, not that Sir Neville would dismiss me, but there's no escaping that a child gets in the way of doing one's job."

Jenny wondered how old Emily might be, and finally decided on somewhere past twenty, but not yet twenty-five. Bert, as she recalled him from their brief meeting the night before, was probably five years older. Young enough, then, to relish an adventure, but mature enough that they could be left to their own devices when Uncle Neville went off wherever it was he was going.

She thought about what he'd said the night before concerning the make-up of that expedition. Three men only, and Bert hadn't been one of them. She didn't think Uncle Neville was such a snob as not to mention a servant in his count, but then she didn't know. There was so much she didn't know, including the most important thing—how to convince Uncle Neville to let her go with him to Egypt.

"Did Uncle Neville tell you where he was going?"

Emily looked puzzled.

"Why, to Egypt, Miss. Kay-ro or so such heathen place. At least that's where Bert and I will be stopping. Sir Neville said he might need to go elsewhere, but that he'd make certain we had a respectable place to stay while we're waiting for him."

"I'm sure," Jenny said.

She would have asked more, but she noticed that Emily had lifted a smaller box from inside one of the trunks and was shaking out a ring of keys, clearly looking for the one that would fit the lock.

"No need to unpack that one, Emily," Jenny interjected with enough haste that Emily gave her a rather quizzical look. "I mean, I don't think it's anything I'll need for a while."

Emily set it back inside the trunk, though not without a questioning glance. Jenny, thinking of that ring of keys—keys she could certainly reclaim, since they were her own property, but which Emily in turn could easily reacquire for long enough to open the box—made a decision.

"Go ahead and open it," she said, "but take care with the contents."

Curiosity and apprehension warred for a moment on Emily's face, but curiosity won—a thing Jenny wholly appreciated. Turning away to brush her hair, her hand never staying in its rhythmic stroke, she continued to watch through the mirror.

Emily set the black box on a chest of drawers, and unlatched the top. Opening it, she halted, her hand still resting on the lid, her mouth a round circle of surprise and astonishment.

"Miss!" she said. "Miss! These are pistols in here!"

Jenny nodded. "That's right. Matched set and a boot-top derringer. Bowie knife, too, in the lid. They make it through all right?"

Emily snapped shut the lid as if she were closing it on a box of scorpions: quickly, but with great delicacy.

"I wouldn't rightly know, Miss."

"I'll check them later, then. Salt air might not have done them too much harm, locked away like that."

"I suppose so, Miss . . ."

Emily folded some of Jenny's undergarments in silence, but finally curiosity got the better of her.

"Were those your late father's, Miss?"

Jenny felt that familiar sense of unreality, as if Pierre Benet somehow weren't dead, though she knew all too well that both he and Mama were gone.

"No, Emily," she replied, her voice softer than she'd intended. "They're mine. Always been mine."

Emily looked at her, eyes impossibly wide. For the first time, Jenny noticed they were blue and that Emily had freckles.

"Oh."

If Emily excused herself a few minutes later, Jenny, carefully relocking the weapons case, could hardly blame her.

Neville returned shortly before lunch and found Jenny awake, dressed, and in the front parlor, a book spread out on the table before her. When he entered, she leapt to her feet with spontaneous pleasure, a sunny smile all at odds with the unrelieved black of her dress lighting her face.

"What are you reading?" he asked.

"Belzoni's account of his travels in Egypt."

"Still interested in Egypt then?"

"Very much so!"

Neville smiled to himself. Perhaps Egypt would lose some of its charm if Jenny knew what other delights awaited her in England.

He seated himself in one of the high backed overstuffed chairs that remained from his parents' day, steepled his fingers, and began:

"This morning I went out and investigated options for you here in London while I am away. I spoke with Lady Lindenmeade, a good friend of your grandparents. She has said she would be delighted to have you stay with her while I am abroad. The Lindenmeades are quite well connected, and one of Lady Lindenmeade's granddaughters is coming out this year. I am certain you would receive the best introductions. Margaret is a fine young woman and would only be too happy for your company."

Jenny bit her lip, clearly not wishing to seem ungracious in the face of an offer that many young women would be only too delighted to accept.

"If it doesn't make much of a difference, Uncle Neville, I'd still rather go with you."

Neville realized he was pleased rather than otherwise.

"Well, I spoke with Lady Lindenmeade on that matter as well, and she pointed out to me that as you are still in mourning for your parents, you could not be expected to be enthusiastic about teas and balls."

"That's true enough," Jenny said, though something in her tone suggested that she might be less than enthusiastic at the best of times.

Neville wondered if the American version of the balls and parties that would fill the winter season was less entertaining than the English. Hadn't Boston been settled by Puritans? Perhaps that explained Jenny's lack of enthusiasm. He put the matter from his mind.

"Lady Lindenmeade assured me that your reputation would be undamaged if you traveled in my company to Egypt. She is writing to some friends of hers who are wintering there, and believes she can arrange for you to remain with their party when I must leave Cairo."

Jenny nodded, but Neville thought that some of the brightness in her features dimmed. However, she was too polite—or too prudent—to press the matter. All she said was, "Then I can go with you?"

"That's right, my dear. You will winter in the land of the pharaohs!"

At this, Jenny's happiness returned.

"I have arranged," Neville went on, "for you to meet Lady Lindenmeade for tea tomorrow. She can better advise you on what you will need for a sojourn in Egypt as she wintered there herself a few years ago."

"Thank you, Uncle Neville. You seem to have thought of everything."

"I try," he said. "Emily—you have met Emily, haven't you?"

"This morning. She seems quite sweet, and very efficient."

"Emily has agreed to accompany us, and act as your chaperon. She and her husband will wait on you when I am away."

"Wasn't Emily going with you before this? She mentioned that she was going when we spoke this morning."

Neville shook his head.

"No, I only just asked her and Bert last night."

Jenny looked puzzled, then she grinned.

"You guessed all along that I'd rather go to Egypt than stay here!"

Neville nodded. "I know determination when I see it."

And I don't think you've quite finished being determined, Miss Benet. There will be time enough to deal with that once you've seen Egypt for real. I suspect that you will change your mind about going into the desert without my pressing.

Jenny touched his hand.

"Thank you. I won't let you down."

Neville accepted this as a promise.

"Would you be willing to grace me with your presence this afternoon? Our other traveling companion is coming to call. I should like you to meet him before you finalize your decision."

Jenny frowned.

"I've made my mind up, sure as anything, Uncle Neville. What's wrong with this man?"

"Mr. Holmboe is . . ." Neville hesitated, searching for the right word. "Very clever and very talented. He is also a bit odd—annoying some find him, though I do not."

"He is abrasive and argumentative? Or is he one of those learned fellows who has to let you know just how much smarter than you he is?"

"I would prefer for you to make your own decision regarding Mr. Holmboe. However, I thought it only fair to warn you that he is not terribly popular in some circles."

Jenny toyed with the lace edging on one sleeve, clearly fascinated.

Neville continued, "I had reasons other than Mr. Holmboe's talents for hiring him. One is that I do not wish news of our planned venture to spread. He is outside the usual circles, and therefore not likely to gossip."

"You're not doing something illegal?" Jenny asked sharply.

"Perhaps on the fringes of legality," Neville admitted. "I will explain everything at tea. Then you will have time to consider whether you wish to continue associating yourself with this venture by traveling in my company. Lady Lindenmeade would be happy to have you."

Jenny frowned, but no matter how much she wheedled, Neville would say no more. There were things he would prefer to talk about as little as possible.

The hours between Uncle Neville's arrival home and when high tea was served late that afternoon dragged interminably for Jenny. Belzoni's book, once so fascinating, could no longer hold her interest. After she'd read the same half-page three or four times, she marked her place and set the book aside.

Then she went up to her room. She hadn't had much need for her guns on the steamer across from Boston, but even with them locked up in their case, the salt air wouldn't have done them much good. Taking out oil and cloth, she methodically cleaned both six-shooters and the derringer. Emily hadn't found the Winchester in its fitted box that was flush with the bottom of her longest trunk—or, if she had, her curiosity had been amply satisfied that morning. In any case, the rifle remained in its padding, nearly as pristine as it had been on the day its custom-made beauty had arrived at the finishing school, along with a note from Papa promising that they would go hunting soon after the term ended.

Jenny had taken the rifle out and practiced assiduously when visiting tolerant friends in the Massachusetts countryside, but she had lost heart for the sport the day the telegram had arrived announcing the burning of her parents' new ranch and their deaths in the fire. Now she stared down at the polished metal gun barrel, the shining oak stock, the fanciful curlicues etched along its length and shaping her initials.

She briefly wondered if Mama and Papa had argued over this peculiar gift, then felt certain that they had not. Mama might have been startled by Papa's selection, but she wouldn't have argued about its aptness. Both Jenny's parents knew that their daughter's goal was to become a frontier doctor like her father, though the question of whether Jenny would go to medical school or acquire her training more informally from her father had not yet been settled.

Indeed, though Madame's institute was commonly called a finishing school, subjects other than deportment, music, and art were available to those young women who chose to indulge—and Jenny had indulged with enthusiasm in case the medical school option seemed wisest. This coming summer she was to have been her father's full-time assistant, expected to rise for every call, depart every social engagement as he did, and otherwise learn whether she was prepared for those grueling professional rounds.

A tear splashed from her eye, staining the velvet lining, and bringing Jenny back to the present. Somehow she must acquire ammunition. It shouldn't be too difficult, though. Papa had made certain the rifle's caliber was one commonly used by both the military and civilians. If Uncle Neville would not approve the purchase, Jenny would take care of it herself some day when she was supposed to be buying ribbons and handkerchiefs.

This practical line of thought was more attractive than her grief, and Jenny sat down and began making a list of things she would need if she was to be ready to go into the desert with Uncle Neville. That he planned to leave her in Cairo, she had no doubt. That she would do her best to change those plans, she already knew.

Writing out that list forced Jenny to go back and forth between her newly unpacked belongings and the writing table. She wondered what Emily had thought of her well-worn calf-high riding boots, stack of folded bandanna handkerchiefs, and the soft-brimmed slouch hat, stained by sun and weather, but that was as neat a fit on Jenny's head as her own hair. Probably none of these items of clothing had puzzled the maid as much as the selection of denim trousers, tailored to Jenny's measurements, with belt loops wide enough to accept her gun-belt with its ornamental hammered silver coins.

The trousers had been Mama's idea. She herself rode sidesaddle, managing the awkward seat so well that one time she'd gone straight up the side of a mountain after a strayed cow and calf. Jenny, however, had favored riding astride, long after she should have given up such childish practices.

Mama was no fool. In return for Jenny's agreeing to learn to ride sidesaddle well enough to pass on social occasions, she had agreed to let her daughter wear trousers when no one was around who could be shocked. Like most compromises, it made no one perfectly happy, but as none of those whom it made unhappy were within the Benet family, it worked just fine.

I wonder what riding a camel is like, Jenny thought. *Or will Uncle Neville get some of those magnificent Arab horses I've read about? That would be splendid. I suppose it will depend on where he plans to go, and how deeply into the desert.*

One way and another, Jenny filled the hours until tea. Even so, she'd been dressed in her new tea gown—simple and black, as appropriate for a young woman still in deep mourning—for quite a while before she heard the clock chime the hour and knew she could descend without seeming too eager. Not seeming too eager was part of her plan for convincing Uncle Neville, for if he was anything like Mama, pushing was just the way to get him to dig in his heels like a bronc determined not to ford a flood-swollen river.

Tea was being served in the parlor, and Jenny didn't miss the appreciative look in Uncle Neville's eyes as she glided in.

He really does think I'm pretty, she thought, and felt a trace surprised.

Out west any white woman was still awfully rare. Even a plain as dirt spinster of forty might find herself getting loaded down with marriage proposals, so Jenny hadn't taken too seriously the calf-eyes that followed her around at just about every box social or church dance. Back east, the recent war had done its part to whittle down the number of eligible bachelors. She hadn't had suitors lining up to visit on Sunday afternoons like some of the girls.

There had been a few, of course, the nicest of them Tommy Mullens, the middle brother of one of the girls in Jenny's year, but nothing had come of that other than a few good conversations. Uncle Neville's obvious admiration felt just like Papa's had—warming and completely nonthreatening.

They hadn't gotten much beyond Jenny's thanking her uncle for his compliments on her dress when a solid rap on the front door announced their caller.

As soon as Stephen Holmboe crossed the threshold into the parlor, Jenny knew that she was encountering a genuine English eccentric. Later she would learn that Stephen was in his mid-twenties, but at that moment he appeared both older and younger. Part of this was due to his attire which was, even to Jenny's American eye, at least fifteen years out of date. Men's fashions hadn't changed as dramatically as had women's, which had gone from hoops to bustles, and from bonnets to dainty hats. However, it had not remained stagnant.

Stephen Holmboe wore checked trousers with a matching loose-fitting jacket designed in the high-buttoned style. His cravat was wide and flowing, matching the solid off-white of his shirt. In short, he was quite the swell—but a swell who would have been out of style even a decade before. Mr. Holmboe's manner of dressing his brilliant golden blond hair continued this motif. It was longer than was currently fashionable, as were his bushy side-whiskers and mustache. Curtseying to Mr. Holmboe's bow, Jenny felt rather as if she were being introduced to an enormous ambulatory dandelion.

She might have been put off by this eccentric vision, but the blue gaze that met hers and darted quickly away was both shy and sweet. Stephen's smile was kind, and his mannerisms closer to those of a boy of fifteen than a young man of twenty-five. Within moments of their being introduced, it was evident to Jenny that Stephen Holmboe possessed both energy and enthusiasm in abundance.

"Hullo, Sir Neville," he said. "Yes, I'll have a cup of tea. These ginger biscuits look smashing."

Stephen loaded one broad-palmed hand with sweets, took his cup in the other, and only afterwards seemed to realize that seating himself without spilling something all over the carpet was going to prove difficult. Jenny inclined her head toward a chair with an end table conveniently near.

"Perhaps there?" she suggested.

Stephen grinned, managed to drop his cookies onto the table, and then set the tea cup down after.

"I certainly won't starve you, Stephen," Uncle Neville said tolerantly. "Cook has even supplied more than sweets."

"Smashing!" Stephen repeated. "Viands suitable for a king. I shall probably devour everything in sight and then start on the upholstery. I think I forgot to eat today. Got absorbed in reading up for our expedition. Lost track of time. Would have forgotten this except that you'd dropped such ominous hints—and my sister dragged me out of my book."

Jenny helped herself to a small iced cake, more to cover her amusement than because she was very hungry. Having expected another stiff and formal Englishman—quite possibly one with a chip on his shoulder—and who would certainly disapprove of her, she found this ebullient young man a relief. However, she could understand why the conventional and conforming English might find Stephen annoying.

Neville dismissed the maid, settled a plate of dainties that he promptly ignored on the table near his elbow, and became quite solemn.

"I do have some rather serious matters to confide in you both," he began. "Before I begin, I must impress upon you how very important it is that none of this go any further than ourselves. I believe you will understand why once I have finished, but I must have your word."

Stephen nodded crisply, boyishness vanished.

"You have my word," he said. "Not a peep to anyone."

"Mine, too, Uncle Neville. I'll swear on anything you'd like."

"Your word is enough, Jenny," Neville replied, "as is Stephen's. If I didn't think you were trustworthy, I wouldn't be confiding in you. However, I must warn you that this could be a dangerous secret to hold."

Neither of his listeners expressed any reluctance to hear, but still Neville paused for a long moment more before going on.

"My story begins when I was still in active service in Egypt. My commanding officer called me to him and told me I was being delegated to escort a visiting German archeologist, one Alphonse Liebermann, during his travels into Upper Egypt."

Speaking tersely, yet sparing no detail, Sir Neville related how Alphonse Liebermann had been seeking the lost burial complex of a pharaoh known to him only as Neferankhotep. He told about their journey up the Nile, and about their arrival at the Hawk Rock. In less dispassionate tones, he related how on the brink of their great discovery they had been assaulted by Bedouin tribesmen.

"We were forced to flee for our lives," Sir Neville concluded, "and without a great deal of luck and some elaborate trickery we would not have escaped. The event soured Liebermann on searching for buried tombs. We returned to Luxor and toured extensively before he returned home."

Sir Neville drank deeply from tea that Jenny knew must be stone cold, but he didn't appear to notice. "Events might have soured Alphonse on archeological exploration, but I fear that for me the attraction became only more acute. My duties did not permit me to pursue this interest full-time, nor even to always remain in Egypt, but when I could, I continued learning everything possible. My interest meant that I was frequently assigned as liaison to archeological expeditions—a courtesy the army was happy to extend for diplomatic reasons. However, though I came to know various archeologists very well, I never confided in them what I had learned from Alphonse Liebermann. That was to be my discovery, and mine alone.

"I continued planning on mounting an expedition to find the Valley of Dust. The winter two years after the first venture, everything fell into place. I had been detailed to escort a group as far as Luxor. However, once in Luxor, my time was to be my own. I had leave coming to me, and I arranged to take it. I made other arrangements as well, and one night, a few days before I was to depart, I was returning rather late to my quarters when my plans were scotched for good.

"By this time, I knew Cairo quite well, and did not always remain on the main thoroughfares. This proved to be a mistake. A group of men—Arabs, I could tell, but not more than that—emerged from an alley and attacked me. I would like to say that I fought them all off, or even that I fought brilliantly, but the reality is that when five men attack one, even if that one is armed, the single man is doomed to failure.

"I believe that they intended to kill me, but the noise of our battle—and I assure you that I did not hesitate to shout for help at the top of my lungs and in every language I could remember—brought some brave men to my rescue. They were Greeks, I believe, and their arrival forced my assailants to flee.

"I survived, but only barely, and only because the doctor who first treated me was a very clever Egyptian *hakeem* who had studied both abroad and in his own land. However, I was no longer fit for duty, much the less for a demanding trip up the Nile. I was put on medical leave, and when some of my injuries festered and would not heal, I was rotated home. Arriving, I discovered that my mother was not well.

"Faced with a need to regain my own health and to tend to my mother in what proved to be her final illness, it was not difficult for me to resign from the service without a stain on my character. After Mother's death, I did not return to the army. Part of this was because my father, much older than my mother and devastated by his loss, begged me to remain. However, I would be less than fair to you if I did not admit that there was another reason."

He paused, and it took all Jenny's reserves of self-restraint not to urge him on. Stephen, however, either knew Sir Neville well enough to feel no such compunction, or was simply too impulsive to care.

"Tell on," he said. "What could keep you from going after such a find?"

Sir Neville lifted his tea cup, seemed vaguely surprised to find it empty, but made no effort to refill it. When he spoke, his voice was hushed, as if speaking of the matter aloud was somehow to be avoided.

"The reason I did not return, Stephen, was that as I lay bleeding out my life onto the cobbles, one of the Arabs bent to cut my throat. As he did so, he hissed, 'So is the Lawgiver avenged against sacrilege. So is the good king's peace preserved.' "

Stephen shuddered. "Not really!"

"I assure you, my friend," Sir Neville replied. "I did not invent the item to amuse you."

Jenny, who had been thinking that perhaps this final flourish had been included to scare her off, heard the sincerity in her uncle's voice and rejected the idea.

"One of the Greeks fired even as the Arab spoke his curse," Sir Neville went on. "I do not think the shot hit my would-be assassin, but it did frighten him off. Instead of a cut throat, I received this."

He indicated the long slash that still disfigured his face.

"Those words remained with me through the long illness that followed. Indeed, I came to feel that they had an element of ritual to them, as if they were sacred words that must be spoken. Or perhaps I was merely feverish, and attached too much importance to the chance words of an unbalanced assassin.

"Before you reject the former out of hand, however, let me add this. A friend who came to visit me in hospital reported that my rooms had been ransacked. He thought it simple robbery, notified the appropriate authorities, had the rooms sealed to await my return, then commiserated with me on my foul luck. When I returned to those rooms, however, I began to wonder if mere robbery had been the burglars' goal. The rooms had been thoroughly searched, but many small items of value remained. What had disappeared was every trace of anything having to do with archeology. Every book, paper, map, and notepad had either been removed or burned in the hearth. I could not help but consider a connection between this robbery and my being attacked. Yet very few knew that I intended to do archeological exploration over my holiday, and fewer still knew my goal. The idea seemed fanciful, yet it would not leave me."

"Half a tick," Stephen interrupted. "You say that few people knew what you were after. How about the soldier who accompanied you on your first expedition? What's his name? Bryce? Could he have told someone what you were after? Or that Arab girl? She helped save you, but might she have talked afterwards?"

Jenny thought Uncle Neville must have considered this, but it didn't hurt to present the matter. It might even prove soothing.

"Mr. Holmboe does have a point, Uncle Neville. For that matter, what about Alphonse Liebermann or his valet? Might they have said something to someone? Were they involved in this venture?"

Sir Neville steepled his fingertips.

"I am pleased you are willing to take me this seriously. Stephen, if you would not be offended, I would like to address Miss Benet's query first."

"Good right ahead, old fellow."

Sir Neville inclined his head in thanks.

"Very well. As far as I know, and I think I would have known, neither Herr Liebermann nor his valet were in Egypt at the time. Herr Liebermann returned to Germany following our travels that winter, and though we continued to correspond until his death, I do not believe he ever again ventured to Egypt."

"He's dead then?" Jenny asked, feeling an odd pang at the loss of this man she had never known, but who had become quite real to her in her uncle's account of their adventures together.

"He died two years ago, at home in Germany. I had a card from one of his relations in response to my last letter. His valet, Derek Schmidt, remained in his service, but I do not know what has happened to him since."

Stephen leaned forward.

"So they weren't in Egypt when you were attacked. Right. Does that mean they didn't speak to anyone about old Neferankhotep?"

"It does not," Sir Neville admitted. "However, when I recall how carefully Alphonse guarded his secret, and how reluctant he was to confide it in anyone, I do not think he would have turned it into a mere fireside tale. Schmidt might have been more loquacious, but he was also quite loyal to his master."

Jenny picked a line of pink frosting off one of the tea cakes.

"But the point is not whether they told anyone at some other time," she said. "It is whether what they said would have been likely to set someone out to dry-gulch you and search your rooms right then. You didn't write him about your planned venture?"

"I did not," Neville said. "As I indicated earlier, Herr Liebermann acquired moral scruples regarding the wisdom of unearthing the good king. I did not wish to trouble him further."

Jenny wondered if Uncle Neville himself might have some scruples, but did not pursue the point.

Stephen eagerly asked, "And the other two? Bryce and the Arab girl? He knew what you were after. How much did she know?"

Sir Neville frowned.

"I dislike thinking that Bryce could have had anything to do with what happened to me, but it is possible that something he said did alert someone. At that time—two years, as you must recall, after our initial venture—Bryce had altered his circumstances. Shortly after our return, his term of service ended and he left the army, though they would have been very happy to keep him."

Stephen grinned. "This doesn't have anything to do with that girl, does it?"

"Miriam," Sir Neville said. "Best you recall her name. Yes, it had everything to do with Miriam. Eddie had fallen in love, but in order to win his bride he had to satisfy her family."

"Even after everything her father and brother did," Jenny interjected indignantly. "Abandoning her and all?"

"Even so," Sir Neville said. "Arab women are legally subject to their men. Ali formally kept his rights regarding his daughter, and Miriam used his abandonment of her quite to her advantage."

"You mean," Jenny said with a grin, "she hounded Ali into making him accept Bryce as a suitor."

"Correct," Sir Neville said with an answering smile. "Ali set some rather rigid conditions, including that Eddie must convert to Islam and make the pilgrimage to Mecca, but Eddie met those conditions. He and Miriam were married about three years after their meeting.

"At the time I was planning my venture, Eddie was living with a foot in each world. Since he already knew the secret of Neferankhotep and the Valley of Dust, and since I knew him for an excellent quartermaster, I enlisted him in my cause. He, in turn, was eager to assist. Like me, he had felt the job was only half-done."

"So Eddie could have let something slip," Jenny mused, "even if accidentally."

"That is true," Neville replied. "And I prefer to think that any betrayal would have been accidental. Who knows? Perhaps Neferankhotep does have guardians. Perhaps they are alert to certain signs. Perhaps they watch any expedition into Upper Egypt, and if it ventures into questionable territory, they strike."

He spoke lightly, but it seemed to Jenny that he believed there was at least some truth in what he'd said. For her part, Jenny put her bets on Bryce. A man who would forsake religion and country for a woman couldn't be trusted.

As soon as she formed the thought, Jenny felt a wash of guilt. How was what Eddie Bryce had done any different from what her own mother had done? Hadn't Alice Hawthorne disobeyed her parents? Fled her native country for another? Abandoned civilized lands with churches for the sort of generalized Christianity available on the frontier? Furthermore, Alice had married a Catholic, which many Englishmen would think was almost as bad as marrying a Mohammedan.

Stephen seemed to share Jenny's reservations. "It doesn't look good for Bryce. I dare say you've broken ties with him."

"Actually," Sir Neville looked rather uncomfortable, "I have not. I have already written to Eddie, informing him in a roundabout fashion of my intentions and requesting his assistance."

He clearly took their silence as criticism, as in Stephen's case it might well have been, though Jenny was still too overwhelmed by her own insight into her personal hypocrisy to feel very critical of someone else.

Neville spoke out in defense of his friend. "Bryce is a good man. Solid. I have no proof that he was involved with the attack on me, and every reason to be grateful to him. He was the one who thought to check with my landlord after I was attacked, so that I would not lose my rooms. He convinced the *hakeem* to continue treating me once the initial emergency was over, when I might have been left to the dubious mercies of some ham-handed army surgeon."

Jenny held out one hand in a mollifying gesture. "I don't condemn the man without proof, Uncle Neville. However, it does make sense that these mysterious Arabs might have learned of your intentions through him. You mentioned watchers. How better to watch than to watch those who organize caravans and such?"

"I second Miss Benet," Stephen said. "If Bryce did betray anything it might well have been accidental, fault of the job rather than the man. Probably should write him, tell him to watch out so he doesn't make a similar slip this time round."

Neville relaxed. "I have already done so," he admitted. "Eddie did not appear offended. Indeed, he was so circumlocutious in his reply that I wonder whether he might have come to a similar conclusion. Anyone reading his letter would think I am only coming to Cairo this winter for my health."

Neither Jenny nor Stephen raised the possible complicity of Miriam, daughter of Ali, wife of Edward Bryce. Perhaps because he had his own doubts, Neville Hawthorne did not pursue the matter either.

3

A Letter from the Sphinx

STEPHEN HOLMBOE did not linger at Hawthorne House long after the discussion ended, though Sir Neville invited him to remain for dinner. Neville rather dreaded that Jenny would take the opportunity to once again press him to permit her to take part in the expedition proper, but perhaps his account of violent assault and nameless assassins had dampened her ardor, for she did not mention the subject.

"Our departed guest is certainly an interesting person," she said instead. "Where did you find him?"

At this Sir Neville's mood, which had begun stern and become quite grim, lightened somewhat. "As I mentioned earlier, when I returned from Egypt, I decided to continue my studies in Egyptology. Stephen was recommended to me as a tutor in hieroglyphs and ancient Egyptian history. You can imagine my surprise to find him so young, but I assure you, he knows what he is about."

"I'm sure he does," Jenny said. "Still, you must admit he is an odd character. Am I correct in assuming that his clothing is badly out of date?"

"You are indeed, dear niece."

"Ah. I wondered whether Fashion had made one of her radical turns once again. Certainly what I've heard about the new 'aesthetic' dress reminds me of the French court's fashion for shepherdess costumes and simplified gowns not long before the French Revolution. Fashion always seems to return in some new version of itself."

Neville smiled. Earlier that morning, Emily had come to him, anxious and upset, to report that Jenny's trunks were packed tight with firearms, trousers, and other unladylike items. Emily seemed to think that Jenny might have somehow managed to sneak a male compatriot into Hawthorne House, and felt she must report the possibility.

Neville, familiar with Alice's ongoing battles with her daughter over civilized dress, and his sister's own musings over what was reasonable or logical given the Benet's current area of residence, had been able to reassure the maid. He heard echoes of those mother/daughter debates in Jenny's most recent comments, but had resolved not to raise the matter unless Jenny did so herself.

"Stephen possesses a colorful, if not completely creditable history—or I should say, his father did. The senior Stephen Holmboe came from money if not title. However, had he applied himself, I do not think a knighthood would have been out of reach for him. Such titles are more easily gained than you might imagine."

Jenny raised a finger in interruption. "That reminds me. Did Herr Liebermann manage to acquire a knighthood for you?"

Neville shook his head, but his smile did not diminish.

"He did not. However, he did commend me to the queen's attention. When some years later my deeds were such that my name was suggested for the awards list, the honor was quickly granted. I suspect that good Victoria did not forget her cousin's request, even if it wasn't appropriate at that time."

"Ah," Jenny said. "I didn't think Mama said you'd been honored for saving some German, but in light of the rest of the story I thought you might have altered the report you wrote her. But were you saying that the elder Mr. Holmboe was not similarly honored?"

"Correct," Neville replied. "Stephen's father had wealth, physical robustness, intelligence, and an attractive person. However, he squandered these resources, alienated his wife and broke her health, and finally shot himself over unpaid gambling debts."

"Goodness!" Jenny gasped. "How terrible for his son."

"I believe these events scarred the boy—then nearly a young man—deeply. Some of Stephen's foolish manner may be an effort to conceal that shame. He eschewed his father's vices and from an early age became quite a scholar. There was not sufficient money both for books and for a fashionable wardrobe, so Stephen took to wearing his father's clothes—he'd had a rather extensive wardrobe. Later, when styles changed, Stephen did not bother to have the clothes altered to a more modern cut. I think that Stephen's defiance of fashion is also part of his continued rejection of the parental mold—though it could be he's simply too absorbed in languages and history to care about the outer man."

Jenny mused in silence for a moment. "And his mother? Does Mr. Holmboe have any siblings?"

"His mother is an invalid. He has two younger sisters as well. The first came out in a quiet way a few years ago and made a modest, though apparently happy, marriage. The second sister has not been so fortunate. She is bitter about her lack of suitors, and has loudly complained that her brother's eccentricities have harmed her prospects. Having met her, however, I think she has no one to blame but herself—and perhaps her family's lack of fortune.

"Mrs. Holmboe has a small income from a brother, who has otherwise distanced himself from her. I believe her elderly parents are even less kind. Stephen augments this income with what he earns tutoring and doing research for scholars of greater reputation."

"Whew!" Jenny exclaimed. "I guess I can be patient with Mr. Holmboe, if he has had to put up with all of that. After all, there are worse things than dressing rather odd."

"Mr. Holmboe was on his best behavior this afternoon," Neville warned. "You have not seen my talented tutor at his most outré."

"Well," Jenny replied thoughtfully, "he hasn't seen me at mine either."

Neville thought she might be about to raise the question of attire, or perhaps of her collection of firearms, but though she paused, she said nothing and Neville kept his resolve to have her be the one to bring up these matters.

The following morning, Sir Neville found a dirty and tattered envelope mixed in with his morning post. His first impulse was to set it aside, believing that the butler had misdirected it when he sorted out the servants' mail. On closer inspection, he saw that the envelope was addressed to him in a clumsy hand, with much blotting of ink.

He had just slit the envelope and unfolded the contents when the butler came to the door. "Mr. Stephen Holmboe, sir. He says he realizes that he has not made an appointment, but hopes that you would do him the honor of granting him a moment of your time."

Neville suspected that Stephen had actually said something more like, "Morning, Weatherington. Is Sir Neville in? I just need a quick chat."

"He would be very welcome indeed, Weatherington. Show him in directly."

Perfect timing, Stephen, Neville thought in amusement. *I wonder if he was outside waiting for the post to be delivered.*

Stephen breezed in moments later. The portfolio tucked under one arm was the only neat thing about him. His golden whiskers were in disarray, and his clothing was subtly misaligned. Neville fancied that Stephen must have dressed in the dark, and the visitor's first words confirmed that supposition.

"I had my final lesson with the Meadowbottom brat this morning. I don't know which of us will be happier to see his lessons end. One thing's sure, his father is going to hate losing my services. Won't find anyone who'll tolerate that imp of Set for less than twice what he was paying me."

Neville made sympathetic noises, then pushed the letter across the desk.

"I received your missive this morning," he said with a chuckle. "Very clever. Haven't had a chance to work it out though. You overestimate my skill—or at least how quickly Weatherington brings the letters around."

Stephen had automatically picked up the sheet of paper, and was staring at it with what Neville could have sworn was genuine amazement.

"What are you talking about, Neville?" he asked, lapsing into the informality they had adopted during their teacher/student days. "I didn't send this. Do you think I have the time for something this elaborate, what with everything to be finished before we depart?"

Neville wasn't taken in.

"A letter in hieroglyphs? Come now. Who else would do something so elaborate? You must admit it's right in line with your idea of a joke."

Stephen raised his gaze from the letter. "I tell you, I didn't do it. Moreover, it's all wrong as a teaching exercise."

"What do you mean?"

"No determinatives, for one," Stephen said, frowning. "No syllabics, only the simplest phonetics . . ."

He trailed off, his gaze returning to the letter. Then he started, glanced around the clutter of the small room Neville used as an office, and said almost frantically:

"Neville, can we go into the library? I need to write something down and there's no room in here. Do you still have those texts we used for your lessons?"

"Of course," Neville said, leading the way across the hall to the library. "What's wrong?"

"What's wrong is more like what's right," Stephen said cryptic in his enthusiasm. "Wait just a moment or two and I'll show you."

They entered the library, and were halfway to the large, round table that stood invitingly in the morning sun, when they realized that Jenny was there before them. She had Mariette's recent volume, *Itinéraire de la Haute Egypte*, open in front of her, and had been so absorbed in her reading that she hadn't noticed them any more than they had noticed her.

"Uncle Neville. Mr. Holmboe. What is going on?"

Neville might have tried to distract her, but Stephen felt no such compunctions.

"Look at what came in the post for your uncle this morning."

"Why it's written in hieroglyphics," Jenny said in astonishment.

"Hieroglyphs," Stephen corrected absently, rummaging where he knew blank paper and pens were kept. "You wouldn't call the letters we use 'alphabetics'— same principle."

"Oh," Jenny looked temporarily stunned, but recovered quickly.

"Why is someone writing to Uncle Neville in hieroglyphs?"

"That is what we're about to find out," Stephen said. "Mind if I sit? This is going to get tedious."

"Of course I don't mind," Jenny said, making room next to her. "Sit here. Uncle Neville can have your other side. This way we can both see what you're doing."

Stephen dropped into the indicated seat without hesitation.

"Neville, before you join us, would you grab that basic text we used for your class?"

Neville had already taken the requested volume and several others from their places, and he set them on the table.

"Now," he said, "what is this about the message being 'all wrong'?"

"All wrong as a teaching exercise," Stephen clarified. "That's what I said. Look at what we have here."

They did. Clusters of hieroglyphs were drawn with elegant perfection on the page.

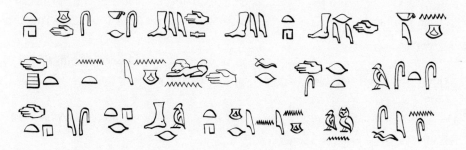

Jenny frowned. "They look all right to me. I even recognize a few—that owl and that reclining lion."

"They are correct," Stephen said, "as far as they go. What is wrong is what is missing."

"I'm terribly confused," Jenny admitted. "Would you mind explaining?"

"What do you know about hieroglyphs?"

"That it was fancy picture writing," Jenny said, hesitantly. "The ancient Egyptians didn't have an alphabet. Instead they had hundreds and hundreds of pictures, and none of them meant the same thing."

"Accurate as far as it goes," Stephen said, and Neville recognized the pedantic note creeping into the younger man's voice, "but only as far as it goes. Actually, the Egyptians did use the same sign for more than one thing. That owl is a good example. It could represent the bird, but it could also mean the sound we associate with the letter 'M.' "

Jenny frowned. "If you say so, but I'd think it would be confusing."

"No more than our silent letters, once you know the rules," Stephen replied with a shrug. "Though it's something of a miracle that anyone ever translated the system at all. It would have taken much longer without the Rosetta Stone."

"That's the one found by Napoleon's expedition," Jenny said, "the one with the same text is a bunch of different languages."

"Right." Stephen waved a dismissive hand. "You can read about the Frenchman Champollion, and how the Rosetta Stone was the key to his discoveries and all the rest in a dozen books. What is important for our purposes here and now is a very odd fact. The Egyptians actually had a perfectly good alphabet. They just didn't use it. Apparently, they preferred their cumbersome ideographs. Sometimes they even went to the trouble of writing redundant texts, including both the pictures and the phonetic signs."

"Why?" Jenny asked.

"No one knows," Stephen said. "Maybe they did it as a pronunciation guide. Egypt was a large and populous kingdom. Quite likely spoken Egyptian had dialects, just like modern English. Heaven knows, there are times I can't understand what you Americans are saying."

"Or I our own country folk," Neville hastened to add, seeing Jenny's brow cloud, "or, I suspect, them me. Stephen, stop lecturing, I want to know what this says."

"A minute, Neville. You have a smart niece here. We shouldn't quash her enthusiasm."

Neville wasn't so certain, but he knew dissuading Stephen would take longer than letting him finish his explanation.

Jenny also wasn't about to give up.

"If they used the same sign for more than one thing," she asked, "how did they know what was what?"

"The same way we do, pretty much," Stephen said. "By context. I mean, if you say 'Hello, Mrs. Jones. How is your son?' that good woman won't think you mean the sun in the sky. However, if there could be any doubt, the scribes added what we call determinatives."

"You're losing me," Jenny warned him.

"Right. Let me slow down. The Egyptians were a lot like us in that they named their children after important people. So a village might have lots of Rameses, if that was the current pharaoh's name. Well, to tell all these Rameses apart, they'd use nicknames. Let's say the village strongman, Rameses, is nicknamed 'Bull.' With me?"

"All the way," Jenny answered quickly. "So if you wanted to write about this strongman, and make sure no one would doubt you meant the man named Bull not the bull in the field, you'd add one of these determinatives."

"I wish all my students were so quick," Stephen said. "Sure you're not pulling my leg about not knowing hieroglyphs?"

"Sure," Jenny affirmed. "But my father was French, and I grew up with two languages in the house, and learned Spanish soon after, and scraps of various Indian languages as we traveled. I'm not stuck to one language."

Neville thought with some amusement that Stephen was looking at Jenny with genuine admiration, her command of languages having impressed him where her beauty had not.

"Right," Stephen said. "Now, before Neville hits me over the head with the poker, I'd better finish this fast. You were right when you said that Egyptian writing was more ideographic than alphabetic, but you didn't go far enough. Ideographs could be made up out of syllable signs. I noticed right off that there were none of these, no determinatives, and none of the ideographs for very common words. In fact, every sign here is one that has a simple phonetic value."

"So this text," Neville said, reaching for his beginners textbook, "is written in an alphabet—not ideographs." He started scribbling down the equivalents he could remember, glad to be making progress.

Jenny looked down at the letter. "But how do you tell in what order to read them? I see that several signs are repeated, but sometimes they're side by side, and sometimes they're heaped on top of each other."

"Very observant," Stephen replied. "And when you're looking at genuine inscriptions, it's worse. The Egyptians would write a text left to right or right to left, or even in columns."

Jenny stared at him.

"Why would they do that?"

"Our best guess is because they liked their texts to fit in the most attractive way possible into the available space. Another probable reason is that hieroglyphs take up a lot of room, so you want to fit them efficiently into the space. That's the reason for the stacking you noticed."

"So how do you know which way to read them?"

"It's fairly simple," Stephen said. "Characters that look like an animal or person—like that quail chick—always face toward the head of the line. I assure you, there are a lot more of this type of symbol in a real text than are represented here."

"I'll take your word for it," Jenny said.

"Then you read upper before lower, whether in a column or in a compressed word group."

Neville had been copying fairly mechanically while he listened to Stephen's explanation. Now he looked up in concern.

"Stephen, this text doesn't look anything like the Egyptian words I remember," he said. "I'll be the first to admit that I need the dictionary more often than not, but . . ."

"You're onto something, my good knight," Stephen said, obviously in high spirits. "Now give us a good morning and let us finish the basic transcription before we go on."

Neville agreed, and with Stephen helping him, it wasn't long before the hieroglyphic text had been reduced to strings of letters broken into word groups.

TH GDS KRS BYDS BY TH BRYD KING DPRT NT INGLND FR DSRT WSTS DTH IS THR BWR TH GRINING WMN SFYNK.

"But it doesn't make any sense!" Jenny protested. "There are too many consonants, not enough vowels."

"Actually," Stephen said, his good humor persisting, "there are no true vowels in written Egyptian. The Egyptians didn't bother writing them, anymore than the Hebrews did."

"And I bet they figured them out by context, right?" Jenny said. "I could write my name Jni Bnt and someone familiar with French or English might guess what to fill in."

"That's about how it went," Stephen agreed. "I see you scowling at our humble transcription, thinking I'm teasing you again. The characters Neville and I keep filling in as an 'I' are technically weak consonants, but don't let that bother you. I believe our writer here has included the feather to make his meaning more clear."

"More clear?" Jenny asked dubiously.

"Well, he could have left it out altogether," Stephen said. "He didn't use the signs that might fill in for the letter 'A' for some reason. So, Neville, you've had time to study this. What do you make of it?"

"I think," Neville replied, feeling his way toward what he had felt as he began to transcribe the text, "that this is not written in Egyptian, but in some other language—most probably English."

"English!" Jenny said. "Show me what you mean."

Neville pointed to a word about a third into the transcribed text.

"That for one. It says 'king' as clear as anything. The one three words later could be 'England' without too great a stretch of the imagination."

"Inglnd," Jenny said, sounding it through. "There's no hieroglyph for 'E,' right? Anyhow, we don't so much say 'eh' as 'ih.' L-N-D sure does look like 'land,' though I suppose it could be 'lend.' "

"Think like an Egyptian," Stephen urged. "What makes sense is probably what we want. Shall we start at the beginning?"

"I'll wager that 'T-H' is 'the,' " Neville said without hesitation. "It occurs several times in the text."

"Gods!" Jenny exclaimed, nearly shouting her discovery. "The next word is 'gods.' "

"Now, K-R-S doesn't look like much," Stephen said, "but take a page from our Germanic cousins. Don't look at it, sound it through."

"Krs," Jenny said obediently. Then her eyes widened. "Curse!"

"That's my guess, too," Stephen said. "We must remember that English is completely illogical and we have hard C's that sound like K's and soft C's that sound like S's. Our correspondent here is giving us phonetic equivalents."

"I think," Neville said, "that this is why he didn't use the character for 'A.' As I recall, the Egyptians didn't have a character that differentiated between the long and short forms of the vowel, while a long 'I' sounds like 'Y'—which was represented by the doubled feather character."

"The letter y is long 'I,' " Jenny murmured. "That means the next word is 'bides.' "

Using these rules, they quickly translated the remainder, with only a few words causing them to pause long enough for the ink in Stephen's pen to blot.

THE GODS CURSE BIDES BY THE BURIED KING DEPART NOT ENGLAND FOR DESERT WASTES DEATH IS THERE BEWARE THE GRINNING WOMAN SPHINX.

"I admire this manner of spelling," Jenny said, comparing the original to their transcription. "It makes more sense than ours. I mean, look at 'death.' D-E-T-H would do just as well."

"For spelling, maybe," Neville said, "but I don't much like our correspondent's content. It's rather hard to make out precisely what is meant without punctuation, but this is clearly a threat."

"Or a warning," Stephen said. "That last line isn't particularly threatening. Now, I would punctuate the text this way."

He took the pen and jotted a few marks.

THE GOD'S CURSE BIDES BY THE BURIED KING. DEPART NOT ENGLAND FOR DESERT WASTES. DEATH IS THERE. BEWARE THE GRINNING WOMAN SPHINX.

"Woman sphinx?" Jenny asked. "Aren't they all women?"

"Not at all," Stephen said. "The Egyptians apparently adored sphinxes. They depicted them with male, female, and even animal characteristics—hawks spring to mind, rams, too. So we apparently are being warned to be wary of a specific female sphinx."

"If we take the 'buried king' to mean our Neferankhotep," Neville said grimly, "that means someone knows our purpose for going to Egypt."

"Not necessarily," Stephen said breezily. "I mean, who else do archeologists want to dig up? Certainly not commoners. The occasional queen is nice, but kings are the prize."

"Maybe so," Neville said, but he was not convinced.

Jenny looked up from the message, her expression solemn. "Are you planning to cancel your trip, Uncle Neville?"

"No!" he replied a trifle sharply. Then he softened. "However, if you wish to remain here in England, it is not too late for me to speak with Lady Lindenmeade."

"I'm going," Jenny replied. "I've already started shopping. This is just going to make me expand my list—unless I can borrow your primers. We'll have lots of travel time, and I think I'd like Stephen to start teaching me hieroglyphs."

Neville forced a laugh. "You may have the books, Jenny, but I'm beginning to think you'd better buy spare ammunition for your guns."

It was hard to say who looked more surprised, Jenny or Stephen. Jenny's surprise rapidly changed to delight.

"I have a rifle, too, Uncle Neville, a new Winchester, custom-made. Can we get ammunition for that, too?"

"Of course."

Stephen sputtered, "Guns? For a lady?"

"Jenny's parents had rather peculiar ideas as to how best to raise a lady," Neville said, "and since you have no doubt that Jenny is a lady . . ." He trailed off challengingly.

"Not a bit," Stephen replied a trifle over-heartily, "and given I can't even knock off the coconut at the village fair, it's probably a good idea that Miss Benet can compensate for my deficiencies."

"We should make certain you know the basics," Neville said. "But that will need to wait. We leave in two days."

"For the desert wastes," Jenny said, looking down at the letter.

Where death awaits, Neville thought.

Unexpected Traveling Companions

JENNY THOUGHT the amount of fuss her English companions made about the journey to Egypt almost funny, given what they claimed to be ready to attempt once they were in Egypt. They were traveling through parts of the world civilized since the time of Julius Caesar—though Caesar certainly wouldn't have said the Gauls were civilized—to one of the cradles of human culture.

The distance involved was tremendous, but they were traveling by train and steamship. Thanks to Uncle Neville's wealth, they would travel first class all the way. Jenny was rather looking forward to the journey—especially when she compared it with some of those she'd taken with her parents. Those had involved buckboards, covered wagons, and in a few cases barely broken Indian ponies.

Sir Neville intended to arrive in Egypt around the ebb of the inundation of the Nile. Travel upriver would be easiest then, and the whole of the cooler winter season would remain for exploration. He admitted that he had no idea how long it would take for them to locate the Valley of Dust once they reached the Hawk Rock, and even less idea how long they would wish to remain there when—and Jenny noted with some amusement that Uncle Neville persistently said "when," never "if"—they found it.

At this point, "they" and "them" still referred exclusively to Uncle Neville, Stephen Holmboe, and the mysterious Edward Bryce, but Jenny felt certain that long before the time came for the members of the expedition to board the steamer that would carry them upriver, she would be included in their number.

And if not officially, she thought, *I'll just stow myself in a trunk 'til they can't possibly leave me behind.*

With the aim of making herself as useful as possible, Jenny applied herself to learning basic hieroglyphs—at least this way she'd recognize characters, if not always be able to interpret their meaning. She also took advantage of the long days traveling by train across France to demonstrate her skill for accurate sketching. Uncle Neville had decided not to trouble with the delicate and expensive bother of a camera, so an artist other than the already overextended Mr. Holmboe would not come amiss.

Jenny's thoughts were so focused on Egypt that France went by in a blur. Only after they had reached the port where they would board the steamship that would carry them across the entire length of the Mediterranean Sea did she wonder if this had been deliberate—an avoidance, not so much of the country, as of the inevitable memories of her French-born father that it would bring.

When they arrived aboard *Neptune's Charger,* a not completely pleasant surprise awaited them. Bert and Emily had gone ahead to settle their belongings while the remaining members of the group took care of some last minute shopping. The shops were crowded, and the French merchants obstructive until Jenny flourished her best French at them. Consequently, they arrived just before departure. *Neptune's Charger* had left port and was well out to sea when they discovered who was among their traveling companions.

Jenny was standing on an upper deck, looking down at the churning water, when a light, laughing voice spoke from close beside her. "I do always wonder why Homer called the Mediterranean the 'wine-dark sea,'" the voice said. "It looks rather like water anywhere. Maybe these blues and greens are more lustrous, but certainly the waters are not wine-purple."

Jenny turned to find Lady Audrey Cheshire leaning with studied elegance against the rail. Her first inclination was to blurt out "What are you doing here?" Her second to wonder if this meeting was completely coincidence. She might have gaped open mouthed for a moment, but her reply pleased her with its cool control.

"Lady Cheshire, is it not?" Jenny said, giving a slight dip of her skirts. "I believe we met on the day I arrived in England."

"Was that the very day you arrived?" Lady Cheshire asked. "I recall Sir Neville saying you were newly come from America, but I hadn't realized you had landed that same day. Are you then leaving again so soon?"

Jenny nodded. "Uncle Neville offered me the opportunity to accompany him to Egypt, and I was happy to take him up on his kind offer."

Lady Cheshire looked more interested than that simple response deserved. "Surely you must be apprehensive about venturing into the Egyptian wilds."

"Wilds?" Jenny laughed. "I understand Cairo is very civilized. It was an old city before London had its Great Fire."

"True." Lady Cheshire opened a fan and waved it languidly, though the sea breeze was fresh and pleasant. "Cairo *is* rather marvelous. I have visited her many times, and would be happy to show you the sights."

Knowing her uncle's desire for secrecy, Jenny didn't know how to respond to this ostensibly kind offer. She was saved from needing to do so by the arrival of that gentleman himself.

"Lady Cheshire?" Sir Neville said. "Is that you?"

Audrey Cheshire turned and subjected him to the full glow of one of her magnificent smiles. "Surprised, Sir Neville?" she said archly. "Well, you have no one but yourself to blame for my being here."

"Oh?"

Although the fashion in which Sir Neville bowed over the lady's hand was perfectly cordial, Jenny could hear the suspicion in her uncle's voice. She wondered if Lady Cheshire heard it as well. If so, she did not give any indication.

"That's right," the lady continued. "Thinking about your traveling to Egypt awoke in me a longing for those happy winters I spent in the Land of the Pharaohs with my late husband. Suddenly, the prospect of another winter in London, another dreary round of the sparrow chatter of gossipy matrons, of making calls and attending dressmaker's fittings, seemed overwhelming rather than inviting. My man of business made some inquiries, and here I am."

Her explanation seemed to relax Sir Neville somewhat, but Jenny was not convinced. The explanation seemed too pat to her. Hadn't Lord Cheshire been an archeologist? Might not his widow have gotten wind that Sir Neville was onto something big? Anyhow, Jenny didn't like the way Lady Cheshire was laying on the charm. She'd seen the same smiles on the faces of dance hall girls, and those women usually had only their own gain in mind.

Jenny hid a smile as she imagined what Lady Cheshire might think if she knew herself compared to those soiled doves of the West. Then she remembered that lady's comments about the dubious reputation of young widows, and wondered if Lady Cheshire might be cynical enough to see the similarities for herself.

Sir Neville was making conversation, comparing notes on their journeys across France and about the high prices the French charged for everything. Jenny knew it was only polite for her to join the pair, but felt rather thankful that it was a young woman's place to be seen but not heard.

Lady Cheshire was not traveling alone, and soon Mrs. Syms joined her on deck. Mrs. Syms was very excited about returning to the Land of the Pharaohs.

"They had secrets, you know," she said, animation lighting her rather horsey features. "Those pyramids were meant to focus psychic emanations, and they still do so today. The people of Egypt are wonderfully spiritual. Our own gypsies are debased Egyptians, don't you know, and even in their degraded state can still tell fortunes and all that kind of thing. One can expect marvels from the undiluted stock."

Jenny managed to keep a straight face. There was something pathetic about the woman's enthusiasm that made it easy. She was willing to bet anything that when in England Mrs. Syms attended seances and spiritualist lectures.

With the arrival of Mrs. Syms, they drifted over to a sheltered grouping of chairs, and there Captain Brentworth found them. Jenny saw the dark look he shot Uncle Neville, but that gentleman was too busy laughing over one of Lady Cheshire's witticisms to notice.

If she's not careful, Jenny thought, *there will be trouble between them over her.*

She wondered if this was precisely what Lady Cheshire desired. Perhaps Captain Brentworth was becoming too proprietary, and Lady Cheshire wished to keep him in line. That theory didn't seem to quite fit with the way she kept turning those green eyes on Captain Brentworth, drawing him in even when he grew sullen and distant. Maybe Lady Cheshire was simply one of those women who couldn't bear not to captivate each and every male around her.

If this was the case, she was going to have a good audience aboard *Neptune's Charger.* Among those aboard were a smattering of military men moving to new posts, a clergyman off to convert the heathen, and a few business travelers representing interests that supplied cotton to England's mills.

One of the military men, a Colonel Travers, had served with Sir Neville at some point in their overlapping careers. He seemed rather glad to renew their acquaintance, though perhaps with a trace of condescension on his part since Sir Neville was no longer in active service. Doubtless some of Colonel Travers's eagerness was due to the fact that he was senior among the military contingent and thus was barred from undue fraternization. Another reason was that he was traveling with his wife and daughter, for the posting to Egypt was intended to last some years.

Jenny's presence meant that the daughter, Mary, was supplied with a companion of about her own age. However, Jenny thought that Sir Neville, though over forty, was still considered a potential catch in the marriage sweepstakes, his former military connections, current knighthood, and tidy fortune outweighing any disadvantage that age might convey. For her part, Mary made polite conversation with Sir Neville, but Jenny thought her preference was for any of several of the younger officers under her father's supervision.

Over the next few days, several of these young men paid Jenny a fair amount of attention, more so after Emily rather acidly commented to her mistress that gossip had confirmed that Jenny was the likely heir to her uncle's estate. However, having been belle by default of many a frontier post, Jenny was pretty well able to judge men. Alice Benet had met with her share of flirtatious advances herself, and had not left her daughter unequipped with the benefits of her experience.

There was one man—or youth—who did catch Jenny's eye, though not for his marriageability. On the second or third day out from their original port, Jenny was enjoying the pleasant weather on one of the forward decks in company with Lady Cheshire, Mrs. Syms, Mrs. Travers, and Miss Travers. Several of the men were playing cards a short distance away, Captain Brentworth among them. He looked into his cigarette case, found it empty, and barked at the nearest steward.

"Hey, you. Call my boy and tell him I need more cigarettes."

The steward made some polite response and vanished. Jenny was musing over how the English treated their servants rather like Southerners had treated slaves, when a slim, dark youth emerged on deck. He was dressed in a hybrid of English and Arabic costume, trousered, but turbaned, the lines of his attire looser and more flowing than was usual. The light color of the fabrics contrasted handsomely with the warm golden brown of his skin. He looked, Jenny thought, her mind filled with her daily lessons in Egyptology, like one of the young men in the tomb reliefs come to life.

The young man salaamed deeply, extended what should have been a filled cigarette case but proved to be a single carpet slipper.

"Cigarette case!" Captain Brentworth bellowed, throwing his empty case at the boy in illustration. "Why the deuce would I want a slipper?"

The young man bent and picked the empty case from the deck, salaamed again, and went below, leaving the slipper behind.

"Idiot!" Captain Brentworth fumed. "I have half a mind to return him to the orphanage when we arrive in Cairo. Natives are often slow, but this one can be positively moronic."

Captain Brentworth's rant was interrupted by the return of the boy, his cheeks flushed, his gaze downcast. He flung himself clumsily to the deck, extending a filled cigarette case with one hand.

"Take this," Captain Brentworth growled, tossing the slipper at the boy, "and listen to what I say from now on."

The boy took the slipper and was about to withdraw when Lady Cheshire called out.

"Rashid! Come here, please."

Jenny gave the woman a point for the "please," but Lady Cheshire's tone was as imperious as that with which Captain Brentworth had addressed the steward.

"I feel rather dull," Lady Cheshire said when the youth had hastened over, salaamed, and stood waiting, his unfocused gaze on the deck. "Do you have mischief with you?"

Jenny was still puzzling over this odd question when Rashid bowed again, and, reaching into the folds of his shirt, removed a small monkey from where it clung against the warmth of his chest. Slender and long-limbed, the monkey possessed a graceful tail nearly as long as itself. Bright eyes, far more alert and intelligent than those of its master, surveyed the gathering from a face furred mostly white, white face and ruff providing striking contrast to the monkey's nut-brown coat.

Rashid presented the little animal to Lady Cheshire, who took the monkey without any of the shrinking that so many women seemed to think was required if the animal in question was anything other than a lapdog, a very somnolent cat, or a riding horse.

Reluctantly—for several days further acquaintance had not made Jenny any more willing to trust Lady Cheshire—Jenny was forced to award her another point. After further consideration, Jenny realized she was not certain what game she was scoring, or whether Lady Cheshire even knew they were playing. All she was certain of—this with no evidence at all—was that Lady Cheshire's departure for Egypt on the very ship on which they themselves were traveling could not be coincidence.

However, Jenny was very aware that she had no evidence to support this certainty, so said nothing of her suspicions to either Uncle Neville or Mr. Holmboe.

Mischief turned out to be the monkey's name, and he had a half-dozen or so tricks he would do, including putting a handkerchief over his head like a bonnet and peeking out. He had clever little fingers, and delighted at being given something to handle. It was almost as if Mischief saw the world through those agile little fingers, not through the slightly worried eyes that darted from face to face as he performed, as if the monkey was wondering which among his audience were the screamers and which might become friends.

"Rashid seized Mischief from some street performer in London," Lady Cheshire explained, while Mischief clung to her arm and chattered nervously. "I don't know the exact circumstances, but the poor little beast was very ill when Rashid brought it back. Rashid nursed him as faithfully as any mother, and now Mischief is completely devoted to him—though I like to think that the darling little creature knows his friends."

Jenny longed to hold the monkey, but knew without asking that this was Lady Cheshire's show. Still, she could assert herself, too, and did so by opening the book of hieroglyphs that Uncle Neville had loaned her and making a point of attending to her studies, rather than to Lady Cheshire.

This didn't bother Lady Cheshire one bit. That lady's intended audience was not the small circle of women, but the men gathered over at the card tables. Before long, a deep voice interjected itself into the female twittering, and then another, and when Jenny slipped away to her cabin, no one noticed her departure.

Emily was in the cabin, folding away some freshly laundered clothing. She offered to excuse herself, but Jenny was glad for her company. Both Emily and her Bert were the kind of direct, honest hardworking folk Jenny had frequently met on the frontier, and seemed more real to her than the majority of the first class passengers.

For her part, Emily had forgiven Jenny for the incident of the six-guns, especially after Jenny had told her any number of stories about real Indians and cattle drives—the retelling of which had made Emily very popular with her associates.

"Emily," Jenny asked, "had you met Lady Cheshire before this voyage?"

"Her?" Emily said, pursing her lips in a momentary frown. "We haven't been introduced, if that's what you mean, she being gentry and all."

"Did she ever call on Uncle Neville?"

Emily considered.

"I believe she might have been to Hawthorne House a time or two, for the master's lecture nights. He was holding those fair regular for a while, belonged to some association for antiquities. They met at the houses of the members until the group grew so large they thought a hall might be better."

"And Lady Cheshire came to some of those?"

"I think so," Emily said. "She seems familiar. I'd be helping out you see, with coats and things, and she's a striking lady, with those green eyes and all that dark hair."

"Yes, she is," Jenny agreed. "So she's genuinely interested in Egyptology, then."

"I believe so, Miss. Lady Cheshire's maid was saying that the lady has all sorts of horrid things at her house: mummy cases, bones, bits of hair and linen." Emily shuddered. "I don't mind saying, Miss, that I wouldn't want to have the dusting of such trash. Sir Neville's collection is much nicer. The alabaster is lovely stuff and so is that fay-ance glass, though why anyone would want broken old pots is beyond me."

"I like them for the wonder of touching something made by people who lived so very long ago," Jenny said. "So you know Lady Cheshire's maid?"

"Can't hardly help it on a boat like this," Emily sniffed, "though I fancy she wouldn't give me the time of day in other circumstances. She's French—gives herself airs for knowing about high fashion and being able to do delicate lacework and such. The other woman's maid, she who waits on that Mrs. Syms—Polly, her name is—she's a simple countrywoman with no nonsense to her."

"Not very much like her mistress, then," Jenny said with a light laugh. "Mrs. Syms believes all sorts of nonsense."

Surprisingly, Emily, who was a good churchgoing woman and should have no truck with things like spiritualism, softened.

"Ah, but then the poor woman has had her share of hardship, she has."

Jenny tilted her head inquiringly.

So encouraged, Emily went on, "You knows Mrs. Syms is a widow, but do you know how her husband died?"

"I do not. Mrs. Syms is remarkably silent on the subject, given how much she likes to talk on other things. Only yesterday Mrs. Travers was talking about how her sister had recently lost her husband. I noticed that Mrs. Syms became quite pale, and soon after she excused herself."

"Mr. Syms died saving her life, he did," Emily explained in hushed tones. "They were traveling by carriage from some country ball and highwaymen pulled them over and were going to rob them. The thieves hit the coachman over his head and left him senseless. Mrs. Syms was quite terrified, so Polly says, especially when it came clear that the men were more than a bit gone in drink and might be thinking of more than robbery.

"Mr. Syms was having none of that, though. He hit one man and took his gun, then shot another. The highwaymen ran for their lives, then, but not before the good man himself was shot. Mrs. Syms herself drove the coach to the nearest house, but there was no saving her husband. They had no children, being young married then, and she never looked to wed again. Lord Cheshire was some sort of a cousin to her and gave her a roof so her small inheritance wouldn't be wasted, and Lady Cheshire has continued just as kind."

Another point to her, Jenny thought with a certain desperation. *I don't want to hear good things about Audrey Cheshire. I can feel in my bones she doesn't mean well by us.*

"Poor Mrs. Syms," Jenny replied with real feeling. "I can indeed see why she might be interested in spiritualism. I wonder if she has ever forgiven herself."

Emily sighed agreement. "I can't imagine how I'd feel seeing my Bert bleed out his life to save my honor. It's romantic enough in stories, but I think it would really be quite horrid."

"You are a sensible woman, Mrs. Hamilton," Jenny said. "The ladies' servants may be chatty, but I saw Captain Brentworth's boy for the first time today, and he's quiet enough."

Emily's eyes grew round.

"You mean the Mohammedan lad?" she said. "Oh, he's quiet, and like to stay that way. Polly tells me he's a mute and an idiot. Captain Brentworth hired Rashid from some orphanage or poorhouse in Cairo. The lad cannot say a single word, only makes a sort of flat noise like a goat bleating that's supposed to be laughing. He fair gives me the creeps, never looking you in the eye, though I suppose he's a good enough soul. He's kind to that queer pet of his, and they do say you can always judge a man by how he treats his creatures."

"Mute?" Jenny said. "Is Rashid deaf as well?"

"No, he can hear right enough, just can't make his throat shape talking sounds. Can't write, neither, on account of not being very bright."

"So how does he make his master know what is needed?"

Emily grew guarded.

"I don't suppose Captain Brentworth is the type to take much direction from a servant, Miss."

"But what if Rashid needs supplies? Needles and thread or something?"

Jenny felt rather vague about those things a manservant might use to tend his master's needs, but Emily understood.

"I think Rashid has a few signs he can make, gestures and suchlike," Emily replied. "They must get by, since Rashid has been in Captain Brentworth's service some years now—though Polly says the captain is always threatening to get rid of him."

"True."

Fascinated by the exotic young servant, Jenny found excuses to have her path intersect Rashid's and to offer a pleasant nod or a polite greeting in her rather stilted Arabic. Such opportunities were not difficult to find. Rashid seemed to be the favorite errand boy for both Lady Cheshire and Captain Brentworth, as Babette, Lady Cheshire's French maid thought herself above such tasks, and Polly was not taking well to sea travel.

The number of ladies traveling on *Neptune's Charger* was not large, so even if Jenny had wanted to avoid Lady Cheshire, she could not have done so. However, she did not wish to do so—not with Uncle Neville forming a member of Lady Cheshire's court more often than Jenny felt was wise.

Sir Neville had even taken to reading poetry to the lady. His selections were not in the least romantic, but Captain Brentworth, who could not read aloud without making the verse sound like barked commands, clearly envied the other man his delivery—and his proximity to the lady. When Lady Cheshire suggested that Sir Neville read for one of the entertainments the passengers regularly got up for their mutual amusement, Captain Brentworth was clearly irate.

Stephen Holmboe had already participated in one of these entertainments, reading the grisly "Murders in the Rue Morgue" by the American author Edgar Allan Poe, and afterwards arguing quite engagingly about the merits of pure deduction as a means of solving mysteries. Sir Neville had taken the opposite side, and the pair had been applauded for their skill in arguing black white, which Mr. Babellard, the clergyman, had said verged on the Jesuitical.

Jenny was considering what she could offer as her portion of one of these entertainments—perhaps some of the frontier tales that had so fascinated Emily would do—when another communication in hieroglyphs jolted her party out of their more casual preoccupations.

The missive had been handed to Stephen along with the rest of the Hawthorne party's mail when he went below to fetch a book he needed to consult during one of Jenny's lessons on Egyptology.

"Whatever is wrong, Mr. Holmboe?" Jenny asked, when Stephen returned, an envelope held awkwardly in one hand.

"Something rather curious," he said, moving his hand so that she could see that a series of hieroglyphs had been written at the bottom of the envelope below the otherwise very usual routing instructions. Had it not been for their earlier experience, she might have dismissed them as decoration.

Stephen lowered his voice. "I fear we should not discuss whatever this contains in such a public area. If you will locate your uncle and ask him to meet us at his stateroom, I will gather up our books and will join you shortly."

Jenny did so. She waited until Uncle Neville had concluded the long passage he was reading from one of Browning's dramatic monologues, and had received the gushing praise of Lady Cheshire, before saying rather petulantly:

"Uncle Neville, I wish you would resolve an argument between myself and Mr. Holmboe. I tell him that his interpretation of one of the exercises he has set me cannot be correct."

"Oh," replied Sir Neville, obviously amused. "You wish me to defy my own instructor on your behalf?"

Jenny pouted slightly. "I think you could help. This lesson reminds me of the first lesson we did back at Hawthorne House, the one on phonetics. You were able to offer some valuable clarification then, and I do wish you would do so now."

For a moment she thought he might not remember that first lesson, but the momentary flicker of puzzlement departed his features almost as soon as it formed. He laughed, perhaps a trifle theatrically, and rose to his feet.

"If you ladies will excuse me," he said, bowing around the small group. "Mr. Holmboe forgets himself in his enthusiasm. It may be that a more recent student such as myself may indeed be able to offer some assistance."

The ladies did excuse him, though Jenny thought that Lady Cheshire would have liked to have had a reason to attach herself to their party. However, she had already admitted ignorance of all but the most general principles of hieroglyphic writing, so there was no reason why her presence might be helpful.

Jenny followed her uncle to his stateroom, where Stephen Holmboe joined them almost immediately, firmly closing the door into the small room.

"Same correspondent," he began, dropping the envelope onto the table for their inspection. "I recognize the hand."

Jenny was now familiar enough with hieroglyphic writing to know that the signs were shaped slightly differently by every scribe. Still, she thought Stephen's distinction unnecessary.

"I should hope so," she said. "I can hardly imagine two such cranks!"

Stephen cocked a bushy blond eyebrow at her.

"We should not make assumptions," he said. "When you assume, you make an ass out of you and me."

He grinned then, and Jenny, remembering that "ass" was not as rude a term in British English as it was in American, stopped being shocked and caught the joke. She snorted and returned her attention to the envelope.

"It's addressed to you, Uncle Neville. Open it!"

Neville Hawthorne was frowning at the routing instructions. Except for the line of hieroglyphs, they were in keeping with the other letters that had arrived in the same post—although the postmarks were somewhat blurred, as if the envelope had been splashed.

"I wonder who is sending these to us?" he said.

"Let's look at what's inside," Jenny suggested. "Maybe this one will be easier to read."

Nodding, Sir Neville slit open the envelope and removed a folded sheet of paper, neatly lettered with a series of hieroglyphs. Jenny bent forward, eager to see if she could read any of them.

"Our correspondent has used some of the same words," Jenny said, recalling

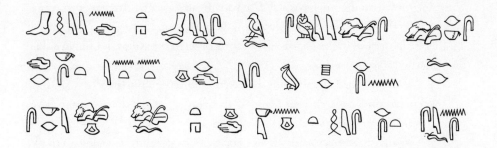

the previous letter, which she had poured over repeatedly with a sort of horrified fascination. "Isn't that 'the'?"

Uncle Neville nodded. He had taken one of the chairs, and motioned Jenny toward the other.

"Let us see what we can make of this," he said.

In a few moments, they had come up with a list of letters nearly as unintelligible as the original.

BHYND TH BRYTST UF SMYLS LRKS DRKST INTNT GRD IS A PR RSUN FR SCRILG LF THE GD KING T HS RST SFYNKS.

"I think it's going to be easier this time," Stephen said. "We know it's in English, so we can fill in fairly easily."

Jenny nodded. "That's 'the good king' there toward the end."

Sir Neville raised a hand. "Let's start at the beginning, shall we? 'Behind the brightest of smiles . . .' "

" 'Lurks,' " Stephen said, not so much interrupting as letting his enthusiasm rule his tongue. " 'Lurks darkest intent.' The next word is a poser until you read on, then it just has to be 'greed.' "

"Yes," Jenny said, continuing his translation. " 'Greed is a poor reason for sacrilege.' But lf? Leaf is all that comes to my mind, and that makes no sense at all."

"Laugh?" Stephen suggested, but he didn't sound convinced. "Luff? Rather too nautical, I fear."

"Luff . . . That rather reminds me of old Alphonse Liebermann," Neville said. "He always transformed his 'V's into 'F's so whenever he spoke about 'love'—as he did frequently when Eddie's attraction to Miriam came apparent—it sounded like he was discussing a high wind."

"Love is rather like a high wind," Stephen said. "Blows you away."

He grinned, and Jenny groaned. She had already learned that Stephen was a punster—and she could imagine just how popular this trait would have made him with the serious archeologists who might otherwise have found him a valuable assistant.

Sir Neville frowned at this levity, his attention fixed on the letter.

"Stephen, am I remembering correctly that the Egyptians don't seem to have had a phonetic equivalent for 'V'?"

"That's right!" Stephen said. "If our correspondent hadn't been able to think of a way around using a letter that, after all, is very common in English, he might have had to resort to the next best choice—an 'F.'"

"So 'love' is an option," Jenny said, "but it doesn't make any sense."

"Look at the text that follows," Stephen urged. "'Lf the good king,' then a single 'T'—it just has to be 'to.'"

"'To his,'" Jenny said, filling in the next words, "'rest.' And the last word is . . ."

"Sphinx!" Stephen said. "With that, I'm betting then that 'lf' is 'leave.'"

Sir Neville pushed his notes forward so they could read the finished text. "'Behind the brightest of smiles lurks darkest intent. Greed is a poor reason for sacrilege. Leave the good king to his rest.' And it's signed 'Sphinx.'"

"A good name for him, since he persists in speaking in riddles," Neville said. "If it is indeed a signature, as this seems to indicate, it rather changes our reading of the first letter, as well."

He pulled out their translation.

"The last sentence becomes, 'Beware the grinning woman. Sphinx.' It's a warning against a specific person—a grinning woman."

Stephen looked rather uncomfortable. Jenny glanced over and met his eye, but neither of them spoke. Over her lessons they had traded a few confidences, and she knew that he too had his doubts about Lady Cheshire and her winning smiles. Uncle Neville, however, seemed unaware of their suspicions.

"I suppose we'll know this grinning woman when we see her," he said. "I'm less happy with the rest of this. It does seem as if the blighter knows what we're after, and has the effrontery to warn us off."

Unable to make herself address the matter of Lady Cheshire, Jenny brought up the other thing that had been troubling her.

"We've been referring to whoever's writing these as 'he,'" she said, "but wasn't Oedipus's sphinx, the one who spoke those famous riddles, wasn't that one female?"

"A point," Stephen said. "Well, if so that rather narrows the field, doesn't it?"

In answer to Jenny's questioning look, he said, "I mean, there aren't that many women who read and write hieroglyphs, if you see what I mean."

"I would have said," Jenny replied a bit stiffly, "that it broadened the field to include the entire human race."

Then she relented. "But I see what you mean. Really, there aren't that many people who read and write hieroglyphs at all."

"Unfortunately," Neville said, "we are heading to a part of the world with what I suppose must be the largest concentration of hieroglyph readers *per capita*. Does anyone have a nomination as to who our correspondent might be?"

Jenny shook her head.

"It would be easier if we could limit ourselves to people on this vessel. Unhappily, there is daily contact with land that includes the same postal delivery that brought us this. Lots of people in England and a few in Egypt know we're on this ship."

"So the writer could be anyone," Neville said, "in two countries—including those frustrating Sons of the Hawk. Stephen, are you willing to continue with me in my search for the Valley of Dust?"

Both Jenny and Stephen nodded, and Jenny felt a thrill in her heart at not being excluded. That thrill faded some at Uncle Neville's next words.

"Jenny, I think you had better unpack that little derringer of yours and discreetly wear it about your person. Stephen, I have delayed your shooting lessons too long. Colonel Travers was speaking just the other day about his concern that his men were doing too much flirting and too little soldiering. I believe he will be quite happy to include you in the training sessions he plans."

Uncle Neville stared down at the papers spread on the table, glowering at them for a long moment before beginning to fold them away.

"We will take precautions," he said, "but I have come too far and waited too long to be turned away by a few riddling words."

Auguste Dupin

WHEN *NEPTUNE'S Charger* was only a few days out of Alexandria, a tremendous uproar broke the lazy hour between tea and dinner. First the passengers visiting on the shaded promenade deck observed the purser, Andrew Watkins, hurrying to the first class cabins. Not long after an assortment of the ship's officers—including, astonishingly, Captain Easthill himself—hurried in the same direction.

Neville, who had been enjoying a quiet conversation with Lady Cheshire while supervising Jenny's lessons, was amused when his niece, obviously curious about what was going on, excused herself, saying she needed something from her cabin. She was turned back politely but firmly by one of the purser's flunkies. Even this was news of a sort, so she returned to her companions and reported.

"We haven't seen the ship's surgeon go by," Lady Cheshire commented. "Otherwise, I might hazard illness."

"He might have arrived from another direction," Stephen Holmboe commented, marking his place in Scott's *The Heart of Midlothian* with his thumb. "The one is not ruled out by the other."

"*Oui, Monsieur Dupin,*" Lady Cheshire responded with a charming laugh.

Mr. Holmboe apparently did not take well to the lady's teasing, for he colored deeply, and prepared to hide his embarrassment in the pages of his book.

"Look," Jenny said. "I believe we are going to learn something. Here comes Mr. Watkins."

Andrew Watkins had been in the Royal Navy, and something of that service's discipline remained with him, even on purely social occasions. This afternoon, however, his hat was off and his thinning hair was in disarray. He paused a short distance from the gathered passengers, clearly looking for one in particular, then hurried over to where Mary Travers was taking advantage of the rare absence of both of her parents to flirt with a few of her favorite soldiers under Mrs. Syms's indulgent supervision.

"Miss Travers," Watkins said, barely concealing his agitation, "if you would come with me, your mother is in need of you."

Mary might be flighty, in Neville's opinion, but she was a good girl at heart. There was nothing at all affected in the way she sprang to her feet, her face suddenly pale.

"Is Mother ill?"

"It seems so," Mr. Watkins admitted. "Doctor MacDonagal says there is no danger, but your presence may be beneficial."

"I'll come right away," Mary said, and did so, not even bothering to reply to the several earnest offers of assistance proffered by the young officers who moments before had been so central to her attention.

Neville frowned. He genuinely liked Colonel Travers, even if he thought him a bit by the book and unimaginative. Mrs. Travers had all the best qualities of a career military wife. Indeed, Neville privately thought her permitting Mary a bit of flirtation out from under her mother's eye was an indication of this, the wisdom that an easy hand on the rein kept the mouth soft and sensitive to guidance.

Jenny looked after her departing friend with real concern in those remarkable violet eyes.

"Uncle Neville," she said, "do you think I should offer my help? Perhaps Dr. MacDonagal is unaccustomed to treating ladies."

"If he's an officer on a passenger ship, he most certainly has done so," Neville assured her. "I'm certain that they would be as happy for your offer later as now."

Jenny sat back and picked up her book, but Neville doubted she saw anything before her. Her downcast eyes had clouded, and before she could stop it, a tear leaked from beneath her lashes. She quickly mopped the betraying drop away, and Neville thought it better not to comment. Clearly, these were not tears of pique, but of sorrow at the memory of her own mother's death when she—unlike Mary—had been far away and unable to help.

There seemed to be a singular dearth of servants about. Even Captain Brentworth's strident bellows for Rashid produced no result.

"They must be being kept below," Stephen ventured. "If they were above deck I think we would have heard them—or they us."

He glanced over at Captain Brentworth, who was moodily puffing on a cigarette as if Rashid's failure to appear were a personal insult.

Sometime later a steward who professed to know nothing about the earlier commotion appeared on deck and asked if he could bring anyone some light refreshment. Dinner would be served on schedule, but for the time being the passengers were asked to remain where they were. Not long after that, Mr. Watkins returned. He walked directly over to Stephen Holmboe.

"Mr. Holmboe," he said, "if I may trouble you, your presence has been requested by the captain."

Stephen rose from his chair, putting his book aside.

"Certainly," he said. "Lead on."

"Half a moment," Neville said. "Mr. Holmboe is in my employ. I cannot have him involved in something without my knowledge."

Mr. Watkins frowned, but did not seem inclined to argue.

"Very well, Sir Neville. If you gentlemen . . ."

Jenny interrupted.

"I'm coming, too," she said. "Wild horses wouldn't stop me."

Mr. Watkins obviously knew when he was beaten. "If your uncle desires your presence," he said.

Neville knew he'd rather have Jenny under his eye than spend his energy worrying about what ingenious methods she would be devising to satisfy her curiosity.

"I do," he said firmly. "Come along, Genevieve."

The use of her formal name was as an adequate reminder to be on her best behavior. Jenny followed demurely, not asking any of the questions that normally would come tumbling out.

Mr. Watkins explained the details of the situation, once they were below. "The difficulty is with Colonel and Mrs. Travers. They are waiting in the ship's library. As the matter is somewhat private, I would rather leave it to them to explain."

The small library was impossibly crowded. Colonel Travers was bending over his loudly weeping wife, while Mary knelt at her mother's feet. A servant was setting down a tray with teapot and cups, his expression neutral but his eyes alive with interest. Captain Easthill was just departing, smoothing a scowl of annoyance from his features when he saw the new arrivals.

"Carry on, Watkins," he said gruffly to the purser. "It's stormy weather in there. Mr. Holmboe, thank you for your assistance. I sincerely hope you can re-solve this very difficult matter."

"I shall endeavor to do so," Stephen replied. Then he addressed the Travers family. "Perhaps one of you would like to explain what has happened?"

Colonel Travers rose and glowered at the servant who was fussing with the tea tray.

"That's enough idling. Get on with you. Mary, pour your mother some tea and make her take the powder Dr. MacDonagal gave her. Teresa, for heaven's sake get a hold on yourself. Mr. Holmboe and Sir Neville have come to help, and they can't learn anything with you yowling like that."

Neville noted that Jenny had done the seeming impossible, slipping past the colonel into the library, and was now helping Mary with the tea and medication.

Colonel Travers glanced up and down the passageway. Finding it clear of everyone but their immediate group and Mr. Watkins, he made a production of clearing his throat.

"Thank you for coming, gentlemen. We have a bit of a problem. My wife's jewel case has been stolen."

Stephen's eyebrows shot up. "Certainly you can't believe I took it!"

"Not at all, not at all, Mr. Holmboe. It is simply that this ship has nothing that remotely resembles a police force. We can report the theft once the ship docks in Alexandria, but Teresa fears that the jewels will be spirited ashore long before then."

Stephen blinked, interested, but obviously wondering what any of this had to do with him. Indeed, Neville could have understood if Colonel Travers had called on his soldiers to form a search party, but what use did he have for an eccentric linguist?

From within the library proper, Mrs. Travers swallowed her sobs enough to speak. "Mr. Holmboe, I recalled your reading from Poe, and how admiringly you spoke of the science of ratiocination. I thought that if anyone aboard this vessel could recover my jewels, it would be a man of science and learning like yourself."

The wind and weather to which Stephen's fair skin had been subjected of late could not hide the color rising to his cheeks.

"Madam, I am only an admirer of Dupin's methods, not a practitioner of the science, except within the limits of my profession. I am a linguist, a translator. I fear I know little about the criminal mind."

Mrs. Travers began to weep again uncontrollably. Jenny left Mary to comfort her mother, and came to the door, speaking in a soft, urgent voice hardly above a whisper.

"Mr. Holmboe, don't you think you could at least try? Mrs. Travers is genuinely upset, and I fear she will do herself an injury if she continues on this way."

Colonel Travers seconded the request. "Please, Mr. Holmboe. If you learn nothing, I will not hold the failure against you. My wife had several items of great sentimental worth in the case. She would never have brought them with her, but this posting to Egypt is to be for some years and she was reluctant to do without her treasures."

Neville hated to see the colonel at such a loss. "What do you say, Stephen? I will gladly assist you in whatever way I can. We certainly can't do more harm."

Mr. Watkins, the purser, who until then had been standing against the passageway wall and looking helpless, stepped forward.

"Captain Easthill has assured us that we have his permission—indeed, his encouragement—to undertake such an investigation. He will ensure the crew's cooperation. I firmly believe that the captain would prefer to have this matter settled before we make port in Alexandria, and the criminal has a chance to jump ship."

"Very well." Stephen nodded decisively. "I suppose we can do no more harm than has already been done. Mr. Watkins, ask the quartermaster, or whatever you call that officer on a ship, to make certain that nothing is handed off board when a supply ship calls. Can you make certain that those men who handle such interactions are completely trustworthy?"

"I would like to say that everyone aboard is trustworthy," Watkins replied, a trace stiffly. "I cannot. However, I can request that only old hands be employed in such tasks. In event, we've already had our daily supplies."

Stephen smiled. "Wonderful. One more question. How widely is Mrs. Travers's loss known?"

Watkins clicked his tongue against his teeth. "Fairly widely, at least among the crew and servants. We thought at first the case had been mislaid, perhaps accidentally carried off with the laundry. That meant we had to speak with the servants, then with the officer of those departments. Then Colonel Travers insisted on speaking to a ranking officer. Then the doctor had to be called when the lady grew hysterical . . ."

"Then news will be all over, like fleas on a stray dog's back," Stephen concluded. "Very well. We must accept that the thief will have hidden the case as carefully as possible. Perhaps we can deduce where, before we do a compartment-by-compartment search."

Mrs. Travers sniffled loudly. "If the thief knows we are closing in on him, he may throw my jewelry into the sea."

Stephen shook his head solemnly. "Reason dictates otherwise, madam.

Thieves work for profit, and there is no profit in throwing jewels into the sea, especially when there are so many admirable hiding places on the ship for the case. There would be even more if he removes the jewels from their case and hides each piece separately."

Seeing Teresa Travers about to begin sobbing again at this new thought, Neville hastened to interrupt. "I think he will not remove them, Stephen, for if he does so he increases the likelihood that a single piece will be discovered, and so give us insight into the hiding places of the rest."

Jenny added, "Or that someone will find a bit of the swag and keep it for himself . . . or turn it in and hope for the Traverses' gratitude."

"Good thinking, Miss Benet," Stephen said. "Colonel, why not let it get about that you're willing to offer a reward if the jewels are found? To anyone but myself, of course," he added hastily, obviously eager not to be thought grasping. "The thief may decide that it is in his own best interest to pretend to find the jewels and return them."

"I can do that," Colonel Travers said. "However, I would prefer to wait until you have completed at least a preliminary investigation. You may make offering a reward unnecessary, and I dislike the thought of paying off a thief."

"However you decide to handle the matter," Stephen said breezily, "will suit me. Now, Mrs. Travers, tell me: when did you last see the jewel case? In fact, why not start by telling us what it looks like?"

Mrs. Travers seemed finally to have gotten control of herself, or perhaps the mild sedative prescribed by Dr. MacDonagal was taking effect. She sipped her tea, then answered with almost military precision.

"I saw it last this morning," she said, "when I took out this little cameo clasp to wear with my dress. The case is a polished walnut box about six inches deep, six or eight inches long and slightly less wide. My initials are inlaid in mother-of-pearl on the lid, surrounded with scrollwork. The case itself is lined with velvet, and contains a shallow upper tray. It is locked, and I always carry the key."

Stephen nodded. "Are you certain you didn't see the case again at tea time?"

Mrs. Travers paused to consider. "I had no need to check for it. My dress was quite suitable for tea. I only discovered my loss when I went to select what I would wear for dinner. I opened the cabinet beneath the lower bunk where I had been keeping it, and found that it had vanished!"

She started to sob again. Stephen waited for her to continue, his expression growing faintly annoyed. Neville suspected that even having two sisters and an invalid mother had not inured Stephen to the fashion for decorous female tears.

"Colonel Travers," Neville said hastily, lest Stephen voice his impatience, "who has access to your cabin other than yourselves and your daughter?"

The colonel frowned thoughtfully.

"My man, Atkins. He 'does' for both of us. Mary and her mother have been assisting each other with feminine things. We plan to hire servants once we get to Egypt. Then there is the steward who cleans up the place, fills the water bottle, makes the bunks, and suchlike."

"That would be Timothy Hamlin," Watkins supplied. "I have spoken with him. He claims not to have had reason to go into the Traverses' cabin since he made up the bunks this morning. He has been with the ship since her launching, and we have had nothing more than the occasional complaint about him—laziness mostly—certainly none regarding his honesty."

Stephen took out a sheet of paper and jotted down names. Neville wondered if Stephen had noticed, as Jenny certainly had, judging from her slight smile, that Mrs. Travers's tears had ceased as soon as she saw that further sympathy was in short supply.

"Anyone else?" Stephen prompted.

"No one but members of the family," Colonel Travers said. "I was in a few times, once to get a book I wanted to show Sir Neville, another time for my pipe. Atkins was busy mending some things, and I didn't want to take him from his work."

Stephen made a note of this. Neville had the sneaking suspicion that these notes were more to reassure Stephen's audience that he was attending than because he needed them. Surely a young man who could keep the complexities of ancient Egyptian verb tenses in his memory could remember a few names.

"Mr. Watkins," Stephen said, turning to the purser, "has the cabin been carefully searched?"

"As soon as Mrs. Travers reported the case missing," Watkins replied, clearly relieved to be able to report something positive. "We thought the case might have fallen to the floor or become buried under something else in the cabinet. I assisted Colonel Travers in making a careful inspection of both these areas, but we found no sign of the missing jewels."

"Colonel Travers, have either you or Mrs. Travers had reason to be discontent with your man Atkins?"

The colonel shook his head decisively.

"None. Atkins has been my man for years. I have even spoken to him about his remaining in my service when I retire from the Army."

"And Mr. Watkins speaks equally well of Mr. Hamlin," Stephen mused. "Are there any others you would add to my list of suspects?"

Clearly he expected no reply, but what he received was a stream of loquacious abuse from Mrs. Travers. The words were so incoherent that Mary had to calm her mother.

"Mother, please slow down," Mary said soothingly. "Mr. Holmboe cannot help if he cannot understand you."

Mrs. Travers obeyed, but her ample bosom heaved with barely suppressed passion.

"I said that I was certain that my jewel case has been stolen by that skulking Arab servant of Captain Brentworth! I've seen the dark-skinned rascal prowling about where he has no right to be. Those natives are all thieves, anyhow. I'm certain that the sneaking scoundrel wanted my jewels to sell so he could have money with which to indulge in his barbaric pleasures."

Neville shot a glance at Jenny. He hadn't missed his niece's interest in Rashid, and he had heard her voice her displeasure with how whites treated native peoples. Jenny's full lips were pressed into a tight line, but she said nothing.

Personally, Neville agreed with Jenny's unspoken advocacy of the Egyptian. From what he had observed, Rashid was dully polite, if vague and rather stupid. He brought a bovine patience to his attendance upon his rather tyrannical master. However, nothing would be gained from saying so now, and Neville had no desire to make Mrs. Travers so angry that she rejected Stephen's advice. Besides, Captain Brentworth was a stiff-necked customer, likely to take offense if someone attached to him were accused of theft.

Stephen made a note of Mrs. Travers's accusations, ascertained whose cabins were nearest to the Traverses' own, and then rose to his feet. "I would like to begin by examining the cabin," he said. "If Sir Neville and Miss Benet would assist me?"

Colonel Travers stepped forward. "I don't quite . . ."

Stephen gave a very urbane smile. "Quite simple, really. You and Mr. Watkins are both overly familiar with the place in question. We all know how easy it is to overlook something in a familiar place . . . Certainly you have mislaid a favorite pipe or some other trifle only to find it in some obvious place?"

Since Colonel Travers was already becoming legendary aboard *Neptune's Charger* for how easily he mislaid his pipe, he had the grace to grin acknowledgement.

"Now," Stephen continued, "neither Sir Neville or myself have been in your cabin. Miss Benet will make certain the proprieties regarding female attire are attended to. No shocks among the stockings, eh?"

They were excused without further delay, and when they were alone Stephen said, with a dry chuckle, "Actually, I had to get Miss Benet away before she flew to defend the young Egyptian's honor. I quite liked Mrs. Travers before all that rot came driveling out. I'm sure if I'd asked for more suspects she would have been accusing the Africans in the boiler room next. However, since we are away, let us go and search the room."

"Do you have any thoughts, Mr. Holmboe?" Jenny asked. "Since you rightly dismiss that accusation of Rashid?"

"A thread of a thought," Stephen admitted. "Sir Neville, you seem to know Colonel Travers fairly well. Have you heard any rumors that he or his wife are in financial difficulty?"

"It has been years since Travers and I served together," Neville said, "but I still have friends at the military clubs. I didn't hear anything there, nor have I caught any such hints from the other officers aboard—a few of them are real gossips, too, and not so fond of their commander that they would hesitate to spread scandal."

"Jenny, anything on the ladies?"

"Nothing," she replied promptly. "Both Mrs. Travers and Mary's clothing is fashionable, but not beyond what would be reasonable for them. They certainly aren't spending overmuch in the shops. Neither seems to gamble—at least Lady Cheshire hasn't been able to get either to take a flutter when we're playing cards."

"Fine," Stephen said. "There are other ways of running into debt—someone could be being blackmailed, for example."

"Really, Stephen!" Sir Neville protested. "I hardly think that likely."

Stephen grinned a trace sheepishly. "Very well. For now we'll work from the assumption that no one in the Travers family pretended to steal the jewels either to claim on the insurance or in order to sell them in Egypt. Besides, they were willing to let us search their cabin. That speaks well for them."

"And the servants?" Neville asked. "Atkins and Hamlin?"

"Both men," Stephen said, unlocking the door to the Traverses' cabin, "have good characters. Let us not sully them until we have exhausted other options."

"Then what shall we do?" Jenny asked.

"Mrs. Travers appealed to Auguste Dupin, not to me. I keep thinking of one of Dupin's adventures. Therefore, like Dupin, I shall not pursue the unlikely until I have exhausted the likely."

"Whatever do you mean?" Jenny persisted.

Stephen leaned against the edge of one of the bunks and began speaking as if he were a lecturer before a much larger audience. "We all agree that none of the probable thieves—the Traverses themselves, their man Atkins, the steward Hamlin, and, of course, young Rashid—are likely to have taken the jewels. In most cases they have opportunity and means, but not motive. The servants especially have more to lose than to gain, for they might lose their character and position simply on the suspicion of being involved. The profit gained from selling Mrs. Travers's jewels would not be sufficient to repay them for this—at least I have not seen Mrs. Travers wearing a rajah's crown or wielding a diamond-tipped scepter."

Jenny laughed. "I hadn't thought of it that way, but you do have a point. All this talk of jewels has made me forget what Colonel Travers himself admitted: Their value is primarily sentimental. Who would risk everything for the price of a few cameos or a matched set of garnets?"

Stephen maintained his pose of urbane sophistication, but Neville was certain the younger man was pleased with this praise.

"Let us examine the cabin," Stephen continued, "keeping in mind that most of the disarray we see is most likely the result of the earlier search."

"I'll start here," Jenny said, kneeling next to the bunk and opening a drawer built into its base. This revealed a frothy mass of lace-trimmed white and ivory fabric. "I suppose the idea is to see if the case is buried under some of these rather generous underthings?"

Stephen colored slightly, but nodded.

"Sir Neville, why don't you and I take the rest of the cabinets? I'll start with those on the right, you the left. Miss Benet, when you are finished there, would you check the area around the washstand? Mrs. Travers may have absentmindedly tucked the case into one of the cubbies when she was attending to her toilette. I know my sisters are always doing such things."

They conducted their search steadily until not a cabinet had been left un-opened or a drawer unprobed. They confirmed that the Colonel had laid in a con-siderable supply of his favorite pipe tobacco, that Mrs. Travers had a fondness for candied violets, and that someone—Jenny suspected Mary—had hidden a par-tially eaten box of chocolates beneath a pile of writing paper. However, they did not find the jewelry case.

"What next, Dupin?" Neville asked, closing the last cabinet drawer, and turn-ing to where Stephen stood with head propped against his fist.

"I'm thinking," Stephen muttered. "My instincts tell me that the case is still in this room. I must be right! Too many innocents stand to lose if I am not. I will not let that happen."

"But where can we look?" Jenny asked. "Will you have us prying up the floor-boards next?"

She looked quite ready to attempt this, so Neville was relieved when Stephen replied, "No, not the floorboards . . . The mattresses!"

"I looked under these bunks already," Neville reported. "No luck."

Stephen's grin did not fade.

"We are not inspecting, sir, we are ratiocinating! Put yourself in Mrs. Travers's place. She is a woman, no longer young and not in the best condition. She has dressed for the day, and needs to put her jewelry case away. However, she has chosen to keep it in a drawer that requires her to kneel beside the bed. She is stout, and tightly corsetted."

"A discomfort you have to feel to fully appreciate," Jenny interjected, poking at her own less than fashionably restricted waist.

Stephen began to mime out Mrs. Travers's presumed actions.

"She sets the jewelry case on the lower bunk, but she needs both hands to open the drawer. See, it sticks a bit. Something halts her—a servant with hot water, a question from her husband, Mary asking her to do something to her hair. What it is does not matter. Mrs. Travers leaves the jewelry case on the lower bunk. Later, something pushes it back—perhaps someone sitting on the edge of the bunk to put on shoes. The case is slid back, and . . ."

Stephen leaned over the mattress and poked his hand between it and the wall.

"The case falls into the crevice and becomes wedged there."

He felt around, seized something, and drew it forth.

"Voila, *mes amis!* The missing jewel case!"

Neville and Jenny burst into spontaneous applause. Mr. Watkins, who had apparently been waiting in the corridor, flung open the door. His face lit with joy when he saw the box in Stephen's hand.

"Oh, Mr. Holmboe, you are a wonder! That must be the very box. See, there are her initials on the lid."

Stephen gave the box a slight shake.

"The box is locked, but from the sound I believe you will find the contents intact. Let us hurry to the library and inform the Traverses of our find."

"I wonder," Jenny said as she hurriedly led the way, "why Hamlin didn't find the case when he was making up the bunks."

"Quite probably because he was not looking for it," Stephen said. "He may even have heard a faint thump when he was tucking in the bedclothes, but thought nothing of it. Those bunks are deuced hard to make up, as I found when attempting to spare Bert a bit of bother."

The fuss Mrs. Travers made was tremendous. To Neville's heartfelt relief, nothing more was said about thieving natives. Jenny might not have been so restrained once the lady was no longer suffering from her loss.

That evening at dinner, Captain Easthill reported the day's events, obviously to forestall gossip that might cast a less than favorable light on his vessel or its crew.

"I have said little about the methods by which Mr. Holmboe recovered the missing jewel case," Captain Easthill concluded. "Perhaps Mr. Holmboe would favor us with a more detailed discussion in place of the planned entertainment."

Stephen waved a hand in a self-deprecating fashion.

"Actually, Captain, if everyone would permit, I would rather offer a reading from Edgar Allan Poe, the very story that set me on the track of the missing jewels. It's a grand little piece called 'The Purloined Letter.' "

Alexandria

BY THE time *Neptune's Charger* arrived at Alexandria, Jenny had memorized a handful of useful phrases in Arabic, but felt she was no closer to getting a grasp of the language than before. She actually felt better about elementary hieroglyphs. Stephen had assured her that there was so much repetition in the texts carved and painted onto the walls of burial complexes that she would be able to recognize common names like Osiris and Isis. She greatly looked forward to doing so.

However, her first glimpse of Egypt came as a complete surprise. Along with most of the other passengers, she was gathered by the rail, watching Alexandria's square skyline take shape.

"It's so green!" Jenny exclaimed. "I thought Egypt was all golden brown desert."

"There is plenty of desert," Uncle Neville assured her. "This, however, is the Delta region. It is one of the most fertile areas in all the world. With the inundation of the Nile just ended, it is also a very busy farming area. The Turkish rulers have tried to introduce some modernization, but most of the farming is still done by hand, and at the caprice of the floods."

Stephen added with a pedantry that still seemed jarringly at odds with his love of a pun, the worse, the better, "It is astonishing to realize that the greatest advances in Egyptian farming were brought in by the Hyksos in the late Middle Kingdom. They introduced both the *shaduf* and the horse and chariot, yet remained reviled by the Egyptians until they were unseated from power."

Colonel Travers snorted, "Damn natives are all alike. Here we've been helping them along since we ousted Napoleon for them in 1801. Does that make a difference? No. Their educated classes are still more likely to go to France than England for their education. They affect French fashions, blending them in with their Turkish ways in the most peculiar manner. Still, England will stick by them."

Jenny had been reading something about contemporary Egyptian history. Now the grinding annoyance that had been building within her at the British imperial assumption of superiority boiled to the surface.

"Don't the British rather have to stick by them?" she asked, not bothering to keep her tone respectful. "It seems to me that I have read about how deeply in debt Egypt is becoming to various British banking and commercial interests. Those same interests hound Parliament to make certain Egypt pays those debts."

"Man's got to pay his debts," Colonel Travers huffed. "Don't see why it should be different for a nation."

"I'm not saying it should be different," Jenny protested, "but it seems unfair to criticize a country for being primitive and in debt, when it's running up those debts in an effort to become less primitive."

"Wouldn't expect a slip of a girl to understand international economic policy," Colonel Travers responded condescendingly.

Jenny was so certain that he understood even less than she did that she lost her temper completely.

"And I don't suppose the Suez Canal has anything to do with the kindness that England offers to Egypt. I don't suppose it has crossed anyone's mind that the canal serves as a straight line for invasion of British interests in India?"

Colonel Travers was shocked out of speech, and to Jenny's embarrassment, Uncle Neville stepped in to defend her.

"Forgive my niece, Colonel," he said. "She is not only young, she is American, and they are rather unsophisticated in their view of the world."

Jenny colored, then paled, and lest she be further humiliated, she left the deck. As she did so, she saw Rashid crouching in a shadowed corner. His eyes remained downcast, but his mouth twisted with sympathetic concern.

————

With some dismay, Neville watched Jenny retreat, but he didn't pursue her. Being guardian to a seventeen-year-old American woman was proving to be more difficult than he had ever imagined. The fact that she looked so much like her ostensibly more tractable mother didn't make his task any easier. He kept expecting her to act as Alice would have—while his all too practical memory made it impossible to forget that Alice had been tractable only on the surface.

The lightest of feather-touches on his sleeve brought Neville back into awareness of his surroundings. Audrey Cheshire was looking up at him, her impossibly green eyes alive with sympathy and just a touch of humor.

"Would you like me to speak with Miss Benet?" she asked. "Perhaps something is troubling her that she would more easily confide in a woman."

"You are too kind," Neville replied. "I think her problem goes beyond mere femininity. I think she is an American—a frontier-reared American—facing the larger realities of civilization for the first time."

Lady Cheshire slipped into a chair, and somehow Neville found himself seated next to her.

"I thought you said Miss Benet had been to boarding school in Boston," Lady Cheshire said. "That is a very nice city, or so I have been told."

"So have I," Neville replied. He was about to explain further, but Captain Brentworth came striding over, outrage in every line of his muscular shoulders.

"The ship will be docking shortly, Lady Cheshire," he said, his refusal to acknowledge Neville's polite greeting, making transparent just who was the object of his anger. "I thought you would wish to make certain Babette has correctly anticipated your desires. She is waiting to speak with you."

Lady Cheshire rose, offering Neville a confidential smile that acknowledged the other man's jealousy while dismissing his right to such proprietary emotions. Neville suddenly realized that he would miss her company.

He spoke impulsively after her as she turned away.

"I hope we will meet again, Lady Cheshire."

"I expect that we will, Sir Neville, if not in Egypt, then certainly back in England."

Her words were commonplace, even dismissive, but there was something in her manner of speaking that made Neville's heart rise with hope. Nearly giddy as a schoolboy, he strode briskly below to confer with Bert, whistling a snatch of a romantic air that had been popular over twenty years before.

Ignoring Jenny's rudeness, a grateful Colonel Travers expressed his gratitude to Stephen for his help in the matter of the jewel case by arranging for the Hawthorne party to have seats on a military train from Alexandria to Cairo that was leaving the next morning. Neville mentioned this to Lady Cheshire as the passengers were debarking.

"Then we will be parting sooner than I had anticipated," she said, and sounded honestly sorry. "Where are you staying tonight?"

Neville gave the name of a good hotel frequented by European travelers. He was not surprised when Lady Cheshire admitted that her party was staying at the same place.

"I had hoped we would have further opportunity to visit," she said. "Perhaps you will let us entertain you and your companions to dinner tonight?"

Neville accepted readily, trying not to admit even to himself that he had been hoping for something of the sort. He even managed to not be too disappointed when both Jenny and Stephen agreed to accompany him. He hadn't thought Stephen cared much for Lady Cheshire's circle, and Jenny might have been sulking after her earlier embarrassment.

As was customary in these hot climates, most businesses had closed for the afternoon, so the carriages that took them from *Neptune's Charger* to the hotel passed through an apparently deserted city. After the omnipresent shipboard breeze, the air seemed stifling, its dampness clinging like a second skin.

In the suite he shared with Stephen, Neville found that time seemed to pass with slowness as stifling as the heat. He snapped irritably at one of Stephen's rather stupid jokes, apologized, and retired to his bedchamber. There he undressed and lay on the bed, trying to cool off and rest. He found he checked his watch so often that he finally took it off the bedside table and stored it in his travel bag to reduce the temptation.

What was wrong with him? It must be the heat, or maybe finally returning to this search after so long. It certainly couldn't be that he had fallen for a pair of lovely green eyes. He wondered what Audrey Cheshire's hair would feel like, released from its cunning coils and let hang loose to curl about her . . . shoulders.

Somehow Neville was up again, checking his watch. He was glad he had caught Bert before the other finished consigning their trunks to the military attache who would take them to the train. It wouldn't have done to show up for dinner incorrectly dressed. He hoped Jenny had remembered to keep out an appropriate gown. Stephen was impossible, but everyone from the ship was accustomed to his outdated attire. Indeed, they were so accustomed that the curious glances Stephen had attracted from the few guests in the hotel lobby when they had arrived had themselves registered as unusual.

Neville wished dinner was not served so late in these climates. He wished the train wasn't leaving so early. He wondered if Lady Cheshire would be staying in Alexandria long. Surely Cairo was more amusing. It was certainly less humid. She would stay at Shepheard's Hotel. That was where all the best people stayed. Maybe he should change their reservations to Shepheard's from Casa Donati. He wondered if Papa Antonio would be hurt. He wondered if Captain Brentworth would be annoyed. He wondered if Lady Cheshire would be pleased.

Somewhere amid these wonderings, Neville fell asleep. He dreamed of lovely women dressed in the revealing fashions favored by the Egyptian court. One of these women had emerald green eyes, startling and lovely within their elaborate lines of kohl.

Bert awoke him with ample time to dress.

"I ordered hot water, sir, in case you wished to shave," the former footman said, clearly feeling awkward in his role as valet now that they were ashore and he must adapt to new circumstances. "I did not think you would wish a hot bath, but the kitchens inform me that water can be quickly had."

"You did well, Bert," Neville assured him. "What I want is something cooling. How is Emily?"

"Fine, once she persuaded Miss Benet to stay settled here at the hotel. The young lady wanted to go and tour Alexandria. She said that with the train leaving so early in the morning, this would be her only opportunity."

Neville was stunned. In his own preoccupation, it had never occurred to him that Jenny would decide to go wandering.

"But Emily convinced her to stay in?" he asked.

"She did. Secured her promise. When we retired, Miss Benet was in one of the hotel courtyards playing with the monkey that belongs to that boy, Rashid. Mrs. Syms was with her, and assured Emily that she was going nowhere, so Emily felt safe leaving her there."

"Well done," Neville said, though he suspected that nothing short of leg irons would have held Jenny.

Then he amended his thought. One positive result of her sympathy for the lower classes was that Jenny would never do anything that would reflect badly on Emily. If she had promised Emily she would remain, then even had Mrs. Syms been distracted from her chaperonage, Jenny would not have strayed.

"And has Miss Benet come up to dress for dinner?"

"She has, sir. Emily is helping her with her hair."

Both reassured and vaguely unsettled, Neville proceeded to ready himself for their dinner engagement. Vest, tie, and tail-coat were constrictingly warm, but he donned them with the confident assurance that he would look his best—besides, the dining room was certain to have fans.

He met his companions in the common room of the suite. Stephen wore the same high-buttoned jacket and checked trousers he always wore on more formal occasions. Jenny was still in mourning black, though she had donned jet pendant earrings and a necklace of matching faceted beads.

However, both Stephen and Jenny might have worn the sheer draperies and the leopard-skin mantle of the Egyptian *sem* priest, for all Neville would have noticed once they entered the private dining room reserved by Lady Cheshire, and Neville saw their hostess turning to meet them.

Neville thought he had seen the full range of her wardrobe aboard *Neptune's Charger*, for Lady Cheshire had more frequently varied her gown than any other woman aboard the vessel. Now he realized that these had been her second best. If he correctly recalled what he had overheard of the ladies' gossip about fashion, Lady Cheshire must have paused to do some shopping in Paris.

The colors of the dressmaker's confection she now turned to display were a compromise between the stronger shades that had been popular a few years before, and the paler hues that were just now coming into fashion. Her double-ruffled skirt was yellow, and her close-fitting, low-cut bodice was a deep blue, trimmed with double borders of white sheer. The large, lace-bordered apron draped over the flat front of her skirt was cut from a striped fabric that combined the colors of skirt and bodice, and brought the entire ensemble into perfect harmony.

Yet Neville thought that the dress would have been nothing without the lady's own natural adornments. Her shining black hair was piled high on her head, a few ringlets trained down along the graceful curve of her neck. The lithe elegance of her arms was emphasized by yellow bows at her shoulders, bows that were echoed in miniature at the edges of her white lace-trimmed gloves. She wore a double string of pearls, and dangling pearl earrings, touched with the tiniest amount of crystal so that they glittered in the light.

Ye Gods! Neville thought in astonishment, but he fancied he kept his admiration within acceptable levels as he bowed over Lady Cheshire's glove, and turned to offer the same compliment to Mrs. Syms.

That worthy lady still wore the fuller skirts that had been popular a few years before, a disregarding of fashion that was not at all uncommon among older women, who seemed more comfortable in the fashions of their day. However, Mrs. Syms was not dowdy. Her hair had been styled to show off a pert cap, rather than being hidden beneath a bonnet, and the colors of the fabric were fresh and unfaded.

Captain Brentworth accepted the Hawthorne party's greetings with a cordiality that belied his discourtesy aboard ship. Indeed, he seemed to be going out of his way to offer them welcome.

"Drinks?" he asked heartily. "The hotel has some excellent iced confections the ladies might enjoy. Something stronger for you, Sir Neville? Whiskey? Brandy?"

Sir Neville declined these, but did accept a glass of very dry white wine. Stephen asked for one of the iced fruit drinks.

"It's cooler here than I expected," he said cheerfully sipping, "but this still tastes marvelous. Wonder where they get the ice? Must be shipped in. Wonderful thing, modern civilization."

Lady Cheshire smiled at Stephen.

"It is indeed. This is your first visit to Egypt, Mr. Holmboe?"

"My first visit in anything but imagination," he replied gallantly.

"And it is Miss Benet's also," Lady Cheshire said. "In celebration of this event, I have asked the kitchens to prepare a meal that will combine a mixture of tastes. The local seasonings are wonderful, but often a bit robust for English palates."

Neville knew with resignation that Jenny would feel required to eat the oddest items on the menu, without regard for how they tasted. He hoped she had a strong constitution. Some Egyptian dishes could be very spicy.

Dinner began with a soup that tasted faintly of curry, served with a flat bread that, to Neville, tasted of nothing so much as slightly burned wheat. He much preferred the Nile perch that followed, but for him the real feast was the lady who presided over the table, making sure that each guest was served some special dainty or other, all the while keeping up a lively stream of chatter.

"I do so envy you," Lady Cheshire said wistfully. "The desert is harsh, but the excitement of exploration certainly outweighs the hardships."

Despite how he had relaxed in the lady's company, Neville felt a warning prickle along his spine. Though many of the other passengers on *Neptune's Charger* had asked what he intended to do in Egypt, he had replied only vaguely, saying he intended to visit old friends in Cairo and visit a few former haunts from his service days. That, combined with his taking Jenny along, satisfied most inquisitors. Egypt was known to be a good marriage mart for those who could not hope to make a first-rate match in England. What could be more natural than that the girl's guardian should take her there?

However, Lady Cheshire did not seem to be fishing for information. She spoke as if she were certain of their plans. Had one of the others talked? He couldn't be sure. Stephen had responded to Lady Cheshire's comment with a rather theatrically puzzled look, while Jenny's expression remained so neutral as to be almost rude—at least to any who knew that such maidenly self-effacement was not her usual manner. Had Bert or Emily let something slip? Said something about how they would be staying in Cairo when their master went elsewhere?

Everyone was looking at him, so he must make some reply.

"I think you are mistaken, dear lady," he said lightly. "We are mere tourists, not explorers."

"Oh." Even puzzled, Lady Cheshire was impossibly fetching. "Babette said something about having been with Miss Benet's maid when the maid was taking clothing out of one of the trunks. Babette said she saw a quantity of what looked like field gear, and mentioned it to me."

Neville made himself smile easily.

"Of course I brought some field gear," he said. "English equipment is some of the best. I thought about setting up some sort of trade with the archeological community."

"Samples then?" Lady Cheshire asked.

"Of a sort," Neville replied, wondering why he felt embarrassed. It must be presenting himself as a common tradesman that did it. "In any case, I have Jenny to consider. The desert is no place for a young lady."

"Ah, there you are wrong, Sir Neville," Lady Cheshire said. She put a finger under her chin, and smiled playfully at him. "That is, unless you count *me* an old hag. I accompanied my dear Ambrose on several of his digs, and I thought the desert enchanting and romantic."

"Nasty, hot, sandy places, deserts," muttered Mrs. Syms. Then she brightened, "The Arabs' horses were lovely as gazelles, though, and twice as smart as their owners. Camels are nasty, smelly beasts."

Neville hardly heard her. He was battling several conflicting responses. Lady Cheshire's flirtatiousness seemed to call for a response, but he was all too aware that Captain Brentworth had set down his wine glass, and rested his hands on the edge of the table, as if at the least provocation he would leap to his feet.

Neville settled for sounding stodgy.

"But you were a proper married woman, Lady Cheshire. Jenny is unmarried, and her American ways leave her open to misinterpretation."

Now Jenny was glowering at him, but Captain Brentworth had relaxed and picked up his glass again. Lady Cheshire looked thoughtful.

"If you were to travel," she said, "perhaps Sarah and I could offer ourselves as female companionship for Miss Benet. She has her maid, of course, but no one who is her social equal."

Neville felt that here, at least, he could respond in a fashion that would offend no one.

"I shall keep your kind offer in mind."

"And another armed man would be of assistance," Captain Brentworth said stiffly, almost as if rehearsed. "The ruins by night can be quite dangerous."

Jenny cut in here, her tone playful, even, Neville realized with a trace of shock, coquettish.

"But Captain Brentworth, why ever would we go out at night? How could we read the inscriptions or enjoy the beauty of the carvings and paintings that adorn the monuments?"

Captain Brentworth seemed immune to Jenny's attempt at charm.

"Haven't I seen you reading those books on Egypt? Don't you realize that much touring is done when the sun is low? That often means returning, if not by night, at least in twilight."

Lady Cheshire added much more kindly, "One of my favorite passages is Champollion's description of the enchantment he felt at visiting Dendera by moonlight. Torchlight gives the scene charm as well, and when the shadows dance, it almost seems as if the sculptures are moving."

From that point, the question of where the Hawthorne party was going or whether Lady Cheshire and her companions might accompany them was dropped. Instead, those who had been to Egypt before vied with each other to tell the first timers about the delights that awaited them.

They lingered over sherbets and thick Turkish coffee, but Neville felt that hardly any time had passed when Stephen pulled his watch from his pocket.

"Look at the time!" he exclaimed. "And we've an early train to catch. I fear we must excuse ourselves. Otherwise we'll overstay our welcome and fail to be enter-training."

He grinned foolishly, and the party broke up with disparaging remarks about punsters.

Once they returned to the upper floor, Neville went to his room. Maybe his afternoon nap had rested him too thoroughly, or maybe he had indulged in one too many cups of the deceptively strong coffee. Whatever the reason, he could not sleep, though he did dream.

Before the sun had fully risen the next morning, Neville and his companions had departed Alexandria on a rattling train. Almost all of its length was given over to cargo, but the passenger compartments were comfortable almost to the point of decadence.

"The other side," Uncle Neville said to Jenny, "of that debt we were discussing shipboard. Not all the money the Egyptians have borrowed from Europe has gone to simple modernization. The ruling class has an Oriental taste for splendor, verging on decadence. Colonel Travers tells me that this car was taken in payment for debts from a Turkish princeling."

Jenny frowned, but rather to her uncle's surprise didn't pursue the argument. Now that he thought about it, she had been distracted and quiet since they had met for breakfast. He attributed her quiet to a sleepless night like his own, leaned his head back against the plush velvet, and wondered if attempting to sleep or ordering more coffee would be the wiser course of action.

Most of the other passengers were destined for military or government posts in Cairo. Some were already posted there and had come to Alexandria on business. These were enjoying flaunting their senior residency to the newcomers, and amid this game of precedence, Colonel Travers's guests were left to their own devices. Even Mrs. Travers and Mary had made their apologies and left. Apparently, some general's wife was also traveling by this train, and had invited them to ride with her in what was apparently an even more elaborate car.

Sleep wouldn't quite come, so Neville was drowsily watching the panorama of the *fellahin*, the native Egyptian peasants, planting their freshly fertilized fields when he was jolted to full alertness by the approach of a junior officer, not one of those who had traveled with Colonel Travers, but a stranger.

"Sir Neville?" the officer inquired, raising his voice to carry over the rumble of the train.

"Yes?" Neville replied, trying not to sound as if he had been half-asleep.

The young man extended a slightly grubby envelope.

"This letter is addressed to you, but apparently became mixed up in our post. I apologize for not delivering it to you sooner, but we only just realized the error."

Neville accepted the envelope.

"No problem at all, Lieutenant. Thank you for taking the trouble to deliver it."

When the soldier had departed, Neville stared down at the envelope, vaguely troubled. It was addressed to him aboard *Neptune's Charger*.

With a sense of foreboding, he slit the envelope open, aware that Stephen had laid down his book, and that though Jenny's pencil continued to move across her sketch pad, the majority of her attention was for him.

What if it were a personal letter? he thought, indignantly. Then he realized that they could easily have seen the address when the lieutenant had handed the envelope over, and so had every right to be interested.

In a less guarded manner, Neville slid the paper from the envelope, unfolding it so the text was visible to them all. There was silence as they stared at the string of block letters interspersed apparently at random with the simple yet elegant symbol known as the Eye of Horus.

BE 𓂀 LN GWC QJDN KNNV EJZVNM GWC KNT𓂀 NDN
VW WVN SVWEA EQJB GWC ANNS BQ𓂀VS EN JZN
TNP𓂀 WV GWC JZN 𓂀V MJVPNZ AXQ𓂀 VF

"Heavens!" was all Jenny could manage. Stephen whistled.

Neville glanced around, but no other passenger was occupying the nearer seats. The closest person was a rather portly civil servant, asleep with a newspaper over his face.

"M. Dupin," Neville said, "Jenny, what do you make of it?"

Jenny leaned forward and turned the paper so she could look at it right-side up.

"Uncle Neville, do you have either of the other letters we received with you— and their envelopes?"

Neville removed the two missives in hieroglyphs from where he carried them in an inside pocket of his coat.

Jenny studied them for a moment, her gaze flashing back and forth between the envelopes and the new letter.

"It is hard to be certain," she said, "given the different types of characters, but the envelopes make me certain. These were written by the same person."

Stephen nodded. "I agree. You know, this mishmash of letters rather recalls the cipher Legrand discovered in Poe's tale 'The Gold Bug.' I'll hazard a guess that this newest missive is in a substitution code of some sort, and that the base language in which it is written—as with the first two missives—is English."

Jenny turned her sketchbook to a new page and made a quick copy of the new letter, leaving large spaces between the lines so they could insert their guesses. With a flourish, she concluded by printing "SPHINX" over the final group of letters.

"That," she said with satisfaction, "is my guess. If I'm correct, we now have five consonants and a vowel."

"Bravo!" Stephen said. "Fill in those wherever they occur. We could get another insight from seeing what comes out."

"I wonder," Neville said, watching Jenny's fingers fly over the page, "why he used the Eye of Horus rather than simply another letter for 'I'? The coincidence between 'I' and 'eye' is too great to be ignored."

Stephen grinned, "To be confusing, I think. Or maybe to be helpful."

"You can't have it both ways," Neville protested.

"I can," Stephen insisted. "If our correspondent wanted to confuse us, mixing in a symbol along with the more usual letters would do it. We might have spent hours discussing the Eye of Horus as a protective charm, or the symbol's history, or its meaning as a hieroglyph in the Egyptian language."

"And if he wanted to be helpful?"

"Does he know for certain that we've figured out Sphinx is his *nom de plume*?" Stephen asked. "He does not, for certainly I have not told him. Therefore, he needs to provide us with one letter to help us on our way. He supplies the letter 'I' in symbol form—a pun on 'I,' I might say. 'I' is not only a letter, but it is one that occurs in the final word in each missive. Therefore, he gives us a clue to that final word."

"I suppose you could be correct," Neville said dubiously. "Why this change in format?"

"I don't know," Stephen said. "Perhaps the text when translated will give us some hint. What do we have, Miss Benet?"

Jenny showed them.

--I-- ---H---H--- ---N ---N-- ----I- ---N- -N- -N--S
-H-- ---S--- HIN- -- -- ----I-N--- ---IN--N---SPHINX

"Something springs to mind right away," Neville said. "'N' followed by a space must be 'no.' Something of the same pattern comes immediately after. I am willing to hazard that this must be 'one.'"

"Bravo!" Stephen said eagerly. "Two vowels! Fill them in, Miss Benet."

Jenny was already doing so, pencil working back and forth between text and crib with a speed only moderated by the need to be perfectly accurate. She held up the end result, frowning slightly.

--I-E -O- H--E -EEN---NE- -O- -E-IE-E NO ONE -NO-S -H-- -O- SEE-
-HIN- -E -RE -E-ION -O- --E IN --N-ER SPHINX

"Several words are almost complete," she said. "Blank-E-E-N. S-E-E-blank."

Stephen's lips moved quickly, trying and discarding possibilities.

"Let's see, the first one could be 'been' or 'seen,' but as we have the 'S' already, 'been' it is."

Jenny scribbled in the "B" and sighed. "The next one is even worse. Let's skip it and go on to the other two letter combination: blank-e. That has fewer options: 'he,' 'me,' 'we.'"

"'He' can be discarded," Stephen said. "Remember, we already know that 'H' is represented by 'Q.'"

"Right," Neville agreed. "Shall we try the other options?"

Jenny had been penciling down an alphabet with the letters they had worked out written under their corresponding letter. Now she paused, a strange expression on her face.

"Wait!" she said, holding her pad so they could see what she had written. "There may be a faster way. Do either of you see anything odd here?"

Stephen was the first to reply. "N-O-P and their equivalents V-W-X follow in the same order."

"So do H-I and their equivalents, Q and the Eye of Horus," Neville added. "Why, I believe that the alphabet is represented in the usual order!"

"With one exception," Jenny agreed, pencil working. "'I' is represented by a symbol rather than a letter, interrupting direct correspondence rather neatly between 'H' and 'I,' two of the first letters we might guess. I suppose the Sphinx wanted us to work for our message."

"I wonder why?" Neville asked, but he expected no answer.

"Here it is," Jenny said, looking down at the deciphered text. "Though I don't know what good it will do us."

She had inserted punctuation where it seemed appropriate, so the text she turned for Stephen and Neville's inspection read:

TWICE YOU HAVE BEEN WARNED. YOU BELIEVE NO ONE KNOWS WHAT YOU SEEK. THINK WE ARE LEGION. YOU ARE IN DANGER. SPHINX.

"Blast him!" Neville exploded. "If we're in such ruddy danger, why doesn't he just tell us what it is?"

"Hush, Uncle," Jenny cautioned, indicating where the civil servant was stirring under his newspaper.

Neville nodded apology.

Stephen was frowning at the message.

"I think he *is* telling us, after a fashion. Put a full stop after the word 'think,' and the message becomes a bit clearer. He is saying that we believe that no one knows what we seek, but we should think about the evidence to the contrary. That is, our correspondent knows. Then he tells us that he is not alone in his knowing: 'We are legion.' Then he reminds us we are in danger.'"

"Hm," Neville grumbled. "So why doesn't he tell us who this legion is and stop dancing around the point?"

"Perhaps he is afraid for his own safety," Jenny offered. "This legion who offers us danger would certainly not be kind to a traitor within its ranks. If Sphinx succeeds in warning us off, then he saves us and saves himself."

"I wonder," Stephen said, returning to an earlier question, "why he has switched formats? Twice hieroglyphs, then this."

"Because he's a bloody damn nuisance," Neville replied sharply, "too in love with his own conceit to be direct."

"Perhaps," Jenny said, "but as I transcribed, I came up with another answer. Look at the handwriting. It is in block print, true, but the letters are quickly drawn. Look how the downstrokes on the 'H' and 'K' are extended. The curves of many letters are less than precise as well. I think he wrote this, if not in a hurry, at least with enough speed that he could not permit himself the luxury of drawing elaborate hieroglyphs."

Stephen nodded. "It was addressed to us care of the ship. If he had to make sure his message would not have to be forwarded, he might have felt pressed for time."

"Note," Jenny said, "that this letter is the first not to contain a warning about a woman. Is she then no longer a danger or is it simply that our correspondent wanted us to realize that our danger was offered from multiple sources, not just one?"

"Not enough information to go on to decide that point," Neville said.

He folded the new message and its translation away with the previous missives, and all three fell into thoughtful silence. The train continued to rattle along, but they hardly noticed the small villages and green fields. Throughout the marshy land, ducks and herons, along with many less easily identifiable birds, rose in protest at the tumult of the passing train.

At last Jenny spoke, "Uncle Neville, you may wish to find the pharaoh, but I believe that the one I hope to find is the Sphinx."

Papa Antonio

IN CAIRO, they parted from the Travers family with thanks and protestations
of gratitude on both sides.

"Do come see us," Mary Travers begged Jenny. "We can have so much fun
getting to know Cairo."

Jenny promised she would, but she thought that the parts of Cairo she would
be interested in and those that would fascinate Mary Travers would overlap very
little. Still, Mary would certainly want to visit the standard tourist attractions, and
she was pleasant enough company.

Jenny had an ulterior motive as well. If Uncle Neville thought she was keeping
up her friendship with Mary, Jenny would have an excuse ready if ever she needed
to get away unsupervised. Jenny didn't know if such a need would arise, but she
firmly believed in being prepared.

After collecting their trunks, Uncle Neville selected one porter from the
swarm who converged on the passengers.

"Shepheard's Hotel?" the man asked in fairly good English.

"No," Neville replied. "Do you know the hotel run by Antonio Donati? Papa
Antonio?"

A grin split the man's wiry black beard.

"Sure I know Papa Antonio. That where you go?"

"That's right. We'll need a wagon or donkeys to carry the trunks. Can you get them?"

"I can. A prince among wagons. Strong."

The porter named a price. Sir Neville countered with a much lower figure. They dickered back and forth for a while, settling on an amount that seemed to leave both men well satisfied. Then the same routine was followed with a passenger carriage.

"Bert," Neville said, "do you mind riding along with the trunks?"

"No problem, sir," Bert said with an apprehensive glance at the porter.

"I don't expect you'll have any trouble," Neville assured him. "The porter will follow right behind the carriage. You're simply insurance that he remembers where he's going."

Emily was handed up into the carriage, where she drew her skirts up around her, her attention split between keeping an eye on her husband and staring at the strange buildings and exotic people who crowded around.

Once the carriage was clattering towards their destination, Stephen leaned forward and asked, "Sir Neville, neither of those fellows asked very much. Indeed, their highest price was a great deal less than I saw you present our cabin steward aboard *Neptune's Charger*. Why did you bother to make such a fuss?"

Neville grinned, looking more relaxed and happier than Jenny could recall, even when she included those times he'd been mooning over Lady Cheshire.

"Well, Stephen, bartering is the custom here. If you don't dicker, the word spreads that you're an easy mark, and the natives will try to take you for anything they can get. Can't blame them really. They live pretty miserable lives on the whole."

Stephen nodded. "I noticed that you didn't let on that both you and I understand Arabic. Was that part of the same?"

"That's right," Neville agreed. "Never tell more than you must. It's fascinating what you may overhear."

Jenny smiled at a memory.

"Really," she said, "it's not too different from what we dealt with in the West. Papa always said that the Indians weren't sneaky, but we aren't their people, and they see no reason to give us a fair shake, not when they see we have so much. Until we prove ourselves friends, we might as well be enemies."

"That's not just true in foreign lands," Stephen added. "I've seen a Cockney take a country farmer for everything he's worth, just because the farmer speaks with a different accent."

As the carriage left the train station, nearly naked children ran alongside the wheels holding up their hands and begging for *baksheesh*.

"That's alms," Neville explained to Jenny and Emily. "Islam declares that it is a virtue to give to those less fortunate—that such generosity will be rewarded in heaven."

"Doesn't Christianity?" Jenny asked, puzzled.

"Not in the same fashion," Neville replied. "I believe there is some sort of formula: give so much, get so much credit. The idea is good, but the difficulty is that a class of professional beggars has emerged. In the worst cases, children are deliberately starved or mutilated so they arouse pity."

"Poor mites!" Emily exclaimed.

Jenny shuddered and her hand, which had been reaching for her purse, fell limp.

"There are ways to deal with the beggars, ways that benefit the real poor without encouraging the professionals," Neville said. "I'll explain later."

In addition to the children, scrawny dogs chased after them, barking at the carriage, at the running children, and even at each other, adding greatly to the general commotion. Robed Arabs leaned out to watch their progress from arched windows and doorways, their interest growing more and more intense as the carriage left what even Jenny's inexperienced eye could tell was the tourist quarter near the station.

This curiosity was far from standoffish. Vendors ran alongside the carriage offering fruit, flowers, wooden and clay bead necklaces, and even statuettes and pottery adorned with hieroglyphs and the painted images of Egypt's old gods.

"As ancient as yesterday's mud," Stephen said, speaking just loudly enough that the others could hear him over the noise. "You would think they would take more care."

"Some do," Neville assured him. "However, we have all the marks of being just off the boat. We seem like easy targets. Similar statuettes are often artificially aged, encrusted in sand, then buried where a local guide can lead a susceptible tourist to 'discover' them."

Jenny looked at him quizzically.

"What's the point of that, Uncle Neville? Just a joke?"

"No. There has been an effort since the Egyptian Museum was founded in the late fifties to regulate the removal of antiquities from the country. Tourists are routinely advised of these regulations and of the penalties attendant upon their violation. Therefore, a tourist who believes he has made a find can easily be encouraged to bribe the guide to stay quiet about it—thereby earning the guide a great deal more than he could make by selling the same figure as a souvenir in the bazaar. Another benefit—at least for those who are running the con game—is that someone who is smuggling an antiquity from the country is quite unlikely to show it to an expert."

Emily sniffed. "These Egyptians seem like dishonest sorts."

Neville shrugged. "Many are. Most are simply poor."

Their progress through the crowded streets was slow, providing ample opportunity to study Cairo's polyglot architecture. Squat, practical dwellings built of mud, and not terribly different from what Jenny had seen in the southwestern parts of North America, contrasted vividly with the needle-pointed minarets of the mosques.

Occasionally, they passed a house that would have been perfectly in place in London or Paris. Then there were buildings that showed remnants of Roman construction. Whatever the style, balconies overgrown with vines and flowers abounded. The variety was fascinating, but Jenny rapidly grew tired of the dust and noise—especially after how spoiled she had been on both train and steamship.

I'm getting soft, she chided herself. *This wouldn't have bothered me once—at least not so quickly. If I want to prove myself fit to go with Uncle Neville, I need to show some backbone.*

Despite this resolve, she was relieved when the carriage pulled into a curving driveway before a tidy building faced with white stucco. The hotel's arching doorways and windows belonged to many regions of the Mediterranean, but the style of the trim and the elaborate iron grills that latticed over the windows somehow evoked Italy rather than Egypt.

Reaching from his box, the driver pulled a conveniently placed bell rope. A cascade of chimes rang out, and the passengers had hardly begun to climb somewhat stiffly down from their seats when a small, withered man with snowy white hair and beard, and piercing black eyes emerged from the wide front door. He was tanned as darkly as the Arabs and wore a long, loose robe after their style of dress, but his features were European.

"Leonardo! Leonardo!" he cried out in a sing-song voice that owed its music to Italian. "You have come back to your old friend at last. I had your letters and have set aside rooms for you and your companions. Come inside out of the dust and introduce me."

The old man waved them ahead, stopping only to speak a few words to the carriage driver and baggage porter. To Jenny's ear, his Arabic seemed as fluid and musical as his English.

"Come in, come in out of the heat and the noise," the innkeeper urged, motioning for Emily and Bert to join the others. "The porters will do their job without your watching—I know them. They are good men and hard-working. Surely you need something refreshing to drink."

The servants obeyed, and soon they were all settled in a sitting room that was astonishingly comfortable, especially in contrast with the dry dustiness outside. Jenny knew how well thick adobe insulated against both heat and cold, but Stephen looked as astonished as if he'd been subjected to a conjuring trick.

"Ah," said their host, "you notice how fine and pleasant it is. Enjoy. Now, Leonardo, though I think I can guess, introduce me to my new friends."

Neville complied. "This young lady is my niece, Genevieve Benet, the daughter of my late sister, Alice, and her husband, Pierre. Jenny, this is Antonio Donati, a very old friend of mine."

"Pleased to meet you, Mr. Donati," Jenny said, curtseying.

The old man's face crumpled. "Please, Miss Benet, call me Papa Antonio, as my Leonardo did when he was younger and not so grand."

Jenny smiled, "I would be delighted, Papa Antonio. Would you please call me 'Jenny'? I get so tired of all this 'Miss Benet' stuff."

"I, too, would be delighted," Papa Antonio replied. "Now Leonardo, you move too slowly. This young man like a flower in sunlight with his golden hair and beard, this must be Stephen Holmboe, the linguist."

Stephen bowed acknowledgment, saying something in what must have been Italian.

Papa Antonio beamed and turned to Emily and Bert. "And these are the good people who care for you, Mr. and Mrs . . . Hamilton, yes? Now, take seats and I will give you chilled wine and perhaps some bread and fruit to nibble, and you will tell me about your journey."

Jenny accepted the wine, noting with interest that the bottle had been kept cool in a small well at one corner of the room.

"Papa Antonio . . ." she began.

He interrupted, his expression anxious. "You perhaps do not like this wine? Perhaps as a young lady you would prefer fruit juice or even tea?"

"The wine is wonderful," Jenny assured him.

Papa Antonio beamed. "It is from Italia, from the vineyards of my own family. I, of course, am very proud of it, but perhaps I think it is not to English tastes."

"I am American," Jenny replied. "And it would be excellent wine to anyone with taste. What I wanted to ask is why do you call Uncle Neville 'Leonardo'?"

She saw a half-smile quirk the corner of her uncle's mouth.

"Ah," replied Papa Antonio with a wide flourish of his hand " 'Neville'—that sounds to me like a horse. Hawthorne is a tree, and this man is many things, but he is not stolid like a tree. He tells me his second name is 'Leonard,' which is nearly as stiff, but Leonardo, that slips off the tongue as good wine down the throat, yes?"

Jenny laughed.

"Yes, it does. What will you call Mr. Holmboe?"

"If he wishes, I shall call him that, since we are only newly met . . ."

Stephen interrupted, and Jenny suddenly realized that he was probably as weary as she with the enforced formalities of the voyage. What did his sisters call him, she wondered, Stephen? Stevie? Certainly not "Mr. Holmboe."

"My first name is Stephen," Stephen said, almost as if reading her thought, "which is what my family calls me. However, if it does not flow like wine for you, you are welcome to use another name."

Papa Antonio tugged at his beard in contemplation.

"Stefano is easier on my tongue," he said, "if it suits you."

Stephen smiled, a thing that was hard not to do when confronted with Papa Antonio's enthusiasm.

"I would be very pleased."

Bert and Emily were spared rechristening, perhaps because the old man was wise enough to see that they were rather overwhelmed by all the newness. While wine and refreshments relaxed his guests, Papa Antonio explained his rather peculiar hotel.

"It is more, I think Neville say to me once, like what you English call a boarding house. I do not rent a room for a night or two, but have visitors who stay with me for months and even years. Many of my guests are military men or business travelers. These are assured that when their duties make them go elsewhere their belongings will be safe."

As he said this, Antonio Donati cast a quick, guilty look toward Neville, and Jenny realized that this must be the very house which had been broken into by the mysterious burglars all those years before. Suddenly, the elaborate grates covering the exterior windows did not seem so much adornment, but more obviously protection.

Neville gave Papa Antonio a small smile and, so encouraged, the old man returned to his subject.

"As you will see, this house is arranged around a central courtyard, very pleasant in the evening, very nice all the time, I think. Your rooms are along one side on the lowest floor. There is only one floor above, and right now no guests are using those rooms so there will be no trampling of elephants over your sleeping heads. Good, yes?"

They agreed, and pleased, the innkeeper went on.

"Now, I am too old to much like going out into the markets every day or doing laundry and cleaning, so I have a good family who lives here and does such things. They are Copts, as you say, Egyptian Christians. You will like them very much. They have rooms on the second story, over this section of the house. This way if the *bambinos* wail in the night they do not trouble the guests."

Stephen dove into the gap when Papa Antonio paused to sip his wine.

"Are we your only guests? The place seems remarkably quiet."

"It is so quiet because the train bring you in as the hot part of the day is ending. Soon you will hear more noise, this I promise. However, it is true that I have fewer guests here than is usual. Winter is the best time for travel, and many of my guests are away for days at a time. Some will come in and out, but I do not think they will trouble you. All are lovely people or I would not have them."

He smiled warmly at them all. "But now my helpers will have had time to put water and other comforts into your rooms. Perhaps you would like to have a rest from the heat and maybe wash off the travel dirt? Do not worry that I will let you sleep too long and miss your dinner. I shall come myself and rap gently on your doors, waking you with plenty of time to spare."

They accepted their host's invitation. The rooms proved to be large and airy, with a curtained sleeping area in one corner and the remainder furnished as a sitting room. Jenny, Sir Neville, and Stephen each had their own rooms, while Bert and Emily shared a fourth. Emily and Bert were obviously surprised to discover that their room was in no way inferior to those assigned the other guests, and Bert even drew his master to one side.

"Sir, there must be a mistake. Mr. Donati should be told."

Jenny saw her uncle's grin and realized that he had been waiting for this.

"No need, Bert," he assured the man, clapping him genially on the shoulder. "If you and Emily are to stay on when I go elsewhere I wanted you to be comfortable, not cramped in servant's quarters. I hope you won't find one room too small."

Bert answered politely, "Not at all, sir. Thank you, sir." The delight he was too well-trained to express in words was evident as he gathered Emily to him and they went into their assigned place. Emily appeared a moment later to help Jenny undo her laces.

"Will you need anything from your trunks, Miss?" she asked.

"Nothing I can't get for myself," Jenny assured her. "Go rest."

Emily turned to go, then turned impulsively back.

"Your uncle's a good man, Miss Benet."

"He is indeed," Jenny agreed with a smile. "I could have done far worse for a guardian."

It seemed for a moment Emily might say something more, but she grew suddenly shy, bobbed a curtsey, and hurried away.

The evening meal was magnificent, prepared by Papa Antonio himself with the assistance of two young Copts, twins of about thirteen whom he insisted on referring to as Castor and Pollux, though apparently they possessed perfectly normal Christian names. Afterwards the group retired to the central courtyard, which was every bit as pleasant as their host had promised.

Date palms taller than the second story roof granted both shade and privacy. Water trickled from a vase cradled in the arms of an Italian Renaissance cupid into a basin tiled a delicate rose pink. Honeyed dates and enormous golden sultanas were set out on a gauze-covered tray for those with an inclination to nibble. More of Papa Antonio's family *vino*—this a sweeter, dessert vintage with a faint undertone of oranges—had been offered as an alternative to dark, almost muddy coffee.

Neville and Jenny accepted small cut-crystal goblets of the wine, while Stephen happily indulged in the coffee, sweetening it almost to syrup and adding thick cream.

Papa Antonio held his wine up to the candlelight to admire its delicate color.

"Like amber, no? Or translucent gold, perhaps." He sipped and sighed happily. "Beauty is everywhere if you know where to look for it, I think. In memory or in color or in a dream about to be realized. How long do you plan to remain in Cairo, Leonardo?"

Sir Neville stretched lazily. He had discarded his formal English clothing and sat in his shirt and a loose pair of trousers, rather as if he were in his private quarters at home. Jenny made a mental note that formal etiquette was apparently dispensed with at least here within the walls of Papa Antonio's inn.

Tomorrow she would have Emily help her unpack some of her lighter dresses, including those with the shorter skirts. She was certain that Uncle Neville would agree with her that ankle length made more sense when one was going to be trailing about on dirty pavement. Trousers would be out of line, at least until they entered the desert and there was no one to be scandalized but gerbils and camels.

"I need to contact Eddie Bryce," Neville said in response to Papa Antonio's question. "Do you know where we could reach him these days?"

"Write to Ibrahim Alhadj ben Josef on the Street of Potters," came the reply.

"Gone completely native then, has he?" Neville said. "I thought as much. My letters reached him though, under his other name."

"They would," Papa Antonio agreed, "for he continues to do a great deal of work for the English. Many scorn him for his choice, but cannot quite give up the usefulness of one who speaks both Arabic and English fluently, and has such good contacts within the Arab community.

"I'll send the letter out this evening," Neville said, "if one of your servants would deliver it."

He did so, and a reply was waiting for them when they came out into the courtyard to breakfast. The waiting letter was addressed in a sloppy masculine hand on rough paper of local manufacture.

Delighted to learn you have arrived safely. I have a job that will take up the better part of today. If I do not hear otherwise, I will call this evening after dinner.

Edward Bryce

"That's fine, then," Neville said, folding the note away. "Stephen, before the day gets too hot, why don't you and I go out to the bazaars and see about a few supplies?"

"Can't I go, too, Uncle Neville?" Jenny asked.

"It would probably be best if you did not," Neville replied. "The bazaar I have in mind is not one usually frequented by the tourists. Even we Englishmen may find ourselves treated coolly, but I expect our knowledge of the local languages to get us through. If we took a young woman with us—especially one who went unveiled—the Arabs would consider it an insult. Tomorrow when we have spoken with Eddie, I will arrange for you to see something of Cairo. Perhaps you can look up Mary Travers and go visiting."

Had Jenny not already resolved that appearing tractable would be her best way of achieving the greater goal of accompanying the expedition when it left Cairo, her temper would have boiled over at this casual dismissal. Go look up Mary Travers, indeed!

As it was, she kept her opinions to herself, and when the men had left without her she trailed after Papa Antonio as he tended the plants in the courtyard. Holding the basket into which he dropped the dead flowers, she couldn't help but feel a bit like a discarded blossom herself. The image made her smile. The men might see her as some delicate flower, but she knew different.

Papa Antonio glanced sharply at her, but asked nothing, only handed her a sprig of some exotic flower, glowing white and strongly perfumed.

"Put it in your hair, Jenny," he coaxed. "You are a pretty young woman. You should take more pleasure in your beauty."

Jenny sighed, rolling the stem between her palms and sniffing the blossom's fragrance.

"There are times that I get so tired of being a woman, Papa Antonio. It seems that there are so many things a woman—especially a young, unmarried woman—should not do, and all of them are more interesting than what I am supposed to like doing."

"I think, in time, you will learn that there are things a woman may do that a man may not," Papa Antonio said, placidly clipping off a few dead leaves. "Remember this and be patient."

Jenny shifted. Even her ankle-length skirts felt awkward, the gown's bodice clinging and the stays stifling.

"I don't much like being patient," she admitted. "Right now I'm wondering if I should have stayed in America. Uncle Neville would have made sure some banker gave me a proper allowance, and Madame turned a blind eye on my 'frontier' eccentricities. I didn't need to dress for company so often, and when I reached my majority I could have convinced Uncle Neville to let me go back West. I know I could. He's a decent sort."

Papa Antonio smiled at this compliment to his friend, but he hadn't missed her restless impatience with her costume.

"A lady's dress is like a cage, no?" he said. "They wall in the ribs with something tight. These days they give you a fat tail of heavy cloth that drags behind. Not so long ago, I recall that the ladies surrounded themselves with great hoops of whalebone and wire—very real cages, indeed, that made their skirts stand out like sails on a ship. I think you don't like these cages at all, no?"

"Not one bit!" Jenny replied firmly. "They're stuffy and they're uncomfortable. I can't see how making a woman into some sort of funny shape makes her prettier, either. A man gets to be shaped like a man. Why can't a woman be shaped like a woman?"

Papa Antonio chuckled comfortably.

"Perhaps because not all women have such a pretty shape as you do," he said gallantly, "and they are happy to hide under petticoats and layers of skirts."

Jenny snorted, but she couldn't help but share his laughter, imagining some stout matron wearing trousers that exposed the breadth of her backside for all to see.

Papa Antonio grew serious. "Perhaps it is that men fear that if a woman was shaped like a woman he could not trust himself to behave as less than an animal."

Jenny had seen too much on the frontier to dismiss this, much as she would have liked to believe finer ideals. She was struggling to find an appropriate retort when Papa Antonio continued,

"In all sincerity, Jenny, while I understand many of your complaints—How could I not? I who have given over my European clothing for the pleasures of an Arab robe—While I understand this, I cannot understand why a woman like yourself who is wise enough to resent the cage of a gown would want to put herself into a much more permanent cage."

Jenny stared at him, open-mouthed.

"What do you mean?"

"Why just a moment ago you were wondering whether you should have stayed in America. You were speaking of going to the West where you think you could make rules for yourself, no?"

Jenny nodded, uncertain what the correct response would be.

"I know that the American west is a great, vast place, bigger than much of Europe, but even so compared to all the world it is a very small place indeed. If you go back, certain you can live nowhere else, you will have put yourself into a cage of your own making."

Jenny sank down on the edge of the fountain. Trailing her fingers in the water, she considered what the old man had said.

Papa Antonio poured them both lemonade from a thick stoneware pitcher placed ready by one of his attentive Copts. Then he stood, listening to the sounds of his household going about its duties, and waiting for her to speak. His silence was so unusual that Jenny bit back a hasty retort about the frontier being plenty big enough for her and spoke more carefully.

"It would be a cage, wouldn't it? My mama was a nurse during the War Between the States, helping my papa. Later she encouraged me when I wanted to be a doctor. She always said that a woman should know more than the kind of chatter that fills the spaces between the fashion plates in *Godey's Lady's Book*. Papa agreed with her. I guess they spoiled me some, even though they tried not to. They even made sure I went back East for a proper education, though I couldn't see the need. Maybe Madame was the one who was right after all."

Papa Antonio patted her on one shoulder.

"No need to go so far the other way, Jenny. Be happy being Jenny Benet, with all the sides she has. What I do not want you to do is to put yourself into any cage, just because you are hoping to make life simple. One thing this old man has learned is that life is never simple."

"I promise I'll try," Jenny said.

"Now I must ask you to try another thing," Papa Antonio said, and if anything he looked more serious than before. "I think I must ask you to protect your uncle."

"Uncle Neville?" Jenny restrained an impulse to jump to her feet like a dog hearing an intruder. "What's wrong? Is it the people who nearly killed him before? Have you learned something?"

"I have learned many things," Papa Antonio replied, and there was that in his tone that made Jenny unwilling to challenge his evasion. "The danger to which I refer is not from without. It is from within. You say Leonardo has told you about what happened those many years ago."

Jenny glanced around the courtyard, confirmed they were alone, and nodded.

"He told us about going after the tomb that he'd learned about from the German archeologist, about how they were chased off and the German fellow went home. And he told us about how he planned to go back, and how he thinks that his 'accident' was no accident, but a deliberate attempt to stop him."

"I am just a little surprised he told so much to a young lady," Papa Antonio said, "but then I know he thinks highly of you."

"He told me because he knew I was nosey," Jenny said, "and that if he didn't I'd snoop around until I found something out. I think Uncle Neville hoped to scare me off, too."

Papa Antonio smiled sadly. "That, at least, has not worked, I think. Well, Jenny, we will not argue that point. I wish to tell you of my fears for your uncle."

He settled himself next to her on the fountain's edge, refilled their glasses, and looked down into the water with such intensity that it seemed to Jenny that the old man must be seeing more than bubbles and froth.

"I think that Leonardo really believes that what he wants is to find this tomb and make himself some name for a great discovery. He has written to me about that other German, the one who has found Troy, or so they say. I think Leonardo would be another like that one.

"But I think there is something else driving him as well. I think that he felt great shame when the Bedouin forced him to retreat short of his goal. The German left for Europe. Eddie found his love, Miriam, but Leonardo, he only finds disgrace. I think it was to wash clean this disgrace as much as for anything else that he always plans to go back."

Jenny sipped her lemonade and listened, sure there would be more.

"Once when we were discussing a battle, Leonardo says to me, 'There is no shame in strategic retreat if it lets you remain strong enough to go after the enemy later.' I think that until he returns to the desert, he will feel he ran rather than retreated.

"But there is more. After his second attempt, when he is beaten so terribly and nearly dies, then I think this becomes more than a matter of transforming flight into strategic retreat. From his letters I realize that my lion is very angry, that he wants more than to find this tomb, he wants revenge on those who hurt him. Sometimes he may still say he is unconvinced that the two events are connected . . ."

"He connected them for me and Stephen," Jenny interjected.

"He was trying to be honest with you, and as you yourself say, to scare you. To me he has said one and the other, but I think that in his deepest heart he is certain, and that even deeper than that certainty he is very, very angry. I think that now he not so much hunt for this old king of Egypt. I think he hunts for these Arabs who so greatly harmed him. He wishes to fight them again, this time prepared, and this time to win and so wash himself clean of the bitterness of two losses."

Jenny frowned. "I don't know. He asked us to be very careful, not to say anything to anyone but you and Mr. Bryce."

"And yet the first thing he does when coming here is to go out into the bazaar? Not a bazaar where Europeans go, but to an Arab bazaar? If he had taken you where tourists go, or to one of the archeological finds, I would not worry as I do, but though Eduardo could make all arrangements while Leonardo remains safe under my roof, the first thing Leonardo does is go out and be seen. I am greatly troubled by this."

"Me, too," Jenny said, "now that you put it that way. I'm real scared. Are you going to talk to Uncle Neville? You're pretty sharp at making someone see when they're fooling themselves."

Papa Antonio surprised her by slowly shaking his head.

"I have tried, directly and indirectly. I have made no more headway than a sea gull into a tempest. So I warn you, who are his niece, and who truly cares for him."

"What good can I do," Jenny said, bitter once more, "stuck back here in Cairo while the others go off after Neferankhotep?"

"Two things you can do," Papa Antonio said, undaunted. "One, by your very presence you may convince your uncle to change his mind, to reach after the new, good things life offers."

"I don't know if that will work," Jenny said. "Uncle Neville was so set on this trip that he almost missed meeting the ship that brought me from America. Even after he remembered, he didn't change his plans, just gave me the choice of staying in London or coming with him. What's your second plan?"

"It is not, I think, unsuited to your own desires," Papa Antonio said, and though he smiled his impish smile, Jenny thought that something sad remained around the edges. "You wish to go with him. Very well. I will help you to go—not because I think it is wise, but because I think that short of locking you in your room there is no way to discourage you. While I will be your host, I will not serve as Leonardo's jailer."

"And then you want me to stop him?" Jenny asked in disbelief.

"Rather I want you to force him—by the need he will feel to keep you safe, if no other way—to think carefully, and listen to the counsel of others. He will still be in danger, yes, and so will you all, but at least the danger will be from those he has somehow made his enemies and not from himself."

Jenny swallowed hard. Contemplating murderous assassins was one thing when safely in London or even on shipboard, but hearing this sane old man speak so calmly of them made her realize that they were a real threat, not some fancy of her adventurous uncle. Papa Antonio believed in them—but then he'd seen his friend beaten, had his home robbed. He had reason to believe.

For a moment Jenny toyed with the idea of letting Uncle Neville persuade her to stay behind. Then she realized that she'd never forgive herself if anything happened to him, anything she might have prevented. She hadn't been there when the Indians killed her parents. She'd be there when whoever it was came for Uncle Neville.

"I'll go," Jenny said, making her voice as firm as possible. "If you can't convince him to give it up, I'll go."

Bazaar

THAT EVENING, as members of Papa Antonio's apparently innumerable family of attentive Copts were clearing away dinner and the guests were adjourning to the courtyard, Eddie Bryce arrived.

Neville was startled by how much his old friend had come to resemble an Arab. Always lean, now Eddie was spare, his flesh sapped of any excess by constant exertion in the heat. His skin had browned to the color of dark toast. Brown hair and beard were worn long, neatly trimmed around the edges. Like Papa Antonio, Eddie wore the long, loose cotton robes of the Arab, but he also wore a turban that made him look oddly, instantly, exotic.

At closer inspection, Eddie's English heritage was still evident. His nose was short, his weathered skin—where it was not covered by beard—showed a faint patterning of freckles beneath the tan. His hair had bleached slightly from exposure to the sun, giving the effect of greying, and thereby added dignity to the man's overall presence.

The stiff bow with which Eddie greeted the company mingled the oriental and the occidental in style, but when Papa Antonio gave his newly arrived guest a chiding look, Eddie grinned and embraced the old man. Introductions followed,

and soon their party was settled in the courtyard, where the plashing of the fountain waters would assure that they not be overheard by the other residents.

The father of the Copt family, serving in the capacity of butler, brought coffee, sweet wine, and desserts, then withdrew. Neville suspected that the butler's
frequent forays over to the two or three other clusters of guests spread about the
courtyard were as much to assure that they were not in a position to overhear this
conference as to assure their comfort.

Neville longed to move directly to business. His trip with Stephen into the
bazaar earlier that day had made him even more eager to move his project forward.
However, he knew such directness would be rude, even in England, and certainly
here in Egypt. He wasn't certain how much Eddie had embraced oriental custom
along with the outer appearances, but that turban and all it implied warned him to
take care.

"How are Miriam and the children?" Neville began.

"Very well, thank you," Eddie replied taking out tobacco pouch and papers, and
beginning to roll a cigarette. "Allah has blessed us with three sons and two daughters. If He continues to favor us, we will have another child before the end of spring."

In response to questions from Papa Antonio, and spurred by Stephen's desire
to make certain he understood the dynamics of an Arab family, Eddie discussed
his children, his wife, his wife's relatives (many of whom lived with them), and
something of his business.

Neville had known Miriam's father and one of her brothers, and considered
them ample reason for Eddie to avoid the entire clan. He thought he was hiding his
impatience well, but before he had smoked his first cigarette, Eddie gave him that
wry, irreverent look that had made him so unpopular with many of the Army officers under whom he had served.

"But I see that Neville is fidgeting," Eddie said, "impatient to get on to business. I'll start. I can go with you, Neville. Your letters made clear when you
planned to arrive, and so I haven't accepted anything that would take me from
Cairo overlong. I have a few day jobs to complete, but since these can be combined
with making arrangements for you, they will not delay you."

Neville nodded. "We'll need camels, but it would be best if we were able to
pick them up at Luxor rather than bring them from here. Can you arrange that?"

Eddie puffed a smoke ring.

"I can. Now that the Nile is subsiding it's easy enough to get messages upriver. May I assume you are going ahead with your mad venture?"

Stephen interrupted, a good thing, for Neville had felt an unwise spike of
anger at Eddie's manner of referring to his dream.

"Mad venture, Mr. Bryce?" the young man said. "Do you mean Sir Neville's expedition specifically or archeology in general?"

The corner of Eddie's mouth lifted in half a smile.

"I do," he said, "though I have my doubts about archeology."

He paused.

"By the way, I'd prefer if you'd call me Eddie or even Eduardo as Papa Antonio does. I'm neither your master nor your servant. You're going to be trusting your lives to my skills, and so we'd better start being friends."

Stephen beamed at this, his momentary defensiveness at Eddie's criticism of archeology vanishing, just as, Neville suspected, Eddie had known it would.

"And you should call me Stephen," the linguist replied cordially.

"And me Jenny, please," that young lady said. "You, too, Stephen. I'm getting real tired of this Miss Benet stuff."

Neville noted that departure from *Neptune's Charger* and the English passengers had had a deleterious effect on Jenny's English. It was becoming more and more broadly American, and at that not American of the best. However, he had other things to worry about than his niece's diction. Before he could return to matters of transport and supply, Stephen was pursuing Eddie's aversion to archeology.

"Why do you dislike archeology, Eddie?"

"I don't dislike archeology as such." Eddie spoke slowly, as if determined to find precise words to express his objections. "I'll even admit to finding some of the conclusions archeologists reach interesting. I just wonder at the amount of energy smart people put into digging up other people whose only wish for the afterlife was that they wouldn't get dug up. Seems a bit wrong, when you look at it from their point of view.

Stephen leaned forward. "Actually, as I understand it, the first wish of the ancient Egyptians was that they not be forgotten. Their entire mortuary tradition has evolved from the making of offerings by the living to the dead, offerings that were meant to assure that those who had died would continue in comfort in the afterlife."

"The tomb treasures," Jenny added, obviously eager to show she had done her lessons, "were meant to represent those things the departed would need in the afterlife. Some archeologists think that even the poor had similar items placed in their graves, though they had to make do with simple drawings and clay figures rather than elaborate painted frescos or statues made from gold and alabaster."

Eddie nodded that he understood. "But you do admit that they didn't want to get dug up."

"No," Stephen admitted. "They didn't, but mostly because that would hurt their chances of being remembered after death and receiving offerings from their descendants. For an ancient Egyptian, being erased from memory was a fate worse than death."

Neville interrupted, aware that his tone was a touch mocking, and wondering where that mockery came from. "So in a sense, we could be doing old Nefer-ankhotep a favor by finding his tomb and making his legend current once more. He certainly has been forgotten."

Eddie directed a too sharp glance toward Neville.

"Has he?" he asked softly.

Speaking in a more general tone, Eddie turned again to Stephen and Jenny.

"Still, you'll admit that the majority of archeologists aren't motivated by a desire to keep the dead from being forgotten."

"True," Stephen said. "Yet, without archeological excavation and the information we gather, the history and culture of the ancient Egyptians would be completely lost to us."

"Does that matter?" Eddie asked, clearly enjoying his role as devil's advocate.

From the eagerness, completely free from any anger, with which Stephen responded, Neville guessed that the young linguist saw this in the light of an intellectual debate and did not feel personally attacked.

"Certainly," Stephen said. "Without the work that archeologists have done, we would still be in the position of those who saw the ancient Egyptians as peculiar magicians or as all being like the horrid tyrant mentioned in the Bible."

Jenny added, "In your work, Eddie, you must have met those people who still want to think of the ancient Egyptians as having some arcane powers. We traveled on the steamer with a woman who could go on for hours about how the pyramids could not have been constructed without magical assistance, or how the hieroglyphs were magical symbols, potent in themselves."

"Seems to me," Eddie said with a grin, rolling another cigarette and accepting a fresh cup of coffee from the curiously silent Papa Antonio, "that even the ancient Egyptians themselves felt that way. Weren't things like the Eye of Horus or the scarab beetle considered talismans to ward off evil and misfortune, the way a Christian might use a cross?"

Neville interrupted. "There will be ample time to discuss such matters on the way upriver or in field camps—more than ample."

"Fine," Eddie replied. "However, this hasn't been as useless as you might think, Neville, old man. I do need to know what you're hoping to bring out. If it's just knowledge, well, we don't need as many pack camels, but if you're for looting the tombs . . ."

Stephen flared, honestly offended. "Collecting artifacts is not looting!"

Eddie looked at him levelly. "If we're going to work together, Stephen, we're going to need to be honest. You know as well as I do that the majority of archeologists aren't motivated by a desire for knowledge. They toss old pots aside in their eagerness to find gold and precious stones, even though those pots and the things written on them could teach a whole lot. Most of the people funding expeditions are hoping to find some of the beautiful things the ancient Egyptians buried with their dead. Interest in the relics of the ages—and the value some people give them—has been a later development, and one that is far from universal."

Stephen paused and Neville could see him swallowing some angry retort.

"Eddie, I agree," Stephen said a bit woodenly when he finally spoke, "Archeologists like Belzoni at the beginning of this century were little more than tomb robbers. I'll admit it. But what about Denon? He worked even earlier, and certainly his painstakingly careful renderings of the tomb paintings and the tombs themselves were not motivated by greed."

"They didn't need to be," Eddie said. "Denon was on Napoleon's payroll, so he had the luxury to indulge in art."

Jenny pressed Stephen down when the young man surged to his feet.

"Mr. Bryce—Eddie—why are you baiting Stephen? If you don't want to be part of Uncle Neville's expedition, for any reason, then I think you should say so and why. Whatever people did fifty years ago, whatever some of them are still doing now, Stephen isn't responsible."

Eddie laughed, a drawn-out, good-natured sound that immediately eased the tension.

"You're right, Jenny. I was baiting him. I have my reasons—and some of them are as practical as how many camels I should arrange for us to take with us. It's one thing to talk about Denon's paintings and ancient knowledge, but if in the end I'm going to find myself being asked to haul out gold-plated furnishing and statuettes I need to be ready in advance. A camel's a good beast, and strong, but it isn't a steamer that can be loaded to the capacity of the hold, and fed brush because the coal has been left behind to make room for artifacts."

"Have people really done that?" Jenny asked.

Before Eddie could answer, Neville cut him off.

"Eddie, you said you are willing to work for me. Have you changed your mind?"

"Certainly not based on anything these young folks have said. You, though, you've been remarkably quiet, Nev."

"Can't get a word in," Neville replied, forcing a laugh. "Can we start making arrangements?"

"First one question," Eddie said. "Does Stephen—and Jenny, since I understand you're the only family she has left—do they know about how your last attempt to go after this Neferankhotep got stopped?"

"I told them," Neville replied, "even before we left England. I told them everything, even what I thought I heard the one would-be assassin say."

" 'So is the Lawgiver avenged against sacrilege. So is the good king's peace preserved,' " Eddie replied. "I still think that this good king is not forgotten, Neville. If I am to assist you, I insist on one term. We will not speak of this expedition to anyone. You have been convinced to take a trip to Luxor—perhaps by Mr. Holmboe, who wishes to see the Valley of the Kings. I have a very reliable agent in Luxor, a cousin of my wife's mother. Cambridge-educated man. Daud knows how to keep silence. So do I."

Neville sensed the other man's implied criticism.

"And so do I," he said indignantly.

"Do you?" Eddie said. "You just admitted that you have confided in your niece and in Stephen."

"That's different."

"How?"

"She's my family—my only family, as you so aptly reminded me. Mr. Holmboe is an expert I need in order to do my work. I don't read hieroglyphs well enough to translate any inscriptions we might find. However, I won't take him out without giving him fair warning."

"And what would you have done if he'd been scared off? How would you have stopped him from telling your story to others?"

Neville felt himself growing unreasonably angry.

"Would you have had me kill Stephen if he had refused to take the risk? I think you have been living among the Bedouin too long, Mr. Bryce."

"I think," Eddie replied, "that one reason there is no trace of Neferankhotep—at least under that name—or of the circumstances of his burial is that there have been many who would kill in order to keep his secret."

The two men glowered at each other, and what might have been said next—for accusations of cowardice and being wife-ridden were rising to Neville's lips—might have ended that long friendship. Stephen spoke first.

"I say, gentlemen, isn't this rather moot? I mean, I did come along. I don't plan on betraying any secrets, and all that."

Eddie ground out his cigarette.

"You're right, Stephen. However, from this point on, I must be considered to be in charge—not of the archeology, but of all details of the planning. There will be no more trips to the bazaars unless I am there, and even those trips will be to the bazaars frequented by tourists. You will investigate the local monuments, go to the museum, take a picnic to see the pyramids and the Great Sphinx."

He looked at Neville. "All of you. I don't know if these intervening years have been enough to erase all memories of the gallant army captain with the archeological interests. Some might even remember how you got that striking scar on your never too lovely mug. Do you agree?"

For a fleeting moment, Neville considered refusing, considered firing Eddie and getting help from elsewhere. The army surely had some men who could use a bit of field experience. Colonel Travers would assist him in recruiting appropriate candidates. Or there was Lady Cheshire. Captain Brentworth had worked for Lord Cheshire in much the same capacity as Eddie would for Neville.

But the others were already agreeing, even Papa Antonio, and Neville realized he could not fire Eddie when all the man wanted was to assure the safety and secrecy of the expedition.

"Very well," Neville said. "I agree. It's going to be bloody hard playing tourist though, when so much waits to be done."

Jenny turned a shining face toward him, mischief dancing in her violet eyes.

"Oh, I don't know, Uncle Neville. You know how very much I've wanted to see the Sphinx."

Jenny knew that in their protectiveness the men were likely to keep her nearly imprisoned at Papa Antonio's. Doubtless there would be jaunts to the Egyptian Museum or the Great Pyramids, but these would be so very European in their orientation she might as well be part of some Cook's tour.

Stephen's enthusiastic description of his trip to the native bazaar with Neville had made her hungry to see something of the Mother of Cities, and while she'd prefer that something was off the beaten trails, after hearing Eddie lay down the law the evening before, she didn't dare press too hard. However, she didn't see that there would be any harm in reaching for the stars and seeing where the others compromised.

Therefore, as they were breakfasting that morning on fresh fruit over light wheat cakes, she began her assault on the bastions of masculine privilege.

"Uncle Neville, I have a wonderful idea," she said, making her voice light and yet confident. "I want to go out to the bazaar with you and Stephen. I can borrow some long robes from Papa Antonio, wrap my hair up under a turban, and go as an Arab boy."

Papa Antonio choked on his coffee. Stephen suddenly found his melon fascinating. Even Uncle Neville was struck silent for a moment trying to find some excuse other than the obvious—that it would take more than robes and a turban to make Jenny Benet look like a boy of any race—for refusing her request.

"Has it occurred to you that you speak no Arabic?"

"I have a few phrases," Jenny replied defiantly. "Or I could pretend to be mute, like Captain Brentworth's servant, Rashid."

"The merchants would still expect you to understand them," Uncle Neville replied, "and before you say you could pretend to be deaf as well, let me tell you that there is no way you could ignore the noise of a typical bazaar—at least not with sufficient skill to convince anyone you were deaf."

"In any case," added Eddie Bryce, who had arrived in time to overhear, "your eye color would give you away. We might darken your skin with some stain, but there are few Arabs with eyes that deep violet. We might find ourselves made offers for you by one of those less than scrupulous men who continue to defy regulation and deal in human flesh. They are dangerous people, and I, for one, would not care to anger them."

There was a twinkle in his eye as he made this speech, and Jenny gave him an answering smile.

Eddie went on, "I don't see why you should not go to the bazaar as yourself. Escorted by Neville and Stephen you should not have any trouble, at least not in those bazaars accustomed to Europeans."

"But is it safe for her?" Stephen asked anxiously. "The place I went with Sir Neville yesterday made the worst London market I've visited seem a quiet village fair."

"She'll be safe if she isn't permitted to wander off on her own," Eddie assured him. "Indeed, there is nothing some vendors like as much as a European woman accompanied by a gentleman—especially if it looks like he has deep pockets. Jenny may provide some protection for Nev as well."

Jenny flushed, wondering if Eddie had noticed the derringer that she still carried with her.

"Protection?" she asked.

"That's right," Eddie replied. "We were talking last night about Neville's 'accident' a few years ago. It is just possible he will be recognized, or someone in the wrong will hear he is back in Egypt. If he is seen squiring around a pretty young woman, buying her trinkets or such, that will provide excuse enough for his return. Whether they take you for a new wife, or note the family resemblance and take you for a daughter, they won't be as curious as they would be if he were out buying rope and shovels."

Uncle Neville agreed.

"But no Arab costume," he commanded, "and make certain your walking dress is modest. None of those short skirts like you were wearing yesterday."

Jenny agreed with becoming meekness, quite content to relinquish the comfort of ankle-length skirts in her greater victory.

When she came out, appropriately attired, with both wide-brimmed hat and parasol, she found the men waiting. Eddie had arranged for a light trap with a reliable Arab driver. He made sure that each man carried a flask filled with good clean water, and advised them to drink frequently.

"Once you're in the market, stick to tea or coffee, or water you can be sure has been boiled. The water sellers tend to pull their wares directly from the Nile. If you become overly hot or tired, find a shady place and rest. Sunstroke is a real risk in this climate."

He addressed his remarks to Jenny, but she felt fairly certain they were intended for Stephen. That young man, accustomed to England's milder sun, had already been told to put on a wide-brimmed straw boater rather than his usual heavy bowler.

As the trap rattled through the streets, Jenny soaked in every little detail of their surroundings, peppering Uncle Neville with questions. Whether he thought she was entering fully into her role as newly arrived tourist, or thought her enthusiasm genuine, didn't matter. She doubted that he would guess that beneath her honest interest lay a desire to acquire enough knowledge of the city that, if necessary, she could find her way back to Papa Antonio's if she went out alone.

At the edge of the bazaar, Uncle Neville paid off the driver.

"We walk from here. The stalls are arranged too haphazardly to make anything else practical."

He was not exaggerating. The bazaar merchants only grudgingly allowed for paths between their stalls, and the amount of foot traffic made these avenues seem even narrower than they were. This didn't stop some shoppers however, and frequently even foot traffic was halted when cart or donkey met with horse or carriage or camel. Someone, usually the person of lower social rank, was forced to give way. Jenny wondered aloud if some of those donkeys didn't travel as great a distance backward as they ever did forward.

As some sort of compensation for the immediate chaos, the bazaar district they had entered had different quarters for different trades. If there were signs telling which area was which, or whether one needed to rely on a trained guide, Jenny never learned. What was clear was that the places themselves advertised what was being sold. Here were slippers of every type piled up in heaps. These, Uncle Neville explained, were an essential part of daily life, for no one entered a mosque except barefoot or in slippers reserved for that use—the wearing of other footwear on holy ground being considered as sacrilegious.

Then, just when one was thinking there was nothing in all the world but slippers, a turn of an alley, perhaps passage through an ancient stone arch, and everywhere were saddles: camel saddles, horse saddles, donkey saddles. Intricately worked saddles in leather, embossed and polished. Plain, workaday saddles. Used saddles, newly refurbished. Camel saddles, bright with tassels.

Then another twist and a few turns and they were in a world of carpets. This bazaar was huge. Jenny was enchanted by the shimmer of silk and the solid beauty of dyed wool, captivated by the patterns woven into the fabric—each, or so she was assured, containing one little flaw deliberately made, for only Allah is perfect.

After the carpet bazaar, they went to the coppersmith's bazaar. Here Sir Neville bought Jenny a jewelry set made of copper adorned with polished stones cut like scarabs for her to wear when her mourning had ended. Stephen had already indulged himself in a little sack of fake scarabs, though he refused a "real" mummy's arm offered to him by a man passing in the street.

"It's someone's arm," he admitted after inspecting it, "but I for one don't think it would be disarming to any but the chappie who lost it."

Once their initial curiosity was satisfied, Uncle Neville took them to a sidewalk cafe. They drank coffee and ate very sticky clumps of honeyed almonds while watching the polyglot crowd push and shove about its business. The mixture of peoples was amazing, even to Jenny who had the western American's familiarity with people in black and pink and various shades of brown, of people who spoke English and Spanish, or any of a wide variety of Red Indian languages.

Here the differences were so great that the American mixture might well be one people. Skins shown black, brown, olive, sunburned red, and parasol pale. Eyes were dark and light, round and slanting, sometimes in the oddest combinations. Hair was brown and woolly, or shining black and oily, or the odd russet tinge that spoke of mixed blood. It was curly or straight or set in braids or left loose like pictures of prophets depicted in the family bible. Heads were left bare or adorned with beads or caps or hats or veils.

Ethnic differences were accentuated by the varied styles of native dress—for these seemed to persist whether or not they were particularly suitable for the climate. Certainly the shirts and fitted trousers of the Europeans—even when topped with a broad-brimmed palm-leaf hat as a concession to the brilliance of the sun— seemed far less appropriate than the flowing robes of the Arabs or the loose cotton shirts worn by the Egyptian fellahin. However, even when the European in question belonged to a community—such as the Greek—who had dwelt in Cairo for generations, a style of dress derived from their land of origin persisted.

Jenny was just debating whether she wanted to continue exploring or to go back to Papa Antonio's, where she could dispense with the restrictive weight of bustle and petticoats in favor of a loose house dress, when she noted Uncle Neville gazing with fixed intensity toward the nearest edge of the bazaar.

She followed the direction of his gaze, and saw Lady Cheshire, of all people, bending gracefully to inspect a brilliant piece of woven silk the merchant was holding up for her inspection. Captain Brentworth stood protectively close. Mrs. Syms and Rashid waited a few paces away, their arms filled with packages.

At that moment, almost as if aware of the intensity of the gazes resting on her, Lady Cheshire turned and looked their way. Her face lit with such pleasure that Jenny was not at all surprised to note that Uncle Neville was beaming back rather stupidly. Captain Brentworth's expression became stormy, before he schooled his features into rigid neutrality.

There was nothing to be done but to motion for the Cheshire party to join their own, and these did so with alacrity, leaving the silk merchant to look after them, his bearded features almost comic in the broad lines of his disappointment.

"Sir Neville, dear Miss Benet," Lady Cheshire gushed, extending a slender hand gloved in lace. "Mr. Holmboe. How delightful to see you all."

Jenny tried not to feel self-conscious as she extended her own, ungloved, hand. She'd taken advantage of the men's ignorance of fashion to slip off the ones Emily had supplied for her that morning, but now her informality seemed glaringly obvious.

She need not have worried. Uncle Neville had no eyes for anyone but Lady Cheshire, and Stephen, quite oddly, had no eyes for anyone but Uncle Neville. The younger man's normally open, cheerful features were stern, but what Jenny read there wasn't envy, but concern.

The coffee shop owner was only too happy to let them draw several tables together, especially when Lady Cheshire ordered not only coffee and sweets, but a pastry tray. Rashid was permitted his own cup of coffee and a share of the goodies—not, Jenny suspected, so much out of anyone's awareness of the youth's obvious weariness, but because it kept him conveniently near to guard the packages.

Jenny smiled at Rashid and was rewarded with a slow smile before his expression settled into its usual dullness. She wished they could sit and, well, "talk" wasn't exactly the right word, since Rashid had no words, but play with Mischief as they had that afternoon in Alexandria when everyone but themselves and Mrs. Syms had retired to nap.

That worthy woman was holding up to the heat here as easily as she had in Alexandria, her leathery skin smooth and dry as some exotic lizard's. She was wearing a walking dress in a vibrant red watered silk, and when Jenny complimented her on it, she immediately turned to Rashid.

"Hand me the silk I just bought, Rashid," she said. "There's a dear boy."

She rewarded him for his service with a flaky pastry topped with thin slivers of toasted almond, almost as if he were Mischief, but Jenny thought her kindness no less genuine for that.

"Look at this," Mrs. Syms said, unrolling a length of golden tissue. "Audrey tells me such strong colors are going out of fashion, but I could not resist."

As Jenny expressed her genuine admiration for the fabric—while reserving her opinion as to how it would look on the older woman—she couldn't help overhear the conversation at the other side of the table.

"We came up to Cairo rather earlier than planned," Lady Cheshire was saying. "Captain Brentworth heard from an old friend that the museum library might be interested in buying some of my late husband's papers. I have some reservations about parting with them, but certainly it would be better for them to be available to scholars here than moldering away in his files in England."

Sir Neville commented, "The museum director is interested in making Egypt's collection the first in the world—as it should be, given that Egypt is the source of the artifacts. Still, not all English scholars would thank you. The Egyptian Museum is more French than otherwise in its affiliation, and that is deeply resented."

"I know." Lady Cheshire paused. "Perhaps you would permit me to consult you further on this matter. You are on the fringes of the archeological community, and therefore might advise me more wisely than those involved in its intrigues."

"I would do what I could to assist you," Sir Neville said, and Jenny thought that he sounded disproportionately pleased.

"Where are you staying?" Lady Cheshire asked. "We inquired after you at Shepheard's, but you were not there, nor were you at the other better hotels. I was going to send a note around to dear Teresa Travers and ask if she knew where we might find you, but then we had the good fortune to encounter you ourselves."

Jenny found herself wondering just how much luck had to do with their encounter. The bazaar was so large that even a planned meeting might go awry. However, it did seem unfair to accuse the woman of subterfuge.

"We are staying with an old friend of mine," Sir Neville responded easily. "Antonio Donati. He runs a small rooming house in another section of the city. It is really quite nice, though without many social amenities. I lived there when I was a soldier, and wanted some relief from military life."

Lady Cheshire leaned over to Mrs. Syms.

"Make a note of their address, would you, Sarah? It is a pity you aren't staying at Shepheard's, but I can understand you would not wish to overwhelm poor Miss Benet with Shepheard's social whirl. It is *so* nice to be able to stay with friends. We could entertain you at Shepheard's there if you are staying in Cairo long. That way Jenny could at least say she's been to Shepheard's when she returns to England."

"We will be here some time, yet," Sir Neville said. "We have hardly begun to show Jenny the sights. Eventually, Stephen and I may take a short jaunt or two, but we will never be away for long."

He led the conversation away from their plans for the future with such determination that Jenny felt almost guilty at her relief. It made her feel very peculiar to see a man of Uncle Neville's years—he was over forty, after all—acting like a besotted cowhand. If he could continue to mislead Lady Cheshire, then all hope was not lost.

They visited with the Cheshire party for some time more, then Sir Neville made their excuses.

"I know that our host has special plans for dinner, and I promised to do some shopping for him on our way back. I would not wish to disappoint him."

This white lie surprised Jenny a great deal, but any hope that she had that it indicated Uncle Neville was immune to Lady Cheshire's charm evaporated as soon as they relaxed in the trap that carried them back to Casa Donati.

"I would very much have liked to visit with our friends longer," he said, his tones those of one who thinks aloud. "However, Captain Brentworth was clearly growing impatient. I cannot see how Lady Cheshire has tolerated his service for so long. He is quite a tyrant."

"Probably," Stephen said with a dryness that was not usual for him, "she tolerates him because the captain worships the very dirt Lady Cheshire treads on. Such dirt-termined devotion is not easy to find here on earth."

He chuckled a bit at his pun, but Jenny thought Stephen intended a genuine warning. Sir Neville shook his head.

"Lady Cheshire should not permit it. The captain is not worthy of her. Doubtless he is interested only in her fortune."

Stephen's gaze met Jenny's and she favored him with a shrug.

"None are so blind as those who will not see," Stephen said, and Jenny was certain that he meant someone other than Lady Cheshire.

Anubis

EDDIE BRYCE arrived in time to join them for dinner, an excellent meal built around wild duck served on a bed of rice and ornamented with apricots.

After dinner, they retired to their favored table in the courtyard, the one where the noise of the fountain neatly covered their conversation. This evening the precaution hardly seemed necessary. One of Papa Antonio's regular tenants, a dealer in textiles, had returned from a buying trip, and a steady line of laborers moved antlike to carry his purchases into a ground floor storeroom. They were not precisely noisy, but clearly saw no reason not to liven their labors with jokes and song.

Sighing slightly, Neville drew out his pipe and began stuffing in tobacco he had bought that afternoon in the bazaar. It was a Turkish variety of which he had fond memories.

"I've worked out transportation," Eddie began, accepting a cup of syrupy black coffee from Papa Antonio with the air of a man who accepts not simply refreshment but necessary support. "It's a compromise between caution and speed. If we wanted to involve as few people as possible, we could take a dahabeeyah from here all the way upriver."

"*Dahabeeyah?*" Jenny asked.

She had asked to join them, promising to keep out of the way. Though strictly speaking she had no need to take part in their conference, Neville had taken pity on her. She had brought her lesson books with her, but thus far they had remained closed.

"It's an Egyptian river boat, a sailing vessel," Eddie explained. "The best dahabeeyah are quite luxuriously appointed, and many vessels of all classes are available for hire. However, compared to a steamer they travel very slowly. Since Neville wants to have as much of the cooler months as he can for his desert exploration, a dahabeeyah would not serve for the entire journey."

Jenny nodded her understanding, but Neville thought she looked a bit disappointed.

"A dahabeeyah does fit into my plan," Eddie continued, "but not until after we arrive in Luxor. From Cairo to Luxor, we will travel like any other party of well-to-do tourists. I will act as your servant—easy enough to do, since Bert is remaining behind."

Neville frowned. He had noted how tired Eddie looked, and had anticipated giving him a rest from the grueling life he had inflicted on himself with his marriage to Miriam.

"I had intended to have you travel as comfortably as any of our number," he said.

"And I thank you for your thoughtfulness," Eddie replied, something flowery and Arabian in the manner with which he delivered this simple reply. "However, given the circumstances, I would rather travel as a servant. I may hear things you would not and thus ensure the safety of us all."

"You have a point," Neville said.

He longed to omit all these precautions, to go back to the simple enthusiasm with which he and Alphonse Liebermann had planned their first venture to the Valley of Dust. However, Neville's experiences when he had attempted the second expedition could not be denied. Indeed, Neville suspected that part of the reason he chaffed and fretted at the elaborate care Eddie was taking was because he would like to forget just how dangerous this undertaking might become.

"When does our tourist steamer leave?" Stephen asked, interrupting Neville's inner debate.

"Not for several days yet," Eddie assured him. "The *Lotus Blossom* has just returned to port from her first run upriver. They ran into a snag or two, so she needs to make some minor repairs and re-equip. You have time yet to see Cairo."

"That's jolly fine," Stephen said happily. "I do so want to see the Great Pyramids from other than a distance."

"I will arrange a reliable escort," Eddie promised. "It is a matter of honor for me to see that you are not subjected to the indignities usually inflicted upon tourists."

The conversation returned to arrangements for their journey. The trick was to clarify which items were necessities, which were things practical and useful, and which were luxuries. They had a great deal of difficulty explaining to Stephen that the library of books he had hauled over from England did not need to go into the desert with him.

"Then I don't understand why you didn't have me leave them at home!" the young man said, for once genuinely irritated.

"Had I known you had carried them with you," Neville replied, "I would have done so. I had assumed that your trunks were filled with clothing, and perhaps a few books for tutoring Jenny."

"Clothing?" Stephen said, amazed. "Who would need three trunks filled with clothing? I brought my books, notes, some instruments for measurement, a drawing set . . ."

Eddie held up his hand.

"The books, except for a few basic texts, must stay. They weigh too much and are too fragile. However, your measuring instruments may save me a great deal of all too conspicuous shopping for similar items."

So peace was restored. Jenny looked on and made a few helpful suggestions, but otherwise contented herself with studying her hieroglyphs. Indeed, she remained so meek—not once pleading to be included, even when Eddie began itemizing the various stops the *Lotus Blossom* would make between Cairo and Luxor, so that the passengers could enjoy touring various archeological sites—that Neville became suspicious.

Yawning, in spite of all the coffee he had consumed, Eddie left as soon as they had settled on a list of items to be purchased. He promised to send along a runner mid-morning with arrangements for their proposed trip to the Pyramids at Gizeh.

"You'll want to leave early," he replied when Neville commented that Eddie had better plan some time for sleep. "I'll go home and rest, and speak with one of my nephews about serving as your tour guide. He can arrange for the donkeys and such."

"Let him do the donkey work, eh?" Stephen said, chuckling.

"I'll axe him," Eddie retorted, and with mutual grins for their cleverness they parted.

"That exchange of what passes for wit finishes me," Jenny said, gathering up her books. "I'm going to my room to let Emily unlace me so she and Bert can retire."

"Good thought," Neville said. "Emily will be glad for something to do. I think neither of the Hamiltons quite knows what to do with their leisure."

"Have them start conditioning your field gear," Jenny suggested. "Sea travel will have done it no favors, and they won't be along to put burst seams right. Stephen will need to be measured for his kit, as well—unless his father included desert adventuring among his interests."

"That was not Father's idea of an adventure," Stephen agreed, a trace of sadness coming through despite his determined good humor. "I do hope you won't expect me to give up my sartorial statement."

"That," Neville replied dryly, "is not the type of statement I wish you'd give up."

"Pun my word," Stephen said happily. "A palpable hit."

Once alone, Neville began to review the list he and Eddie had put together. His attention would not stay on the neatly printed words.

I wonder if the others would mind if I invited Lady Cheshire and her friends to accompany us to the pyramids tomorrow. We might even treat them to luncheon. I seem to recall some lovely places along the river. Eddie would know the best.

Imagination wandered through the delights of a day spent in that lovely lady's company. He sketched out details. Eddie had mentioned donkeys. In his day there had been camel rides, too. Harder animals to manage for the unskilled.

Must get Stephen some training, he thought. *Wonder if Eddie can manage something innocent-looking. Might be easier if we just got him a horse. Still, that's a lot more feed. Even Arab steeds are fragile compared to camels.*

He found himself imagining Lady Cheshire mounted upon a camel. The image was not dignified. A horse though, sleek and fine-lined. Black to match the shining glory of her hair? Or white as sunlit sand for contrast? He toyed with both ideas, accessorizing the lady to go with each and deciding in the end that he preferred the black.

Smiling at his own conceit, he finished undressing and retired to the curtained alcove that held his remarkably comfortable bed. The sheets had been scented with something spicier than the lavender used by his housekeeper back in England. Perhaps he should lay in a supply.

On such domestic thoughts, he fell asleep. Perhaps that was why, when he awoke, he thought he was still dreaming.

Afterwards, Neville thought it must have been the sound of the door latch falling shut that had awakened him. At the time, though, he was in the dark, straining to separate form from shadow. Something was moving in the greater reaches of his room, something trying very hard not to make a noise as it felt its way along. He sensed it rather than saw it, felt it in the motion of the air in the enclosed space.

Neville had blown out the candle after he had gotten into bed, but it remained within reach, a box of matches near to hand. He reached toward it, stopped, feeling ashamed, the way he had as a child when he'd been moved from the nursery into his own room and the isolation had awakened fears of monsters lurking in the darkness.

He'd fought the impulse to light the candle then, certain that the maids or someone would guess from the spent taper or the depleted box of sulfur tips that he'd been afraid. Fear of seeming foolish again made him pause, and that pause was a moment too long. When he reached through the netting, something was between him and the candle.

The obstacle was damp, hot, and solid.

Naked flesh, Neville thought, his mind filling with elaborate childhood images of monsters. His hand, jerking upwards and away from that startling contact, touched the hem of a garment.

"What the . . ." Neville gasped, almost more an intake of breath than a word.

As if that sound had been a signal, Neville heard a tearing sound, and felt the bed curtain falling around him, enshrouding him. Something hard hit him in the upper torso, releasing a warm flood of blood. Neville flailed wildly, seeking to free himself from the smothering fabric, thoughts confused, intertwined as they were within the haze of nightmare.

Then, distantly, through the muffling of the thick walls he heard a shrill scream, a snap that his battle-conditioned mind recognized as the report of a gun.

Jenny's derringer! Neville thought, and the sensation of nightmare vanished, leaving his mind clear and his thoughts crisp and calculating. One might scream at a nightmare, but one did not shoot at it. Remembering how flimsy the bed curtains were, Neville stopped fighting against them, gathered both legs, and kicked out.

His bare feet impacted squarely with what felt like the thighs of someone who had presumably been bending over him. The force of his kick was somewhat impeded by the downed bed curtains, but it landed with sufficient power that he heard his assailant stagger back and crash into a chair not far from the bed.

His wound was throbbing, washing his chest with blood. Neville grabbed the bedpost with his right arm, using his left arm to claw away the remainder of the bedclothes.

"Who are you?" he shouted inanely, repeating his question in Arabic, then in French.

His attacker wasn't answering. Neville heard what was presumably the man rising, then the slap of bare feet on the tiled floor. Neville turned, following the sound, willing himself to motion, though he was uncomfortably aware that he was bleeding freely.

The assassin was moving in the direction of the window.

Barred, Neville thought with grim satisfaction. *You won't find exit there, my lad.*

He paused, taking advantage of this moment of opportunity. His fingers found the reassuring weight of the revolver and were bringing it around into line with his target. Then with his first clear look at his opponent, the nightmare returned with staggering force.

Silhouetted, solid dark against the dim rectangle that marked the window from the surrounding wall, Neville saw a long-nosed, pointed-eared shape—unmistakably the head of a jackal, but a jackal larger than a large man.

Neville groaned. What was Anubis, the Egyptian god associated with burials, doing in his bedroom? Had he lost enough blood that he was hallucinating?

"Stop!" he shouted, but the word echoed strangely in his ears. "Stop, I say!"

The jackal-headed figure gave an odd, barking laugh, placed its hands on the broad sill and smashed its shoulder against the bars.

Moving forward, gun held ready in anticipation of his triumph, Neville waited for the impact of flesh against metal. Instead, with a shriek of protest, the bars tore free. Neville heard them hit the street outside. The jackal-headed figure leapt lithely to the sill, barked another high-pitched laugh, then was gone.

At that moment, the door to Neville's room burst open. Jenny, clad in a nightdress of some pale-colored fabric, her hair an unbound tangle, stood there. She held a six-shooter competently, and cast around as if seeking a target. Stephen Holmboe towered above and behind her, the candelabrum in his hand backlighting Jenny while casting himself into grotesque shadow.

Jenny seemed to take in the situation in a glance. She ran across the room, gun in one hand, encumbering skirts gathered in the other. Approaching the window from one side, she peered out.

"Hard to tell in this light," she said, "but whoever it was is gone."

Stephen had brought the candelabrum into the room and was lighting Neville's reading light from it.

"Don't get in front of the window," Jenny ordered. Then she saw her uncle clearly for the first time. "Uncle Neville, you've been shot!"

"Stabbed, actually," he said calmly and, as if the words had been some sort of release, fainted dead away.

Jenny stood frozen as Uncle Neville collapsed, then, lowering the hammer of her six-shooter on an empty chamber, she bolted to his side.

"Stephen, get that light over here, then call Papa Antonio!"

Stephen did so, for once shocked into silence. By the time Papa Antonio arrived, Jenny had ascertained the basics of her uncle's condition.

"He's been stabbed. A long 'T,' but I don't think it did more than slice muscle. I'll need my doctor's bag. It's in my trunk, next to the rifle case. Emily should know. Can you get me some boiled water and clean linen?"

"I can do this," Papa Antonio said.

Stephen returned, bringing with him more light. "Will Sir Neville be all right?" he asked hesitantly. "Should we call a doctor?"

"Help me get him on the bed," Jenny said by way of reply. "You're big enough to lift his shoulders without twisting him about too much. I'll get his feet."

Stephen moved to obey, and Jenny belatedly remembered his questions.

"Yes," she said, lifting Uncle Neville's feet. "With luck he should pull through this. I'd guess blood loss put him out. If Papa Antonio knows a reliable doctor who will come at this hour, I won't complain, but right now I can do as much for his wounds as any doctor."

Stephen didn't protest. They'd had time on *Neptune's Charger* to exchange histories, and he knew she had studied medicine with her father. Jenny appreciated his acceptance. Maybe living with his sisters and mother had helped Stephen accept that women weren't all fools.

Emily brought Jenny's doctor's bag, and for a time the surrounding world vanished as Jenny concentrated on tending Uncle Neville's injury. He had bled a great deal. Traces of the bed netting in the wound showed that the knife had caught in several layers of fabric, which had doubtless lessened the force of the blow. While that had saved Neville from more serious injury, it also meant that Jenny had to painstakingly clean the wound before stitching it up.

Uncle Neville came around while she was still cleaning the slash. After reassuring him that he was in no danger, Jenny said wryly, "Well, Uncle, I don't have anything to put you under, but I can offer you a bullet to bite or a tot of something strong."

Neville merely cocked an eyebrow as if to say that opiates were not to be thought of for such a minor wound, and accepted a piece of soft wood to clamp between his teeth so he wouldn't risk biting his tongue. He didn't refuse the stiff whiskey Papa Antonio brought, though.

Jenny could feel Uncle Neville flinch as she plied her tweezers and needle, but she'd sewn conscious patients before. Her father had begun her training on freshly slaughtered pigs before he let her move on to unconscious patients, but he'd always insisted that she wouldn't know whether she had what it took to be a doctor unless she worked in less ideal circumstances.

She still hated that slight flinch that reminded her she was inflicting pain, but she'd learned to push her reaction into the back of her mind. If sometimes she still needed to retire to a private place to settle her stomach afterwards, she didn't think that invalidated her professional calling.

Tonight, though, she was too keyed up to become nauseated. After she'd finished stitching and bandaging Uncle Neville, she suddenly felt tired, but not too tired to find out what had been going on while she worked.

Bert and Emily had arrived and were curtaining over the window with thick muslin. From outside came the sound of metal clattering, doubtless someone moving the bars which had failed to stop the would-be assassin's escape.

"Would someone," Uncle Neville said, speaking very carefully, as if reluctant to admit that either pain or alcohol were affecting his thought processes, "tell me precisely what happened tonight? I heard noise from outside my room while I was dealing with my own little problem—a scream, I thought, and a shot."

Jenny answered, "Those were me, Uncle Neville. I had just gotten out of bed—too much coffee, I fear—and was answering nature's call."

She colored at this indelicate admission, then went on.

"To my astonishment, I saw the door to my room start to open. I thought it might be Emily, coming for something she'd forgotten, and was about to say something. Then I realized that the shadow this person was casting—it was back-lit from the courtyard—was far too big to be Emily. It was huge . . ."

She paused, and then went on.

"I realized that in the dim light—I had not bothered to light a candle—this stranger didn't know I wasn't asleep. My derringer was on the table next to the bed. I rose quietly, and reached for the gun, but he must have heard me move for he turned with incredible agility and stabbed at me with his knife. I screamed and fired. I saw him stagger, then dive out the window. I'd just gotten my six-shooter from the trunk—the derringer's a one-shot model—when Stephen came banging at my door. He'd barely had time to come in with his light when we realized that there was noise from your room. We ran, then, but we didn't get here in time."

Uncle Neville smiled. "I don't know about that, Jenny."

She returned his smile. "What I still don't know is how Stephen happened to be so opportunely awake."

Stephen looked embarrassed.

"Nothing so grand, I'm afraid. I must have fallen asleep while I was sitting up reading. My candle had guttered to almost nothing. Something woke me—perhaps one of your assailants moving about. I thought nothing of it and had just lit fresh tapers so I could find my things—I'm afraid I'd left them rather higgledy-piggledy when we were making equipment lists earlier—when I heard Jenny's scream. I grabbed up the candelabrum and ran."

"So you were not attacked?" Neville asked.

"No, sir." Stephen looked thoughtful. "Perhaps my light deceived any watchers into believing I was more alert than I was."

"Quite likely," Neville agreed.

He looked straight at Jenny with an odd uncertainty to his usually direct gaze.

"Jenny, you said you saw your attacker fairly clearly. You mentioned he was huge. Did you notice anything else?"

Jenny swallowed hard.

"I did. He . . ." She looked pleadingly at him. "Don't think me crazy, Uncle, but he looked just like one of the pictures from Stephen's books, a man dressed like an ancient Egyptian—wearing one of those short tunics or kilts. He had a broad collar around his neck and over his upper chest."

Uncle Neville continued to fix his gaze on her.

"Is that all?"

She felt suddenly defiant.

"No, that isn't. Above that collar, the man had a jackal's head, just like the god Anubis does in the pictures. I'm not crazy, and the light was poor, but there was enough coming from behind him that I'm sure of what I saw."

She was ready for objections, but none came.

"That matches what I saw," Uncle Neville said, "though I didn't get as clear a look—just a glimpse before my man went out the window—and most of what I saw was the head. He was probably dressed like your assailant, though. I remember being surprised that his legs were bare."

Jenny felt a wash of relief. Stephen seemed about to say something, but Uncle Neville cut him off.

"Did you hit your man?"

"Yes. There was blood on the floor, though not much. I may have only nicked him. I didn't take much time to aim."

"Still," Uncle Neville said, "we may be able to track him by the blood drops. Where's Papa Antonio? Has anyone checked around outside?"

Bert came over in response.

"Mr. Donati has gone outside with several of his staff to check the surrounding area. He left when Miss Benet was performing her surgery, but said he would be available if you needed him."

"Find him for me, would you, Bert?" Neville said. "Emily? Is anyone about in the kitchen?"

"Just about everyone is awake, sir," the maid replied. Unlike Bert, who was acting as if attacks by masked assassins fell into a footman's daily routine, she was clearly terrified.

Jenny reached out and patted her shoulder comfortingly. "Come with me, Emily. We'll go over to the kitchen and see if one of the staff can help us make tea. I'd like Uncle Neville to have some broth as well. It will strengthen him against the blood he's lost."

When they returned with their supplies, Papa Antonio had come in from making his inspection.

"I thought," he was saying, "that it was too much bad luck that both sets of window bars were weak enough for a man to break through. I went out with lanterns and some of my good Copts, and do you know what we find?"

"What?" Jenny asked, setting down her tray and offering her uncle a bowl of beef consomme.

Sir Neville looked vaguely disgruntled at this nursemaiding, but Jenny cocked an eyebrow at him after the manner of a very disagreeable teacher at her boarding school, and he subsided.

Papa Antonio grinned, accepted a cup of tea from Emily, and with a fine sense of theater said, "We find that it is no chance the window bars break so easy, for where they are set into the wall it has been cut away at, even softened with a bit of water beneath where the stucco is. You understand?"

Everyone did understand. Stephen tried to make light of it.

"People who live in mud houses shouldn't hire window washers, I see."

"I not hire these window washers," Papa Antonio replied, "as I think you know. No, what I think happened is this. Someone come along when the street is quiet—as it is on that side of the house, which is why I put my treasured guests there. The guests are away, perhaps at the bazaar. This person chips away the stucco to loosen the bars, then squeezes in some water, just to help."

Jenny shuddered. Suddenly the thickness of the mud brick walls seemed very insubstantial. She controlled her trembling lest she dribble soup onto Uncle Neville.

"I think," that gentleman said, holding up a forestalling hand, "you found more than that, Papa Antonio."

Papa Antonio nodded. "We did. I decide we should check all the other windows. Of all the windows in the house, only one more set of bars is loose—those on Stefano's room."

Stephen's tea cup rattled as he set it in the saucer with a jerk.

"My room! Then I *did* hear someone moving around."

"You did," Papa Antonio said. "I think that someone comes to your room just as to Leonardo and Jenny. He opens the door the littlest bit, but there is light within. He draws back, unwilling to have you give alarm. To permit this would be to stop his comrades who are doing such good work. Perhaps he plans to have them help him after their work is done, perhaps you are to be let live and he will slip away."

The young linguist's mouth was opening and shutting, but no sound came forth. Jenny took mercy on Stephen, inserting a question of her own to give him a chance to recover his equilibrium.

"How did the men get in here?" she asked. "Over the roof?"

"I think not," Papa Antonio said. "The door to the storage room used by my guest the textiles merchant is unlocked. He found it so when in the commotion he awoke. Once he heard there had been intruders, of course he thinks for his wares. There is evidence that several men hid within among the boxes and bales."

"Did he know his porters?" Jenny asked, already knowing how unlikely this would be.

"No. He hired a gang boss on the docks when his boat came in. The boss brought his own men. Probably these three simply picked up bales of fabric, carried them inside, then hid themselves. The lock is not difficult to open. It is meant more to keep someone from wandering in than to prevent the door from being opened."

"They were lucky," Stephen said, "but I see they didn't trust in luck alone to get away."

"No," Papa Antonio said. "Why cross the courtyard twice? That is where they would most likely be discovered. Why chance the locked front door? My porter keeps half an ear awake in case someone needs him. The window is so much easier."

"It seems to me that they may have intended to come in through one or more of the windows," Neville said thoughtfully. "The arrival of your guest with his purchases simplified matters, and they did not hesitate to adapt their plans. Three men could have removed the grille from any of our windows fairly quietly if it had already been loosened, then they would slip in and . . ."

His gaze fell to where Jenny's neat bandaging wrapped his chest.

"What did they want?" Stephen asked plaintively. "I mean, is this the same gang that went after Sir Neville years ago? Are those men connected to the bandits in the desert who foiled Alphonse Liebermann's first venture, or was that mere co-incidence? They were dressed like Anubis, and Anubis is the protector of the dead."

"I wish I knew," Neville said.

He was about to say more when Emily, who had been listening in mingled horror and fascination from one side of the room, gave a sudden sharp cry.

"Is everything all right, Emily?" Jenny asked, turning sharply, her hand dipping to where her six-shooter waited, heavy and reassuring in the pocket of her dressing gown.

"I'm fine, Miss Benet," Emily said, looking nervously at her. "I just remembered something the porter gave me when I went back to the kitchen. I'd forgotten until now."

She held out a flat, white rectangle addressed to "Sir Neville Hawthorne and Companions" at Papa Antonio's address.

Emily continued. "The porter said he found it dropped near the doorway. Maybe one of those men was carrying it."

Jenny accepted the envelope and held it to the light, feeling dully certain what she would see.

"I know the handwriting," she said, tilting the envelope so that Stephen and Uncle Neville could see. "It is our correspondent again."

The two men nodded. Everyone else looked mildly confused. The servants, however, would not pry. Papa Antonio seemed to sense that Jenny must have her reasons for being oblique.

"We'll leave that letter 'til morning," Sir Neville said, taking it and placing it in his bedside table, wincing as he pulled his wound. "Even if it spelled out the situation in chapter and verse, we would be no better off. It is late, and I think we should all endeavor to get some sleep."

"I couldn't sleep in my room," Jenny interrupted hurriedly. "I don't want to seem a coward, but I really couldn't, not with the bars broken out and everything."

Papa Antonio agreed. "For tonight we will change rooms. I have already spoken to several stout young men, older brothers of Castor and Pollux, and they are very eager to sleep in these rooms and forestall unwelcome visitors."

"And we'll take their rooms," Stephen said. "Play ring around the roomies."

He grinned, and Jenny liked him for this evidence of courage. Stephen had been truly frightened when he'd heard that he had been marked for assault along with the others, but he was bearing up well now.

They shifted their accommodations, Sir Neville taking the mysterious letter with him into the room he was sharing with Stephen. Jenny went to sleep with Emily and Bert, those two declaring they would feel much better if they knew that she wasn't alone.

They would even have given her their bed, but Jenny insisted that a pallet on the floor was sufficient, and proving her determination by lying down and closing her eyes. She lay still, pretending to be drowsing off, and listening to the married couple whispering as they settled down.

Somewhere, as the earliest-rising members of the household were stirring the fires to life in the kitchen, pretense became reality and Jenny slept.

The next morning, soon after Jenny had risen, dressed, and inspected Uncle Neville's wound, a young man arrived from Eddie Bryce.

"I don't know if we're going to visit the pyramids this morning after all," Sir Neville began apologetically, when the young man introduced himself as Ahmed, one of Eddie's nephews.

"Ibrahim, my uncle, said nothing to me about the pyramids," Ahmed replied in English heavily flavored with Arabic. He was clearly confused. "My uncle said to me, 'Go to the house of Antonio the Italian. You will find three English who are staying there. Give the oldest among them this letter. It will speak for me.' "

At this, Ahmed held out a folded sheet of paper roughly sealed with wax, but without an envelope. Asking the boy to wait, Neville opened the letter. It was quite short, and he finished quickly, then held it out to the others, his expression impassive.

Neville,

There was a bit of a dust-up here last night. I was assaulted outside my house by a man wearing a jackal-headed mask. Good thing he was wearing that ridiculous head-gear, otherwise he would have had me. As it was, I managed to win out. There are a few problems about the body, but when I have them sorted out, I will be by. I suggest you stay near to home where you will be safe.

Eddie.

"Your uncle Ibrahim is well?" Neville asked.

"Well enough, though he has some business this morning that must be attended."

Ahmed looked positively shifty, and Jenny felt certain that the body of the mysterious assailant was not being dealt with through the usual channels. Was Eddie unwilling to present the police with an assassin who wore a jackal-headed mask?

"Tell him we will wait here as he wishes," Sir Neville told Ahmed. "Tell him, we, too, had visitors last night, but none of them remained to speak with us."

Ahmed nodded, his coffee-brown eyes widening in appalled understanding.

"Uncle Neville," Jenny said, remembering her manners well enough not to embarrass the Arab boy by addressing him directly, "should we let our guest go home through the streets alone?"

Ahmed smiled brightly, appreciating her concern. "I am not alone, Miss. My older brother and two of my cousins are with me. I come inside because I speak English."

"And you do so very well," she replied.

The boy colored under his tan and salaamed himself away, promising to deliver their reply to his uncle.

Uncle Neville's amusement at Ahmed's juvenile embarrassment didn't last beyond the boy's departure.

"This doesn't look good," he said. "I had hoped Eddie wasn't included in last night's fracas. I wonder what he has to tell us? It sounds as if his man didn't escape. Certainly something could have been learned from the costume, if from nothing else."

Stephen fidgeted. "We can guess all we want," he said, "but it won't tell us anything Eddie can't after he arrives. I suggest we look at that letter."

Sir Neville nodded, and removed the paper in question from the inside pocket of his light jacket.

"I'm surprised you didn't remove it from my keeping while I slept," he said as he handed the sealed envelope to Stephen. "I noticed you eyeing it as soon as you awoke. Here. I'm a bit clumsy still. You open it."

Stephen flushed slightly, but took the envelope with such eagerness Jenny didn't doubt her uncle's description of Stephen's impatience was perfectly accurate.

"It's in cipher, again," Stephen said, spreading the letter out for them to see.

"Different," Jenny added. "It's just a long list of numbers, not a single letter."

Stephen produced clean paper and writing implements from seemingly nowhere.

"Let's give it a shot," he urged. "At least working on it will pass the time. I just wish I believed the Sphinx is going to tell us something we don't already know."

"You mean," Jenny replied with an attempt at lightness, "like the fact that apparently we're marked for death?"

10

Miriam's Tale

EDDIE ARRIVED while they were still recopying the long list of numbers that made up the Sphinx's most recent missive. He was not alone. Walking beside him, a veil drawn across the lower part of her face, was a woman whom he introduced as his wife, Miriam.

Neville thought Miriam much changed from the lovely, lithe girl who had courageously stood by Alphonse Liebermann's small expedition ten years before. Her eyes were still dark and lovely, but the bearing of several children had forever robbed her figure of its girlish grace. Yet the change was not without benefit. There was a poise about this older Miriam, a centered strength, that the fiery Bedouin girl had lacked.

A Madonna now, Neville thought, *rather than Joan of Arc.*

The courtyard was quiet now. Papa Antonio's staff was busy repairing the damage from the night before, and his other guests had gone about their business. None had blamed the attack on their host, though a few had looked slantwise at Neville and his associates, and had markedly avoided sitting too near to them at breakfast.

As if cobras might crawl out from beneath our kippers, Neville thought with grim humor, *or scorpions from the sausage.*

In this relative privacy, Miriam put her veil aside. Apparently, living within Cairo had not completely undermined her Bedouin independence—or maybe she simply felt herself among friends. Only the most restrictive Mohammedans kept their women permanently within harems.

Introductions completed, Eddie did not waste breath on idle chatter. "I've heard something about what happened here last night," he said. "My nephews spoke with the servants. I'd like to hear your version, but I think you need to hear what happened at our place."

No one disagreed. Eddie sighed, fumbled with his cigarette papers, and at last began.

"As you recall, I left here fairly late yesterday evening. I went directly home, keeping to main avenues—at least as many as I could, though you must understand that in the district where we live, 'alley' versus 'street' is a fine distinction. I stayed alert, for even without the matters we've been discussing, Cairo streets are not safe for a man alone."

"Woman neither," Miriam said, and from the throaty chuckle that underlay the words, Neville guessed that he was hearing the tag end of a joke.

The flashing smile Eddie gave her confirmed as much, but he did not pause to explain.

"Our house," he said, "is rather like this one in that it's built around a courtyard. However, not having European guests to appease, we don't bother with windows on the outer walls, not on the ground floor at least. The main entrance is a wide door that goes directly into the central courtyard—you pass through a sort of alley between two blocks of the house to do so, if you follow me."

Everyone nodded that they did.

"There's a gate set about a foot inside this alley," Eddie went on, "that we keep locked unless needed. There's another door that goes right into one of the living areas that is more commonly used for visitors anyhow, so keeping the gate locked isn't much of an inconvenience."

Neville had a fleeting memory of himself telling Jenny and Stephen about how he had been attacked on the eve of his abortive second attempt to find the Valley of Dust. Something in Eddie's deliberate, detailed narration bespoke a similar desire to avoid dwelling on the unpleasant climax of the story.

What could be so terrible? Eddie was here, apparently uninjured, his wife with him, as surely she would not have been had a member of their family been hurt. Neville fought back an urge to ask questions or attempt to hurry the other man along, but his sense of apprehension grew.

"Rather than wake anyone in the house, I decided to go in through this gate," Eddie continued. "I was working the key in the lock when I heard a footfall behind me. It was the slightest whisper of leather against dirt, and had I not already been straining to catch the sound of the key turning in the lock, I wonder if I would have heard it. I swung around, one hand going instinctively for the knife I wear at my belt, but I don't think I was really worried.

"Many of my wife's relatives come and stay with us, and with winter making travel pleasant once more, I thought the newcomer might be one of these. I did wonder a bit about the hour, but there were reasons that someone might arrive so late—including that travel after nightfall is cooler and more pleasant.

"However, such thoughts fled as soon as I had a clear look at the figure approaching me. His head was that of a gigantic jackal, his attire beneath the long cloak he now let fall to the dirt almost as fantastic—that of an ancient Egyptian god or king, complete to the ankh he held stiffly in his left hand.

"I was so shocked I couldn't cry for help, though my own house stood at my back. The jackal-headed figure came at me swiftly, that ankh raised as if he'd brain me with it, a long-bladed knife held expertly in his free hand. There was an awkwardness to his approach that permitted me to dodge clear, bringing my own knife into play. That's when I realized that the man wore a mask that covered his entire head, and though the eyeholes were cut large enough that I could see the entire of the human eye within, the mask must restrict his vision.

"I didn't waste my advantage, nor did I give away what I'd realized. I let him see my fear, though it was fear at being attacked, not at some apparently supernatural manifestation. We dodged around each other. He had reach on me, reach and size, but I had greater mobility. He walloped me a few times with that ankh . . ."

Eddie peeled back the sleeve of his robe to show some shockingly purple bruises.

"It was carved from wood, solid as a club. I counted myself lucky, though, because that knife of his worried me and I'd already learned the hard way that the upper part of his tunic was made from overlapping leather scales, while the mask was like a helmet for his head. Neither would have been anything to a gun, but they were plenty to my knife. This chap was bigger than me, too, and had more muscle. My only advantages came from that big mask he wore. It slowed him some, and seemed to be hot and heavy, too, for I could hear his breath rasping like he was panting.

"To make a long story short, I got my knife in, up and under his right arm. I must have hit one of the big veins because blood came out like a torrent. He was on his knees almost before I realized what I'd done. He bled out amazingly fast, but before he stopped kicking I realized I'd better cover my tracks. I finished unlocking my gate, then dragged the body into the courtyard. Then I started hauling buckets of water up out of the well, eager to rinse the worst of the blood off the street outside. When I got out there with my first batch a couple of feral dogs were already licking up the puddle. It fair made me sick, but I was grateful, too.

"I was hauling out a second lot of buckets when Miriam came out; the noise of the bucket crank had woken her." Eddie looked fondly at his wife. "She's not sleeping well, in her condition and all, and she'd been worrying about me being out so late. She saw the body, still in its mask, and smothered a scream in one hand."

Miriam smiled with a sort of shy humor. "You learn not to wake the children no matter what, isn't that true? I will not lie that I wanted very much to scream loud enough to knock the stars from the sky. That dead monster, my husband all wet with blood, it was all so terrible."

"You'd never have guessed it from how she acted," Eddie said proudly. "She realized that no one had better see that body. 'I am awake,' she said. 'Someone else may wake, too. Put it in our room. Only the infant is there.' I did what she said, having already realized that I was wasting my time trying to do what the feral dogs would do much better. I washed up using the water in those buckets I'd just drawn, and by the time I'd made sure my arm bones weren't cracked, Miriam was kneeling by the body, pulling off the mask, cool as can be. What she uncovered gave us both a horrible shock."

Miriam reached out and took Eddie's hand.

"The dead man was one of my cousins, a fierce man, one who lives more in the desert than the city. We saw him once or twice a year when he brought camels into the city. Sometimes Eddie would meet with my cousin's family for trade. We had never been very close—indeed, I thought my cousin held us in some contempt—but it was frightening to see him lying there dead."

"I was worried about more than that," Eddie added. "I'm not loved by any of the authorities. I'm not Arab, so the Arabs don't trust me. The English never do like when one of their own goes native. The French and Turks have each had their go-rounds with me, usually when my ability to translate for someone makes it easier for my client to avoid a whole lot of unnecessary bribes. I'm useful, though, too useful to ignore completely. If I got taken for murder or involved in a blood feud with the Bedouin, I wouldn't be useful anymore—and I couldn't expect much help."

Neville wanted to protest, wanted to say he'd have stood by Eddie, no matter what, but he knew that Eddie was only assessing the situation realistically. Even with Neville's help and the bribes Neville's money could pay, nothing would buy Eddie out of a blood feud, and such a feud within a family could get very ugly indeed. Even Miriam's immediate relations—her brothers and father—might side with the slain cousin rather than stand by an Englishman.

"We decided that we'd better get rid of the body, fast. That crazy costume wouldn't make our job any easier, so we stripped it off, and that's when things got really strange."

"Only then?" Stephen asked.

Miriam shook her head. "I agree with Eddie, but I also disagree. What we discovered was a strangeness that began to lead us to something like sense."

"You see," Eddie said, "when we removed the dead man's tunic we found two tattoos on his chest where they would pretty much always be covered by his robes. I made sketches. I'd like to see if you recognize them."

The sketches were rough, but somehow their very lack of artistry added to their impact. One depicted the head of a hawk shown in profile. Its eye was unusual—at least for the depiction of a natural bird—for it had been outlined in the fashion similar to the cosmetics worn by humans in numberless Egyptian tomb paintings. The second drawing showed a stylized female figure wearing an elaborate headdress, a series of hieroglyphs wrapped in a cartouche at her feet.

"Horus," Stephen said, looking at the drawing of the hawk's head. "With the Eye of Horus. The Eye was a popular protective charm in ancient Egypt."

"I couldn't show it here," Eddie interrupted, "but the eye was done in a different color than the rest of the tattoo. Most of the tattoo was blackish, but the eye was a really shouting green."

Stephen looked pleased. "That fits nicely. The Eye of Horus was frequently carved from blue or green stone. You see, it was supposed to represent the eye that Horus lost while fighting Set . . ."

Jenny raised her hand in protest. "Lecture later, Professor. Who is the woman? The headdress looks like Hathor, sort of, but doesn't Hathor have cow horns?"

Stephen bent over the sketch. "Hathor often does. This looks more like Isis to me, especially given the sun disk between the horns of her crown. Eddie, it looks like you tried to copy actual hieroglyphs here."

"That's right," Eddie said. "It wasn't a new tattoo, and lots of the fine lines had blurred, but wherever I could make something out clear, I copied it."

"What I can read settles it then," Stephen said, straightening. "Isis and Horus: the mistress of magic and her son, the warrior protector, avenger of his father, the god with whom the living king was often identified."

Neville spoke when Stephen paused for breath.

"The question is, what are they doing tattooed on the chest of a modern Bedouin—a man who was presumably a good Mohammedan?"

Miriam spoke, "That is my story, as he was a member of my family."

"You knew then?" Jenny asked in surprise.

"I have just learned," Miriam corrected. "It is not quite the same thing."

Jenny nodded. "I understand."

Miriam looked uncomfortably at Eddie. "I think I must tell you, though I hardly believe it myself, and I must ask that you do not let the story go beyond we few. Should the telling of this tale be tracked back to me, I think that not only myself and Eddie, but all our children and perhaps all who dwell within our walls, would be slain."

After the events of the previous night, no one was inclined to find this statement either melodramatic or unbelievable. Miriam accepted their promises, then took up her tale.

"When we were laying out the body of my cousin, my mother, who has recently come to live with us, entered the room. Now, before you can understand this story, you must understand my heritage. My father and mother are both Bedouin, but my father is more than half a man of the city, a trader in camels and such. My mother came from a wilder tribe, a fierce people who go from oasis to oasis, living on camels' milk and dates—and the spoils they take from softer folk.

"Yet even those fierce people have learned to like certain things that are more easily gotten in trade: guns and ammunition, coffee, strong spices, tobacco. Then, too, sometimes their raids would bring them too many sheep or some other thing not worth the carrying, but worth keeping long enough to trade. It was during one of these trading parties that my father saw my mother and desired her. She was not the healthiest of my grandfather's daughters, and my father had some very good firearms. A trade was made, and for years my father thought he had the best of the bargain, for once fed upon more than camels' milk and dates, my mother grew healthy and bore him many strong sons and daughters.

"Then, when the first of those sons grew to the threshold of manhood, my grandfather came from the desert. He told my father that as each child reached maturity, that child must be tested, and if the test was passed, the child would be initiated into an ancient trust—a trust that would take them from my father's family back into my grandfather's.

"My father protested, as what man would not, but in the years that had gone by since he had married my mother, he had learned real fear of the old desert warrior. In the end, he obeyed. Two of my brothers and one of my sisters went from us in this way. Other brothers and other sisters, however, returned to tell of being given strange things to eat and drink, of being put through great physical hardship, and finally of Grandfather praying over them in strange words before telling them to return to our father.

"I asked my mother if she had been tested in this way when she was a girl, and she admitted that she had, and that she thought that her failure of this test was one reason she had been permitted to marry my father. She did not miss the desert, not one bit. Even the veiled life of a city woman seemed finer to her. I, however, was a romantic child and sought to make myself worthy of my grandfather."

Miriam looked momentarily sad. "I was never given the chance. The old man was shot through the heart when leading a raid. We heard that there was much squabbling among his heirs. Still, when this was resolved someone might have come for me, but before that happened, I had met Eddie and chosen a different life. My mother's kin settled their differences and continued to occasionally trade with my father. Gradually I thought nothing more of it, except to be glad that no fierce man from the desert would come and demand my children of me, as my grandfather had done."

"Your cousin," Neville asked, wanting to make certain he understood how this story related to the previous night's murderous attacks, "he was of this fierce desert tribe?"

Miriam took a deep breath. "He was, and though I spoke the truth when I said he was my cousin, he was more. He was also my brother, the oldest of the sons who had been taken from my parents by my grandfather."

Eddie looked shocked and grasped her hand.

"Miri, I didn't . . . I'm terribly sorry. I didn't know."

Miriam touched the side of his face.

"How could you, when neither he nor I told you? The first time I saw him after he had been taken away, I greeted him warmly and called him 'brother.' He scorned me and my embrace, pushing me aside and telling me that someday I might be his sister, but for now I was simply a cousin, an annoying girl child who should better know her place."

"What a . . . pig!" Jenny cried.

Neville swallowed a smile, certain his niece had been about to use a far stronger term.

"He was really little more than a boy then," Miriam said, "newly taken from all he had known and put under a very hard master. I can understand now why he might have spoken so, but at the time I will not deny that I was deeply hurt."

"He must not have liked your marrying Eddie," Jenny said, still defensive.

"He did not. Indeed, he told me that he would prefer if I did not even name him 'cousin'—though, of course, the relationship was known by then in too many circles and could not be denied. I will admit that I rather enjoyed pressing him to admit our relationship, though there were times he quite frightened me.

"Now, when my mother came in and saw the body of her first-born son upon the floor, tattooed with heathen symbols, and outlandish clothing spread on the floor beside him, she did not weep. She looked at him levelly and said, 'He turned from Allah, and his pagan gods did not defend him.' I said to her, 'Mother, you grew to womanhood in the tents of my grandfather. I think you know more of this strangeness than you have ever admitted. Tell me what you know.'

"She resisted, looking quite afraid, but I was without pity since this danger had come to my husband and might have touched my children. I even threatened to send her back to her father's people, saying, 'And do you think that the sons and daughter you gave away will welcome you, especially when their brother has died on your doorstep?' That frightened my mother indeed, but it still took much effort to get her to talk."

Miriam paused and smiled. "I realize I have talked immodestly long, but bear with me and you will have the story you truly want."

Neville smiled in return. "And in my eagerness to hear, I have been a terrible host. Wait and I will bring refreshments, then you can go on."

Miriam did not refuse, and feeling like six types of monster for making a pregnant woman talk so long with only the splash of the fountain to cool her, Neville ordered the promised refreshments, made certain everyone was comfortable, and then asked Miriam to continue her tale. She did, picking up as if there had been no interruption.

"Perhaps because my grandfather was so confident that none of his children would fail in the test put to them, he was less than perfectly cautious about this mysterious other alliance, at least when only his family was about. The uninitiated were sent away when secret matters were discussed, but not guarded. One day, curious about what might await her, my mother spied on the ceremonies of initiation.

"She saw men and women dressed in costumes not unlike the jackal-headed one we have all seen, but the jackal was only one of the strange creatures represented. There was a hawk-headed man and a woman dressed like this Isis." Miriam indicated the sketch of the tattoo. "And others. The initiates were given hashish to smoke—my mother knew the smell—and what she suspected was wine. They were told to stand without crying out while their skins were marked with needles. While this was being done, for it was a long process, the man wearing the hawk's head—Mother thought it was her own father—told a strange tale.

" 'In the days long, long ago, when our people built the mountains of rock called pyramids and carved tombs into the cliffs, and raised great cities that were the envy of all the world, there was a king who was praised by even the gods for his goodness, honor, and sense of justice. When this king grew old and knew he would die, he did not wish that wealth be spent on an elaborate burial, as was then the custom. He told his people to bury him as the most common men were buried, and that he would be content.

" 'The gods of those days, for this was before the time of Allah, did not fault men for obeying the good king's request, but took it upon themselves to raise for him a pyramid grander than any ever seen. The people who had loved their king were glad at this sign of favor, but the priests grew envious. When they thought enough time had passed that the gods would have forgotten the good king, the most greedy among them came to rob and despoil.

" 'But the gods had not forgotten the good king, their brother, and raised a great wind to carry sand and hide forever both the tomb and the evil men who would desecrate it. The people in the nearest village were awakened by the windstorm and trembled in fear, weeping and praying that the wrath of the gods would spare them. At last every man, woman, and child fell into a deep sleep. The children dreamed of the good king as he had been in life, so that even those who had never seen him felt his seal on their hearts. The adults dreamed differently.

" 'Two gods came before them, a great hero with the head of a hawk, and a woman, human in all ways except for her beauty, which was divine. The hero and the lady said with one voice, "To you is given a great honor and a wondrous burden. The memory of the good king must not vanish with the unfolding of the ages, for there are too many corrupt kings and too few just ones. Tell stories of the good king to your children, and to your children's children. Bring them to the valley in which he is buried, a valley you shall know by this sign—it is protected by images of four gods. By this sign, they will know the tales you tell are true."

" ' "Yet," the hero and the lady continued, "even as this legend lives, so it will arouse greed in the hearts of the weak. Thus we give you a second charge—to guard the good king's rest throughout the ages. When, lured by hopes of treasure and glory, those come who mean to loot what we have buried, it is your task to stop them before they can defile the good king's rest. Know that we will watch you, and hold you to this trust. From this day forth, you are the Sons of the Hawk and the Daughters of Isis, together the protectors of this good king." ' "

Miriam paused. "So ended the story my mother told me. She is not an imaginative woman, and she cannot read nor write. She is little interested in antiquities as are most of our people—seeing them as things to sell if found, but otherwise not worthy of consideration. I cannot help but believe that my grandfather was descended from these villagers, and that somewhere still there are those who guard this ancient trust."

Neville felt both angry and afraid. "And would kill us to do it?"

"Yes, Sir Neville."

Miriam raised her chin defiantly, and in that gesture Neville saw again the valiant Bedouin girl who had saved his life ten years before.

Stephen shook himself as if coming out of a dream.

"The thing I find most fascinating about that tale—other than the obvious, I mean—is that it has a ring of truth to it. Most Arab legends say nothing about the pyramids or the old gods. At best they equate them with genies and efreet or other mythical creatures of the desert. This story, though, takes a historical view."

Neville had to agree, but being practical did not wish to discuss it at the moment. Instead he turned to Miriam.

"Do you think your father and brother who were my camel drivers all those years ago knew anything of this story?"

"Yes, and again, no," Miriam said. "I do not think my father and brother knew all this, but I think they knew that men of my grandfather's clan followed us, and that was why they abandoned their responsibility to you and left me. I was with them on that trading trip, contrary to usual practice. Now I suspect this was because someone may have sent for me to undergo my test. Indeed, there were times I thought the entire adventure was part of some such test. Now, though, I do not."

Silence fell as everyone mulled over what they had learned. Neville wondered if this last would finally be enough to make the others pull out. He wondered if he could go on alone. Then he saw how Stephen was studying the sketches of the tattoos, not with fear but with fascination. Eddie, too, looked defiant, and he realized that the other man felt deeply both the assault on himself and the old insult to his wife. Neither of them would give up, not unless he did first.

And should I defile the good king's rest? Neville thought. Then he shook himself violently. *To be turned away by this would mean I believe these tales of heathen gods, and wouldn't that be blasphemy? There is one God only. Isn't that the first commandment?*

He felt unsettled, and that made him even angrier.

Are you so afraid of a pack of Bedouin wearing fancy dress that you'll turn back? he thought. *No!*

Trying to keep his qualms to himself, Neville turned the blandest face he could to the others.

"So," he said. "Are we still on?"

Stephen grinned. "What an amazing discovery this would be! Legends surviving from the time of the ancient Egyptians. Why, if I can reliably document any of this, my contribution will be rated right up there with Champollion's revelation that Coptic is a survival of the original Egyptian language!"

Eddie was more grim.

"I'm with you. Miriam and I already went through it. I don't want to back down. What if these Sons of the Hawk decide they want my sons? I won't have it."

Jenny said hesitantly, "Uncle Neville, let me go with you. It's going to be dangerous, and none of you are doctors. You know how well I can stitch a wound. If these Sons of the Hawk try again, you'll need me."

Neville shook his head. "No. I'm not bringing a woman into danger."

Jenny sighed and changed the subject, "Well, after everything Miriam has told us, our story is going to be a bit dull; but don't you think we should tell Eddie about the Sphinx?"

They did so, producing the various missives as evidence, the final, still encoded one, last of all. Miriam lifted it and studied it curiously.

"You say it was dropped by one of the jackal-headed men last night?"

"Emily said the porter found it on the ground," Stephen said. "It must have been dropped by one of them."

"Odd," Miriam said. "The Bedouin are not highly literate. Still, my brothers learned to read and write Arabic before they left my father. One of them could have learned English in the intervening years. But why would they warn you so strangely?"

"And this grinning woman," Eddie said. "Could the writer mean Isis? Seems rather disrespectful, given she has nicer titles."

"Maybe the new letter will clear some of this up," Jenny said, "now that we know more about the situation."

"I need to take Miriam home," Eddie said, "and make certain there has been no further trouble. After my mother-in-law told us what she knew, we realized that we could get some help from the nephews who are living with us. They're kin on Miriam's father's side, and would dread a blood feud with the Bedouin. They'll keep their mouths shut."

"And the body?" Neville asked.

"Croc food," Eddie replied shortly.

After Eddie and Miriam had left, lunch was served. Most of the household retired for the afternoon rest, but Neville was amused to find his young associates unwilling to retire with the cipher unsolved.

"Let's look at it, then," he said. "My wound aches enough that I doubt I'll sleep."

Jenny rose without comment, got some ice from the kitchen, and very efficiently cleaned and packed the injury. She said nothing further about his refusal to take her along, but Neville felt her every motion as a rebuke.

Jenny was determined not to lose her temper, but it wasn't easy. She felt that her cool, controlled response to the previous night's attack deserved acknowledgment. She didn't like the way Uncle Neville persisted in treating her as though she were the kind of woman who fainted at the sight of blood.

Stephen seemed unaware of the silent conflict raging between uncle and niece—or if he knew of it, he was too smart to comment. He finished writing out the lines of numbers while Jenny tended Sir Neville's wound, then held out the re-copied letter for them both to inspect.

17-9-4-23-18-7-16-3-11-7-22-3-3-8-7-15-6-6-3-11-7-
3-20-16-3-8-22-26-19-15-18-15-2-18-21-3-26-18-16-19-11-
15-6-19-8-22-19-24-19-15-26-3-9-7-13-3-20-3-2-19-
11-22-3-22-15-7-16-19-19-2-7-22-3-8-11-23-8-22-
21-3-26-18-11-22-23-26-19-22-23-7-16-19-26-3-10-
19-18-7-22-19-15-6-8-23-7-26-19-15-18-17-15-6-19-
26-19-7-7-11-3-6-18-7-22-15-10-19-6-19-15-17-
22-19-18-26-23-7-8-19-2-23-2-21-19-15-6-7-26-3-
17-25-15-11-15-13-13-3-9-6-8-6-19-15-7-9-6-
19-7-15-2-18-26-23-2-21-19-6-2-3-8-15-26-3-
2-19-2-3-6-15-11-15-13-20-6-3-1-22-3-1-19-
15-20-8-19-6-6-15-22-15-7-26-3-11-19-6-19-
18-22-23-7-11-15-8-17-22-20-9-26-21-15-14-
19-7-4-22-23-2-12

"Whew!" Jenny said, staring at it. "No word breaks, no punctuation. No anything."

"I notice," Neville said, "that none of the numbers is higher than twenty-six. That seems to indicate that there is one number for each letter of the alphabet."

"The last six letters are 7-4-22-23-2-12," Stephen protested, working something out with pen and paper. "If that is our correspondent's signature, as has always been the case before, then 'SPHINX' should work out to something like 19-16-8-9-14-24."

"Still," Jenny said, "Uncle Neville has to be right. It can't be just coincidence."

They all stared at the sheet of paper for a long moment. Stephen's pen scratched as he tried the alphabet against the cipher.

"Q-I-D-W-R . . ." he muttered. "That can't be right."

"I've got it!" Jenny said excitedly. "You're working it out as if 'A' corresponds to 1, and 'B' to 2, and so on, but what Sphinx has done is start in the middle of the alphabet. 'M' is 1 and the rest seems to follow directly in order."

"How do you figure that, Jenny?" Neville asked.

She pointed to the line of numbers.

"See here how in Stephen's first attempt to work out Sphinx in numbers 'H' and 'I' become 8 and 9? Well, in this letter we have the fourth and fifth numbers in that last sequence of six falling in that order, too. If we make 22 stand for 'H' and 23 stand for 'I,' they fall in sequence just as they do in the alphabet."

She took the pen Stephen extended to her and wrote the entire alphabet in a line. Over 'H' she wrote 22, and over 'I' 23. Then she wrote rapidly until she reached the end of the alphabet.

"Then we just start with 1 over 'M' and continue until we have wrapped around to 'H' again," she said, doing so. "Gentlemen, your key."

A   B   C   D   E   F   G   H   I   J   K   L   M
15 16 17 18 19 20 21 22 23 24 25 26 1

N   O   P   Q   R   S   T   U   V   W   X   Y   Z
2   3   4   5   6   7   8   9 10 11 12 13 14

With the key in front of them, it was a matter of minutes to decipher the newest message. Breaking the letters into words wasn't as easy as it might seem, for what Stephen termed "phantom words" kept jumping out to distract the eye. The phrase "words have reached" became for a moment "word shaver each." Common sense and patience split the letters into words, then the words into likely sentences. Unhappily for their hopes of revelation, the completed message only added to their confusion.

Cupid's bow shoots arrows of both lead and gold. Beware the jealousy of one who has been shot with gold while his beloved's heart is lead. Careless words have reached listening ears. Lock away your treasures and linger not alone nor away from home after Ra has lowered his watchful gaze. Sphinx.

"What," Neville asked, "does this about Cupid have to do with murderous tattooed Arabs wearing jackal masks? Certainly they're not concerned with Eddie Bryce's courtship of Miriam after all this time!"

"I can't figure it out either," Stephen said. "There was something about arrows of lead and gold in Roman mythology as I recall, but up until now we've been being warned away from the 'good king' and's he's Egyptian. Is this even from our Sphinx?"

Jenny felt a flash of exasperation.

"Of course it is, Stephen. He—or she—uses his name, and the assumption we'd know it, as the key to the entire cipher. Without that, we could have solved it, probably by frequency patterns like in one of those Poe stories Stephen loves so much, but we'd have been longer about it."

"What I can't figure out," Stephen said, "is why the Sphinx would go to all the trouble of creating ciphers, then make it so easy for us to solve them. It took longer to recopy this one than to solve it."

Jenny wanted to shake him.

"Does that mean then that you've figured out what this message is about?" she asked a trace sharply.

The young linguist blinked at her, then colored from his high-buttoned collar to his blond hairline.

"Uh. No idea."

Jenny didn't believe him, but she also knew why Stephen Holmboe, linguist, wouldn't say anything. It looked as if speaking like a Christian would be her job, and given how she was feeling toward her uncle right now, she wasn't even unhappy about the possibility of embarrassing him.

"Well, I have a pretty good idea," she said. "Surely you gentlemen must have noticed that Captain Brentworth does not care to have anyone pay attention to Lady Cheshire but himself."

Uncle Neville replied with what Jenny knew must be feigned nonchalance. "I have, but the lady in question does not seem to care for him a whit."

"Exactly," Jenny said. "Captain Brentworth has been shot with the arrow of gold—the arrow that inspires love—while Lady Cheshire has been shot with lead and feels nothing but indifference."

And I'd swear she is indifferent to you as well, Uncle Neville, she thought. *But she has her reasons for making sure you think otherwise.*

Uncle Neville gave his niece a hard look, and Jenny wondered if she'd spoken aloud.

"Now," Jenny continued, "apparently our Sphinx thinks that Captain Brentworth feels threatened by one of our number—one of you two gentlemen."

"And how do you know it is not the reverse?" Uncle Neville said sneeringly. "How do you know that perhaps Lady Cheshire is not threatened by your youth and beauty?"

Jenny flushed. For a moment they ceased to be uncle and niece. She was simply a young woman who had been belittled by an older man.

"For one thing," she said, pointing with her index finger, "the message expressly says 'his beloved.' For another, the only member of our group who has been indulging in flirtation is you."

Neville Hawthorne colored, but Jenny knew the difference between embarrassment's blush and anger's flush. This was anger. She didn't care.

"Stephen's only beloved is his books," she said. "You, however, continue to melt at Lady Cheshire's least smile. I thought you might even take her up on her offer to accompany you on your expedition—this despite the fact that since before we left England we have been warned against a 'grinning woman' and bright smiles."

Jenny thought she might have gone too far. Uncle Neville was a gentleman of the old school, son of parents whose narrow-mindedness had forced their daughter to elope with her beloved. Neville had been kind to his niece thus far, but Jenny was uncomfortably aware that modern English law now considered women little better than chattel. If he chose, Uncle Neville could do whatever he liked with her.

"I see how you draw your deductions," Neville finally said. "However, I do not know if you have sufficient information on which to base them. How do you think those last few sentences fit into the matter?"

Jenny drew a deep breath, refusing to be cowed.

"I would set them as a separate paragraph," she said bravely. "These seem to be more in kind with the warnings about those who are legion—those who know what we have attempted to keep secret."

"Then this portion of the message," Stephen said, obviously eager to leave the question of his patron's romantic entanglements aside, "could indeed be tied into the attack we suffered. The reference to Ra—the Egyptian god of the sun—also seems a connection. Seems rather odd to leave a warning after attempting to murder us, don't you think?"

Sir Neville shrugged.

"Perhaps they did not believe they could slay all of us—after all, they failed to slay even one. This warning could be meant for the survivors and be yet another attempt to frighten us from our goal."

He rose, his hand moving toward his bandage, then resolutely dropping.

"I refuse to be frightened away—from anything I choose to pursue."

With those ominous words he stalked across the courtyard and shut the door into his room firmly behind him. In the quiet, Jenny heard the latch drop into place. She looked at Stephen who said very quietly,

"I think you're right, but what can we do?"

Jenny felt hopeless, but wouldn't let her despair show.

"Figure out who this Sphinx is, then shake her until she tells us straight what we need to know."

Stephen grinned. "Great idea. Any thoughts how to go about it?"

Jenny shook her head. "If I'm right about these messages at least partially referring to Lady Cheshire, then one of her party would seem likely."

Stephen nodded. "So, Mrs. Syms, Captain Brentworth, or one of the servants: Babette, Polly, or Rashid."

"I'll sound like the kind of snob I'm always complaining about," Jenny admitted, "but I don't see any of the servants being up to this. I'd bet on Mrs. Syms. She would have ample opportunity to observe and leisure to work something like this up."

"Does she know hieroglyphs?" Stephen asked dubiously. "I thought she denied any knowledge of them."

"Could be a blind," Jenny said.

"What if it's Eddie Bryce?" Stephen said. "He could have been playing dumb when we showed him the letters. He might have known about these Sons of the Hawk longer than he admits."

"But Lady Cheshire?"

"He's no idiot. Maybe he knows Sir Neville has a romantic turn of mind and decided to send a few general warnings. This last message is the first to get at all specific."

Jenny frowned. "Maybe. I think I'd place my bets on Captain Brentworth before Eddie Bryce. A few strange messages would be a far better way to chase Uncle Neville off than dueling. These days killing someone in a duel counts as murder."

"And Captain Brentworth," Stephen assented eagerly, "could have knowledge of hieroglyphs. He was Lord Cheshire's assistant, after all."

"Next time we see any of these," Jenny said, "let's drop a few hints and see who looks guilty."

Stephen nodded.

"I'm game, but we must be very careful. I can't forget that this Sphinx is someone who seems rather free about handing around warnings of death. I don't want him to decide it is time for him—or his Legion—to make another try."

The Great Pyramid

THAT EVENING after dinner, as they were sipping more of the delightful orange-tinged dessert wine and contemplating turning in early, a note arrived from Eddie Bryce. Sir Neville skimmed it, then read it aloud to Stephen and Jenny:

> *Dear Neville,*
> *I've made arrangements for you and your guests to tour the pyramids tomorrow morning. I know Jenny will not wish to sully her pretty frocks crawling about such dirty structures, but tell her not to worry. There are all sorts of amusements for the ladies including camel rides and a fortune teller called the Sphinx. I shall be there to pick you up around dawn. Dress for riding, and ask Papa Antonio to pack a light refreshment.*

As Neville had expected, Jenny had nearly swollen up with indignation at the implication that she would be too concerned with clothing to tour the buildings, and Neville resigned himself to having her ruin her frock. However, he read on before Jenny could spout forth her indignation, and as soon as she realized the implication of the subsequent sentences, her mood calmed as quickly as it had darkened.

"The Sphinx!" she said, a thrill in her voice. "Imagine. Eddie must have been very busy since he left us."

"Very," Neville agreed. He still felt uncomfortable when he recalled their earlier dispute, and was eager not to dwell too long on the subject of their mysterious and increasingly annoying correspondent. "Shall we turn in early, then? I'm tired, and Eddie says he will be by at dawn."

The others nodded agreement, and vanished almost as quickly as the genies in Burton's *Arabian Nights*. Neville also went into his room. The bars across the window had been repaired and reinforced. Moreover, teams of Papa Antonio's Coptic servants were keeping watch from the shelter of the roof. This was no hardship post, since in the dry season the roof was used as a porch might be in an English country home. The watchers were well-supplied with rugs for when the winter night grew chilly, and judging from the several pots of strong black coffee Neville had seen carried aloft, they were unlikely to fall asleep.

He was grateful for the precautions, especially for the relief they gave to Jenny and Stephen, both of whom had been more unsettled than they would admit. However, he did not think they were likely to be attacked again—at least not here.

After laying out Sir Neville's riding clothing, Bert retired. He and Emily had been invited to join the expedition tomorrow, but the maidservant was still so nervous that she hardly would leave the room the couple shared.

Sir Neville sat at the small desk in one corner, penned a quick reply to Eddie and set it aside to dry. Then he paused, studying the blank sheet that rested in front of him. Finally, he penned a few lines, blotted them rather more quickly than neatness demanded, and sealed both letters with his ring.

He stepped across to the porter's station, still manned at this hour, for residents might be out at any of the many entertainments around the city.

"Can these still be delivered this evening?"

The porter, a handsome man with a nose like the one Rameses the Great had caused to be carved on his numerous portrait statues, glanced at the directions, and smiled as that same Rameses was never shown smiling.

"I can arrange for that, Sir Neville."

As he turned back to his rooms, Neville saw that not one, but two strong-bodied, square-shouldered young men had emerged in answer to the porter's summons. Papa Antonio was clearly not taking any chances with his staff's safety, either.

Before blowing out the light, Neville took the time to clean the handgun that was his own personal favorite. He decided he wouldn't look too closely come morning at Jenny's attire, but felt fairly certain that somewhere among the voluminous folds of her skirts she would be carrying something rather more lethal than her handy little derringer.

Jenny's delight the next morning when Eddie Bryce arrived atop a camel, leading a string of three more of the magnificently ridiculous beasts, was slightly modified when, upon rushing out to see them more closely, she discovered that the animals possessed a powerful and unusual odor. That Eddie's mount, an impressive animal with a tightly curled coat the color of a cougar's hide, wrinkled back its lips and spat at the sight of her did nothing to renew her enthusiasm.

Uncle Neville strolled out behind her, natty in his riding kit. He stood in the doorway, tapping the top of his riding boots with a crop, and looking amused.

"Couldn't get horses, Eddie?"

Eddie said something to his camel that caused it to lower itself to the ground. This was a complicated maneuver that involved the camel first falling onto its front set of knees, then lowering its rear parts, then—with an audible sigh of protest—working its forequarters so that its bent forelegs extended neatly in front.

Stepping from the elaborate saddle, Eddie said in low tones that hardly carried even to where Jenny stood, "I thought you might need a refresher. Stephen will definitely need to learn to ride a camel, and I thought that Jenny wouldn't much like being singled out to miss the experience. Besides, horses don't much like the smell of camels, not unless they're trained to it. I'm going to have enough to do without minding a mixed string."

Jenny wondered if Papa Antonio had spoken to Eddie about their intention of having her accompany the expedition. Certainly, the two men seemed friends, but what if Eddie was one of those men who thought women were safer at home? What if he tried to stop Jenny from coming? Remembering how Miriam had helped save Alphonse Liebermann's expedition, and Eddie's evident respect for his wife, Jenny thought Eddie was unlikely to be so conventional. If so, this was her first chance to prove her eagerness to be part of the expedition.

She hastened to assure Uncle Neville that she was quite eager to ride a camel—though to be honest, after seeing one up close, she was less certain.

For one thing, she hadn't been prepared for how big the camel would be. For another, the camels seemed completely disgusted by humans. She'd met skittish horses, wild horses, and even mean horses—including one bronc who had tried to stomp a fallen rider to jelly. The camels were completely different. Except for random muttering apparently addressed to each other, they simply chewed thoughtfully and looked superior.

She mentioned this apparent disgust to Eddie, who grinned.

"Well, they do say that the camel is the only living creature who knows the final, secret name of Allah. Must seem rather hard on them to be stuck hauling us around."

Stephen had emerged by now, a satchel of books and notepads slung over one shoulder, an expression of dismay on his face.

"Are they tame?" he asked as the third camel in line spat a thick gob of green goo in front of his booted toes.

"As tame as camels ever get," Eddie assured him. "These are pure sweethearts. The one I rode is called—if we translate from the Arabic—Angel. The other three are Tiny, Honey, and Flat Foot."

"All the camels I've seen seem to have rather flat feet," Stephen said, bending to check and earning a shriek from Flat Foot.

"They do," Eddie agreed, moving down the line and making the remaining camels kneel. "Cloven, with two huge toes. Permits them to walk over the sand without sinking down the way we would. Now, are you ready?"

Three nods, two hesitant, answered him.

"Very well. Neville, you take Angel. I'll let you lead, since you know where we're going. That leaves me to watch from the rear, in case either of our novices has trouble. The camels will follow each other sure enough."

Uncle Neville nodded. "Let me show them how this is done."

He strode over to Angel, slung himself into the saddle, fastened the lunch basket behind, and then gave the camel a slap on the shoulder. Angel emitted a mournful moan, and unfolded herself in the reverse of how she had reclined, Neville swaying easily with the motion.

"You guide them with the nose rope," he said, "but just as with a well-trained horse, they learn to respond to other signals."

"You next, Jenny," Eddie ordered.

Jenny crossed to Tiny, who didn't seem one bit smaller than his companions. Her skirts would have made getting into the saddle difficult, but Eddie had arranged for a sidesaddle arrangement not dissimilar to the one used for horses. Jenny neatly arrayed herself and Eddie raised his hand.

"Hold tight," he warned.

Jenny did, and at Eddie's signal Tiny rose. The motion had seemed awkward but smooth when Uncle Neville demonstrated how to move with it, but now she felt herself jerked up and back, then up again. Tiny craned his neck to look at her, veiling his long-lashed eyes in disgust at her ineptitude.

"Now Stephen," Eddie said without a pause.

Stephen held on for dear life, but something of his apprehension must have transmitted itself to Honey, for the camel would not obey the command to rise. Finally, Eddie resorted to a sharp jerk on the nose peg and up she came, screaming protest.

"She'll be all right now," Eddie reassured Stephen as he handed him up the reins. "Keep these in hand, but don't tug. A camel's nose is more sensitive than even a good horse's mouth, and you could tear the flesh."

Flat Foot gave Eddie no trouble. He accepted a second provision basket that young Castor brought out from the kitchen, thanked him, then called: "All right, Neville, get us on our way."

Jenny's first experience of a camel in motion was as remarkable as its rising. The animal swayed slightly, in a motion nothing like the walk, trot, or even the smooth canter of a horse. Once she had adjusted to the strange feel, she noted that unlike a horse, Tiny was moving the legs on either side of his body in unison. This pacing gait was surprisingly smooth, but her body, accustomed to other balance, fought it.

They were out of Cairo city limits before she adjusted enough to look around, and when she did she noticed that Stephen looked positively ill.

"I'm sure," the young man said when queried, "I would do as well walking on my own two feet."

Although other tourists were heading for the pyramids, none were close. Eddie therefore spoke freely.

"You might, for a short time, but you'd wear out fast, twist an ankle, or over-heat. If you want to be part of Neville's mad venture, then you'd better get accustomed to riding a camel."

"What about a horse?" Stephen protested. "Everyone has heard about the magnificent Arab steeds: subsist on a handful of dates and a half-cup of water and all that."

"Ah, but a camel doesn't need even that half-cup of water," Eddie said. "A properly trained camel—by which I mean one accustomed to desert work—can go without water for a couple of weeks. Some trainers swear that they do better if you don't feed them either, but force them to live off their own resources. I wouldn't go that far, but a camel would spit at that handful of dates. It would rather have thorn bush or sagebrush—both of which should be plentiful this time of year."

Stephen looked unconvinced, but Jenny was impressed.

"Do they really eat thorns?" she asked.

"I've seen them eat thorns long enough to use for sewing needles or as tent pegs," Eddie responded with perhaps slight exaggeration, "and like it."

Neville, as easy in his saddle as if it hadn't been years since he was last astride, looked back. "Since we don't know where we're going or how much water and forage will be there, we can't risk horses, Stephen. We need beasts that will take punishment. Understand?"

"Yes, sir," Stephen replied, rather like a schoolboy chastised by his master, and made no further complaint.

The journey from Cairo to the pyramids at Gizeh took about an hour and a half, and carried them mostly through farmland. The road was fairly busy in both directions, with early tourists heading out, and farmers and merchants heading into the city. It provided a good test for their camel riding, and if Eddie hadn't been alert, more than once Jenny or Stephen might have failed to handle their mounts. Being thrown was only one among their concerns. More likely—and more embarrassing, especially to Jenny's pride—the camel would simply refuse to move ahead, but would stop and browse on some interesting bit of foliage.

When Jenny felt confident enough with Tiny's gait to look ahead toward their destination, she had to fight a feeling of disappointment. She had already glimpsed the pyramids several times—from the train and from various points around Cairo. They had seemed small, worn, and rather insignificant. However, she had reassured herself that this was only in contrast to the multi-faceted architecture of the modern city.

Now that they were away from that distraction, the pyramids looked, if anything, worse, mere broken heaps of sandy colored stone. They hardly seemed worth the effort to reach.

Still, the Sphinx will be there, and maybe a few answers, she consoled herself. *And I am learning how to ride a camel. How I will ache tomorrow!*

Her initial disappointment was completely forgotten as they mounted the last, long, sandy slope to the plateau on which the mortuary complex had been built. Suddenly, the pyramids were revealed in their great size, mountains built by human hands, the last surviving of the Seven Wonders of the ancient world, showing without a doubt that they not only deserved their title, but held it still, even in the face of trains, steam liners, and other technological marvels.

The golden brown of the stone mellowed to gold in the light of the sun. Rough surfaces were solid, rebuking efforts to undermine their power. The rest of the complex had fared rather less well than the pyramids. The three lesser pyramids did show ruin; one of them was more a giant cairn than a structure. The temples, minor tombs, and other outbuildings were tumbled down, only hinting at their former orderly magnificence.

But the three large pyramids were everything one could hope for, and Jenny forgot her sore and stiffening muscles, forgot Tiny's irritability. When Eddie made Tiny kneel, she slipped down from the saddle, her head thrown back so she could stare to her heart's content.

Even in her dreamlike enjoyment, Jenny was very glad for the tart lemonade contained in the bag on Eddie's camel. Uncle Neville, however, waved away the lukewarm cup and crossed to one of the water-sellers and came back with his flask filled with water so cold that it seemed that it must have been iced. Jenny expressed her astonishment, and Uncle Neville smiled, well-pleased.

"They keep it in special pottery jugs which are slightly porous. The water dews on the outside, and the resultant evaporation cools the water within."

"Marvelous!" Stephen said, and Jenny, despite mild concerns about where the water might have been drawn, had to agree. She supposed that similar things were done in the American southwest, but she'd never bothered to notice or inquire. That was just life. This was adventure.

Climbing to the top of the Great Pyramid was an adventure—especially since to do so in long skirts required that Jenny be helped by three strongly built Arabs, all of whom were completely respectful, but who she thought were having far too much fun alternately pulling and pushing her up the uneven and awkward "stairway" created by the sandstone blocks.

Once the view from the top had been fully enjoyed, she turned to Stephen. The linguist was breathing a bit hard, having insisted on making the climb unassisted. Jenny herself was rather glad for the jumble of blocks that were all that remained of the next tier of the pyramid. She seated herself in a shady patch, and Stephen eagerly followed suit.

"Tell me, Stephen, what is less respectable—a young woman in trousers that cover her limbs as effectively as any skirt, or the same young woman being manhandled by three strange men?"

Stephen wiped his streaming forehead with the back of his hand before remembering to fish his handkerchief from a trouser pocket.

"I refuse to enter into a debate on that matter. I will say that both would provide a certain degree of visual interest—indeed, in the case of the latter I should say 'does.'"

Jenny leaned forward, folded her fan with great deliberation, and used it to hit him sharply across the arm. The Arabs, who waited for them a few paces away, howled with laughter. Stephen colored, and was about to say something when his gaze caught something of interest below.

"I say, Jenny, look down there, over by our camels."

Jenny did so, shading her eyes with her hand, for as the sun had risen higher, the glare off the surrounding sand and rock made her wish for smoked glasses.

We must get some, if Eddie hasn't already done so, she thought idly. Then such idle musings were replaced by pure astonishment.

"That's Lady Cheshire!" she exclaimed. "And Captain Brentworth and Mrs. Syms, I'm sure of it. Can it be a coincidence that they chose this day of all days to visit the pyramids? Were they newcomers to Cairo I might think it more likely, but these must be as familiar to them as the British Museum."

"It might be coincidence," Stephen said, but his tone did not express belief. "I did wonder that your uncle didn't escort you to the top of the pyramid."

"Are you saying that he might have been waiting for them?"

"I don't think that is impossible."

Jenny didn't either. She began the descent so precipitately that her Arab escorts had to pinch out their half-smoked cigarettes to assist her.

At the bottom, Jenny left them to apply to Eddie Bryce for their tip, and crossed—Stephen only a few steps behind her—to the little group. She didn't know what she was going to do or say, only that she didn't wish to leave Uncle Neville alone with Lady Cheshire a moment longer.

Alone was probably a poor choice of terms, for in addition to Lady Cheshire's constant escort, there were Arabs selling lemonade, cool water, and "genuine anteekahs" milling around the fringes. Still, Jenny couldn't help but feel she was somehow right. Any man—at least any man as susceptible as Uncle Neville—who spent too much time beneath the gaze of those pale green eyes might as well be alone.

Lady Cheshire greeted them as casually as if they were on the front porch at Shepheard's Hotel, offering no explanation for her presence. Nor, Jenny realized, could she demand one without seeming rather more aggressive than she wished. Instead, she accepted the glass of lemonade offered to her, made some enthusiastic comments about the view from the top of the pyramid, and waited to hear what would next be said.

"I suppose you plan to go inside the pyramid?" Lady Cheshire asked in notes of playful mockery.

Jenny nodded. "I would like to very much. However, I would rather walk around and see the rest of the complex while the day is relatively cool."

Everyone assented to this suggestion, and they trooped off, Eddie acting as their guide. Jenny noted that he had adopted a slightly sing-song accent to his speech, and somewhat simplified his vocabulary. She doubted that the Cheshire party even realized he was English rather than Egyptian, a suspicion that was confirmed when Lady Cheshire asked him a question, addressing him as "Ibrahim."

"A bit of a joke," Uncle Neville said softly, almost in her ear. "When we saw them coming, Eddie bet me he could completely take them in. I think I'm going to lose."

"Did you . . ."

Jenny resisted the sudden impulse to ask if Uncle Neville had had anything to do with the others' arrival, changing her question in mid-phrase.

"Did you learn anything about that fortune teller?"

"We did indeed, scouted while you and Stephen were making the climb. She pitches her tent over by the Great Sphinx himself."

"Isn't the sphinx a her?" Jenny asked, recalling their earlier discussion.

"Some are," Uncle Neville agreed, "but not this one. I believe it's thought to be a portrait of one of the pyramid builders—Chephren, I think."

The Great Sphinx was on a different, slightly lower section of the plateau than the pyramids, more detached and therefore even grander than usually depicted in drawings. Jenny liked the statue immensely, though she wished the nose hadn't been broken. It made the stern nobility of the features slightly pathetic.

"Is it true that the damage was done by Napoleon's soldiers?" she asked.

"I don't think so," Uncle Neville replied. "I heard that it was done much earlier, but for all he did for Egyptology, Napoleon was not loved—I don't suppose conquerors ever are—and the story spread."

True to form, Mrs. Syms was the first to call attention to the fortune teller. She came bustling over to where they were trying to make out some of the writing on the sphinx, full of excited importance.

"I went over to see what that was," she said, indicating a pavilion pitched on the shady side of the towering monument, "and it's just too thrilling. There is a fortune teller there, a woman. She calls herself the Sphinx and claims, so the boy told me, to directly channel the wisdom of the ancients through the statue itself."

Jenny tried to deduce if there were anything suspicious in this presentation, but Mrs. Syms was very much in her element, thrilled by this evidence of occult science. Jenny glanced at Captain Brentworth and Eddie Bryce, but the one looked bored and the other impassive.

"Of course we must have our fortunes told," Mrs. Syms went on. "Imagine what my friends in the Silver Twilight will say when I come home and tell them."

"Imagine," agreed Lady Cheshire, a trace dryly. "Well, if you insist, Sarah, I certainly do not mind. There is shade near the tent, and we can make a comfortable seat on the sand."

Jenny dove in before the lady's apparent indifference would make participation seem foolish.

"Well, I'm going to try it," she said. "I've had my palm read, and my fortune told in cards, smoke, and tea leaves, but I've never met anyone who claimed to channel the ancient Egyptians."

"Through a statue, what?" agreed Stephen. "All too marvelous. I want a go at it, too."

Uncle Neville's air of detached amusement was perfect. One would never have guessed that they were all hoping for the solution to a mystery that had been dogging them since before they had departed England.

"Then let us all go that way," he said. "Who knows? Perhaps I shall ask the lady what joys may lie in my future?"

"Not sorrows?" Lady Cheshire teased.

"Never," he replied gallantly. "I refuse to admit to the possibility of sorrow."

"I," Jenny said, rolling her eyes, "am going. Follow as you wish, Uncle. Coming along, Mr. Holmboe, Mrs. Syms?"

The three walked ahead, followed more slowly by Lady Cheshire flanked by Captain Brentworth and Sir Neville. Eddie had melted back into anonymous servility a few paces to the rear, but Jenny felt certain that should anything happen, he would be ready.

The Sphinx's pavilion was everything even Mrs. Syms could desire. Flame-colored silk curtains painted with curious signs and sigils adorned the sides and rose cupolalike from a center post. Inside, elaborate oriental carpets were piled, gleaming jewel-like in the sunlight.

The seeress herself was seated before a low table in the center of this splendor. She did not deign treat with them herself—indeed, she didn't even turn her head when they approached. Instead a young man, almost a boy, ran out.

He wore his hair in the curious style called the "sidelock of youth" common in ancient tomb paintings, and, so Jenny had been told, still worn by some of the fellahin. His only garment was a loin cloth or kilt, remarkable mostly for the heavy triangle of stiffened fabric that hung in front, swinging as he moved. His wide brown eyes had been outlined with kohl, and he stood very stiff and straight as he inspected them.

"Someone has taken a look at a few tomb paintings," Stephen murmured softly. "That's an Old Kingdom style, I believe."

Mrs. Syms hurried to meet the boy.

"We wish to consult the Sphinx," she said formally. "Myself and my two young friends here."

The boy looked them over, his gaze almost insolent.

"You three," he said. "All together or private?"

He had a way of saying "private" that made quite clear that the greater revelations were reserved for such audiences.

"Oh, private, most definitely," Mrs. Syms said.

There followed a brief negotiation over the price. Having seen what a small amount of money would purchase in the bazaar, Jenny thought the price Mrs. Syms agreed to rather steep, but she was too excited to argue.

Mrs. Syms went in first, and with great ceremony the four side curtains were rolled down. Stephen and Jenny fidgeted in listening silence, but heard nothing but the rise and fall of two voices.

After a while, Mrs. Syms came out. Her face was flushed with more than the heat, and she carried with her the heavy scent of some exotic incense.

"It was wonderful, wonderful!" she said. "The Sphinx told me ever so many interesting things, and she knew things, too, about my late husband, and about things that have been worrying me. I must go tell Audrey and convince her to give it a try."

She bustled past, and Jenny looked at Stephen.

"You or me next?"

"You," Stephen said. "That way if there's anything you want me to check, you'll be able to tell me."

Jenny nodded. The Sphinx's boy was waving a languidly arrogant hand.

"She will see you now," he said.

Jenny dropped the agreed upon sum into his hand, and stepped through the curtain he held open for her. The only light within was sunlight filtered through the silk from which the pavilion was crafted. The rosy glow immediately made Jenny feel detached from the world without, a sensation enhanced by the intense fumes from the incense burners placed around the tent.

"Come here, daughter," came a creaking, ancient voice. "Seat yourself before me and tell me what you wish to know."

Jenny did as she had been commanded. There was a chair she didn't recall hav-

ing seen before, one more suited for European styles of dress than the heap of pillows on which the seer crouched. She settled herself carefully, for the first time getting a close look at this woman who called herself the Sphinx.

The Egyptian motif had been continued in the seer's attire as well. Old and
wrinkled as she was, the Sphinx did not sport the naked upper body that even the
better class of Egyptian woman seemed to flaunt, but her striped and pleated linen
robe was topped with a broad enameled collar. She wore wide disk-shaped earrings, and her head was covered with the strange vulture crown that Jenny couldn't
help but think looked rather as if a dead bird had been carefully balanced upon her
head. Her eyes had been rimmed with kohl, and her wrists and upper arms were
heavily burdened by wide cuff bracelets. She held a large looped cross—the Egyptian symbol for life—in one hand.

"What do you wish to know?" the Sphinx repeated.

"I don't know," Jenny said. "Can you really tell the future?"

"I tell what the Great Sphinx tells me," came the reply. The old woman moved
very little, only her lips and her bright eyes within their dark cosmetics seemed
alive. "Shall I tell you about yourself?"

Jenny nodded.

"You come from far away, a long journey first across the cold sea, then across
the warm. I see a girl weeping for lost parents, lost when she herself was far from
them."

Jenny stiffened. She realized that the Sphinx might have informants at the hotels and train stations. The Sphinx could even have learned this much from Mrs.
Syms, for the woman was both talkative and credulous.

The Sphinx didn't appear to move, but a light silk scarf that had rested over
the top of the table drifted to the carpet, revealing an odd assortment of items:
coins, scarabs, the bowl of a clay pipe, shards of pottery, a carved foot from a figurine, polished stones, even the lead seal from a bottle of champagne.

"Close your eyes," the Sphinx commanded. "Let your hand drift over the table
until it is drawn down. From what you touch, from these I shall tell your future."

Feeling both a little frightened and rather foolish, Jenny did as she had been
told. She didn't feel any particular guidance, but moved her hands and let them
drop three times at random. Opening her eyes, she discovered she had touched the
foot, the scarab, and the lead seal.

"You have traveled far," the creaking voice said, "but your journeys are not
ended. There is a long road ahead of you, one filled with heartache, before you find
what will satisfy your soul. You will see wonders in this land and elsewhere. You
will find both less and more than you desire."

This was apparently the message from the figurine's foot, for the Sphinx now moved to the scarab.

"I see two lives before you. One is broken by many dangers, hard and yet ultimately fulfilling. The other is full of peace and contentment, bliss without end, joy without ceasing."

She touched the lead seal. Her voice cracked and rose, becoming shrill and hollow, echoing strangely in Jenny's ears.

"Choices made in the Land of Egypt will decide your fate. Walk carefully in the Red Land. Watch carefully in the Black. Beware the Hand! Beware the Eye!"

The old woman's entire body slumped forward, her vulture-crowned head clattered among the bric-a-brac on the table, scattering the scarab and a coin to the floor. Jenny leapt to her feet and was raising the old woman when the boy came in and waved her imperiously back.

"The Sphinx is well," he said. "The power often leaves her thus. Go. I will summon your companion anon."

Jenny went out, distinctly unsettled. She hadn't thought the Sphinx seemed well at all. In fact, for a long moment she hadn't been certain the old woman was even breathing. Seeing her emerge, Stephen came over, a cup of cool water in one hand.

"You look white as a ghost," he commented. "Was she that good or was it just hot in there?"

"Maybe a bit of both," Jenny said, accepting the water gratefully. "The air in the tent was rather close. Lots of incense, too. I can't say I learned much useful. She puts on a good show, but whether or not she's our correspondent . . ."

Jenny paused. She had learned enough about diagnosis from her father to know that you shouldn't tell your patient what you hope to find lest your own comments skew the results. She stopped short of mentioning anything about how the Sphinx's voice and manner had changed and the odd final warnings before the woman had collapsed.

"Pretty standard stuff," Stephen said, unimpressed by this expurgated report, "except for that bit about your parents. Is there anything you want me to look for?" Stephen asked.

"You might take a look at her table and the other ornaments in there," Jenny said. "There were hieroglyphs painted on them, but I'm not good enough to tell if they were in the same hand as our correspondent's."

"The ones on the tent curtains aren't," Stephen said with a chuckle. "They're just monkey-copies. A few bits make sense, but most just look good. They don't say anything."

Jenny sighed.

"I wonder if this matter of names is just coincidence," she said. "Still, we're here. We may as well be as thorough as possible."

"Right," Stephen agreed. "Besides, I want to hear what she says lies ahead for me."

He grinned easily, and after a time the boy beckoned him forward.

"Wish me luck," he said.

"Luck," Jenny replied.

She wanted to stand watching, but Mrs. Syms was crossing over, her eyes bright and eager.

"Tell me all about it," she said.

Jenny, still suspecting that the woman might be the genuine author of those strange letters, complied, editing her account much as she had for Stephen. Mrs. Syms made a very good audience, but like most enthusiasts, what she really wanted was a listener for her own adventures.

With minimal encouragement, Mrs. Syms began a detailed account of her own audience with the Sphinx. Jenny listened with only half her attention, noting that there were similarities between the two meetings, including the selection from the odds and ends on the table. When Mrs. Syms concluded, Jenny frowned.

"She didn't faint or anything like that?"

"Why, no," Mrs. Syms sounded vaguely affronted. "Did she when she spoke with you?"

"Well," Jenny paused, "it sure seemed like that, but I think," she added, unwilling to hurt the older woman's feelings, "I think you had a much more detailed fortune."

Certainly, a much more intelligible one.

More than the Sphinx's failure to provide a spectacular conclusion to Mrs. Syms's session was troubling Jenny. After all, the Sphinx might be savvy enough to realize she didn't need to go to such extremes to impress Mrs. Syms. What troubled Jenny was that nowhere in Mrs. Syms's account had she said anything about any of her companions. It seemed unlikely that she had glossed over any part of her account—she had even described the furnishings.

So how did the Sphinx learn about my folks? Jenny thought. *Could she really have some sort of second sight?*

Eventually, Stephen emerged, looking flushed from being closed up in the tent, but more amused than anything else.

"How was your session?" Mrs. Syms asked eagerly.

"Right enough," Stephen replied politely. "I have been assured that Mother and my sisters are both well. Indeed, Ida has apparently had a proposal of marriage."

He chuckled.

Jenny had heard enough about Stephen's acerbic spinster sister to understand his amusement. Ida's betrothal seemed as unlikely as snow falling on the pyramids.

Mrs. Syms asked a few more questions, then trotted across to where Lady Cheshire was keeping court in the shade of some fallen masonry.

"I really *must* convince Audrey to try," she said in parting.

Stephen let Mrs. Syms get out of earshot, then began to follow more slowly, Jenny walking beside him.

"The hieroglyphs on the table were not in our correspondent's hand," he said. "That isn't conclusive, since there is no reason to believe the lady seer did her own decorating. However, it rules one clue out."

"Anything else, M. Dupin?" Jenny asked with affected lightness.

Stephen ran a hand through his side-whiskers.

"There was something odd," he admitted. "Did she say anything to you about a Hand or an Eye?"

Jenny nodded, aware that her heart was suddenly beating far too quickly.

"She did. Does it mean anything to you?"

Stephen shook his head.

"No. I wish it did. I even asked her if this had anything to do with the grinning lady."

Jenny caught her breath.

"And?"

"And she looked at me with extraordinary blankness, then her eyes rolled up in her head and she toppled forward onto the table."

Stephen walked a few more steps, then stopped.

"The odd thing is," he concluded, "is that I could have sworn she was dead to the world, but sound came from her lips nonetheless. She gave the most horrid gurgling laugh and then said quite distinctly, 'No. Far better for you if they did.'"

Mozelle

THE SERVANT boy rolled down the crimson silk curtains after Stephen's departure from the Sphinx's pavilion, nor did they rise again. When Eddie, impeccably Arab, went to inquire, he was informed that the lady had been overwhelmed by the strength of the communications that had passed through her. There would be no further seances today.

Privately, Neville was relieved. Despite the glowering presence of Captain Brentworth, he had been much enjoying his quiet conversation with Lady Cheshire and had no desire to interrupt it in order to lurk within some incense scented bower with a woman not half as comely. If anything was to be learned from the fortuneteller about their mysterious correspondent, the two young people would ferret it out. In any case, he thought he had already worked out the solution.

Who better than Stephen Holmboe himself as the source of the mysterious messages? His earlier denial meant nothing. Of course he would deny being the Sphinx. Why ruin his game before it had hardly begun?

Stephen was fluent in Egyptian hieroglyphs, and admittedly loved tales involving ciphers and puzzles. He also was well-known for his rather low sense of humor. If Stephen Holmboe was the Sphinx it would also explain why the warnings were so vague regarding the "good king," but so singularly and annoyingly pointed when making reference to Neville's interest in Lady Cheshire.

Those comments might be only mischief on the younger man's part, but Neville was willing to bet that there was a degree of jealousy involved as well. That was why, once he had decided who the Sphinx must be, he had written to Lady Cheshire. The note had merely been an apology for his not calling yet, explaining how busy they were, and how busy they were likely to be. If he had made mention of their plans to go see the pyramids at Gizeh the following day and the likely time they would be there, he wasn't precisely inviting the lady . . .

But he had been delighted when she had arrived. He had kept general his conversation regarding their plans for the immediate future, and had been all too aware that she was probing. But then what woman worth her salt wasn't curious? They were always dropping little hints, and creating mysteries. It was part of their charm. Jenny's blunt directness was almost masculine, and completely unsettling to an old-fashioned man like himself. He preferred the artistry involved in gentle flirtation.

So it was when Eddie reported that the Sphinx was done reading fortunes for the day, and Jenny and Stephen had returned dusty and dirt-smeared from touring the interior of the Great Pyramid, that Neville made his suggestion.

"You hosted us in Alexandria, Lady Cheshire," he said. "Why not let me return the favor? We will make our leisurely return to Cairo, freshen up, and then meet again at Shepheard's for dinner."

His suggestion was accepted with alacrity. They rode back to Cairo in company, their camels proving not unduly offensive to the jaded nag that drew the carriage within which Lady Cheshire and her friends had arrived. When their roads parted, Neville scribbled a note and entrusted it to Mrs. Syms.

"Give this to whoever is in charge of the front desk, and they will make arrangements. Until tonight, then."

"Until tonight, Sir Neville," Mrs. Syms said happily, obviously anticipating a treat. Lady Cheshire merely looked demure and mysterious, and Neville's heart sang within him.

Jenny's silence said more than any words would have done regarding her disapproval of her uncle's dalliance, especially in that she remained quiet after they had returned to Papa Antonio's and there was no longer the excuse that she needed to mind her camel. Stephen would not have said anything in any case. He had a nice sensitivity regarding his place, both as a younger man and as a subordinate.

Of course, if Stephen is the Sphinx, Neville thought, *then he has said enough already, though in cipher.*

They went their separate ways. As he let Bert draw him a bath, Neville began to fume.

It's not like I need to have an unmarried chit manage my affairs, he thought, his temper steaming like the bath water. *I wonder that it bothers me at all. I wonder if it's because she reminds me of Alice. Family can always get under your skin like no one else. Well, Jenny is a mere niece. Moreover, she is less than half my age—and too impressionable by half—to be so swayed by a handful of anonymous letters when anyone can see that Lady Cheshire is a fascinating and intelligent woman.*

He snorted aloud, startling Bert, who was pressing Neville's evening dress.

Bert poked his head around the carved wooden screen that provided a semblance of privacy.

"I'm sorry, Sir Neville," he said when he saw his master still in the bath. "I thought I heard you call."

"No, Bert. I can handle getting out of the bath by myself."

"Very good, sir."

Bert began to withdraw, then poked his head around again.

Really! Neville thought. *He's still more footman than valet. I must arrange for him to have some coaching. Perhaps someone at Shepheard's would undertake it while we are away.*

"Sir Neville," Bert said. "I forgot to mention, but a letter was slid under the door a few moments ago."

"Thank you, Bert. Put it on the secretary and I'll have a look at it when I'm dry."

"Very good, sir."

Stephen's working quickly, Neville thought, amused, rising from the water and beginning to towel off. *I wonder if he had his newest cipher worked out in advance. I must be particularly dense in assisting to solve this one.*

But the missive was neither from Stephen, nor from the mysterious Sphinx. It was from Eddie Bryce.

I received word that the Lotus Blossom is ready to depart as of tomorrow morning. Apparently, earlier notification was mislaid in the confusion at my house. I hope you and your companions will be prepared to depart on time, as with the tourist season beginning in force, it will be more difficult to book appropriate accommodations and we may lose a week or more.

Eddie went on to set a time they should be ready to depart, noting that he would arrange for both carriage and luggage wagon. He reminded them that secrecy was of the essence, and said that he and Papa Antonio had worked out some appropriate misdirection. The letter concluded rather surprisingly.

> *I would like to advise you to bring Miss Benet with you. We know that we have enemies here in Cairo. For ourselves to escape them while leaving a lady vulnerable would be less than proper. I have made arrangements for my family's safety. I would hope that you would do no less for the only surviving member of your own bloodline.*

Neville read over this last paragraph repeatedly, then folded the letter and set it aside. Eddie did have a point, and he knew he would worry about Jenny were he to leave her, even if he had her move to the comparative safety of another house-hold—say, with the Travers family. The Anubis-mask-wearing assassins could slip in under any number of guises: porter, household servant, messenger.

He made up his mind, and before dressing for dinner donned a dressing gown and crossed to rap on his two charges' doors. Both answered promptly, Stephen al-ready clad in his out-dated formal wear, a book in his hand, and Jenny in a long robe. Something about her hair suggested that Emily had been dressing it.

Neville showed them both the envelope.

"The Sphinx?" Stephen said, with what Neville thought—knowing what he did—was admirable promptness.

Jenny, clearly still annoyed with her uncle, said nothing, just stood quietly. Her posture reminded Neville of a junior officer who did not dare speak out against a superior, but was determined not to offer anything that could be con-strued as support. For a moment, Neville considered not taking Eddie's advice and leaving her aggravating presence behind.

But weren't you just telling yourself that she's the child and you the adult? he chided him-self. *Would you ever forgive yourself if something happened to her because you answered childishness with the same?*

The answer was so obvious that Neville didn't even bother to answer, not even to himself.

"No, not the Sphinx," he said. "From Eddie. He says our steamer is ready to depart tomorrow morning. Apparently, an earlier notification was mislaid. Give any orders you have for your baggage to Emily and Bert before we depart for Shep-heard's. Have them leave out what you'll need in the morning, but pack the rest away. Apparently, Eddie has some dodge in mind, and I wouldn't be surprised if our luggage is gone before we return."

"We?" Jenny asked, for he had clearly been addressing them both. "Our?"

"That's right," Neville said. "Eddie has convinced me that the safest place for you may be outside of Cairo, where we can keep an eye on you."

Jenny was too pleased to be offended by this indication that her uncle thought she needed looking after. The annoyance that had been coloring her manner since she had realized that Sir Neville intended to continue associating with Lady Cheshire slid away.

"I can be ready," she promised. "Thank you, Uncle Neville!"

She bounced to her toes, kissed him on one cheek, and hurried back into her room, doubtless to tend the dual chores of readying for departure and finishing her preparations for the evening.

Stephen smiled at her exuberance, then looked more seriously at Neville.

"Are you certain this is a good idea, sir?"

"I do," Neville replied with more confidence than he felt. "Jenny seems to have inherited a rebellious spirit from her mother. I dread what mischief she would get into without us to mind her."

"We won't have a lady's maid for her," Stephen reminded him, "not unless you intend to bring Emily and Bert after all."

"I think Jenny can do without," Neville replied. "Indeed, I suspect she has done more without than with in the course of her life. There will be ample female company aboard the steamer to safeguard her honor, and when we leave . . ."

Stephen shrugged, and finished the sentence with a poor attempt at lightness, "We'll need to safeguard far more than mere honor."

Their dinner that night at Shepheard's was quite elegant, and very tasty, though Neville was perhaps more absentminded than his guests might have expected, judging by the pleasant sociability with which he had visited earlier that day. Catching himself musing over whether Eddie would have laid in all the necessary supplies Neville excused himself with a laugh.

"I must have worn myself out riding that camel," he said. "Takes more out of one than you'd imagine. I expect Jenny and Stephen will feel it in the morning."

"I feel it now," Jenny said, her slight shifting in her chair inviting laughter. "My body still seems to be swaying back and forth."

When the dessert course was being served, Lady Cheshire presented them each with little gifts. Stephen and Jenny received detailed figurines depicting camels in all their caparisoned glory "to commemorate your first ride." To Neville she presented a fine calfskin-bound volume of the works of the poet Algernon Swinburne.

"I know that his poetry has been rather . . . controversial since its first appearance," she said, pausing slightly, so that Neville had time to recall that "controversial" was a mild way of stating the matter. "Swinburne has been faulted both for his wealth of pagan allusion and for his openly sensuous imagery. I recalled from one of our discussions that you were unfamiliar with his work, and when I saw this in the bazaar, I resolved to make you a present of it. I shall enjoy having the opportunity to discuss his work with you."

Neville gave appropriate thanks, doing his best to ignore the angry expression Captain Brentworth turned in his direction.

Jenny's right, Neville thought. *For whatever reason, Lady Cheshire does enjoy reminding the man of his place.*

Shortly thereafter, they departed. A slim, dark figure darted out to their carriage. It was the Arab boy, Rashid, the monkey Mischief hanging off one of his arms. Unable to speak, the boy contented himself with a smile, then pressed a small cloth bag into Neville's hand before vanishing into the darkness.

"What is it?" Jenny asked, leaning forward to see.

Indulgently, Neville handed it to her and let her open it. Nothing could be better than that slim volume of poetry—and the implicit promise it contained.

Jenny untied the drawstring, and with a small clattering sound the contents spilled into her palm.

"Scarabs!" she exclaimed. "Three of them. Nicely made, too, carved from stone rather than cast porcelain. There's writing on them, but I can't read it in this light."

When they were back at Papa Antonio's and enjoying a final glass of their host's familial wine, Jenny opened the bag again and put the scarabs on the table.

"See if you can read them, Stephen," she prompted.

Stephen slid the nearest to him.

"Lapis lazuli," he announced, inspecting the material. "Poor quality, but genuine. I understand that modern artifacts merchants import the stone much as their ancestors did. Lapis lazuli was thought lucky, and was sacred, I believe, to the goddess Hathor."

"She's the one who looks like Isis except that she has cow's ears?" Jenny said tentatively.

"That's right." Stephen turned a scarab over and studied the inscription. "A very ancient goddess, sometimes represented as Horus's wife, other times as his mother—a role also held by Isis. Sometimes Hathor shares with Anubis the role of protector of the dead."

His voice trailed off as he polished the scarab against his arm to better inspect the carving, then he resumed: "There are two hieroglyphs here—neither simply phonetic, I am happy to announce. One is the *crux ansata*, the cross with the looped top, also called the ankh. It indicates a wish for life—not only on earth but throughout eternity. The other is harder to make out. I thought at first it was the reed, but I rather think that it is a feather."

"Feather?" Jenny repeated. "And what does that mean?"

"Drawn by itself like this," Stephen said, "it could either mean 'truth' or 'justice' or even a wish for the same. It certainly does not indicate any ill-wishing."

"Than I think we can rule Captain Brentworth out as the giver," Jenny said, giving Neville a sidelong glance, but otherwise not pursuing the point. Do they all say the same thing?"

Stephen inspected them, then nodded. "I wouldn't doubt that the makers of 'anteekahs' have learned a few propitious signs, and reproduce them for the delight of the semi-educated tourist."

His self-deprecating shrug as he set the scarabs on the table indicated that he was classifying himself with all humility as one of those obvious marks.

Jenny picked up the nearest scarab and turned it idly in her hand. "I wonder why Rashid gave them to us?"

Neville smiled, "You have been very kind to him, my dear. He probably picked the scarabs up in the bazaar with no idea of what they say or indicate, just seeing them as the type of trinkets we Europeans seem to covet."

"And we do not even know if they are from Rashid," Stephen added. "They could be from Mrs. Syms. Native lucky amulets seem rather more in her line."

Jenny nodded, "I still imagine Rashid is the giver. Mrs. Syms likes explaining the occult significance of such items far too much to lose an opportunity, and she doesn't know we are leaving in the morning. There would be ample opportunity for her to give us a gift and pontificate to her heart's content."

"Rashid, however," Stephen agreed, "would need to make his little gesture whenever he could—preferably when his master would not think he was getting above himself."

"Odd isn't it?" Jenny mused, "Rashid is a dutiful Mohammedan, and yet he gives us pagan charms as a gift. Papa Antonio trots off to daily Mass, but in his courtyard is a fountain with a pagan god at its center. And look at Mrs. Syms and her obsession with the occult. Seems to me that the tradition that began with the Hebrews and continued into Christianity and Islam advocates one god, but there is something in the human spirit that longs for a more immediate and personal contact with the divine."

Neville rose and stretched.

"We must rise early tomorrow," he said. "Enough time for philosophical and theological speculation when we're on our way."

The *Lotus Blossom* was contracted to Cooks, and their fellow passengers were as varied as could be. They were mostly English or American, but a fair smattering of Germans, French, and other representatives of the wealthier European nations rounded out the group. The reasons for taking the tour were as varied as the passengers themselves. Some had come to escape the European winter, others for the opportunity to view exotic sights, still others were painters or writers seeking material. There were even a few game hunters, all but panting for the opportunity to shoot crocodiles, hippos, and other exotic game.

Neville had thought Jenny might have joined the hunters at their sport, but she seemed content to take a seat where she could see the newly planted fields and picturesque ruins slipping by, her sketch pad in her lap, but her hands idle more often than not.

One afternoon, several days out of Cairo, she poked Stephen, who was dozing beneath the brim of his straw boater.

"Uh?" Stephen said, sitting up straight, his book sliding to the deck.

"I was wondering," Jenny said, as if picking up an interrupted conversation, "if the people who live here along the Nile still feel some respect for the old gods, and that's why they haven't broken up the temples for building stone."

"That's a nice, romantic notion," Stephen replied, "but from what I've read, the fellahin are perfectly willing to sell their heritage for whatever they can get for it. You know that it wasn't until fairly recently that there were any controls on the sale of antiquities, and those were mostly imposed in response to pressure from without."

Neville stopped trying to get his pipe to draw long enough to add, "It helps that archeologists themselves are growing increasingly jealous of their rights to their finds. The Egyptian Museum, although administered by the French, works in cooperation with the Egyptian government. One of its jobs is to issue *firman*—that is, permits—for excavation, and to make certain the artifacts are properly cared for afterward. Modern competition for permission to dig is quite intense."

Jenny raised the elegant twin arches of her eyebrows. "Do we have a firman, Uncle Neville?" she asked softly.

"We aren't excavating," Neville replied brusquely, "merely exploring."

"Ah," Jenny said.

"Your uncle is right about the competition for firman," Stephen said, his tone implying that he thought Neville had been right to avoid bureaucracy until it was unavoidable. "The system has its advantages, though. Any peasant who finds a site and sets about looting finds himself in a great deal of trouble with the authorities. I understand the fellahin find it very annoying. For some of the fellahin, tomb robbing is an old family business."

"And has been," Neville said, "since the earliest days of the pharaohs—the Great Pyramid can testify to the truth of that."

Jenny gave a rueful smile, "An ancient if not honorable profession."

"True," Stephen agreed. "Rather like . . ."

He stopped in mid-phrase, his fair skin blushing ruddy, even beneath its sunburn. Apparently his intended jest had not been appropriate for a lady's ears.

"So why are there still so many ruins?" Jenny asked, a twinkle in her eye suggesting that she knew perfectly well what Stephen had just saved himself from saying. "If respect for the old gods and the old ways hasn't kept them intact, what has?"

Stephen looked at the tumbled heap of sandstone blocks and laughed. "First I would have to disagree that 'intact' is a fair definition for the condition of most remaining monuments."

"Oh, do agree," Jenny said, "for the sake of argument, if not just to humor me."

"Very well. The most practical reason that so many monuments remain intact is that those blocks of stone take a tremendous amount of labor to move. The fellahin have very little incentive to do so much work to build their own homes—especially when mud and straw are lighter, and make perfectly practical building materials.

"Most obelisks and statues that have been moved are moved during the Inundation, when the fellahin cannot farm and so are eager to hire out as labor. I don't think any study has been done, but I believe that were you to inspect any area near where a nobleman's residence or other grand structure has been built, you would find a notable paucity of ruins."

Neville nodded his agreement. "Think about the destruction we saw at the Gizeh. Most of the sheathing stone from the pyramids was removed for use in Cairo."

"I do think," Stephen said, "that superstition might have played some role in preserving the monuments of ancient Egypt, but I take that as something different from religious respect."

"Indeed," Jenny agreed.

"In my day," Neville said, "that is, when I was a dashing young captain with a gift for translation and an interest in archeology, many of the fellahin considered the archeologists sorcerers. They greatly distrusted their ability to read hieroglyphs, and their apparent intimacy with the secrets of ancient peoples."

"And today?" Jenny asked with a laugh. "In these far ages into the future?"

"Have more respect for my advanced years," Neville protested. "Sometimes those days do seem farther away than the ages when the pharaohs reigned, but I do think the attitude has changed some. Worldwide interest in Egypt's archeological treasures has created work for the fellahin. I suspect that instead of magicians, these days they see archeologists as bank accounts."

"Good for them, then," Jenny said, "but I do feel rather bad for the old pharaohs. They went to so much trouble to ensure that they would rest in peace, and peace seems to be the last thing that anyone will grant them. All that work for nothing."

"Now, Jenny," Stephen said. "I don't think several additional centuries of se-cure burial is nothing. Remember, the worst thing those pharaohs could contem-plate wasn't being dug up—it was being forgotten. Modern archeology assures that they will never be forgotten—that they will have a new life in modern memory."

Jenny's pensive expression did not change.

Neville said softly, "It's our own plans that bother you, isn't it?"

Jenny nodded. "I can't help but feel like what we're doing is sacrilege or some-thing. And what will we do if we find the Valley of Dust? Will we go out and get a firman for excavation? Grab a few treasures and take them home as mementos? Leave it all behind, and try to be satisfied that we've solved the puzzle?"

She spoke very softly, but her words seemed to ring in Neville's mind rather than merely in his ears. Here, unavoidably spoken, were the protests and objections he had struggled not to face. He shrugged, and chose not to face them now.

"Egypt certainly has her claim," he admitted, "but the people of a land are of-ten the last ones to appreciate her history and treasures. Worry over it if you must, Jenny, but don't fret too much. After all, we still have no guarantee that we will find anything at all."

The *Lotus Blossom*'s route up the Nile was punctuated by regular stops at the most popular ruins. Memphis and Sakkarah, forty-some miles outside of Cairo, were the first stop. They were satisfyingly spectacular, possessing sufficient pyramids, temples, tombs, and colossi to delight even the jaded heart.

Other stops were shorter, the highlight a single temple, cluster of tombs, or a native bazaar. Assiut, the Lykopolis of the ancient Greeks, was fascinating, as were

Abydos and Denderah. Jenny began to recognize various clusters of hieroglyphs, just as Stephen had predicted, and felt almost indecently pleased with herself.

At Eddie Bryce's suggestion, they kept to themselves their knowledge of all but the most routine aspects of archeology, and mingled with the tourists. For Stephen and Jenny this was a delight, but Jenny suspected that Sir Neville was growing impatient.

Although no jackal-masked assassins haunted their cabins, and the Sphinx seemed to have ceased correspondence entirely, their days were not without excitement. Stephen got into a fist fight with a fat English tourist—a minor lord or some such—who was determined to break off a section of relief sculpture as a souvenir.

For her part, Jenny garnered some startled and disapproving stares when she not only encouraged Stephen, but offered to help him. Eddie, who continued to blend in with the Arabs, intervened before more than a few blows were exchanged, and both sculpture and tourist escaped relatively unscathed.

When they were not touring monuments and temples, there was the Nile itself to enjoy. The coordinator of the Cook's tour arranged entertainments similar to those on *Neptune's Charger*, but in the interest of not attracting too much attention, Sir Neville requested that they keep their participation to a minimum. Watching for crocodiles was a favorite pastime, despite—or perhaps because—the reptiles seemed scarce on this heavily traveled stretch of the Nile.

At every halt in the steamer's route robed and turbaned Arabs sold "anteekahs"—real and manufactured. The sight of women who had only moments before been exclaiming in squeamish horror over a lizard on the deck or a rat swimming through the water, now digging up to their elbows in cases containing fragments of bone and cloth presented by their sellers as "real mummy" brought the twist of a cynical smile to Jenny's lips.

For Jenny's part, she found herself remarkably free from the universal passion for relic-hunting. She didn't resist when Uncle Neville bought her a few pretty strings of glass beads, nor did she chide Stephen for the growing collection of figurines, scarabs, and the like that cluttered his cabin. However, she felt no desire to grub in the dust and make a find herself.

Denderah's archeological sites were nearer to the river than was usual along the Nile, where every bit of arable land was kept under cultivation. This made it a natural stop for the Cook's tour, and the Hawthorne party mingled with them. Jenny trailed toward the rear of the group, but the late period temple of Hathor, magnificent as it was, failed to hold her attention.

The weather had grown progressively warmer as the steamer carried them south along the Nile, and while some of the women had been heard complaining that they should have remained in Cairo's more temperate climes, Jenny—who had laced her stays as loosely as she dared—was quite content.

She wandered off through the newly planted fields, stepping over thin irrigation rills, and admiring the stark beauty of the temple without the annoying interference of tourist chatter. Distance made it easier to imagine the temple as it might have been. In her imagination Jenny replaced the broken stone that remained where Hathor's face had been hacked from the columns with the goddess' benign features.

A shrill, piercing cry broke into Jenny's imaginings. For a moment, she thought it was the high-pitched voice of one of the women on the tour carrying from the echoing halls of the temple. Then she realized it had come from much closer.

One of the fellahin? she thought. *The women do bring their babies with them into the fields.*

With more urgency, she continued her search, imagining a child abandoned or forgotten. What she found seemed just as pathetic.

A litter of kittens not more than a few weeks old were nested in a grassy hollow near one of the irrigation streams. All were stiff, still, and cold, all but one who cried from the center of the huddle, its little pink mouth opening and shutting, its cries growing suddenly more intense, as if it sensed Jenny's nearness. There was no sign of the kittens' mother, and judging from the way their ribs were outlined beneath their fur, she must have been gone for several days.

"Oh, you poor darling," Jenny said, scooping up the kitten.

It was a miserable scrap of an animal. Its ragged coat was a deep, golden brown, the hairs ticked at the tips with a darker brown—more like a rabbit's coat than a cat's. Its wide blue eyes could not have been open for more than a few days, but the kitten already viewed the world with suspicion. It didn't even struggle when Jenny picked it up, just drooped limp and resigned.

"You," Jenny said, stroking the kitten's fur, "need something to eat. Can you handle goat's milk, I wonder? You'd better, since I don't think the steamer has a resident mother cat."

She hadn't noticed Stephen and Uncle Neville crossing the field, the curiosity writ large on their features making them look oddly alike.

"What did you find, Jenny?" Uncle Neville asked.

"A kitten," she said. "The rest of its litter is here, dead. It's nearly starved, poor darling."

Stephen looked at it critically.

"You're not taking a kitten with us," he said.

"And why not?" Jenny replied stubbornly.

"They won't want a kitten on the boat," Stephen said reasonably. "Give it to one of the merchants. They'll be glad for a cat. Or maybe the temple custodians would want it."

"Lady Smitherington has her obnoxious pomeranian with her," Jenny replied stubbornly. "No one will complain about my having a kitten. I want to keep it."

Eddie Bryce came up to join them, having apparently grasped the situation by osmosis.

"It is cute," he admitted, using one finger tip to pat the tiny head, "but we're due to leave the Nile in a few days. We'll be hard pressed to keep ourselves alive then. You'd be dooming the little thing."

"It isn't at all strong," Uncle Neville added. "I don't mind if you bring it with you now, but we'll find a home for it in Luxor. Otherwise you'd save its life for nothing."

Jenny felt unreasonably stubborn, and Stephen must have seen this, for he wheedled most unfairly, "The ancient Egyptians considered the cat a sacred animal. You said you were worried about the sacrilegious aspects of our expedition. If you leave the kitten behind in Luxor, you will have gained the merit of saving a life, but if you selfishly take the kitten with you and it dies, you will have slain a holy animal."

Although she was fully aware that leaving the kitten behind was the most reasonable option, nevertheless, Jenny turned a deaf ear to the men's words. She carried the kitten back to the *Lotus Blossom*, cleaned it up, and even went as far as to give it a restorative from her medical kit. With stubborn disregard for gender—for the kitten was female—she planned to name it Moses.

"I found it among the bulrushes," she said, "and the name means 'saved from the water,' which is certainly appropriate enough."

Stephen looked up from his book. "Why not Mozelle?" he asked. "That's a feminine form of the same name."

Jenny liked his suggestion, and so the kitten became Mozelle.

The Sphinx Again

KARNAK AND Kurneh, both of which had yielded so many monumental finds in the early and middle years of the century, were their last major stops before Luxor. The natives here were accustomed to tourists, and the local authorities expected "gifts." Fortunately, the *Lotus Blossom*'s captain had standard arrangements in place, and made a great ceremony of handing out mirrors, fountain pens, and bags of good tobacco.

This ceremony occurred on the Hawthorne party's last day aboard the vessel. Eddie had booked them passage only this far, and Neville had explained to any who inquired that he had business in the area, but hoped to rejoin the vessel when she returned from Aswan.

The city of Luxor was rich with history, even discounting the tombs in the Valley of the Kings. Named Waset by the Egyptians, rather confusingly, the city had been called Thebes by the Greeks. The Greeks' other name for the city, Diospolis Magna—the Great City of the Gods—made more sense, for Luxor was amply supplied with temples and shrines, as well as numerous structures dating to important periods in the New Kingdom and before.

The Arabs, arriving with very little sense of the previous inhabitants, had

called the city Al Uqsur, the Castles, doubtless in reference to the ruins that remained—though some argued that what had impressed the Arabs had been the
towering cliffs that framed the relatively flat area.

Neville noted with some amusement that Europeans tended to refer to the city
as Thebes, as if they were visiting it in an incarnation of its older glory, while residents and Egyptian "old hands" referred to it as Luxor. It made for a certain amount
of amiable confusion, a confusion not lessened by its proximity to Karnak, which
tended to get conflated by the less knowledgeable into the much-renamed whole.

Reis Awad, captain of the dahabeeyah on which Eddie had made arrangements for them to travel onward, was not there to meet them, but a representative
of his family brought word that the *Mallard* was expected any day now. She had
gone upstream with a small group of hunters who hoped to find crocodiles.

Neville was inclined to be annoyed at this, and Eddie reproached him.

"It was the best thing Awad could have done," he said. "A dahabeeyah sitting
idle at this busy season would have attracted attention. Gossip is the very life of
any port city, and I told Awad in my letter—without explaining precisely why—
that we were very eager not to make ourselves conspicuous."

Not knowing precisely when the *Mallard* would return, Stephen and Jenny
urged Neville to help them plan an itinerary that would let them see as many of
the sights as possible. Neville fell in with this, not wanting Eddie to be distracted
from the last-minute preparations that he had not been able to attend to before
they reached Luxor. Therefore, he was rather surprised when Eddie heard their intentions and nearly took their heads off.

"Don't you people realize that this is the most dangerous portion of our trip
since we left Cairo?"

Stephen blink owlishly, but found the courage to reply. "I admit, I *do* fail to
understand. We have had no difficulties—not even a letter from the Sphinx—
since we boarded the *Lotus Blossom*. Shall we not assume that we have shaken our ad-
versaries from our trail?"

"Use your heads for something other than filling out your hats," Eddie said.
"Yes, we seem to have shaken them, but if those people have agents anywhere other
than in Cairo, it's going to be here. We're not terribly far from where Chad Spice's
journal indicates he emerged from the desert. Right?"

Three heads nodded as one.

"It ought not take a genius to realize that any archeologists who show up here
are going to be watched. They'll be watched by the locals, and they'll be watched by
other archeologists—some of whom have been known to exchange shots when
they're worried that someone is going to try and poach their site. Now, look at that

plan you have laid out—not a single trip to the bazaar, or to watch the dervishes dance, or anything else that isn't strictly archeological."

Three heads bent and inspected the schedule.

"You're right, Eddie," Stephen said, shamefaced, for he had suggested most of the points of interest. "We've been idiots of the worst order."

"I did so want to see some of the more famous sites," Jenny sighed. Mozelle curled asleep in her lap, the question of her eventual fate rather pointedly undiscussed. "I don't suppose there is some way we can see more of Thebes than this hotel, is there?"

Eddie softened. "Oh, I think there might be. We just won't go poking around the digs, and Stephen will have to keep his enthusiasm—and his fists—to himself. You folks will dress up properly English, and we'll tour the sights. Jenny should look a little bored, and whine about wanting ices, and Stephen should talk about how he wants to go shooting. Neville should do a bit of business with the local merchants, enough so that anyone who heard why you left the *Lotus Blossom* won't wonder."

Neville frowned. "I don't mind playing out this charade, Eddie, but will it leave you time to finalize our arrangements?"

"Already taken care of," Eddie assured him. "I've had a note from the fellow who's meeting us with the camels, and he's on his way to the rendezvous. Reis Awad has agents who handle purchasing for the *Mallard*, and I've given them our shopping list. Nothing could be more innocent."

Neville had to be satisfied with this. He even began to enjoy the touring. Luxor was rapidly becoming the second most famous area in Egypt, and its attractions were more apparent than they had been a decade before. Separately, both Jenny and Stephen shared with him their desire to return someday when they would have more time, and he didn't really blame them.

But I have something to do first, before I can rest and tour other people's achievements. I need to achieve something of my own goals.

A few days after their arrival, Reis Awad came into port. He was a short man, stocky, but nimble as a monkey. With considerable pride, he took them on a tour of the *Mallard*. Like all vessels of her kind, she was flat-bottomed, equipped either for sailing or rowing.

"And when the wind fails us," Awad said, "we track."

He showed them the long lines used for towing the dahabeeyah from the bank.

"My sailors pull," he explained when Stephen looked mystified. "It work very well, but maybe you not see this. The wind is sweet and steady from the south this time of year, Allah willing—and we not go so far."

Reis Awad was too polite to state his curiosity openly, and though Neville felt that he could be trusted, Eddie's constant warnings about caution were having their effect. Neville just smiled and ignored the implied question. Let Awad think this was just another mad English venture. In truth, was it anything but?

Maybe, Neville thought, remembering old Alphonse Liebermann, *a mad Teutonic venture.*

The next day they moved aboard the *Mallard*. The cabins for passengers were aft, a roof built between them providing an upper deck furnished as an outdoor sitting room with its own removable canopy. Below was a many-windowed saloon for times when the outdoors might be too hot or windy to be pleasant. The cabins were tiny, but furnished with all the civilized amenities.

"I feel like I'm a little girl playing house," Jenny said, looking at the miniature perfection of her cabin. "I wish we were staying aboard for more than a few days."

Neville was tempted to suggest she do just that, for he still felt a great deal of concern about taking her into the desert. However, he knew Jenny would be indignant if he did, and doubtless there would be a wrangle. There had already been one over the kitten. Before surrendering to Neville's command that she leave the kitten at the hotel, Jenny had proven herself more willing to argue or sulk than to burst into ladylike tears, and Neville didn't know if he wanted the Arab crewmen to see him permitting such behavior.

Though Eddie would be sleeping on the foredeck with the members of the crew, he used the excuse of helping them settle into their cabins to brief them.

"Most of Reis Awad's business is ferrying tourists from Luxor to the nearby sites, so he's done himself proud with all the trims that appeal to Europeans. There are cooking facilities near the foremast, and as long as the wind holds, you won't be bothered by smoke. The cook's good, too. He did a few years in one of the big Cairo hotels, and knows how infidels like their food prepared."

"You've found us a fine boat," Neville said. "Given that I would have settled for speed and a reliable crew, this luxury is almost too much."

Eddie grinned. "Just helping out the family. Awad's a cousin, after all." He grew serious. "From Miriam's father's side of the family—no connection to those peculiar Bedouin."

Neville needed to return to the hotel to settle their bill and pick up some clothing the hotel laundry hadn't had ready when they'd packed. When Neville reentered the lobby, the clerk at the front desk reached into the maze of pigeon holes behind him.

"A letter came for you when you were out, Sir Neville," he said. "It was delivered by hand."

Neville looked at the handwriting on the outer envelope at first with eagerness, but recognition brought with it no joy, only a sensation of dread.

"You say it was delivered by hand?"

"Yes. Some street urchin. That is not uncommon, sir. There are so many steamers this time of year, not to mention the dahabeeyahs and the regular land post. Letters get mis-routed, and then some child gets to earn his dinner running them to their correct destinations."

Neville accepted the envelope, tucking it unopened into an inner pocket. He settled the bill, collected his package of laundry, tipped the clerk, and headed back to the *Mallard*.

Jenny and Stephen were ensconced on the upper deck, watching the activity in the busy harbor while ostensibly improving Jenny's knowledge of hieroglyphs.

"We had a letter today," Neville said after greetings had been exchanged.

Jenny looked up from her lesson book.

"From Papa Antonio?" she asked. "I believe he is the only one who knew where we planned to stay."

She glanced at Stephen as she spoke, with such an obvious undertone in her voice that it made Neville defensive.

Jenny can't know I told Lady Cheshire we were going to the pyramids at Gizeh. Then again, maybe Mrs. Syms said something, and she does know. She certainly suspects.

He dropped the envelope on the table, indignant in his injured innocence.

"It is not from Papa Antonio," he said.

"The Sphinx!" Stephen murmured excitedly.

"I should have known," Jenny said with mock boredom. "He is the only one who ever writes me."

Stephen slit open the envelope and seemed pleased rather than otherwise to find the missive was again enciphered. Turning to a blank page in her sketch book, Jenny made a clean copy.

12-W-11 C-13-3-8-13-X 12-2-13-𓂀-X-F 12-W-11 X-𓂀-U-10
12-W-11 4-U-3-8-𓂀-10-6-Y-𓂀-2-R R-𓂀-F-5-X-13-3-11-F
12-W-11 2-U-Y-𓂀-10-F 11-6-6 X-U-A-11 𓂀-F 4-U-2-11
R-13-10-6-11-2-U-7-F 12-W-13-10 11-𓂀-12-W-11-2 U-10-11

"The last word can't be Sphinx!" Jenny said in alarm. "It doesn't have the right number of letters."

"He gave us one letter," Stephen said soothingly. "An eye for an 'I,' if use in the last missive to include that symbol holds constant. That's a vowel and a common one, too. Surely we can solve the cipher from there."

Jenny looked doubtful, but obediently wrote the letter 'I' under each of the Eye of Horus emblems.

They all stared blankly at the page, then Stephen said, "I would hazard a guess that neither letters nor numbers progress in order. Therefore, effectively, each is simply a blank symbol. He could have drawn squares and triangles or little stick figures and they would have served as well."

Neville snorted, "And doubtless it will come to that if we don't find him out and shake sense out of him."

Stephen smiled. "I'll make another guess. The most frequently repeated pattern is 12-W-11. It occurs four times—including, perhaps significantly, at the beginning of the missive."

He held up a finger when Jenny would have interrupted. "Moreover, 12-W occurs in two other places, suggesting that these letters are frequently found in conjunction. Let's see what happens when we fill in 'the' for 12-W-11, substituting wherever those numbers occur."

Jenny did so, and before either man could speak she said, "The second to last word must be 'either'—which gives us the 'R.'"

No one objected, so she filled in the letter. Then Neville laughed shortly and pointed to a pair of letters.

"Eye-F," he said, "must be 'is.' We know 12 stands for 'T,' which rules out 'it.' 'F' is the last letter of four words, which is reasonable if it is 'T,' but not if it's 'N.'"

"And the Sphinx," Stephen added, "has very helpfully used 'F' as his cipher symbol which rules out 'if.'"

Jenny filled in the "S," and they stared for a long, silent moment.

"Sense of the phrase," Stephen said, "can be as useful as frequency of letters or grammatical clues. Think about the word 'either.' It implies a comparison. We have a four letter word preceding it, ruling out 'or'—even if word order would admit such clumsy phrasing. I would suggest 'than' fits both the letters we have, and the sense of the phrase."

"Oh, good," Jenny said, scribbling away, "that gives us two more letters—and one of them is a vowel."

"If 'than' is correct," Neville said, "the final word must be 'one' and that supplies us with the 'O.'"

"It's beginning to make sense," Jenny gloated, her pencil flying across the paper. "Take a look."

12-W-11   C-13-3-8-13-X   12-2-13-𓂀-X-F   12-W-11
T-H-E   ?-A-?-?-A-?   T-R-A-I-?-S   T-H-E

X-𓂀-U-10   12-W-11   4-U-3-8-𓂀-10-6-Y-𓂀-2-R
?-I-O-N   T-H-E   ?-O-?-?-I-N-?-?-I-R-D

R-𓂀-F-5-X-13-3-11-F   12-W-11   2-U-Y-𓂀-10-F
?-I-S-?-?-A-?-E-S   T-H-E   R-O-?-I-N-S

11-6-6   X-U-A-11   𓂀-F   4-U-2-11   R-13-10-6-11-2-U-7-F
E-?-?   ?-O-?-E   I-S   ?-O-R-E   ?-A-N-?-E-R-O-?-S

12-W-13-10   11-𓂀-12-W-11-2   U-10-11
T-H-A-N   E-I-T-H-E-R   O-N-E

Steven examined the partially completed cipher.

"'The -a—a- trai-s the -ion.' The letter 'X' occurs three times there. Either 'L' or 'N' would work in 'trai-', but we already have 'N.'"

"So it must be 'L,'" Jenny concluded triumphantly. "The -a—al trails the lion."

"Jackal!" Neville said, so loudly that several of Reis Awad's sailors looked nervously toward the shore.

Each of them felt a chill of horror as they recalled their nocturnal burglars.

"Got it," Jenny said, keeping her voice down as she filled in the new letters. "'The -ockin—ir- -is-laces the ro-ins e—,'" she continued. "There sure are a lot of sixes in that line."

"A double letter," Stephen said. "Not overly common in English, especially when you eliminate most of the letters we already have."

"'G'" stated Neville. "It has to be 'G.' That makes the final word 'egg.' I'll bet my estate that the long word is 'mockingbird.'"

"Another bird right after that," Jenny said, already filling in. "Robin."

"The mockingbird somethings the robin's egg," Stephen said. "'Displaces' would be my guess."

"Looks good. We almost have it," Jenny said, continuing to pencil in. "Could the next word be 'love'?"

Neville noticed that she very carefully did not look at him as she said this, and didn't know whether to be embarrassed or annoyed. He settled for reading the completed message aloud.

"'The jackal trails the lion. The mockingbird displaces the robin's egg. Love is more dangerous than either one.' Why bother to encipher this at all? It doesn't make any sense even translated."

Jenny frowned at him. "You're going to be angry with me, Uncle, but I'd say that it makes perfect sense—and fits in with the Sphinx's other messages quite neatly."

Stephen frowned. "I thought that cuckoos were the birds that pushed eggs out of other bird's nests, not mockingbirds."

Jenny scowled at him. "So the Sphinx made an ornithological error. The sense is the same. Jackals are scavengers. Mockingbirds—or cuckoos—push other birds' eggs out of the nest and replace them with their own."

"Mockingbirds," Stephen added helpfully, "could be said to steal the songs of other birds. They're fabulous mimics."

"Right," Jenny said. "In any case, we have animals that have a reputation for living off the labor of others. It sounds like a warning against someone who would try to benefit from our labors."

"And this bit about love?" Neville said, daring her to say it.

Stephen interjected, obviously in the hope of keeping Jenny from being too blunt, "Love itself can be very dangerous. More evil has been done for love—whether for a country or a religion or another person—than we like to admit. We prefer to think of it as a tender emotion."

Jenny wasn't going to be dissuaded.

"Stephen's right. Love makes a wonderful excuse for not seeing the truth about the motives of a country, a religion . . . or a woman. Uncle Neville, don't you see . . ."

"Enough," Neville interrupted sharply. "I assure you I have not betrayed our plans to . . . anyone. If you're so clever, tell me this. Who do you think is sending these messages?"

"We had several candidates," Stephen said cautiously, very aware of his position as Sir Neville's subordinate, "but most don't seem to apply once we left Cairo—if truly no-one knew our plans. Eddie Bryce now seems the best. Can he read hieroglyphs?"

"Not when I knew him," Neville said. "However, that doesn't mean he hasn't learned since then."

"We've shown him the other letters," Jenny said. "I say that this time we confront him with our suspicions. It's only fair."

Neville agreed. He didn't think Eddie was a likely candidate, but if the time had come for confrontations, he wasn't going to let Stephen off the hook.

They placed the deciphered letter on the table, and when Eddie came up to inform them that the wind was so favorable that Reis Awad intended to leave immediately, they showed it to him.

"Another of these?" Eddie said. "Fellow seems to like romance and danger as subjects, don't you think?"

"You should know," Jenny said.

"What?" Eddie looked genuinely confused.

"I said, 'You should know.' Aren't you the author of these fascinating letters?"

Eddie shook his head, laughing. "I am not. Hell, I'm not that clever. Almost all the education I got was in the army, plus what the mullahs drummed into my head after I converted. Ask Neville—I couldn't even read when we met."

His astonished pleasure that they could think him capable of such elaborate games was so genuine that they believed him.

"Anyhow," Eddie added, "didn't you get the first of these while you were still in England, and another one on the steamer you took over from England? I'd like to know how I would have worked that."

"You could have mailed them in advance," Stephen said. "You did know our travel plans, so you seemed the best candidate. And you and the Sphinx seem to think alike. Whenever the Sphinx hasn't been warning us about romantic entanglements, he's warning us off 'the good king.' Other than the Sphinx, you've been the least enthusiastic about this venture."

Eddie smiled. "I don't think I'm the least enthusiastic. Those fellows in the jackal-masks were pretty determined to stop us. I see your point, though. Is this the only such letter you've received since we left Cairo?"

Neville nodded. Nearby, the dahabeeyah's sails were flapping, ready to catch the wind, and Reis Awad was shouting orders to his men, steering them as they rowed the craft out of the harbor.

"Want to turn around?" Eddie asked. "I could make some inquiries. Try to learn which post this came in, which boats just arrived, whether any of our associates are new to Cairo."

He thinks I've told Lady Cheshire something, Neville thought. *Have I been so obvious in my interest?*

Neville shook his head.

"We're finally away. Perhaps we'll slip the Sphinx at last." Then he remembered his own suspicions and turned on Stephen, "Or maybe not. Maybe I've been nursing a mockingbird cuckoo in my breast. I know someone far more likely than Eddie to pull such a trick."

Stephen pointed to himself, "Me?"

"You," Neville enumerated his suspicions on his fingers. "You write in hieroglyphs—and know enough to disguise your typical form beneath an assumed style. You love those mysteries of Poe and might want a hand at creating one yourself. You have had both privacy to create these, and opportunity to deliver them.

You've also been almost indecently eager to decipher them—and have been available to provide little hints to Jenny and myself when we get stuck."

Stephen's mouth fell open.

"Me?" he repeated. "Why would I?"

"For a joke," Neville said, firmly. "You like a good joke—or a bad one. A joke that would enable you to take digs at your employer without seeming ungracious would be ideal."

Stephen colored, and he shook his head vigorously, as if the mere motion alone would be sufficient to prove his sincerity.

"I swear it wasn't me," he said, "on my honor. I appreciate your kindness more than I can say, and while I enjoy a joke as well as the next fellow, I would like to think I'm never mean about it. Anyhow, why would I want to dissuade you from a venture that's letting me to fulfill one of my heart's desires?"

Neville considered. Leaving out the Sphinx letters, Stephen's humor was either clever or self-deprecating, but never cruel. He had to concede that the younger man's defense was reasonable.

"You swear you aren't the author of these?"

Stephen put his hand over his heart. "I do."

Neville offered Stephen his hand. "Then I apologize for thinking you were playing a cruel joke, but I hope you'll understand that I had to ask."

Jenny had been listening to this without comment, but now she rose. "Since we're indulging in confessions—and we're safely on our way—I have one to make. I brought Mozelle with me. She's asleep in my cabin. I think I'll go get her so she can have some fresh air."

Neville buried his face in his hands, suddenly laughing to split his sides. He should have known he couldn't win. In the end, Jenny really was more like Alice—or Alice like Jenny—than he had ever admitted.

Although Neville longed to sail non-stop from morning until night, they had to play at touring and hunting lest they arouse the sailors' interests in their destination. That would be unwise, Eddie warned him, since they did not wish tales of their urgency to be told once they had left the *Mallard*. Better that the crew gossip about Jenny's skill with a rifle, or Stephen's ineptitude with the same.

The sailors were all relatives, by blood or marriage, of Reis Awad. Knowing each other well, they found much of their amusement in speculating about their exotic passengers, talking about what they would do if *they* were rich (Neville knew this would not include cruising up the Nile), gambling, and making music. Lest they have too much time for speculation, Eddie had invested in a drum, a set of pipes, and a tambourine, presenting them to the sailors along with hints that his employers liked the local music.

Neville didn't, particularly, but he felt some nostalgia for the sound. Jenny seemed to enjoy it, but doubtless she heard it as strange and exotic. Stephen evidently disliked it, but seemed to have an infinite capacity for tuning it out—certainly a useful skill for a scholar residing with both mother and sisters.

Reis Awad proved to be an admirable captain, skilled at getting the most out of both the wind and his crew. This did not mean he had absolute control of the situation. Once a sandstorm forced them to tie up along the bank for an entire afternoon. Another time a local sheik tried to charge an unreasonably large sum for viewing a small ruin. When Reis Awad and Eddie refused, the sheik hinted that there were those in his village who would take what they wanted. They spent a tense night anchored in mid-stream, but no assault came.

Watching Jenny and Stephen's delight in every element of the passing scenery—from birds and flowers to hippopotami and crocodiles—Neville felt the years slipping away from him, until he too was once again seeing the Nile for the first time, without goals or dreams to distract him from its beauty. His impatience left him for hours at a time, and he realized with a start that he was closer to being happy than he had been for many years. Like Jenny, he began to wish the voyage would go on longer.

It can, you know, he told himself one night. *Eddie wouldn't mind, and I could convince the other two, especially with the incentive of sailing further up the Nile. We could go up the cataract, into Nubia even.*

But even as he considered this, he knew he was only toying with a fancy. The peace he felt was due in part to knowing he was almost there—almost to the point where the Hawk Rock was just visible from the banks of the Nile. From the upper deck, he kept watch along the west bank and, finally, in a quiet stretch between Edfu and Kom Ombo, they found the landmarks he had set down so many years before.

Seen from the river, there was little enough to attract attention, just a small farming village without even a minor ruin to distinguish it. Beyond this village, deep in the desert, was a rock formation that to the expectant eye bore a distinct resemblance to a watchful hawk. Had it not been for the clear, dry air, and the utter absence of trees, the formation might well have been invisible, or at least too blurred to be seen clearly. As it was, the setting sun feathered the hawk in the colors of blood.

"There it is," Neville said softly. Quoting from memory, he said, " 'Worn and near mad, I stumbled from the desert wastes into a village by the Nile. Joyfully, I went and plunged my head into the silty waters. The natives looked at me as if I were insane, and I fear I did not help myself to gain their regard, for as soon as I was recovered enough to stand, I stood and saluted the Hawk Rock that had been my guide away from the strange Oasis of Statues back to the Nile."

Eddie had also seen the Hawk Rock, and returned from speaking to Reis Awad.

"We'll sail on up for a few more miles. Tomorrow I'll go ashore, and see if the arrangements I made for camels and such have been carried out. Tonight, do your packing, since I want to be ready to leave at a moment's notice. As much as I like most Egyptians, some of the residents in these outlying villages think a deal only holds until they have your money."

"Isn't it unwise for us to leave the river this close to an obvious landmark?" Jenny asked. "If those jackal-headed men really do protect Neferankhotep's tomb, aren't they even more likely to have agents here than in Thebes?"

"It is likely," Eddie said with the air of one who has resigned himself to a course of action that could not be avoided. "However, we cannot make the journey without camels, and we couldn't very well carry camels on the dahabeeyah. That means we had to set a rendezvous point."

Neville added, "Chad Spice's journal doesn't give very clear directions. If we don't start from where we can see the Hawk Rock, we're lost before we begin. We aren't landing at the same village from which Alphonse started us, and people do go out into the desert. I've had Eddie give it out that our destination is the Khargeh Oasis—a place as unknown to most of these river fellahin as the Tower of London."

Stephen grinned, "London Bridge is falling down, but Khargeh Oasis is just across town."

Jenny tried to smile at his joke, but Neville saw her shiver, her gaze fixed on the distant landmark.

"It seems to be watching us, doesn't it?" she whispered.

Neville turned involuntarily to look. Across the reddened sands the massive clump of rock returned his gaze with one that had watched since long before the time of the pharaohs. Its perspective seemed older than Egypt, older even than the gods.

Riskali

EARLY THE next morning, Eddie and Neville took the *Mallard*'s lighter to shore. Eddie had wanted Neville to remain behind, but Neville insisted on going.

"We're going to have to go ashore sooner or later," he said. "I promise not to cause you any trouble. I'll speak only English, and act dumb as a post."

Eddie hesitated.

"Despite what I told Jenny, I'm not comfortable drawing too much attention to ourselves, even here."

"The camels," Neville insisted, "will have drawn attention."

Eddie surrendered. "Very well."

As they drew closer to the village, it became evident that it was unremarkable, even for an Egyptian peasant village. The houses were roughly rectangular structures built from mud brick, brightened here and there with a bit of painted woodwork or a curtain. Goats and semi-feral dogs roamed the twisting alleyways that passed as streets, and the mosque was distinguished only by being slightly taller than the other structures.

The fields surrounding the village were adequately tended, but did not show any great ambition in their planting. The irrigation ditches were minimal. Only a few shaduf were spaced along the banks; apparently, the villagers were willing to settle mostly for what the Nile gave them. This morning, even the shaduf were idle; the men who should have been tending them stood along the riverbank, gaping at the dahabeeyah.

Almost as soon as the lighter bumped against the bank, an elderly man in surprisingly spotless white robes came striding out of one of the largest houses. His aura of confidence and the retinue that trailed him marked him as the village headman. In an isolated place like this, he was probably the religious as well as the civil leader. He might pay token heed to the national government and the regional governors, but doubtless the fact that he knew that, from a practical standpoint, his rule was absolute, accounted for his haughty demeanor.

Eddie and Neville stepped ashore, warning the sailors to be ready to depart at a moment's notice. Then they turned to face the headman.

He greeted them in formal Arabic, and Eddie replied with the same, his own words flawlessly mimicking the dialect of the region. The old man raised a bushy white eyebrow in surprise, but otherwise did not comment.

"I am Riskali ben Ali," he said, "headman here."

"I am Ibrahim Alhadj ben Josef," replied Eddie, stressing the 'alhadj' just slightly.

Riskali was appropriately impressed. Although all good Mohammedans were enjoined to make the pilgrimage to Mecca, in such an isolated place as this, few would have actually achieved that goal.

"You are with the dahabeeyah?"

"The dahabeeyah is with me," Eddie replied. "I am seeking my friend Daud who was to meet me here."

Riskali's expression became guarded. "Daud? Let me think."

Eddie did not move. Neville knew that the natives had become conditioned to expect an extensive series of gifts—bribes, really—from any Europeans. Eddie was doing his best to convince the headman to accept him as another son of Islam. This would not make him immune from the need to offer gifts, but it would mean that the villagers would need to honor any agreements they made with him.

Fleetingly, Neville regretted forcing himself on Eddie. Then he dismissed the thought. The presence of Europeans aboard the *Mallard* could not have been concealed, and his deferring to Eddie, no matter how subtly, would give weight to the other man's claim to be the master of the expedition.

After several moments during which the flies buzzed counterpoint to the silence, Riskali sighed gustily.

"I cannot think of anyone by that name," he said.

This was an invitation to jog the headman's memory with a coin. Judging from the excited shuffling of some of the younger members of the retinue, they knew this as well. What had begun as a simple exchange of information was now revealed as a contest of wills.

Eddie did not look as if he would be the one to give way, but the deadlock was broken by the emergence from one of the huts of a lanky Arab with a short beard. He wore expensive robes of elegant cut that made the snowy whiteness of the headman's robes seem merely over-bleached.

"Oh, *that* Daud," the headman said dismissively. "I thought you were seeking someone important."

Daud waved cheerfully and made his way to the riverbank. Feigning indifference, the headman led his contingent toward a cluster of palms near the center of the village.

"Let's not seem too friendly, old chap," Daud whispered in cultured Oxford English. "The old man has heard tales of the wealth—relatively speaking—that the villages down river are raking in, and he has decided that he deserves his share."

"Has Riskali made things difficult for you?" Eddie asked, bowing formally, so that the watchers would think they were merely exchanging greetings.

"Yes and no," Daud agreed, bowing in return. "I have the camels you requested, along with saddles and such, but I don't think Riskali intends to let them leave the village. He's a farmer, but canny enough to know that good camels will fetch a pretty price in Luxor."

Eddie nodded. "A bit unethical, isn't he? Where are the camels now?"

"I have them around the west side of the village," Daud said. "Let me show you."

All through this exchange they had ignored Neville as if he wasn't there. Now he trailed them as they walked through to village center, still apparently ignored.

Half-feral dogs barked at them as they passed. One, more daring than the rest, darted out and nipped at Eddie's heel. Without looking, he kicked back and the cur ran, yelping. Children ran after them as well, blending in with the dogs, whining for baksheesh.

Daud tossed them a few coins, and they dropped back, squabbling after the largess.

"It does offer such a problem," he said. "Just like in the cities, some of these lazy beggars have turned the Prophet's admonition to be charitable to the poor into *carte blanche* to harass strangers. If you give too little, you are in violation of Islam. If you give too much, you invite robbery. I fear I took pity on them soon af-ter I arrived, and added to the headman's greed."

Eddie reached into a pocket within his sleeve and pulled out a bundle of can-died dates. He stopped long enough to give these to the children, who were much more pleased by this kindness than they were by coins that their parents would take from them.

"A stopgap I use in Cairo," Eddie explained. "It makes the children happy, and keeps their parents guessing."

"I suppose I was too long in England," Daud said, Oxford intonations so per-fect that if Neville closed his eyes he could believe himself in that university city. "After guarding my life and purse from the sharp knife of Riskali's envy, I won't easily forget again."

Their deliberate progress had brought them beyond the tended fields, to where Daud had pegged the camels. There were six, each solemnly masticating the prickly grass growing in clumps from the sand. When the three men approached, the camels raised their heads and glared down at them from beneath long lashes.

"You've a lovely group here," Eddie said, stroking one female along her shoul-der and dodging the wad of green slime she spat in his direction. "No wonder Headman Riskali covets them enough to set aside all provisions against theft from another of the Faithful."

Daud smiled and prodded the nearest camel.

"Pretend to be examining them," he said, including Neville in his directions. "The villagers are too busy seeming indifferent to come close now, but no reason to give them cause to wonder what we're talking about."

Eddie cocked an eyebrow, but obeyed, making a great point of checking one of his slime-spitting acquaintance's big, two-toed front feet. Neville endeavored to look both inexperienced and nervous, neither of which was hard to do. He rode a camel well enough, but was no great expert—and the villagers, whose dark eyes he fancied he could feel watching them, made him very nervous indeed.

Daud pulled a camel's head down and made a great show of displaying its teeth for inspection.

"The villagers welcomed me warmly enough when I first arrived," Daud said, "but when Riskali saw that I could not be bullied out of giving him at least one of the beasts, my welcome grew a bit cold. Good thing I brought a few fellows with me, or you might find no trace of either me or the camels."

"Where are your men?" Eddie asked.

"Near the shore," Daud replied. "When I saw the dahabeeyah coming in, I decided we'd better be ready to flag you down if the headman decided to refuse you landing. My chaps will be out here soon enough. I don't suppose your captain would give us a lift, would he?"

"I'm sure he'd be glad to," Eddie replied.

"Allah bless you," Daud said. "Now, not to make too fine a point of it, but how do you plan to get those camels away from the villagers?"

"I'm thinking about it," Eddie promised. "Do you think the headman and some of his retinue would deign to dine with us on the *Mallard*?"

"Eagerly," Daud said. "It will be the social event of the year—if not the decade."

"Can you get your gear and your men aboard?" Eddie asked.

"Easily," Daud replied. "We don't have much. If anyone gives us trouble, I'll just explain that I have business with you. The villagers aren't much interested in our camping gear. What they want are those camels. The rest would be gravy."

Eddie stepped back and rubbed his hands together. His satisfied smile might have been for the camels. Then again, it might not.

"Very good. Let me go and extend our invitations. We will precede you aboard, and let Reis Awad know what to expect. Oh, and make certain you bring the camels' saddlebags along. Where are the saddles?"

"In the house you saw me come out of," Daud answered. "The old woman who lives there doesn't get along with the headman, but is too venerable or some such thing for him to get rid of her."

"Think she'll let us take them?"

"If it meant putting a finger in Riskali's eye, I think she'd carry them herself."

They parted on that cheerful note. Riskali was very pleased to accept Eddie's invitation—in which, Neville noted, he was very careful to include several of the tough-looking young bucks, as well as the distinguished greybeards. The villagers saw the visitors off with a great deal more warmth than they had greeted them.

When they were rowing back to the *Mallard*, Neville asked, "Are you going to let me in on your plans?"

"I'm still putting them together," Eddie said. "As soon as I know what I'm doing, you'll know."

Jenny and Stephen were enthralled by the report Neville brought back, and immediately started speculating on how Eddie intended to claim the camels.

Reis Awad agreed that a banquet could be put together for that evening. The higher-ranking men would dine in the saloon, while the younger would be hosted on the crew deck. Eddie took several sailors to the village to buy or borrow supplies—including pillows and rugs on which to seat their guests, for the banquet was to be held native fashion. Riskali agreed to slaughter a sheep, no doubt chuckling up his sleeve at being paid to kill an animal he himself would be eating.

When he returned, Eddie briefed the others about his plan.

"Now, even if we're careful," he said, "this is going to be risky."

His auditors nodded, excited, rather than intimidated by the possibility of adventure. The voyage from Cairo had been long and peaceful enough to ameliorate memories of that terrifying night when the jackal-masked assassins had attacked. They all longed for a challenge.

"My plan," Eddie said, "is for us to take the camels from right under their noses while they are banqueting with us on the *Mallard.*"

"Won't they miss us?" Stephen asked.

"They would miss *us,*" Eddie replied, "but they won't miss Jenny."

"Jenny?" Neville and Stephen were both appalled, but Jenny was thrilled. She remembered the tale of how Eddie had fallen in love with Miriam when that woman was young and brave, and she suspected she owed a great deal to Miriam's example.

Eddie silenced the men's objections with a gesture.

"We don't have much choice. The villagers have had ample opportunity to see us. If any of our party failed to appear at the banquet, it could be taken as a slight. I don't trust Riskali enough to believe that he wouldn't take an imagined insult as an excuse for banditry. I have every confidence in the ability of Reis Awad and his crew—augmented by ourselves—to win the day. However, I prefer to avoid the sort of conflict that might make our eventual departure impossible."

Reluctantly, Stephen and Neville nodded their acceptance of this logic. Jenny had the good sense not to gloat.

"I suppose I'm exempted from this banquet," Jenny said, "because I'm a woman, and our Islamic guests would be insulted if they were asked to dine with a woman?"

"Again," Eddie said, "many Mohammedan men make exceptions for European women, but I would not put it past Riskali . . ."

"To take imagined insult as an excuse for banditry," Neville finished. He looked rather sour, but Jenny didn't blame him.

"Since Jenny will not be expected to attend the dinner," Eddie went on, "she will be able to go ashore, go around the village to where the camels are pegged, and saddle them up. She can lead them slightly south, and we will meet her there."

Uncle Neville frowned. "I will admit that Jenny has shown herself capable, but that's a great deal to ask from one person—female or not."

Eddie nodded. "I have spoken with Reis Awad. Two of his men are very good with camels, and they will accompany her. Our invitation should have pulled the best of the village's men away. Jenny and the sailors may need to deal with a few boys or some young men—if there is any guard posted at all."

"And why should there be?" Jenny said, stroking Mozelle, who slept in contorted comfort on her lap. "Daud will be aboard, as will his two men. The villagers don't know the sailors, so they won't know that two are missing."

"That is my precise hope," Eddie said. "I spoke with the old woman Daud befriended, and there will be no trouble about the saddles."

"Will I need to get the rest of our gear ashore?" Jenny asked.

"Most of it," Eddie admitted. "When Daud comes aboard with the saddlebags, we'll need to transfer necessary gear to them and have them ready in the lighter."

Neville straightened. "Wait. Why does Jenny need to go ashore at all? Why can't the sailors handle everything?"

"I considered that," Eddie said, "but Reis Awad could only spare two men, and three sets of hands would make things much easier. Also, Jenny can represent you as the owner of the camels. If this becomes a court matter, our position will be stronger for that. Sadly, the law looks differently upon the actions of Europeans and of Arabs."

"I understand," Stephen said. "Otherwise it's just the sailor's word against that of the villagers that the sailors were fetching the camels."

Neville didn't look pleased, but he accepted the truth in Eddie's statement. Eddie's plan was simple, direct—and, most importantly, was already underway. Jenny wondered if that was why Eddie had waited to brief them. It did rather eliminate argument.

"I have one addition to suggest," Jenny said. "In Cairo I laid in a rather large supply of powdered opium—I thought we might need it if someone were injured. If the cook makes one of his spectacular curried dishes as part of the feast, then enough opium could be added to make certain our guests are less alert than they otherwise might be."

"We don't want them falling asleep!" Stephen protested. "Or us," he added as an afterthought.

"Our people can avoid eating much of that dish," Jenny said. "In any case, I was not suggesting enough to knock anyone out, just enough to make our guests a little slow."

"It's an idea," Eddie said. "Brief me on how much does what, and I'll see what can be done."

The scents of chopped onions and garlic, of roasting and stewing mutton, of baking flat bread, and other such culinary preparations, were heavy on the air when Reis Awad sent the lighter to begin ferrying the guests aboard. The first load brought aboard Riskali and a husky, rather villainous-looking young man Riskali introduced as his youngest son. More sons came aboard on the next trip, and nephews and cousins on the later. Daud and his assistants were last, crowded in with a low-ranking nephew who was hardly showing his first beard. Clearly the village was all one extended family, and Riskali was the acknowledged patriarch.

Eddie welcomed all of their guests in Arabic. He had cautioned Stephen and Neville to keep their knowledge of the language to themselves, and in keeping with his representation that he was the master of this expedition, made Reis Awad his co-host, relegating the Englishmen to a secondary role. Neville and Stephen took their demotion well, restricting themselves to greetings in stilted Arabic that would have done credit to a music hall performance.

The meal's main component was a plentitude of greasy mutton. Whether roasted or stewed, the villagers ate it without utensils—other than the wickedly sharp knives they wore at their belts and used for hacking a chunk of meat into a more convenient size. Eddie ate in the same fashion, wiping his hand—for like a good Mohammedan he ate only using his right hand—on the hem of his robe. Neville followed suit, but Stephen could not bring himself to eat in that fashion, and had cutlery and a plate brought from the galley.

The villagers thought this quite funny, and made a variety of crude jokes at Stephen's expense. Although the young linguist managed to act as if he didn't understand, and that he thought their laughter good-humored, his fair skin flushed with anger.

"Easy, old chap," Daud cautioned him in English, keeping his tone light. "We don't want to make them angry enough to leave. Remember Miss Benet and the risks she is taking."

Stephen nodded, then something of a manic gleam came into his eyes.

"If they think I am such a fop and clown, then I shall provide them with ample amusement." He clapped his hands to summon one of the cook's assistants. "I want a finger bowl with lemon water, two clean napkins, a candle in one of the silver holders, and the low table that is on the upper deck."

The assistant complied, clearly thinking that the Englishman had gone mad. When he returned with the requested materials, Stephen set himself a neat table. With a flourish, he tied one of the clean napkins about his neck and set the other by his left hand. Helping himself to roasted mutton, bread, and rice, he continued with his meal.

Riskali was torn between fascination and appalled curiosity, "What does the man do? Why does he go to such trouble to eat?"

Eddie, who understood precisely what Stephen was doing, shrugged incomprehension.

"Many English customs are strange. They eat their meals with many small tools when a good knife and spoon is enough. In some houses where I have been a guest, they use one fork for the salad, another for the meal, and still another for dessert. They use different knives as well—short, blunt ones for putting butter on bread, sharp ones for cutting meat, and long blunt ones for cutting vegetables or fruit."

The villagers roared amused appreciation of this description.

"If they need all of those blunt knives," Riskali's youngest son gasped between gusts of laughter, "they must be very clumsy and fear cutting themselves."

Similar jokes followed, and Eddie continued to spin tales—all completely true, but with the details exaggerated—that exploited the difference between the urbanized Britisher and the Egyptian fellahin. Daud occasionally contributed, but mostly he kept his silence, willing the villagers to forget both him and the camels.

For her part, Jenny had eaten earlier, and was now double-checking the saddlebags. Her own and Uncle Neville's offered no surprises, but she had to set aside any number of Stephen's books, the weight of which would have been an unnecessary burden to the camels.

With the noise of the banquet in her ears, she and her two assistants loaded the lighter, which was tied to the stern of the dahabeeyah, as far as possible from their guests. Then they rowed quietly for the shore.

Jenny knew that this was one of the two most dangerous moments in the whole venture. If any of the villagers—either on shore or aboard the *Mallard*—noticed their departure, any hope of carrying this off would be ended. Kneeling in the bow, she looked back, holding her breath, waiting for a cry of alarm. All that came was a burst of rowdy laughter and a strain of music as the sailor/musicians prepared to perform.

Her own sailors let the small boat drift downstream. Then, when a clump of reeds growing from a sandbar gave them some concealment, they paddled ashore, heading for an inlet that Eddie had scouted out earlier.

Once the boat pulled clear of the drag of the Nile's current, they unloaded the saddlebags. The larger of the men carried two. Jenny struggled a bit under the weight of her own, too aware of the tenuous nature of her command to ask for help. The second man took only a single saddlebag, and moved ahead to scout.

The night was cool, so most of those villagers who had gathered on the river-bank to enviously gaze at what they could glimpse of the festivities had already re-tired to sleep. Those who remained were huddled under rugs with attention for nothing but the light, laughter, and good smells drifting from the *Mallard*.

A few dogs growled as the three passed the outskirts of the village, but per-haps the slaughtering of sheep, ducks, and chickens earlier had sated even them, for they did not bother to challenge—or perhaps they had learned the wisdom of staying away from those who moved with confidence in the darkness.

Therefore it was without arousing suspicion that Jenny and her escort made their way to the western edge of the village where the camels were hobbled. A low wall designed to keep the sand from drifting into the fields concealed the kneeling camels from casual observation. However, a flickering fire framed by two huddled figures revealed that Riskali had indeed set guards. Doubtless if asked he would say he had done this for the good of Daud, but Jenny did not doubt his motives were less pure.

The two night-watchmen sat close to the fire, something—probably a coffee pot—between them, their attitude that of complete dejection.

"Fools!" muttered the larger of her two sailors, laying his burden carefully on the ground. "They blind themselves by looking into the fire."

Jenny set down her own saddlebags, and studied their surroundings, noting the position of the camels relative to the watchmen, confirming that there was no roving post. Then she bent and extracted her rifle. Its weight was familiar in her hands as she gestured with it towards the watchmen.

"We don't dare let them make noise," she whispered, "but we don't want to harm them. Can each of you get a hold of one of them so they can't yell, just for long enough for me to 'reason' with them?"

Two sets of teeth gleamed in the moonlight. The Arabs were conservative re-garding the behavior of their own women, but their desire to make a profit meant that they were willing to make an exception for infidels. During the voyage up from Luxor most of Reis Awad's crew had decided that Jenny belonged to her own category—not a boy, but not quite a woman, either.

With careful silence, the two sailors made their way across the sand, the larger circling to where he could grab hold of the farther guard. In a trice the guards found themselves trapped, one arm pinning their knife arms to their bodies, a broad, callused palm over their mouths. For a moment, the watchmen were too surprised to struggle. When they did, they found the contest uneven. Both guards were young men, fellahin farmers, strong enough, but lacking the corded muscles of the two sailors. One or the other might have managed to shout alarm, but even as the struggle began, Jenny walked into the firelight.

She lifted her hunting rifle, the sleek Winchester lines no less deadly for their lack of bulk. The prisoners fell slack immediately, eyes widening in grotesque horror as they realized that the person holding the rifle was a woman.

These were no sophisticated Cairo Arabs, no jaded merchants or sailors. These were fellahin of an isolated village whose only contact with Europeans was to watch the vessels that carried them on their incomprehensible journeys along the Nile. Even the tales told by their more traveled brethren had not lessened their isolation. In a sense it had increased it, for the Europeans had become creatures of legend along with genie, efreet, and sorcerers.

Jenny pointed her rifle at the smaller sailor's captive, and tossed pre-cut sections of rope and a heavy length of cloth at his feet. The message was plain, and the young villager all but tied himself up rather than invoke the wrath of the lithe, deadly figure standing over him. The second fellow, crushed almost breathless within the grasp of the stronger sailor, was even easier to restrain.

The two bound men were propped beside the fire, ragged rugs that had served as cloaks around their shoulders. With luck, they would not be discovered until morning, and their only injuries would be stiff limbs and bruised pride.

The stronger sailor went back to the boat for the rest of the gear, while Jenny followed the other's directions. In good order, they saddled four of the camels and settled the beasts' saddlebags into place. The remaining two were loaded with extra gear and quantities of water.

The camels had rested for several days now, so took the attention in what was for camels good humor. One muttered a sulky protest. Another spat, but overall they accepted being disturbed on a night they had every reason to believe should have been peaceful.

Keeping clear of the fields, Jenny and her sailors took the camels south of the village. The night was still, sound carrying easily through the clear air. For Jenny, who had wintered recently in Boston, the temperature was comfortable, but the two sailors shivered.

It is winter here, after all, Jenny thought with a trace of amusement. *And I'm wearing a whole lot more clothing than they are.*

Once they had reached the agreed upon point, a place where sandstone boulders provided some shelter and an easily spotted landmark, the larger sailor salaamed.

"Our orders are to return to the *Mallard*, bringing the lighter so that others may use it." He frowned. "It goes against my honor to leave a woman—even a Christian Englishwoman—alone in the desert at night."

Jenny smiled reassuringly. "I'm American, not English, and the others will be along soon. In any case, I brought company."

She lifted the flap of her saddlebag and extracted Mozelle. She had taken the precaution of doping the kitten slightly, so it wouldn't mew and attract attention to itself.

The sailors visibly relaxed. Several of the more superstitious members of the crew had attached a great deal of importance to the little animal, going so far as to proclaim that Mozelle was a good luck charm.

"We will go then," the sailor said. "Stay near the camels. Even jackals will be reluctant to trouble so many and so healthy. This close to the Nile they can find easier game."

With a final salaam, one that to Jenny's imagination seemed to include the kitten, they vanished into the darkness.

Jenny looked where they had gone, marking their solid forms until they vanished. She felt reassured. Even by moonlight, they would not likely be seen, and she and the camels would simply be more rocks.

The stars were bright and clear. It seemed to her that even out at sea she had never seen so many. It was like gazing up into a jewel box. She thought of a painting of the goddess Nut they had seen at one of their stops, and understood why the ancient Egyptians had chosen to imagine the sky as a woman with stars adorning her diaphanous gown.

Thinking of Nut made her rummage again in her saddlebags. There were adjustments to be made if she was to spend the night riding a camel, and she would do her companions no favors if she waited for their arrival to make them. Mozelle, coming out from under the drug now, but still sleepy enough not to wander, watched with interest.

After enough time had passed that the moon had visibly shifted in the heavens, Jenny heard noise from the direction of the Nile. At long last, the revelers were being ferried ashore.

She smiled. As good Mohammedans, they did not drink, but they would be logy with rich food. Many would also be logy with the dusting of opium powder Eddie had put over the candied dates that were one of the desserts—one he had learned was a favorite of old Riskali. She doubted that many of the villagers would have foregone the treat.

Much could still go wrong, though—especially if someone went to relieve the unlucky souls who had drawn guard duty. She waited in nervous anticipation, her mouth dry, as noise became silence once more. Then, after a longer wait, she heard the sound of people making their way as quietly as inexperience would permit through the fields.

Just in case, she raised her rifle.

"Jenny," came a soft call, "it's me, Eddie, with the others."

She didn't lower the gun barrel until she confirmed that they were alone. Then she slid it back into the long holster already in place on the camel her sailor/drover had selected for her.

All three men were tense, for getting away unnoticed hadn't been easy.

"The villagers kept trooping from house to house," Stephen said, eyeing his camel with apprehension. "I suppose they were telling their story to everyone who would listen. Finally, we had to try for shore and hope no one would see us."

"And we were worried about you," Neville added, looking up from checking the straps on the baggage camels, "what with all that prowling around."

"I suppose," Jenny said, "no one wanted to remember the two watchmen."

"From what I overheard when the men were coming aboard, I got the impression the ones left behind were in disgrace," Eddie said, "and not including them in the round of visits would have been their final punishment. Ready to get moving, all?"

Jenny indicated the camel already loaded with her gear.

"All right if I take that one? It has my stuff. Mozelle's asleep in one of the side pockets."

Eddie nodded. "I'll take the lead camel. Daud already told me which one she is. The others should follow her out of habit. Now, if either of you tyros have trouble, don't hesitate to let me know. Stephen, you take that one with the white blotch on his shoulder. Neville, you get the other, and ride drag."

The humans followed his orders without question. The camels were a bit more difficult, having been rousted out once already that night, but Eddie had worked with far less tractable beasts than these and knew how to be firm with them. Within minutes of the men's arrival, the party was ready to go.

Risking a quick strike of a match, Eddie oriented himself by his compass.

"We need to proceed west and a touch more south to reach the Hawk Rock. For now, let's head west and put some distance between us and the village—I'd like to ride the rest of the night if you're up to it. We'll camp and refine our course come day."

No one disagreed, for they had discussed this before. Still, Jenny was more tired than she had been when they had designed this plan, and wondered if she could hold up her part. Only the certainty that Stephen had to be feeling the same, and the knowledge that he would be determined to hold up as long as she did, made her keep her doubts to herself.

Before dropping his camel to the end of the line, Uncle Neville rode close to her. He removed a greasy paper packet from his saddlebag and handed it down, following it with a still-warm canteen.

"Mutton sandwich," he said, "and coffee. Thought you could use something after all your hard work. We've plenty more for later, so don't hesitate."

Jenny felt indescribably grateful and tucked the packet into the convenient pouch near her knee so she could reach it after she had adjusted to the camel's motion.

Almost as soon as she had finished, Eddie Bryce gave a command and the camels lurched to their feet.

"Everyone still aboard?" Eddie asked, a chuckle evident beneath his hushed voice. "Good. Hold on now. There's nothing to do but stay aboard and let the camels do the work."

One by one, the camels swung to follow the lead of Eddie's mount: Jenny's, then Stephen's, then the two pack animals, and lastly, Neville's. Ahead there was nothing but sand and darkness. Above, the stars continued to glimmer. In the far distance, a jackal barked, but though Jenny's ear strained, there was no reply.

15

Destruction at the Hawk Rock

THE MORNING sun came up behind them, its rays rippling across the sand dunes as if it was hurrying to catch up with the travelers. Although when surveyed from their comfortable perches on the upper deck of the *Mallard* the desert had appeared nearly as flat as a neatly made bed, the night's travel had revealed that it was more like a sea, full of dips and rises. Somewhere in the night, Riskali's village had been lost to sight.

Eddie took care as the daylight brightened to make certain that they kept to the troughs between the dunes, so that they would not silhouette themselves against the skyline. Although the humans were exhausted, the camels had fallen into a steady, uninterrupted rhythm. Clearly the hours of steady walking through the cool night had meant nothing to them.

After consulting with Neville, Eddie went ahead, looking for a good spot to camp. The best candidate, a sheltered hollow that offered some prickly grass and dubious-looking shrubs for the camels, could only be reached by continuing for a while after sunrise. By the time they had unpacked the gear and erected camel's hair pavilions to keep off the worst of the heat, the sun would be high.

"The sand looks so soft," Stephen said, trying hard to keep a wistful note from his voice.

"A bedroll will be softer," Eddie said, "and you'll be stiff enough come evening without lying on sand. Lend a hand, you fellows, and we'll get the pavilion up. Jenny, start unpacking personal gear from the camels."

Neville thought Stephen had done well enough to deserve praise, not censure—and judging from the sour expression on Stephen's face—the linguist felt the same. However, Neville trusted the former sergeant's instinct for knowing the best way to get the most from a newcomer to the desert, and so did not intervene. Even he felt inclined to protest when Eddie cautioned them to take care with the water.

"I won't ration it, quite yet," Eddie said. "But it may come to that. You can drink, but no washing. Use sand. If your lips are dry, there's a grease ointment in each of your kits."

Neville protested, "Chad Spice's journal mentions finding water both at Hawk Rock and the Valley of Dust. You and I know he was right about the Hawk Rock."

Eddie shook his head, stubbornly refusing to be persuaded.

"We can't trust an ancient journal, nor memories ten years old either. Water holes dry up or get fouled by men or beasts. I'm not counting on finding any water at all, and my guess is that we'll have to turn around to resupply just as soon as we find this Valley of Dust."

Neville glowered at him, but he could see the other man's point, and decided not to argue. He turned away, scowling, and for the first time in daylight got a clear look at Jenny's costume.

Instead of the neat and moderate black frocks she had been wearing since her arrival in England, she now wore loose, canvas-colored trousers and an equally unfitted tan work-shirt. Around her neck she had tied a red bandanna, and on her head she wore a wide-brimmed hat shaped from undyed leather. Her feet were encased in low riding boots of soft leather, decorated with beaded patterns.

This was jarring enough, but the wide, dark-brown belt she wore about her waist bore more than its adornment of hammered silver coins. From it hung two heavy holsters, each showing the butt of an efficient-looking revolver. The belt held a sheath for a long-bladed Bowie knife, obviously intended to do double duty as a tool or weapon.

In peculiar contrast, the kitten Mozelle frolicked around Jenny's feet, balancing on her back legs to bat at the long fringe depending from the base of the saddlebags her mistress had just unstrapped from the nearest camel.

Jenny appeared to feel his gaze on her, for she turned to face him.

"I know it's not mourning, Uncle Neville, but I already had these clothes, and it seemed foolish to wear black out under the sun. I'm sure Mama and Papa will understand."

"I am sure," Neville said, finding his voice with difficulty. "I wasn't thinking about that."

"The trousers?" Jenny asked. "You know Mama permitted me to wear them on the ranch. I thought this was much the same."

Neville shook his head vigorously, as if attempting to dislodge a fly. Off to the side, he was vaguely aware of Eddie and Stephen, who were studiously ignoring the discussion as they began erecting the pavilion.

"The quantity of weaponry you are carrying," he said. "I knew you had packed some in your luggage, but . . ."

Jenny dumped a load of saddlebags near where the pavilion would be, and walked over to the camels to unstrap another.

"I have the rifle, too," she said wearily. "You saw it last night. You know perfectly well I can shoot. We're out here in the desert, possibly being pursued by angry villagers, maybe facing bandits, maybe even those same mysterious Sons of the Hawk who attacked us in Cairo. Why would I keep my knife and guns in my saddlebags?"

Neville frowned, then realized the frown was more for himself than for Jenny. He'd been prepared to order Stephen to keep a weapon close at hand, and Stephen could barely shoot. Jenny was not only capable, she was good. He'd seen her form as they hunted along the Nile.

And in memory, he heard himself debating whether or not the expedition should be armed—only then it had been Alphonse Liebermann who had balked at the need for weapons, while Neville had insisted.

Am I somehow becoming Alphonse, now that I've taken on his venture? Neville thought uneasily.

"Are you prepared, then, to shoot a human being?" he asked, trying not to let Jenny sense his own internal unease. "It's not the same as shooting a duck or gazelle."

Jenny's violet eyes met his straight on. "If that human being was about to harm any one of us, I'd feel worse about shooting the duck. It, at least, would have done nothing to deserve a bullet."

The measured brutality of her answer left Neville feeling chilled. Then he remembered Alice and Pierre, dead not from accident or sickness, but from the deliberate calculation of human beings, and thought he understood.

Understanding didn't make him the least bit more comfortable, but it stilled his tongue, and he turned without further comment to help erect their shelter against the innocent ferocity of the rising sun.

Jenny was relieved when Uncle Neville didn't press the point about her clothes or weapons. The fact was, she wasn't going to go unarmed—not out here, not with that certainty she felt that they hadn't seen the last of the Protectors of the Pharaoh.

She'd planned on appealing to Eddie Bryce if necessary. She thought he'd be practical rather than proper—but she was glad not to need to do it. Uncle Neville might not believe it, but she didn't much like arguing with him. He was all the family she had left, and with increased familiarity she saw her lost mother in him. The lines were toughened and masculine, but the kinship was indisputable.

Stephen was probably more shocked than Uncle Neville had been, since he'd never seen anything but her hunting rifle and derringer (that last now tucked in her under-bodice as a weapon of last resort). Jenny doubted he'd ever seen a woman in trousers, either, but figured he was woman-ridden enough to know better than to comment on a woman's choice of attire—at least when there was another man around who'd already drawn the unhappy responsibility for that honor.

They dined lightly on cold roast mutton, flat bread, and onions, Jenny giving some of her share to Mozelle, whose needle sharp fangs reminded her whenever she doled out the shredded meat too slowly.

"I wonder," she said drowsily, "if Mozelle's too young for such fare."

Stephen stopped unlacing his boots long enough to glance over where the kitten now slept, belly visibly rounded.

"I don't know," he said, "I don't think she'd be so cat-atonic, if she didn't think it purr-fectly fine."

Jenny tossed one of her own soft-sided boots at him.

"Nice," he said, handing it back. "Indian work?"

"Apache," Jenny replied. "Hardened sole but softer sides, fastens by wrapping the lace around a button, easier than lacing and unlacing."

Stephen was obviously feeling his way to another pun, when Eddie interrupted.

"I'll take the first watch, since I'm most adjusted to this climate. I'd considered taking one of the village dogs along to help, but I couldn't figure out how to make it keep quiet while we were getting away." He grinned, "Not to mention, Jenny's kitty-cat might have had a problem with it."

Jenny, stretched out on her bedroll now, boots placed where she could reach them, the tops folded over to keep out scorpions and other night creatures, stuck her tongue out at him.

"Wake me next if you want, Eddie," she said around a yawn. "I got plenty of practice sleeping in little bites when I was training with Papa."

Bryce nodded. "Fine. You next, then you wake your uncle, and Stephen will take last. We'll get moving again soon after dark, so Stephen, it'll be your job to wake the lazy bones."

"Right," Stephen said. "Do you know how to find the Hawk Rock without light?"

"I took compass readings," Eddie reassured him, "but in general, we should be able to keep on course by the stars."

Stephen chuckled, the over-tired laugh of one who is starting to find anything humorous. "We're the three kings, following the stars. Eddie, you'll have to be one of the camels or we'll have too many and Jenny'll shoot us if we say she's just a queen."

"Go to sleep, Stephen," Eddie advised kindly.

Jenny fell asleep quickly, but dreamed of jackal-headed sphinxes that wrote her notes in her father's elegant French hand, of women dressed in trousers and stars, and of camels that spat tea. She was distinctly relieved when Eddie woke her.

"Nothing moving," he said. "Except your kitten. I think she's hungry again."

Jenny nodded, tried to rise, discovered her muscles were protesting the long night of camel-riding, and raised herself more carefully. Eddie offered no support or coddling, but went immediately to his own bedroll. She thought she should be more flattered.

To keep herself from stiffening further, Jenny paced under the shaded edges of the pavilion. The sand outside was blindingly hot, so she was glad for her smoked glasses. Periodically, she checked back along the way they had come, but the desert remained empty; even the tracks of their passage were blurring as the sand shifted beneath a gentle wind.

Deeper into the desert, the Hawk Rock bulked large in the bright light, an island surrounded by endless seas of golden sand. She wondered if they would reach it tonight, but could acquire no sense of distance in the trackless waste. She remembered, though, that there had been plants growing on the rock when Uncle Neville had been there before. They were still far enough that the only hints of green might simply have been the natural discoloration of the rock.

Eventually, she woke Uncle Neville, and dropped back onto her bedroll. She was aware of Mozelle curling up beside her, then of Stephen gently shaking her shoulder.

"It's dusk," he said. "Eddie's getting the camels ready."

Rising on legs she thought didn't feel quite as stiff as they had earlier, Jenny discovered that Stephen had taken the initiative to make a small fire and a pot of tea. They all so evidently needed the stimulant that Eddie said nothing about the unauthorized use of water, but Jenny could tell from how he looked between the pot and the nearest water bag that he was estimating just how much had been lost to evaporation.

Breakfast was smoked fish and flat bread for all but Mozelle, who had—more by accident than skill—caught an unwary jerboa. Jenny took pity on the kitten's tiny teeth and slit the mouse-like rodent open with her Bowie knife. Growling with almost comic ferocity, the kitten dined on her kill.

They mounted the camels as the westering sun was reddening the sands, and the stars were spilling out against the darkening blue-black. The sunset contained none of the spectacular colors Jenny had seen elsewhere. There was simply not enough moisture in the air.

With the setting sun behind it, the Hawk Rock bulked blacker and more solid than the darkness, which nonetheless eventually swallowed it into itself.

After another full night of travel, they still had not reached the Hawk Rock, but when the sun rose their destination was close enough that they could better appreciate its stark majesty.

"I'll look ahead for a campsite," Eddie said.

"Can't we just go on?" Stephen asked—rather bravely, Jenny thought, for she had seen him limping earlier.

"Be better to rest," Eddie said.

"But it's so close," Stephen protested. "We could arrive in a few hours, and be ready to start exploring come evening."

"I doubt you'd see much with sun-blinded eyes," Eddie said dryly. "This time of year, light rather than heat is what makes the desert dangerous—light, and dryness that sucks the moisture from you without your knowing. It'll get hot enough, though, when the sand starts throwing the heat back at you. Take my advice and sleep out the worst of the day. We'll be there soon enough, and gone again, too. You forget, this isn't the end of the journey."

Stephen sighed. "It's so close."

"May seem so," Eddie said, "but I suspect it's farther than you believe."

As they settled in for the day's rest, Jenny thought about what an interesting traveling companion Eddie was proving to be. On the journey up the Nile he had proved a good tour guide and superlative dragoman, making arrangements that anticipated every contingency. However, she had never realized what a devoted follower of Islam he was until they had struck out into the desert.

Five times a day at the appointed hours he stopped whatever he was doing and unrolled a small prayer rug that had been woven for him by Miriam. Positioning himself so he was facing Mecca, he recited the appropriate prayers in flawless, sing-song Arabic, completely unlike his usual country English accents.

Jenny, who had woken to take her turn on guard, watched with interest.

"You're serious about that, aren't you?" she asked. That night's journey hadn't been as stressful as the previous night's determined escape, and her normal curiosity was resurfacing—and anything that would stop her from thinking about the Hawk Rock and what might wait for them there or beyond was very welcome.

Eddie finished rolling his prayer rug away and smiled.

"Yes, I am. I converted so I would be permitted to marry Miriam, but somewhere along the way the Prophet's teachings started making more and more sense."

"Aren't there some pretty odd restrictions you have to follow," Jenny asked, "like converting all unbelievers or something?"

Eddie smiled. "I'm not saying that all of it makes sense, any more than some of Jesus's more extreme pronouncements made sense. How many of you would 'turn the other cheek' if challenged?"

Jenny, who had been carefully cleaning sand from her rifle, grinned ruefully.

"I think many Christians try to follow the spirit if not letter of Jesus's teachings," she protested.

Eddie chuckled. "That must be why so many Christian nations maintain flourishing militaries, and why there is not a city in Europe without some form of law enforcement."

"Those are hardly fair examples," Jenny protested. "Nations have the right—the duty, even—to protect their citizens from those who would break the social contract."

"I didn't say they didn't, Miss Paine," Eddie replied. "I was just pointing out that Christianity has its share of extreme pronouncements that the majority of Christians are willing to overlook."

"Touché," Jenny agreed, grinning as she realized the martial import of her own choice of words. "For example, I'm not willing to sell all I have and give the money to the poor just to be a good Christian. I rather like traveling in style with Uncle Neville."

"Don't worry about that," Eddie said, moving toward his bedroll. "I don't think the churches are willing to try that one either, whether they are Christian or Islamic."

Stephen's voice broke in, almost shyly, and he sat up rumpled on his bedroll,

"What about the provision that lets you have more than one wife? Would you take a second wife if you could afford her?"

Eddie shook his head. "I don't think I would, even if I could find another father as willing as Miriam's was to accept an Englishman as a suitor for his daughter. I won't say the idea hasn't crossed my mind when I've seen a pretty girl, but . . ."

"I don't think it's a very fair system for the women," Jenny interjected, amazed to hear herself sounding angry.

"Some women claim to like it," Eddie said evenly, "or so Miriam says. She says that they say there is always someone to share the work and care for the children. I really couldn't say, not from experience. I think I'm too British to be comfortable with more than one wife—though now that I think of it, I've known many a British military man who has managed the equivalent. They've had a wife at home, and a woman with whom they live abroad."

Stephen coughed. "Do you think that is an appropriate topic to mention in a lady's hearing?"

"You raised the matter," Eddie said.

Jenny laughed. "Stephen, I don't know whether to kiss you for thinking me a lady or to kick you for thinking me a moron who's never seen the world." She paused. "I don't think I'll do either. It's too hot to risk making you blush."

Stephen said hurriedly, "Eddie, don't you miss a good pork chop or a glass of fine wine?"

"I did at first," the other admitted, "but not anymore. Still, I'm not saying that if we were out here starving and the only thing between me and death was a haunch of wild pig, I'd starve rather than disobey a dietary provision. Now hush up, you two, I'm not as young as you and I need my sleep."

Stephen snorted something that was probably disbelief that Eddie ever got tired, and lay down again. After a while, Jenny heard their breathing quiet and regularize. She was half-drowsing herself when the sound of Mozelle alternately hissing and growling brought her alert again.

The kitten was backing away from something in the sand, spitting and waving one paw. Her tail was bristled and her back arched in a fashion that should have been ridiculous in one so small, but Jenny felt anything but amused. Rising, she saw that the kitten's foe was a large scorpion.

Scooping Mozelle up in one hand, and ignoring the kitten's wriggling protests, Jenny brought the butt of her rifle down repeatedly on the arachnid's shell, watching the tail curve up and over its back as it stabbed ineffectually at the polished wood. Only when it stopped moving completely did she stop and set Mozelle down.

The kitten sniffed once, then contemptuously scratched sand over its foe.

When she woke Stephen for his watch—Uncle Neville had asked for the last watch so he could start packing the camels—she showed him the dead scorpion.

"Ever seen one before?"

"Not that large," Stephen said, poking the corpse in fascination. "They're poisonous, aren't they?"

"Very. Some can kill you; others just make you wish you'd died. They're one of the myriad creeping and crawling reasons Eddie keeps reminding us to shake out our boots and bedding."

Stephen continued inspecting the dead scorpion, flipping it over with a twig to get a better look at its pincers and curving tail.

"It looks rather like a crab of some sort," he observed, "or maybe a spider. I bet the ancient Egyptians didn't like them any more than we do, yet in their cosmology they made them into wardens of the dead, and associated them with beloved goddesses like Isis and Selket. For all that, the ancient Egyptians are dust while the scorpion flourishes. There's a moral in that somewhere."

"Shake out your bedding and check your boots," Jenny suggested, following words with actions. "See you in a few hours."

Neville had been aware of the various conversations that had interrupted the day's rest, but had refused to take part in any of them. When he woke, it would be time to head for the Hawk Rock. Stubbornly, like a child waiting for Christmas morning, he pretended to sleep.

Sometimes he fooled even himself, but when Stephen woke him, he felt as if he'd already been awake for hours.

"Rest a while," Neville advised the younger man. "I'm going to need your mind sharp and clear when we reach the Hawk Rock."

"Why are we even going there?" Stephen asked. "Didn't you and Alphonse Liebermann already find what we'll need?"

"There may be something more," Neville replied. "As you may recall, Alphonse and I left somewhat abruptly. Even if there isn't, we can refill our water."

Stephen licked his lips as he settled back.

"Right. I'd like to be wet behind the ears in more ways than one."

As evening began to bring some relief from the glaring sunlight, Eddie awoke. After tending to his personal needs, he came to help Neville re-pack the camels. By the time the sun was low but the light not yet gone, they were ready.

There was no need to awaken Stephen and Jenny, nor to ask why they were awake before it was necessary. There was very little conversation as they readied themselves to depart, only orders from Eddie on matters of routine, and a few commands to the camels.

To Neville, it seemed the light took longer than usual to fade that night, for his gaze remained so fixed on the looming presence of the Hawk Rock that he felt he could see it even after reason told him it must have faded into the darkness.

Now that they were closer, Eddie struck a match occasionally, checking their course against his compass. After they had been underway some hours in full darkness, Neville was aware of a change in his camel's bearing.

He commented on this to Eddie, who said laconically, "Scented water or grass, I'd guess. Doesn't feel like nerves to me."

It was still night when the bulk of the Hawk Rock began blocking out the stars. Eddie guided them around to the little canyon where the Liebermann expedition had camped a decade before. The opening was there, and Neville's dread that a landslide or rockfall might have blocked or otherwise altered it vanished.

The canyon itself didn't seem much changed, at least from what he could tell by lantern light. They didn't bother erecting the pavilion, just unpacked the bare necessities and settled themselves to wait for dawn.

"Try to sleep," Eddie advised, and though everyone answered that they would, Neville thought that only Eddie himself would get more than a catnap.

Dawn came at last, a gentle herald to what would be another day of unremitting brilliant light and reflected heat. They welcomed it as if the sun truly were the boat of Ra, bringing the god safely once more from his dangerous journey through the dark reaches of night.

"I suppose," Eddie said, resignation in every line of his face, "that all of you can't wait to hurry up and see if the obelisk is still there."

Neville was too embarrassed to speak. Ever since the first hints of dawn had touched the canyon he'd been looking to see if the trail he and Alphonse had followed was still there. The fact that he knew it couldn't be clearly seen from this canyon had not kept him from trying.

Stephen looked equally uncomfortable, but Jenny spoke easily.

"I'll stay here and start setting up camp," she said. "I can't read hieroglyphs nearly as well as the rest of you, and we'll be glad for shelter when the sun is higher."

Eddie rewarded her good sense with a warm smile before turning to the others.

"I'll stay with Jenny and set up camp," he said. "You two can combine searching for the obelisk with seeing if that spring is still active. I seem to recall that water could be lowered from above, and it would be nice to have a wash."

"And a shave," Stephen agreed.

His blond beard wasn't heavy, but several days of golden stubble marred the line of his side-whiskers. Neville rubbed a hand along his own jaw, feeling the rasping roughness with something like surprise. He must be obsessed. He hadn't even noticed the itchy new growth until this very moment.

Gathering several collapsible buckets, a hunting rifle, and some lengths of rope, Neville led his similarly burdened assistant toward where the base of the trail had been. Like the canyon, it remained little changed. Some rocks had shifted. There were shrubs where there had been none, and none where he recalled some, but otherwise it was as it had been: a steep, pebble-strewn trail, unfit for camels and hardly fit for goats.

Neville took the lead and soon became glad for the rope. Stephen proved as clumsy of foot as he was agile with his tongue. He was game, though, grasping the line Neville strung from the base of a sturdy shrub and using it to help himself over the worst sections of the trail.

"Good thing," Stephen gasped when at last they reached a more level section, "that Eddie insisted on bringing extra pairs of heavy gloves. This pair is going to need some mending."

Neville nodded, hardly hearing him.

The meadow or vale seemed rather more overgrown than he recalled, but was recognizably the same place. He cast around, and spotted the telltale lushness that marked the location of the spring.

It, at least, had changed. When he had last seen it, it had been little more than a drip, but now someone had opened the flow to a trickle. Flat rocks had been set to direct the channel into a tiny basin that held a double handful of water. Neville drank, and found it cool and sweet.

"This is different," he said, explaining the changes to Stephen.

"Different," the other agreed, bending to inspect the basin, "but I don't think recent. The stone has had time to discolor where the water habitually pools, and along the edge where it runs over."

Neville nodded. "Even so, it is evidence that someone has been here, has stayed here, sometime in these last ten years."

Stephen didn't seem much impressed. He hardly attended even to the water, his gaze darting around the overgrown vale. His eagerness to locate the obelisk was obvious, as was his awareness that, unlike Alphonse Liebermann that first time, he was not the patron of the expedition and couldn't rush off without leave.

"Remember," Neville said, balancing one of the buckets beneath the point where the basin overflowed, "that water will have attracted all sorts of creatures. There will be snakes here, as well as scorpions and spiders."

"Yes, sir."

Neville rose, certain his knees hadn't creaked this much ten years ago.

"The obelisk was over there," he said. "Follow me."

Cutting away the thorny growth, they located the obelisk easily enough, but what they found was not what they sought.

The tapering stone column had been broken into numerous jagged-edged pieces, the stone from which it had been carved pounded until only fragments of the hieroglyphic writing remained.

Stephen bent and picked up one of the larger chunks of stone.

"New Kingdom," he said, his voice struggling to remain matter-of-fact, "as I believe you deduced last time."

Neville stared at the wreckage, toeing over a few pieces as if expecting to find the intact monument beneath.

"This is recent," he stated.

"But not too recent," Stephen countered. "We had to cut through the thorn bushes to get to it, and I believe desert plants grow slowly, even where there is some water."

Neville nodded.

"Was this done immediately after Alphonse and I were here?" he asked. "The obelisk had been left fallen but undamaged since the New Kingdom . . ."

"Or at least since the time of a scribe who wrote in that fashion," Stephen said pedantically.

"Why destroy it now?"

Stephen tossed his broken piece of stone to the ground, looking far more mature than he usually did, "Because whoever did this hoped that you had not had time to copy the inscription. Without it, you would have no idea how to reach the Valley of Dust. Even with it, we're taking a gamble."

Neville nodded.

"So it could have been done soon after we were chased away," he said, "and the spring modified at the same time."

Stephen pulled back a few bits of shrub, inspecting the rock wall for other writing.

"It does make Miriam's story about the Protectors all the more believable," he said. "I wonder if it was her grandfather's tribe who drove you away then. Did she seem to recognize anyone?"

"No," Neville said, "but her brother or father may have done so."

"Makes you wonder," Stephen went on, "who exactly was the mysterious woman who delivered Chad Spice's journal to Alphonse Liebermann that long time ago. Could it have been another disaffected female of that tribe, someone else who didn't like their children being taken away as Miriam's father didn't like it?"

"It is possible," Neville admitted. "That bucket should be about filled. Let me change it for an empty one. Then I'll check if the place we lowered water from before is still there. You can look for any inscriptions we might have missed. Be careful..."

"I know," Stephen said, "there are ghoulies and ghosties and, especially, long-legged beasties."

"I just hope," Neville added with a faint attempt at wit, "that those are all that will go bump in the night."

By evening, Stephen found no other inscriptions. After setting up camp, Eddie scouted the area, hunting and killing several dorcas gazelle from a small herd obviously drawn to the relative fecundity of the Hawk Rock. The water bags were refilled, and even the camels had drunk their fill.

"There's no real reason for us to remain," Eddie said, wiping his lips on the back of his hand after finishing a liberal portion of gazelle steak. "We have replenished our provisions, and it seems the only thing we will find here is trouble—especially if someone else comes to use the spring."

"Isn't that unlikely?" Stephen asked. "I mean, this isn't exactly on the beaten track."

"Maybe not by your standards," Eddie replied, "but the Bedouin are sure to know every watering hole for miles, and a spring of fresh water, no matter how difficult to reach, won't have passed notice. The Protectors of the Pharaoh aren't the only ones we have to watch out for. The Bedouin are as different from the city Arabs as you can get. About the only thing they have in common is Islam."

Neville puffed his pipe, remembering. "They're proud of their ability to live in the desert, and consider it their territory. Banditry and stealing aren't immoral, not really, no matter what the Koran says. As the Bedouin see it, if they could take it, the other person didn't care enough to safeguard it."

"No more illegal than picking tuppence up off the street," Stephen offered.

"No more," Neville agreed, "except that they can be a bit rough about the picking up."

Jenny, who had been cutting gazelle into thin strips that would dry quickly over the fire, frowned.

"What should we do if any show up, Eddie?"

"If they don't see you, hide and try to get a warning to the rest of us—if you can do so without giving yourself away. If they do see you and I'm not near, try to fire off a shot, and I'll get back as soon as I can. They may negotiate more honestly Muslim to Muslim."

"So if we're in a group," Stephen said, "we should do like we did at the village—play dumb and let you be in charge?"

"Right."

Jenny said hesitantly, "What if they see us and we're in a position to take them out? Should we try, and keep them from getting away before they can bring in help?"

Eddie shook his head.

"Only shoot if they're obviously out to kill you—and believe me, they're not going to want to kill a pretty girl. Even then, don't shoot unless you're sure you can win. The Bedouin believe in blood feud. If you didn't kill every one, the rest would be back to even out the score."

Jenny shuddered. She didn't need Eddie to be more blunt about what would happen if she were captured. Suddenly, that derringer tucked in her under-bodice seemed comforting.

Stephen looked grim. "I guess we should hope we see them first and can hide."

"Wrong," Eddie corrected him. "You should hope we don't see them at all."

"And we likely won't," Neville said, something in the stiffness of his tone making Jenny think that her uncle thought Eddie had overstepped the bounds of propriety in the nature of his warnings. "Not even the Bedouin have magic to tell them where people are. This time of year, they're more likely raiding established caravan routes."

"Good reminder," Eddie said levelly. "Now, from this point forward, since we don't know where we're going, we're going to need to travel by daylight."

"And which way do we head?" Jenny asked. "I know that the hieroglyphs from the obelisk gave what you thought were directions, but I don't remember specifically."

From a side pocket of his saddlebags, Neville pulled the slim note case that held condensed notes relating to Alphonse Liebermann's quest. The originals were safely in London.

"Let me read the verse we found," he suggested, "and you two can see if you agree with our interpretation. I have the original copied here, too."

Remember that Anubis will bring you before Osiris.
Remember that your heart and your soul will be weighed against Maat.
Remember that the monster Ammit waits to devour the wicked.
The son and the self flies as the Nile and the boat.
The mother and the wife follow as the Nile and the boat.
Under the watching Eye of the Hawk, the homecoming is joyous.

Stephen smiled, his delight in a puzzle banishing the moodiness that had descended when Eddie began talking about the Bedouin.

"I agree that the first three lines are simply traditional warnings—and fairly mild ones at that. The son and the self is interesting, though." He turned to Jenny and Eddie. "Did you know that the ancient Egyptians equated the god Horus with the living pharaoh?"

"I think I remember something about that," Eddie agreed.

"Well, think about our Protectors of the Pharaoh," Stephen said. "Who appeared to the men in that dream?"

"Horus the Hawk," Jenny answered obediently, "and it was his sign that was tattooed on the arm of the man Eddie killed."

"Right," Stephen said. "Now, the son and the self could refer to Horus and the pharaoh. The mother and the wife could refer to either Isis who was the mother of Horus and the wife of Osiris—the other god with whom the pharaoh was identified—or to Hathor, who in some legends is both Horus's nurse and his wife."

"I'm for Isis," Jenny said firmly. "Because she's the one on the other tattoo, and a beautiful woman was mentioned in the dream. Anyhow, she fits for another reason. If the 'son' is Horus, the living pharaoh, then the 'self' could be the dead pharaoh—in other words, Neferankhotep."

Neville shook his head. "It's like that damned—pardon me, Jenny—Sphinx again. All riddles. I'd rather skip the first part and look at the second. That flying 'as' interests me. I've checked Alphonse's translation using some books Stephen loaned me when he was teaching me . . ."

"Ah, not just the attentive pupil," Stephen said in mock dismay.

"And Alphonse was right on target. It's harder to be sure, since just like in English there are words that are defined by context, but his version makes the most sense."

"Or you want it to," Eddie murmured so softly that Jenny thought she was the only one who heard.

"Now, looking at the phrase 'Nile and the boat,'" Sir Neville went on with such determination that Jenny felt fairly certain he *had* heard but was unwilling to argue, "the Nile flows south to north. The sun—if we assume the boat referred to is the boat of the sun—moves east to west. When we combine the two, we get northwest. That is the direction I propose we go."

"I've seen pictures of the judgment of the dead," Jenny said, almost inconsequentially, "and it usually shows a little person in the scale being weighed against a feather—the feather of Maat. Your translation refers to both the heart and the soul. Did the ancient Egyptians believe in souls?"

"Did they!" Stephen said, beaming with pleasure at having an excuse to lecture. "Compared to the Egyptian concept, the Christian idea of the soul is really too simple. The ancient Egyptian soul had seven parts. The *ba* is what is mentioned in Neville's inscription, and that's the part that was weighed before Maat, along with the heart. If the *ba* and heart weighed less than the feather, the person was granted a pleasant afterlife—or in some versions, rebirth into a higher station."

Jenny nodded.

"Odd that this mentions being judged. Do you think that was to scare people away?"

"That's right," Eddie said, putting a low growl into his voice. "Be good, little girl, and stay away from things that don't concern you or the monster Ammit will eat you up. Grrr!"

He growled, and Mozelle scampered to hide behind Jenny.

Stephen laughed. "I'd be afraid of Ammit, if I believed in him, that is. He's a horrible-looking creature, part-baboon, part-crocodile, and part-hippopotamus—and the worst parts of each. I'd hate to have him ready to eat me if I failed judgment."

"So the first part," Jenny persisted, "basically says, 'Be good because if no one finds you out while you're alive, then the gods will find you out after you're dead, and you don't want to be caught and fed to Ammit.'"

"That sounds about right," Stephen agreed.

"And then according to Uncle Neville, it says, 'Go northwest, and the homecoming will be joyful.'"

"Maybe," Neville said somberly, "it would be, for those who have nothing to fear."

"And for how long do we continue northwest?" Eddie asked. "I refuse to go any farther than to the half-way point in our supplies. Moreover, I won't agree to any starvation rations in order to extend that point. As far as we go, we'll have equally far to come back, and we cannot afford being worn out."

Neville caught himself starting to glower, than fought back the impulse. The advice was no more than he himself would have given in Eddie's position. True, Eddie stated matters rather forcefully, but then he was probably right to do so.

"Fine," Neville said. "We'll also turn back if any one of us becomes ill or is injured. The Valley of Dust has waited this long. It can continue to wait if necessary."

He managed to get the words out smoothly, but they burned in his throat.

They spent the rest of the evening filling the buckets with water so that everyone could drink and wash in the morning. This time Eddie assigned himself the last watch before morning, so he could try hunting, since this could well be their last chance for fresh meat.

He succeeded in killing another dorcas gazelle. Snares he had set up the night before yielded a brace of hares. All but one haunch of the fresh meat was already packed when the rest of the party rose, and not even Stephen commented on the novelty of fresh gazelle for breakfast.

They left the Hawk Rock almost before the sun had risen, orienting by Eddie's compass, eyes straining to see something—anything—on the horizon that would indicate they weren't simply riding into emptiness.

After traveling by night, the daytime heat and brilliance were punishing, and everyone had reason to be glad on Eddie's insistence on supplying smoked glasses. The men adopted Arab style head wraps that provided some shelter from the sun. Jenny tied her bandanna to protect the exposed skin on her throat and by demonstration proved the efficacy of her wide-brimmed hat.

They stopped only occasionally to stretch and to refill their personal canteens. Lunch was a dry meal, and a light breeze that otherwise would have been delightful made the repast at least half sand.

Stephen looked back along the way they had come. The Hawk Rock had diminished behind them, but remained clearly visible.

"Chad Spice's journal said he could see the Hawk Rock from the Valley of Dust," he commented. "Shouldn't we be able to do the reverse?"

"He saw it on an exceptionally clear day," Eddie replied. "In any case, the reverse does not necessarily apply."

"No?" Stephen was clearly puzzled.

Neville sought to explain. "The Hawk Rock stands out from its surroundings by virtue of its height, the color of its stone, and even the greenery clinging to it. We are apparently seeking a valley, so that advantage will be lost to us. If it is buried in sand, as legend says, it will blend into the surroundings."

"And," Jenny added, "any greenery will be in hollows rather than growing out in the open."

"But Chad Spice also mentioned seeing the four statues," Stephen protested, sounding a bit frantic. "Why wouldn't we see them?"

"We should," Neville answered, "when we're closer. From this distance, they may blend in with the surrounding natural colors. However, you've done well to remind us. It will give something specific to seek."

They pressed on until evening, and not even Neville could resist Eddie's insistence that they stop and make camp while they had light. Stephen looked ragged, and Neville had observed that he was drinking far more water than the rest of them. Jenny was drinking less, but not holding up all that much better. She might have experience with desert conditions, but the reality was that for the last year or so she had been a privileged boarding school miss, not an apprentice frontier physician.

And Neville himself? He thought he'd prepared himself. He'd followed a detailed training regime to strengthen his injured leg and to stretch ligaments torn by his assailants. He'd ridden daily, gone steeplechasing and hunting. But there had been no way to prepare for a camel's side-to-side gait, and he ached all over. Only Eddie looked merely tired, but then he did undertake similar—if not quite as arduous—journeys on a regular basis.

The area in which they camped was utterly desolate. It was as if they'd entered a completely sterile realm, a thing that shouldn't have been possible only a day's journey from a source of reliable water. They saw nothing alive, not a blade of grass or a bit of shrub. There weren't even any insects, yet Mozelle the kitten seemed preternaturally alert, as if awaiting attack. The temperature seemed higher than usual as well, the sunlight more intense.

The next morning found Stephen feverish from too much sun. Not even Bedouin headwraps and ointment could stop his fair skin from burning. Jenny washed and anointed the places Stephen couldn't bear to touch as gently as if he'd been her brother. Without comment or criticism, Eddie assigned Stephen an extra canteen of water. Neville, seeing their concern, knew he had to suggest turning back.

Stephen flatly refused.

"I'll make it," he said, fiercely. "Chad Spice did it in goatskin slippers and with what water he could carry. I will make it!"

He did make another day, though Eddie insisted they rest in the pavilion when the sun was at its highest, and Stephen was clearly too uncomfortable to protest this coddling. Neville bore but impatiently with the delay. The mid-day sun was too brilliant for him to be sure, but he thought he'd seen a thin line of something shadowing the horizon to the northwest. He said nothing, not even to Jenny who he suspected had sharper eyes than his own. If they had to turn back, he didn't want Stephen to know they might have been within reach of their destination.

That evening the westering sun made certainty impossible, but at dawn he felt sure. Even without his field glasses, Neville could see what seemed to be one towering outcrop, and possibly another.

Eddie came to him as he was lowering the field glasses.

"That certainly might be the statues," he agreed. "What I want to tell you is that we're going through water at a much higher rate than I'd planned—and I'd never planned on rationing too strictly with you three children of the land of mists and fogs in my charge."

Neville thought fleetingly how ten years in Egypt had colored even Eddie's English.

"We're at the half-way point in our supplies?" he asked.

"Just about, at least for water," Eddie admitted. "If Stephen keeps needing liquid at the same rate, we're definitely there before tonight—and I won't hide that Jenny has been drinking more, too. She doesn't know it, but I've filled her canteen when she hasn't been looking."

Neville raised his eyebrows.

"It was that or have her collapse on us," Eddie said, as if confessing a fault. "She's kept her peace and sucked on a pebble, and dosed that kitten from her own share, but she's no camel. For that matter, neither are you. Head hurting? Muscles stiff?"

Neville nodded. "Nothing I can't take."

"I'm sure, but I know I don't much like trying to get all of you back by myself."

"Fair."

Neville took one more longing look toward the rocky outline.

"We'd better tell the others."

But those others had plans of their own.

Stephen licked his swollen lips, then seemed to regret the gesture as a sign of weakness.

"We've seen the statues," he said, his voice croaking. "We can't turn around now."

He lurched to his feet, an act that if meant to demonstrate his strength failed to do so, but one that left no doubt as to his determination.

"We could go back to the Hawk Rock," Neville suggested. "Let you recover, let your sunburn heal. Then we could try again."

He didn't think they'd do any such thing, but he owed Stephen a chance to save face.

Stephen wasn't fooled.

"Chad Spice's journal said he found both water and food," he reminded them. "Tame goats."

"That 'tame' is one of the things that worries me," Eddie put in. "Spice seemed to think that the goats were tame because they were unaccustomed to human contact, but the reverse is more likely."

"Bedouin?" Jenny asked.

"Likely," Eddie said.

"I don't care," Stephen protested. "I want to go on. One more day, that's all it's going to take. I know it."

"There's no promise of either food or water," Neville reminded him gently.

"I know, and I don't care."

Eddie shrugged, and they went on.

They were setting up the pavilion as shelter from the mid-day sun, when Stephen gave a croaking shout and pointed to the sky. A single hawk, every feather delineated against the cruel blue, was riding lazy circles on some wind unfelt this close to the ground.

"A hawk!" Stephen cried. "A hawk. 'Under the watching eye of the hawk, the homecoming is joyous.'"

It amazed Neville how heartening that one glimpse of something alive and moving could be. The hawk remained above all the while they waited out the worst of the sun's intensity, then when they broke camp split off to the northwest.

"Is it leading us?" Jenny asked in quiet amazement.

These were the first words she'd spoken other than to ask Stephen how he felt. Neville was shocked when he noticed the dark circles that had formed, bruise-like, under her eyes, and the hollows under her cheekbones.

No one said anything, but they knew that at least some of them had passed the point of returning even to the relative safety of the Hawk Rock. The desert, even in its comparative winter mildness, was sucking moisture from them, leaching it away even in the gentle breeze that created an illusion of comfort.

Eddie readied the patient camels and they struggled on. Neville tried to sense whether his mount was aware of water nearby, but he felt none of the eagerness that had quickened its step when they had neared the Hawk Rock. Did that mean there was no water, or merely that the camel knew enough to husband its strength?

Gradually Neville's field glasses showed him something at the base of the stone outcrop, not a pedestal or building, but a hill or rise washed with sand about its base. As they came closer, he saw they had come to the base of a rocky rise, steep, and slick with accumulated sand. It extended as far as they could see in either direction, curving away so that they could not tell whether they faced a ridge or a circular barrier.

One thing was clear. The camels weren't going up that. Even a human was going to find it a hard climb.

They arrived near dusk. Stephen was no more than semi-conscious, but his camel continued to carry him as if he was any other burden. Jenny was looking feverish, her eyes unnaturally bright. Neville knelt his camel and walked stiffly over to the rock barrier.

"If there's water," he said, "it's beyond that."

"We've enough for tonight," Eddie said.

"And tomorrow?" Neville asked.

"We'll have nothing but camel blood."

Four Watchers

JENNY COULDN'T help herself. She wanted to stay awake, wanted to help treat Stephen's heat exhaustion, but she was too tired. She sat down for just a moment, and awoke only to the cool of the night and restful darkness.

Someone, Eddie, she thought, was leaning against one of the poles to which they had secured the pavilion, just visible in the moonlight. She caught a whiff of his cigarette and was sure.

Rising to her feet, noticing as she did so that someone had removed her boots, hat, and gun belt, then stacked them neatly at hand, Jenny teetered slightly, her head spinning. For the first time since waking she noticed how dry her mouth and lips were. Somewhere during that day's horrible ride she'd stopped noticing. It must be an improvement that she could notice, though it didn't much seem like one right now.

She didn't see her canteen, so she walked over to Eddie. He turned at the sound of her approach, and she saw he was holding Mozelle. The tawny kitten sat upright on the hand he held cradled against his chest, looking more like an ornament on a shelf than a living creature.

Eddie ground out his cigarette beneath a boot toe, and gestured with his head toward a water bag hanging from one of the tent posts.

"Careful with how you pour it," he said, keeping his voice soft. "That's all we have."

Jenny tried not to show how appalled she was, but something must have come through.

"Had to give it to Stephen—and Neville—or lose one of 'em," Eddie answered her unvoiced question.

"Uncle Neville?" Jenny asked, keeping her own voice soft with an effort.

"Gimpy idiot, him with that injury barely healed, decided to try climbing the rocks when I was busy with the gear," Eddie said, fond irritation in his voice. "Ankle's sprained badly. Might be a break. Had to wrap it in wet cloths to cool it. Hope you don't mind. I borrowed some opium from your kit."

Jenny's hand shook, but she remembered the water and steadied it.

"Probably just a sprain," Eddie said. "Didn't feel the bones grating."

"And I slept through that?"

"You and Stephen both," Eddie said. "Don't blame you. This has been harder than it should have been. We've had plenty of water. You're pretty tough for a city girl. Stephen's game. I don't know ... Ever since we left the Hawk Rock, something's been off."

The water, warm as it was and tasting of goat leather, refreshed Jenny. She crossed to where Eddie stood, and realized he was studying the rocky ridge. The moonlight was hitting it just right, illuminating it, making all the shadows twice as dark and twice as sharp as seemed natural.

"That where Uncle Neville sprained his ankle?"

"No, he tried over there." Eddie paused a long while, his free hand scratching between Mozelle's ears. "I took a camel out once I was sure you all weren't coming around for a while, rode around the edges of the curve. Can't say for sure, but I don't think there's a break in this. I think it goes all the way around."

"Like the crater of a volcano," Jenny said. "Can't be, though. This is sandstone."

Eddie nodded. Jenny felt a sudden rush of excitement.

"I should try to climb it now," she said. "While it's lit by the moon but the rocks are cool. They'll heat up pretty fast come sunrise."

Eddie nodded.

"One of us should," he agreed.

Jenny looked at him levelly.

"I'd better. If I get hurt, you might just manage to get one or two of us out. If you get hurt, there's no way I can do the same."

Eddie didn't even attempt to disagree.

"True. Why not wait until morning?"

"There's light enough now, if I'm careful, and I promise I will be careful. Besides, if there isn't water somewhere up there, you're going to need to start us back to the Hawk Rock right quick. We'll need what cool there is if we're to have a chance. Then I figure one of us will stay with Uncle Neville and Stephen when they can't go on, and the other will press on for the Hawk Rock and try to bring back water. That about right?"

Eddie nodded again. He seemed like an oracular statue standing there, Mozelle a carved figure in his hands. Jenny realized that he was fighting a gallant impulse to refuse her, because he knew they both were right, and if there wasn't water up there, or if she got hurt, he was the only one who had a chance of saving them.

She didn't press him to speak, just crossed back to her gear. Gloves, boots, a couple bandannas, an empty canteen, a length of line twined around her waist, just in case there was something worth lowering. She paused at the gun belt, then lifted it, checked that the weapons were clear of sand, and strapped it on.

"Never know," she said, meeting Eddie's silently questioning gaze. "Goats might not be so friendly this time. Hold onto Mozelle for me. Don't want to step on her."

Jenny started her climb without further comment, positioning herself so her shadow wouldn't block the moonlight. Immediately as she began trying to find reliable foot and hand holds, it seemed darker, so much so that she glanced up to see if some vagrant cloud had covered the moon. The sky remained as remorselessly clear as ever.

She knew it was her own nervousness, the thought of Uncle Neville's sprained—hopefully only sprained!—ankle that was making it seem darker than it was. She cast her memory back to her mother teaching her rockclimbing in the New Mexico Territory on rocks not too different from these.

"Test every hold before you trust it, Jenny. Don't forget you can use your knees to bridge a gap. On a slant, let your weight help you secure your hold, don't fight it. Don't ever reach blind into a hole or crevice. You don't know who might be sleeping there."

Jenny wondered if Uncle Neville had the least idea what kind of woman his sister had become when she'd transformed herself from English lady to American doctor's wife—American nurse—American mother—American rancher.

She didn't think he had the least idea, and resolved to tell him, little bits over time so he wouldn't think she was trying to teach him how to be her guardian. He'd really been trying, poor dear.

I wonder if suddenly finding himself almost a parent of a grown woman is what made him so susceptible to that conniving bitch Audrey Cheshire?

Jenny had to dismiss this immediately as unfair. Lady Cheshire wasn't exactly young, but she wasn't old either, and she had ways that made youthfulness seem a disadvantage.

The rock ridge seemed to go on forever. The rocks started getting larger, so Jenny realized that their assessment of the ridge's height had been all wrong. They'd been judging as if the rocks at the top were just about the size of the ones at the bottom, while actually some were so big she had to go around them rather than over. That meant squeezing through some tight gaps and hoping the cobras were sleeping elsewhere.

I never realized what a polite snake a rattler is, she mused. *At least they give warning—at least most of the time, they do.*

She hardly realized when she had dragged herself to the top. Her hands were reaching for the next rock, anticipating the next challenge. She stumbled forward, her feet surprised to find themselves on relatively level ground.

Moonlight illuminated a sandstone ridge bordering a sandy plain. Again she was reminded of a volcano, but here the crater was filled with sand instead of fire—or as had been the case with a mountain lake she'd once seen—with water.

The memory reminded herself of what she was seeking. At first glance, the crater was featureless, but then she noticed that scrubby grass grew near the edges. More patiently than she would have thought possible, Jenny scanned the rim, unwilling to waste energy trudging through the sand.

There. There was an area where the grass seemed a trace thicker. She trudged over, aware of sand trickling into her boot. She must have cut open the leather during her climb. She'd need to mend it or she'd have blisters to end all blisters.

She distracted herself from hope, thinking about the need to mend her boot. Eddie wouldn't have forgotten something as basic as heavy needles and thread, but if he had she might manage with something from her doctor's bag. There was a probe in there that might work as an awl.

There was grass under her feet, not soft like the groomed lawn at Madame's academy, but uneven and coarse. Then, like a miracle, she scented dampness. The patch was in shadow, but she found matches in her pocket. Striking one, she confirmed what her nose had told her. There was a spring here, hardly more than a damp trickle against the rock, but definitely water.

Removing her glove she touched her hand to the dampest spot, and when it came away wet, licked the water. It tasted of her own sweat, of leather, and of sand, but it was definitely fresh. She dug with her hand, making a catch basin for the water, moving a rock or two so the spring flowed as a trickle rather than spreading its wealth along the rock.

Jenny set her canteen to fill. Then she hurried back to where she'd topped the ridge. Squeezing between two boulders she located Eddie, standing just as she'd left him. Even Mozelle hadn't moved.

"Eddie! I've found it. There's water! Not much, but at least one spring."

She saw the flash of Eddie's teeth as he raised his face and smiled.

"Lower your line," he said. "I'll get the buckets."

At that moment, that practical command meant more to her than medals.

Neville felt many things when he awoke: pain from his ankle, lassitude warring against expectation, a numbness where he'd lain too long on one shoulder. However, it was what he did not feel that first caught his attention. Licking his lips in a motion he'd repeated so many times throughout that last hot ride that it had become reflex, he realized that he did not feel thirsty.

He opened his eyes to early morning light against the golden-brown of the woven camel-hair pavilion and tried again. His lips were dry, but neither swollen nor cracked, and his throat was moist. He decided to try speaking, and though his words sounded rather distant to his ears, they came without the hoarse croaking of a parched throat.

"Eddie? Jenny? Stephen?"

Eddie appeared at his side almost instantly. He held a canteen in his hand and without speaking offered it to Neville. His mischievous grin said more than any words. Neville drank and tasted water, heavily tainted with minerals, but fresh and even cool.

"Jenny climbed up last night," Eddie said. "She found a spring. This morning, when there was more light, she went around and found a second, even better than the first. I've been nursing water into you and Stephen since she sent down the first batch. You've been too dopey to notice, but Stephen's doing well enough to complain alternately about how his head hurts, and how we're keeping him from going up to help Jenny—and to get a firsthand look at what she's found."

Neville felt his heart beating so unbearably hard that it actually hurt.

"Then we have . . ."

"Found the Valley of Dust? Seems like it, unless there are two such places. Seems like we have."

Eddie looked less than delighted, but Neville had grown so accustomed to his friend's mixed feelings about the venture that he didn't even comment.

"Tell me," he ordered, muscling himself upright with the strength of his arms alone. He'd had much practice with this when his broken leg was mending, years before, that he could do this almost without thinking.

"Better," Eddie said. "Do you think you can stay on a camel? Good. Jenny's located a path that—with a little work on our part—will let us bring the camels and gear up into the Valley. It'll save a lot of hauling, and then you can see for yourself."

Neville insisted on rising, though his ankle throbbed beneath the bandages. Using a crutch Eddie put together from materials in their supplies, he took charge of getting their gear ready. Stephen, still red and peeling from exposure to the sun, pitched in with enthusiasm. Between them, suffering only a few mishaps that would be comic later but were insufferably annoying now, they packed and loaded the camels, freeing Eddie to help Jenny clear the promised trail.

With more than the usual amount of spitting—and complete rebellion on the part of one of the camels, who refused to rise even when she saw the rest of her train leaving, but who finally joined them, as if a queen gracing them with her presence—the pack train climbed the narrow, rocky trail.

Neville bit deeply into the side of his mouth lest he show how much the jolting progress hurt his injured ankle. He knew that if any of the others suspected how much pain he was in, they would bar him from exploration.

And I have not come this far and waited these ten years, he thought stubbornly, *to be tucked into bed with bread and milk.*

However, when his muttering and protesting mount topped the rise and descended into the Valley of Dust, Neville forgot even his pain in the intense joy of seeing the place at last.

Jenny had compared it to the interior of a volcanic crater, and Neville fully understood why. The entire of the valley stood higher than the surrounding desert, cradled from sight within ringing walls of sandstone. These rose twenty feet or more in height, cupping them within a peculiar quiet.

Although they could not be seen from the inside, Neville understood that without the valley, built from the same sandstone that walled the valley, stood four monuments. Chad Spice had described them as statues, but Stephen reported they were more like columns or pillars.

"You see figures like them in tombs, painting, and amulets," he said, his cracked lips, now liberally treated with ointment but doubtlessly still painful, not limiting his enthusiasm. "Some say that they're meant to represent palm trees, but there is no doubt they represented stability."

"Stephen says," Jenny added, when the other paused to sip some of the blessedly abundant water, "that the pillars may be later additions, rather like the obelisk on the Hawk Rock. I wouldn't let him stay out there to examine them closely. We did notice something odd, though. It looked as if they may have been damaged around their uppermost reaches—as if something had been broken away."

Neville frowned. He had read Chad Spice's journal so many times that the text was engraved on his memory. Spice said he had taken shelter beneath a statue—not a pillar. He'd even referred to the place as "The Oasis of Statues." Neville considered raising the point, then decided there would be nothing to gain from it. Stephen would be sure to argue that an adventurer like Spice would not bother to differentiate between a statue and a pillar, and he would probably be right.

Eddie and Jenny had chosen the location for their base camp on the edge of the valley, near the more strongly flowing of the two springs. It was sheltered by the crater wall from some of the sun, and their pavilion was to be pitched to provide even more protection from the day's heat.

He could imagine Stephen eschewing this shelter to stand out in the sun and examine the columns. Had he been more mobile, Neville himself might have done the same. After all, one of them was likely the column that had given Chad Spice shelter, guiding him, too, into the Valley of Dust.

Fleetingly, Neville wondered about the conflicting impulses that seemed to exist to hide and yet to mark this place, but he was too excited to dwell on his minor mystery. What mattered was that they were there. With water and what remained of their supplies—not to mention the game they would certainly find—they need not hurry away, but could take advantage of what remained of the winter to find the actual opening into Neferankhotep's tomb.

Already he could see where they would need to begin.

At each of what Eddie's compass confirmed were the four cardinal points stood a statue—or rather a sculpture carved in extremely high relief. Each was at least ten feet tall, and stood guard alongside a smoothed panel of stone upon which long texts had been inscribed in hieroglyphs.

"We start by copying and, if possible, translating those texts," Neville said.

"Good," Eddie said. "I thought you might have us empty all this sand out of the valley, and I was wondering where if I'd brought enough baskets for hauling it away."

Neville felt too good to rise to the tease.

"We've found the Valley of Dust," he said. "After all this time, we've found it. I wish old Alphonse could be here. I can just imagine his excitement."

"I wonder," Jenny said, standing hands on hips and examining the valley, "why old Neferankhotep wanted to be buried way out here? I mean, Gizeh was pretty nice, and the Valley of the Kings seemed a whole lot more convenient."

Stephen nodded. "I've wondered about that, as well. All that legend says is that Neferankhotep asked to be buried in an 'infertile valley.' This certainly fits the bill, but it wouldn't be at all easy for the proper offerings to be made. Without those, our good king would have had a pretty grim afterlife."

Eddie scratched along the edges of his beard.

"I heard once that the Red Land has come closer in toward the Nile over time, that the fertile areas were once much larger. Perhaps in Neferankhotep's day the Black Land extended out closer to this point."

Jenny shivered, "And when the gods took their revenge on those who had attempted to steal from the good king they spread the desert around him for greater protection."

"Don't be overimaginative," Neville rebuked her. "We are here as scientists, not superstitious old women like Sarah Syms. Remember that we arrived here the long way around. First we went to the Hawk Rock, then crossed along to here. If we had gone directly west from the appropriate point along the Nile, we would have cut off some of the distance. Neferankhotep's people would have done that."

Jenny accepted his rebuke with grace. "It's easy to forget what's real and what's legend, when you're out here, and those statues are staring back. All right, we've a good bit of daylight left. Where do we begin?"

"My suggestion," Eddie said before Neville could speak, "is that you and I get camp assembled. I'd rather have Neville not moving around, and Stephen out of the sun, so they can gimp over to the eastern rim. The sun isn't low enough yet to penetrate there, and they can start their recording."

Neville thought Jenny might rebel, but he'd underestimated the discipline acquired in the years she'd spent traveling with her parents.

I really must learn more about what they did, he thought. *I suspect Alice deferred to what she imagined were my sensibilities and didn't tell me the half.*

Before moving to help copy the text near the easternmost statue, he scanned the whole of the valley wall with his field glasses. All four of the statues were worn from millennia of exposure to sand and wind, but he thought he could make out the basic details.

"Stephen," he said, turning to where the younger man was gathering together the necessary equipment. "I agree with Eddie's suggestion, overall, but are you up to circumnavigating the valley first? It isn't overly large, and I am eager to begin by becoming acquainted with the overall layout."

Stephen shrugged. "The walls provide some shade along the edges, at least most of the way. I think your suggestion is a wise one."

Their camp was on the southeastern edge of the valley, so they began with the statue that stood to the east. At any other time, thumping over rock and sand on one good foot and a crutch would have been a disheartening reminder of past, more serious, injuries, but Neville was too intent on his goal to care. Stephen stayed near, carrying their gear, but otherwise not offering assistance.

Tactful blighter, Neville thought.

The sculpture that stood to the east proved to be a masculine figure done in fashion more commonly used in painting than in sculpture—that is its head and lower body were represented in profile, but the torso was a front view. Its most striking feature was the regal hawk's head it bore on its broad shoulders. The beak was short and sharply curved, while the feathered head was shaped in a harmonious compromise between a natural bird's head and a short wig or headcovering. In one hand it bore a flail, in the other an ankh.

"Horus the Avenger," Neville said almost reverently. "Or is it Re of Heliopolis? I believe they both have hawk's heads, don't they?"

"And some say that one is just a manifestation of the other," Stephen agreed. "However, the name Horus appears several times in the inscription, so I would say that this is Horus."

The next sculpture, standing to the north, was obviously a woman. Her slender body was clad in a form-fitting gown that left her small, round breasts either bare or hardly veiled. She wore the vulture crown, over which was the hieroglyph for "throne." She carried an ankh in one hand, a slender staff topped with a lotus blossom in the other. Even in this much worn sculpture, her features were both serene and commanding.

"Isis," Stephen said without question. "That sign over her head means 'seat' or 'throne,' which my teacher said is the original form of her name. Some argue that this suggests a matriarchal past, though others question that since women didn't seem to rate much by the time of the pharaohs."

"Don't tell Jenny," Neville suggested.

"Nope," Stephen replied cheerfully. "I'll just tell her this is Isis, wife of Osiris, mother of Horus, and pretty darn powerful mistress of magic in her own right. If Humpty Dumpty had had her around, he'd be sitting pretty to this day."

Neville blinked, then understood.

"That's right. She's the one who reassembled Osiris after Set killed him and cut him into pieces. Nasty story, that one."

Stephen nodded agreement. "I wonder if we'll find Osiris represented on the western wall? Horus was in the east, and he's sometimes associated with the rising sun. Osiris is associated with the afterlife, and his palace is said to be in Amenti, the land of the west."

Jenny, Mozelle bounding at her heels, came jogging across to them at this point. She arrived in time to hear this last.

"Eddie has gone to see if he can scare up some game. I want a glimpse at the statues before I start the grub."

"Horus is back there," Neville said, "and this fine lady is Isis."

Jenny studied Isis for a long moment then wiped her forehead on the sleeve of her shirt. "Isis had the right idea, didn't she? No corset, no bustle, not much clothing at all when you come right down to it. Wonder she didn't burn."

She glanced sidelong at Neville, and he laughed at her expression—a mixture of rue and pleasure at her own daring. He refused to rise to the bait, but indicated with a gesture that they should continue walking.

"Stephen was hypothesizing that we might find Osiris in the west," he said.

"Because he's associated with the west and the afterlife," Jenny said, showing she'd caught the tail end of Stephen's lecture. "Weren't the islands of Avalon, where Arthur supposedly went after he died, weren't they in the west? And didn't the ancient Greeks think the Isles of the Blessed were in the west, too? I wonder why so many cultures associate the west with death?"

Stephen pontificated, "I was taught that such traditions are rooted in the passage of the sun from east to west. Since the sun seems to go west and 'die,' primitive people assumed that when they died they went west as well."

Jenny laughed. "Well, I'll be . . . Does that ever give a new meaning to old Horace Greeley saying 'Go West, young man!' Someone had better tell the U.S. of A. that sending all its young men west is the same as sending them to the afterlife."

Their arrival at the third sculpture forestalled further discussion on this peculiar point of theology.

The carving this time was of a man wearing the tall white crown of Upper Egypt, adorned with two feathers flaring from the sides. He held a crook and flail crossed on his chest, and his feet were bound so closely that they seemed one appendage.

"I was right," Stephen said with satisfaction. "Osiris. He's been depicted in his role as lord of the underworld. Let's see if you've learned your lessons, Jenny. Why does it look like he has only one foot?"

"Because," Jenny said, her nose wrinkling with distaste, "he is shown wrapped up like a mummy—a living mummy. I think that's a horrible fate, even for a god."

Stephen shook his head at such an unscientific analysis.

"If you look more closely, Jenny, you can see that his hands and feet were originally painted green."

"I've seen that in other places," she said, "and always forgot to ask why. Is it for putrefaction, because he's rotting?"

"So speaks the physician's daughter," Stephen replied. "No, it's green for vegetation. The underworld wasn't like Hell for the Christians. It was the source of growing plants, so Osiris—who died and rose again—is regarded as emblematic of the rebirth of life into the world above."

Jenny frowned. "That dying and rising again sounds almost blasphemous."

Neville cut in, lest Stephen in his eagerness grow offensive, "It can't be, Jenny. Egyptian religion predates Christianity by thousands of years. It's just one of those strange ways that the ancients seem to have sensed the truth, even without divine revelation."

"I guess that's right," Jenny said, "or like I heard a shaman say once, that the truth just might have been revealed to more than one group of people."

"Now that type of talk," Neville said sternly, thinking once again that being Jenny's guardian wasn't going to be easy, "truly is blasphemous. Either of you want to guess who the next carving will be? I can't say the field glasses were much help."

Stephen shook his head. "There are too many options. It could be Hathor, who was Horus's wife, and Isis's ally in her quest to resurrect Osiris. Or it could be Maat, the principle of justice and truth. Or maybe Thoth, the god of learning and wisdom, who was, like Isis, skilled in magic, and was often associated with Horus."

Jenny grabbed his arm and tugged.

"Stop talking. There's a really easy way to find out."

They crossed the sand, feeling the reflected heat and doubly grateful for the shade cast by the wall and the knowledge that their canteens were full and that plenty more water waited in camp.

Mozelle romped around them, apparently untroubled by the heat. She chased a lizard into a cleft in the wall, challenged a beetle, and then ran right up Jenny's pant leg when she wanted to be carried. Neville couldn't help but be glad that Jenny had defied him and brought the little cat. They seemed to have bonded, and the girl seemed happier and more alive freed of the restrictive mourning black, with the tiny creature on which to lavish what was clearly a generous heart.

The final sculpture proved to be neither Hathor or Maat. Nor was it Thoth, though the figure was theriomorphic, the human head replaced with that of a jackal, a jackal's tail depending from beneath his linen kilt.

Not one of them needed Stephen to tell them who this was. They all knew too well, for the enigmatic smile that curved the jackal's lipless muzzle was familiar to them from the masks worn by the Cairo assassins.

"Anubis," Jenny said softly. "Protector of the dead, patron of embalming."

Neville found his own voice. "That's why he carried the scroll and the jar. They're the tools of his trade. Legend says that his mother abandoned him, and Isis and Osiris raised him. When Osiris was murdered, Anubis helped Isis repair the body and so learned the arts of mummification."

As Neville had hoped, love of the old stories won over Stephen's disquiet at finding this reminder of their enemies in this place.

"There's an older story," Stephen said, "that makes Anubis a son of Ra. Far from being a miserable orphan abandoned by his mother, in this version Anubis had a daughter of his own and was greatly honored by gods and men for his wisdom and abilities. Either way, those Protectors did him a great disservice using his face as a cover for their nighttime raid. Theirs was an act more worthy of ass-eared Set, murderer of his own brother, not of noble Anubis."

"I'm sure," Eddie said, climbing down to them over the wall nearer to camp, "if the god exists he would be grateful to hear you speak so well of him. Now, would you two invalids get out of the sun, and would Jenny come here and help me? I think I've located a herd of sheep, of all things, and we've got work to do."

Eddie's commonplace practicality broke the eerie mood that had stolen over the other three, and they did as he suggested. "I think I found the ruins of a village," Eddie explained after Jenny had joined him. "It might even be the one mentioned in the legend, if I felt like stirring up Neville's hopes even more. What is more immediately useful is that I spotted a few date palms there, and some wild onions. There seems to be another spring, too."

Shifting and sliding down what might charitably be termed a game trail, they reached the ruined village. Wind-blown sand had all but buried it, leaving the occasional protruding wall or a mound that might conceal a structure beneath. The date palms were there, and Eddie boosted Jenny up so she could gather some of the ripe ones.

Backing the "village" was a rocky slope that concealed pockets of grazing. Following the signs, they tracked a mingled herd of wild sheep and goats. The goats bolted, but the sheep were less swift, and Jenny shot one while Eddie marked the likely direction where others might be found later.

They cleaned the carcass where it fell, leaving the entrails for the jackals, but taking the hide. Eddie knew how to treat it so it would remain supple, and didn't see any reason for waste, especially since they were likely to be in this area for a time to come.

That evening as the sheep roasted over the fire, Jenny peeled thin green onions. Neville and Stephen had copied part of one panel of hieroglyphs and were now trying tentative translation as a means of filling in characters that had been partially smoothed away by the wind. Turning from where he'd been stretching the sheepskin, Eddie broke the comfortable silence.

"What I want to know is why we don't see any signs of people here?"

Stephen looked at him in surprise.

"We do," he said, gesturing to where the statues stood guard over the hieroglyph ornamented panels. "There are the artifacts in this valley, the ruins of the village you found, the pillars on the slopes. That's quite a lot for only a day. Who knows what we will find after we've been here a week."

Eddie shook his head. "That's not what I mean, and Neville, at least, knows it. Why don't we see signs more recent than those? There is ample water here, and forage for animals. We should see evidence of recent Bedouin encampments—maybe even run into a poor tribe that doesn't want to compete with the larger clans for grazing."

Although Eddie had addressed his comments to him, Neville remained silent, so Jenny spoke up, feeling like she was somehow defending her uncle.

"We did see some evidence of people," she said. "The sheep showed signs of having originally been domesticated. One of the horns had been trimmed where it curled too close to the skull, and I'm sure you noticed that that sheep didn't bolt from us with the same energy the goats did. Seemed to argue it knew people."

"Sheep are stupid," Eddie said. "Goats would have the sense to get away from humans, whether they were semi-domesticated or not. Bedouin may be nomads, but they do plant little pockets of crops that they return for at the end of the season. I didn't see any sign of that."

"What about the onions?" Jenny countered.

"Still . . ." Eddie let his words trail off, clearly not satisfied.

"Maybe," Neville said, his voice curiously husky, "it's like the legend says and people shun this valley."

No one even smiled at his suggestion, instead the silence that met it said that this was the explanation that had been lurking in everyone's mind, but no one had wanted to be the first to mention it.

"What could they fear?" Eddie said at last, his irritable tone not for Neville, but for the mystery. "Certainly they don't fear the ghosts of dead pharaohs or the wrath of ancient gods. The Egyptians themselves are the longest running crew of tomb robbers in the land."

Stephen nodded, taking refuge in pedantry. "Belzoni wrote of the primitive natives of Kurneh—or was it Karnak—who lived in the outer chambers of cliff tombs with the bones of the dead scattered about their feet. Certainly, they preserve no wholesome, Christian fear of the dead."

"So what keeps them away?" Eddie persisted. "The journey wasn't easy for us, but it would be nothing to a Bedouin. What keeps them from profiting from this valley?"

No one had an answer. The setting sun cast shadows that seemed to make the statues of the gods move, but they retained their silence. In the rocky canyon below, a jackal found the entrails of the sheep. Its bark carried through the still air, chilling the souls of those who heard it with its note of triumph.

Better and Verse

BY THE middle of the next day, they had fallen into a working routine. Neville balked when he learned that Stephen planned to copy all of the inscriptions before making a serious effort to translate any of them.

"But if something interrupts us," Stephen said, startled at his employer's protest, "then we will have the texts. We can work on them anywhere."

Neville had to agree that this reasoning was scholarly and sound, but he wanted to know what the writing said. The bits and pieces he could read only whetted his interest, hinting as they did at a more complex meaning.

"Jenny and I will take over the copying," Neville said. "You start translating the Horus text we finished this morning. Eddie, can you handle camp chores?"

"Easily," the other answered. "I'd like to go down into the canyons below and cut some extra fodder for the camels, but I'll let you know before I leave."

Neville hardly heard him.

"Jenny, I know you don't have much knowledge of hieroglyphs, but your sketching is excellent. Can I trust you to make a perfect copy of one of the panels? Don't omit a line or a dot. Sometimes that's enough to change the meaning."

"Like leaving out a single line would transform a 'q' into an 'o,'" Jenny said.

"If I'm in doubt whether some mark is intentional or just a flaw in the stone, I'll sketch it in lightly."

"I'll do the same," Neville said. "The Anubis text is closest to camp, so I'll hobble over there."

"And I'll take Isis," Jenny said. "Can't have you gentlemen consorting with a woman in such a state of undress—especially when she's another man's wife."

Favoring them all with a deliberately saucy smile, she scooped up Mozelle and her sketchbook, then trotted across to where Isis held her unspeaking court.

"That girl," Eddie said, "is going to be trouble for some man someday."

"She's trouble for one now," Neville said. "I don't know whether I should try to marry her off or tuck her in a nunnery."

"She wouldn't thank you for either," Eddie prophesied.

Stephen remained unnaturally intent on his notes during this conversation, and Neville found himself wondering if the linguist was smitten with his niece. Jenny was certainly lovely enough to turn a man's head, but there didn't seem to be any sparks flying between the two.

Crutch firmly anchored in his armpit, Neville thumped across the sand. He distracted himself from the pain attendant on this slow progress by thinking of Audrey Cheshire. There was loveliness and more, no doubt about it.

That evening, Stephen announced he had translated two portions of the inscription near Horus.

"There is more than one text," he explained, "as can be seen by the varied directions in which the hieroglyphs are oriented. I started with the one from the upper section of the panel."

"Stop playing professor," Neville said, irritably. His eyes hurt from the glare, and his copying had been less than swift. He'd kept stopping to try and make sense of what he was working with, and succeeded only in frustrating himself.

Stephen cleared his throat. "I went for speed, and accuracy, not artistry. Forgive any awkwardness."

"We do," Jenny said, "in advance."

Stephen cleared his throat once more, and Neville was just feeling guilty about pressing someone who had just a day or so before been nearly killed by heat stroke, when the young man began:

From the East comes he, Horus the Hawk, Horus the Avenger.
With the Sun comes he, Horus the King, Horus the Son.
Born of living mother, murdered father, comes he who causes the wicked to flee in terror.
He thrashes them with his flail, herds them with the wind
    rising from the beating of his strong wings.

He tramples them, as the Pharaoh tramples all who threaten the Black Land.
He is terrible in his wrath, yet tender in his protection of those who dwell beneath
    the shelter of his wings.
From the East comes Horus, and with him comes the wind.

Stephen's recital was met with respectful silence, and he commented rather shyly, "That's all of the first bit."

"It was lovely," Jenny said, "but frightening, too."

Stephen looked pleased. "I remind you that my interpretation may not be exactly what the writer intended. I had to guess where hieroglyphs had been partially effaced. The tone is not precisely traditional, at least from what I know . . ."

"Is there more?" Neville interrupted. "I realize that piece is quite long, but if you have any others, we would enjoy hearing them."

More relaxed now, Stephen did only a minimal clearing of throat and shuffling of papers before beginning.

"This one seems to be cautionary in nature, perhaps a curse against impious behavior. Quite the thing for a place like this."

Forget not that the Eye of Horus is the Eye of the Hawk,
The keen Eye that sees the evildoer and the just man alike.
Horus shreds the evildoer with cruel curving beak and punishing claws.
The wind from the wings of Harakhtes, the wind from the east,
    buries the evildoer beyond the sound of prayer or the gifts of his kin.
In the afterlife the evildoer will be a slave and no wine will ease his hours.
He will dine upon excrement and the leavings of monsters.
When he comes before Osiris, he will have no gifts for the father of his slayer.
Osiris will condemn him.
Anubis will refuse the opening of his mouth.
The evildoer will long for nothingness and be denied.
He will slave forever in filthy darkness and rank starvation.

"The other was frightening," Jenny said. "This one is plain horrid."

"Ironic, too," Stephen commented, "since the tomb robber would probably be illiterate and not understand the warning."

"I wonder," Neville said, "if that's correct in this case. The legend of Nefer-ankhotep says that priests, jealous of the pharaoh's favor in the eyes of the gods, were the ones who attempted to rob him. They would have understood this well enough."

"You sound," Eddie said with a thin smile, "as if you believe all that nonsense about the gods."

"I don't," Neville said quickly—perhaps a touch too quickly, for Eddie's smile only broadened. "However, the people who reburied Neferankhotep here would have known the story."

Eddie let the matter drop.

"What fascinates me," he said, "are the references to the wind from the wings of Horus. As I recall—and I don't claim to be an expert, but I have lived here over ten years—the prevailing wind in Egypt blows from the north, the opposite direction from the Nile current, which is why it is such a friendly river for navigation. This 'wind from the east' seems to be something other than natural."

Jenny cut in before anyone could respond to Eddie's challenge. "By the way, who was Harakhtes? He's the one with the wind in this verse."

"It's another name for Horus," Stephen said. "Horus of the Horizon. I think later periods merged him with the sun god, Ra. It's an appropriate title for Horus in his role as all-seeing god, just as Hor Nubti, Horus of Gold, was the common name for Horus in his role as avenger of his father. I took a few liberties there . . ."

Neville interrupted. "Eddie has an interesting point. I hadn't thought about the wind from the east being a supernatural wind. I guess I thought it was a reference to the *khamseen*."

"The *khamseen*?" Jenny asked.

"It's a wind that comes from the southwest, usually in early summer," Neville explained. "It's quite terrible. It can last for up to fifty days without much of a break. Dust clouds blot out the sun, temperatures rise, sometimes destroying the crops. As if that wasn't enough, the *khamseen* seems to encourage flying insects. I can't think of a more vivid curse."

"But you said this *khamseen* comes from the southwest," Stephen protested. "I took no liberties with the direction mentioned in the text. This Horus wind definitely comes from the east."

Neville shrugged. "I am sure you translated accurately. After all, this is a ritual inscription, not a guide to advise travelers. As I see it, Horus is usually associated with the east. Here he is also associated with the sun god, Ra. The sun comes from the east, and so would Horus, and so would any wind he brings to punish the wicked. I think we are unwise to imagine more."

Jenny looked as if she wanted to agree, but stubbornness wouldn't let her.

"But shouldn't we take the legend seriously, Uncle Neville? You didn't believe Alphonse Liebermann was onto anything, but here we are. And it wasn't that long ago that that German . . ."

"Schliemann," Stephen interrupted.

"That German," Jenny persisted, "found Troy by following descriptions in Homer. I'm not saying there's any truth to the story about gods burying the original mortuary complex, but I'm saying that Eddie's right. We should take notice of any oddities. If you and Eddie are right, a wind from the east might stand out to an ancient Egyptian like someone putting the Rockies running wrong way along North America would stand out to us."

"We'll see what the other texts tell us," Neville promised. "In the meantime, the light is growing too poor for us to continue, and I'd like to preserve our lamp oil for if we find something underground. Shall we entertain ourselves with something other than archeological speculation for the evening?"

"Papa Antonio taught me how to play *senet*," Jenny suggested. "That doesn't take much light."

The evening passed quickly, all the more so in that everyone was tired enough to go to sleep early. Eddie insisted that they continue to post watches, though Stephen was omitted from the rotation until he was recovered from his heatstroke.

In the morning, they continued copying and translating. Eddie went out and shot a goat. Once the meat they couldn't hope to eat before it spoiled was curing, he occupied himself poking around the bases of the statues and looking for other areas that might hold inscriptions. He found a few, but Stephen judged them hieratic texts, much later than the elegant inscriptions on the panels near the statues.

"We'll get to them later," Stephen promised, his fever now purely scholarly. "A history of the occupations of this place would be fascinating."

"I just hope we don't need to empty all the sand out of this valley to find Neville's ruins," Eddie said grimly. "That would take an army, and even his fortune isn't up to hiring that much labor."

Neville heard, but didn't comment. Stephen had started on the Isis text, proposing to work his way around the four cardinal points, but nothing he had read to them when they'd taken a mid-day break had seemed particularly promising. Isis certainly was expected to do her part in protecting the area against evildoers, but thus far her role fell neatly within the parameters described in mythology.

Neville had greater hopes for the Osiris texts, since Osiris was the lord of the underworld, but Stephen grew fussy when pressed to change his plans, and Neville was a good enough commander to know when to back down.

It's not like I haven't waited this long, he thought. *And in any case, why would the texts do more than caution? It isn't like they're going to provide directions into the tomb where anyone could find them.*

But he couldn't help but hope they would find something. The ancient Egyptians had firmly believed that the dead flourished through contact with the living. Offerings were not mere ritual, but were thought to offer nourishment for the dead. The dead were thought to offer counsel and intervention from their transformed state. Surely, the "good king" would not have been completely cut off from his people.

Surely not.

Jenny wondered if anyone else was aware just how tense Uncle Neville was becoming. She faithfully worked away as a copyist, but she had little hope that the texts would tell them anything. Eddie's probing around the edges of the valley seemed a more reasonable route toward finding the tomb of Neferankhotep, but it would be several days before Uncle Neville's sprained ankle would permit him to join Eddie at this work. For now he was restricted to carefully copying the hieroglyphs, and to pretending that he didn't care if they found anything more than these few texts.

She didn't believe him. Uncle Neville wasn't a looter, not even in the way Belzoni or the other early archeologists had been, but somehow, someway finding proof of Neferankhotep's existence had become irrationally important to him. She also suspected that nothing short of finding the good king's tomb would satisfy her uncle's mania. Even if they found the entire legend written on a wall somewhere, he would persist.

Jenny decided to spend some time making careful examinations of the areas surrounding the four statues. Now that she had access to ample water, the climate of the Egyptian winter didn't bother her a bit. She'd experienced far worse during summers in the southwestern United States and, unlike Stephen, she never forgot to protect exposed skin.

She finished the panel she'd been copying, and brought the finished sketch over to Stephen.

"That's all of the second one," she said.

Stephen looked up at her, his expression so blank that she realized his mind was still thinking in Egyptian.

"I'm going to take a break," she said, "or I'll be drawing vultures for owls, and confusing ankhs with the Girdle of Isis."

"That wouldn't do," Stephen said, truly appalled for a moment. Then his natural sense of humor reemerged. "We'd be writing 'wife' for 'life.'"

Jenny mimed throwing a handful of sand at him, and then paused to decide where to start exploring.

While copying Isis texts, Jenny had been given ample opportunity to inspect the area around the statue of that mysterious goddess. Anubis—completely unfairly, she knew—continued to make her skin crawl. Sir Neville had staked out the area near Osiris, and her uncle's temper was such that Jenny had no desire to remind him by her own crawling and climbing that his impulsiveness was what had shackled him. That left Horus, who offered the added advantage of being directly across the valley from her uncle, and thus completely out of his line of sight.

Therefore, scooping up Mozelle, who was burrowing among Stephen's notes, Jenny crossed to the eastern edge of the valley.

First she walked around the Horus sculpture, carefully examining it from all angles, trying hard to think like Auguste Dupin and see with her mind as well as her eyes. Neither approach seemed to do much good. Her eyes saw a statue carved from the rocky wall behind it, the stone polished and smoothed so perfectly that she found herself fighting the impulse to believe it had been made not by human hands, but by divine will. Her mind suggested that the statue might hide a door, but she found no indication of this.

What she did find didn't seem overly useful. From the start it had been evident that the sculpture stood on a base of some sort. Stephen had brushed away the sand that had accumulated around the feet and ankles to see if there were any texts there. What Jenny's investigation showed her was that the base went a whole lot further down than any of them had realized. She hadn't carried tools over, but little casual digging showed that it went down a foot without any sign of stopping.

Recalling how the legend told of the valley being buried in sand to hide Neferankhotep's tomb and all its lavish appointments, Jenny found herself wondering if rather than this being a statue set flush with what they thought of as "ground level," it might rather be the top of a massive pillar.

Thus far Uncle Neville had not turned from his laborious copying of the text over by Osiris. However, the sun was reaching its noontime height, and soon Eddie would demand that they break for an afternoon siesta. Jenny cast about for Mozelle, and spotted the kitten crouched belly to the sand, intent on a long-tailed lizard that had emerged onto a flat piece of rock.

Amused, Jenny watched as Mozelle began her stalk, golden-brown fur blending perfectly with the sand as long ago the now vanished Egyptian lions must have done. The tip of the kitten's tail twitched, then her entire rump wiggled in an ecstacy of enthusiasm.

Mozelle leapt too late. The lizard darted away, slipping up and over the sand, dodging into a crevice in the face of the polished panel. That should have ended the hunt, but Mozelle continued scrabbling determinedly at the rock and sand, unwilling to accept that the lizard could go where she could not.

"I believe," Eddie said, the sound of his voice making Jenny jump, for his soft-soled shoes had made little sound on the sand, "Mozelle wants to be an archeologist. Look at her dig."

Jenny was wondering if she dared make a more indelicate joke, and had just reluctantly decided that this would be improper when she realized there was something strange about where the kitten was digging.

"Eddie, look," she said, keeping her voice low, though every fiber of her longed to shout. "The sand is draining away faster than Mozelle's digging should account for."

Jenny dropped to her knees and pulled the kitten back. Then she saw a small piece of flat sandstone knocked to one side.

"This crack is longer than it seemed," she reported, "and either Mozelle or the lizard knocked away the bit of stone that was chinking it. I can hear the sand trickling in somewhere, like there's a hollow space behind."

From that moment, translating hieroglyphs took second place to clearing away the sand. Stephen and Neville were called over to view Jenny's discovery, and were equally excited.

"The stone has been dressed here," Neville said. "Carefully and so as not to show the marks, but once you know where to look for a seam, it's quite clear. I think we have found the upper edge of a doorway."

Jenny didn't mind that "we," not one bit, for the tension had melted from Uncle Neville, and his eyes shone with even more intensity than they had done for Lady Cheshire.

Eddie was wise enough to know that this was not the time to insist his charges take their mid-day break. With Jenny's assistance, he broke out the gear that had been brought along in case they found anything worth digging after. Among the most useful items were a selection of wide, shallow baskets, tightly woven enough that they could be used to carry away sand. Although bulky as individual items, the baskets could be nested inside each other, and so Eddie had brought a good many.

This proved wise, for moving sand was their primary task. They shoved, swept, and even scooped with their hands, but there was no rapid way to clear the stuff, and soon all had been given ample demonstration of sand's insidious ability to trickle, to collapse, and to otherwise make itself persistently difficult to remove.

After a time, they yielded to Eddie's persuasion that they would get more done if they were rested and cool. Back beneath the shelter of the camel-hair pavilion, Sir Neville presented Mozelle with a sliver of roasted mutton.

"I take back everything I ever said about this kitten, Jenny," he said, his high good humor evident, perhaps because despite his exertions the swelling in his ankle had not increased appreciably. "Mozelle has earned herself a lifetime of cream and mice once we return to England."

Jenny smiled, and scratched the little cat between its tawny ears, obliging with a tummy tickle when Mozelle rolled sleepily onto her back.

"To think," Stephen added, "the entire interior wall here could be honeycombed with doors hidden beneath that sand, and we would never have known."

"Don't say that," Jenny requested with a shiver that had nothing to do with the lengthening shadows. "It gives me goose pimples just thinking about it. What if they should all open at once?"

"They'd fill with sand," Stephen said dryly.

Removing the sand proved to be only part of the job, carrying it away was another—one that devolved largely on Jenny and Eddie, for Stephen still needed to avoid the sun and so was delegated to digging beneath a tarpaulin erected to assure shade. Sir Neville, also restricted to digging, insisted that the sand be carried to the "plain" at the center of the valley.

"Otherwise we may end up moving it all again to get at something else along the edge, or the least breath of wind may blow it back."

The camels were drafted for some of this labor, but human hands had to carry the stuff, and human arms and backs to lift and load it. Within a few hours, Jenny's back ached abysmally, and she was having second thoughts about her find. Copying had been dull, but decidedly unpainful.

She was almost grateful when Eddie ordered her in the most matter-of-fact way possible to return to camp and cook the evening meal. He had shot another goat earlier that morning, but the flat bread—more a cracker than a bread by this time—beans, and dried fruit that were to accompany the meat needed preparation.

When dusk forced them to stop, they had the upper portion of a doorway cleared. Based on other structures of that type, Neville seemed confident they would be finished the next day. They had also uncovered along the sides of the door a short series of incised hieroglyphs accompanied by sunken relief pictures. Stephen had made a quick sketch of these, which he now tilted to the firelight to better study them.

"I can't work out the entire meaning," he said, "since the text runs top to bottom, and so I'm missing a good half. What I can read seems to indicate that entrance through this door is forbidden to all but those confident in the justice of their actions."

"Another curse," Neville asked, masking a yawn, "or a more specific warning?"

"It seems to be just another warning or curse," Stephen admitted. "The writing on the other side of the doorway has something to do with sand. I can't guess what that has to do with anything. It's in a different hand, and the writing is less deeply incised, and in a later style."

"Like what we saw at the Hawk Rock?" Jenny asked.

"Very similar," Stephen said, folding the cover shut over his notes. "I should light a lantern and go finish my copying, but I will admit gratitude that Neville has forbidden gratuitous burning of oil. I, for one, am a spent candle. I understand why most excavators hire native help."

"We couldn't have done that this time," Jenny reminded him. "We didn't know for sure that we were going to find anything."

"And," Eddie said, staring over where the statue of Anubis kept its silent watch, "it might not have been wise."

No one chose to comment on the warning implicit in Eddie's statement. Since they had arrived in the Valley of Dust, it had become increasingly difficult to believe in the world without. Their entire existence seemed to have been bounded by the golden glow of the curving sandstone cliffs. The lush green Nile on which they had so recently traveled had become nothing more than a rather unlikely and extravagant dream.

Eddie, however, continued watchful, and until full darkness fell, he frequently strolled to one or more of the watch posts from which he had earlier established he could see out of the valley and into the surrounding desert.

Speculation as to what they might find when they finally opened the door lapsed as exhaustion made its claim. With very little comment, those who were not on watch retired to their bedrolls until only Sir Neville and Mozelle remained awake. He was so intent on his thoughts, that even when a miniature fox, lured close by the tantalizing scent of their dinner, barked indignantly from the edge of the firelight, he didn't stir.

As always, dawn provided their wake-up call. Stephen had tended a pot of stew made from dried fish, onions, and beans, which he insisted was just as nice as dining on kippers and eggs. No one bothered to ask whether he liked that particular meal. Their supply of tea was holding out nicely, augmented with mint from one of the canyons.

Then the digging began again. Neville, noting how stiffly Jenny was moving, gave her his place digging, and worked with Eddie on loading sand onto the camels. From time to time, he had to lean against the reclining beast to relieve the pressure on his ankle but he managed well enough.

"I've found bottom," Jenny sang out sometime around mid-morning. She put the trowel she had been using aside, and began brushing the sand away with her hands. Mozelle, who had retained proprietary interest in the humans' odd behavior, thought this was a wonderful game and began scrabbling with her.

"Here, Jenny," Eddie said, leaning down over the edge of the excavation. "Try this."

He handed her a small, stiff-bristled broom which she used to clear away the remaining sand.

At last the door stood revealed much as it must have been on the day it was first constructed. Hieroglyphs ran down both sides and adorned a middle panel of the door itself. The base of the pedestal on which the sculpture of Horus stood was revealed as level with the bottom of the door. Jenny and Stephen now stood on rock, rather than sand, though whether this doorstep was a ledge, or the true bottom of the valley could not be told without digging away even more sand—labor no one felt an immediate inclination to undertake.

"The door has neither latch nor hinges," Stephen said. "How are we to get it open without breaking it?"

"Jenny, come out and let me have a look," Neville ordered. "I learned a few tricks when on archeological escort duty."

Eddie, his usual watchfulness vanished in the general excitement of discovery, helped Neville down.

"If you don't have any luck," he offered, "I'll give it a try."

Stephen, meanwhile, was inspecting the hieroglyphic writing on the side panels, concentrating on the less deeply incised, presumably newer text.

"I admire your devotion to scholarship," Jenny said, leaning back to watch as soon as she had climbed out.

"Not scholarship," Steven admitted, "at least not in the purest sense. I've been wondering if these might be directions for opening the door. What if after some years had passed, such guidance was viewed as prudent by some Protector?"

"Like the obelisk that gave directions to the valley?" Jenny asked.

"Exactly," Stephen said. "From what I can make out, the text does apply to the door, but it's as annoyingly vague as the obelisk was, full of references to Nekhebet and Wadjet."

"Who?"

"The patron deities associated with upper and lower Egypt, the vulture goddess and the cobra goddess," Stephen replied. "Elegant in their strange ways, but hardly useful."

Neville had been making a meticulous inspection of the interior of the door frame, and now he gave a grunt of satisfaction.

"Found something?" Eddie asked.

"I may have," Neville replied. "Hand me that whisk broom."

He knelt, and carefully swept all traces of sand from the base of the door leaving it, as Stephen commented with fascination, "Clean enough to eat from."

"Now some water," Neville said. "It doesn't need to be much."

Eddie handed down a canteen. Neville poured a small stream of water on each corner of the door. It pooled, then began to sink into the stone. Neville did not seem disappointed, but rose to inspect the top of the door.

"One of you," he said to Eddie and Jenny, "climb around and take a close look at the top of the door frame. Try not to knock too much sand down."

Eddie obeyed, crossing to the top of the rock and leaning down awkwardly.

"What am I looking for?" he asked.

"Try to feel if there is any indication of an opening—a small one. You'd be feeling for motion in the air or a change in temperature."

Eddie probed with his fingers.

"Maybe."

"Stronger on one side over the other?"

"Maybe on the right, but I wouldn't swear to it. Are you going to tell us what you're thinking?"

Neville nodded.

"I think that the door doesn't move back and forth, but sideways along a track. There's enough space in the cliff wall to admit it. The fit is tight, but I think it moves right to left. The water I poured on the stone seemed to leak away just the smallest amount on the right, where on the left it soaked into the stone."

"The sandstone could have been more porous on the right," Eddie objected.

"It could," Neville agreed. "However, take a look at the crack—the one Mozelle's lizard slipped into. It's also on the right, as if someone knew it opened that way and tried to pry it open, but failed."

"Or was stopped," Eddie said darkly.

Neville looked up at him.

"Or was stopped. Come on down. The next step is seeing if we can figure out what holds it in place. Otherwise, we'll have to try and break through the stone, and I'd hate to do that."

Throughout the morning, they remained unable to move the door. When they retired to escape the greatest of the sun's intensity, Neville decided to hint that the time had come for them to simply break it in.

To his surprise, both Jenny and Stephen objected strongly, and though Eddie said nothing, his aversion to the idea was evident.

"We've hardly looked, Uncle Neville," Jenny said sternly. "If you really want this discovery for the sake of science, you can't behave like a tomb robber."

"I'm sure you're on the right track," Stephen added. "I think the mentions of Nekhebet and Wadjet are just elaborate ways of referring to south and north—or, since the doorway is on the west side of the valley, to left and right."

"Which is which?" Jenny asked quickly, and Neville felt rebuked for his impatience.

"Well, if you face the door—and from other parts of the text, I think that is indicated—then the right is Upper Egypt or Nekhebet, while the left is Wadjet. The text talks about Wadjet going to visit Nekhebet."

"Or, as Uncle Neville has been saying all along," Jenny completed triumphantly, "that the door slides from left to right. We are on the right track!"

"No pun intended," she added as the three men looked at her and groaned—Stephen the loudest of all.

Perhaps Stephen's translation provided enough encouragement that they took more care on their return examination, perhaps they would have worked the puzzle out eventually. Whichever was the case, Eddie eventually detected the small piece of stone that kept the door from sliding. It was a skilled bit of carving that looked like just another section of the solid stone, but once his patient investigation of every inch of the upper door frame found that one piece moved, removing the chock offered no difficulty. Grating on the sand that had drifted into its track, the door slid easily enough, vanishing into a recess to the left of the opening.

"What astonishing engineering!" Stephen marvelled, dusting his palms on his trouser leg when they stopped for breath. Track or not, the sandstone panel was heavy.

"These are the people who built the pyramids at Gizeh," Neville said, feeling as absurdly proud as if he'd done the work himself.

He noticed his niece was no longer peering over the edge. "Where's Jenny?"

"Here, Uncle Neville," the head framed by the wide-brimmed hat reappeared.

"I went to get a lantern. We may need light to see what's inside. Go on, finish opening it!"

The men did so, the door moving more easily now that they could step alongside it and push. Jenny leaned down to lower the lantern, but it proved to be almost unnecessary. Once opened, the chamber proved to be lit from within by narrow slits cut in the rock above.

"I am an idiot," Neville said, striking himself on the forehead. "I should have thought to look along the ridge line above for indications of caverns below."

"The openings must be covered," Eddie said reasonably, "otherwise the sand would have filled the place long since."

Debate as to whether this would have been possible, or whether such coverings would have perished long before died away, for at last they could see what had waited behind the door, unseen for who knew how many millennia.

Dire Warnings

THE ROOM was quite deep and square—excavated, as best they could tell, from the surrounding rock. The floor was covered with a layer of sand that had drifted in through the ventilation slits and the crack in the door, but otherwise it seemed as pristine as the day the workmen had left it.

The back wall was dominated by a painting of Maat represented as a lovely, winged woman crowned with a single white feather. She was depicted in stylized Egyptian fashion. Her head with its single feature was turned in profile. Her unnaturally long arms—from which depended heavy, hawk-like wings, their feathers painted in white, black, and blue—were presented along with the torso in a front view. Her lower torso and kneeling legs were again in profile. Lest anyone fail to recognize her, her name and a brief hymn of praise were painted above her in gold.

On the left-hand, or northern, wall was painted the monster Ammit, She Who Devours the Wicked, waiting for her prey, surrounded by swarms of vipers and scorpions. Green, red, and black had been used to depict Ammit's crocodilian snout, her leonine mane and forequarters, and her hippopotamus hindquarters. The monster's divinity was asserted by the striped *nemes* headdress she wore.

Jenny forced herself to study the horrible creature, and concluded that no other monster could so perfectly represent watchful punishment. With her long, many-toothed snout tilted upward toward the underside of an empty set of scales, Ammit didn't even seem particularly ferocious, more like a mastiff waiting for her master to drop her a tidbit.

The right-hand wall showed Osiris in a similar fashion to his sculpture on the other side of the valley. In this depiction he carried the flail and crook loosely, as a living man might, rather than crossed over his chest. Unlike the worn statue, here the green hue of the god's exposed skin was vivid, the expression in his eyes could be seen as stern, but not unkind. He wore a jeweled collar, and the tall crown of upper Egypt was shining gold rather than the more usual white. His wrappings were elaborately adorned with curving lines rather like the letter 'U', ending in tiny dots of yellow, blue, and red. The overall effect was light and elegant. Jenny found herself thinking the design would make a pretty summer dress.

When Jenny would have brought the lantern into the room, Neville stopped her.

"We don't want the smoke to stain the paintings," he said. "These have been untouched for millennia. It would be a pity to ruin them now—especially since we have light enough."

Jenny smiled. She thought some of the fervor for discovery had eased now that they were in the chamber. Stephen was busy trying to spell out the texts alongside the painting of Osiris.

"What does all of this mean?" she asked.

"I won't know for sure until I translate it thoroughly," Stephen replied, his tone distracted. "I will make an educated guess that this chamber is intended to show the options that await at judgment. On one side stands Osiris in his glory, ready to welcome the just. On the other is Ammit, waiting for her supper."

Jenny tried to sound casual. "It ties in rather nicely with the inscription alongside the statue of Horus, doesn't it?"

Stephen nodded, "Though it doesn't explain those references to the wind. I don't see anything here about it, either. This is all about the wonders that await those whose souls are in balance with Maat. They will go to the fields of Amenti, where the grain grows taller than a tall man, and all the delights of life flourish under the light of Ra."

"Sounds almost as good as the Muslim paradise," Eddie quipped, examining the drawing of Maat with more than scholarly interest. "I wonder if the Egyptians believed in houris?"

Jenny saw Neville shoot his friend a dirty look, but Stephen nattered on unaware of the breach of propriety.

"They believed in something like that. The paintings on the walls, and the little carved figures—shabtis—were meant to supply all the luxuries the deceased might need in the afterlife. This included someone to do your chores for you, and all the rest."

"I wonder," Neville said, speaking quickly enough that Jenny knew he was trying to make sure Stephen didn't forget himself and talk about that provocative "rest," "if there are any doors out of this chamber and into the tomb proper?"

"Maybe so, maybe not," Stephen said, shrugging, and moving from Osiris to Maat. "Doorways into key areas of a tomb were usually very carefully concealed so that tomb robbers wouldn't have easy access. Sometimes there were entire false passages, done up with art and polished stone floors."

"I remember," Jenny said, "something about that from our tour at Gizeh. I think it must have been a terrible amount of work for the laborers."

"True," Stephen agreed, "but what was being protected was more than gold and precious goods. If the body and its substitutes were destroyed, so were the essential elements for continuing in the afterlife. The laborers might have felt pretty good about being in on the deception. In the afterlife, the pharaoh became one with Osiris, and he would be more welcoming to someone who served him well."

"Or," Eddie said sardonically, "the laborers might have liked knowing what passages were good and which were dummies. After all, the robberies were probably inside jobs."

There was an uncomfortable silence following that, and Jenny knew that, like herself, the men didn't know whether to classify themselves as thieves.

If we don't take anything, she thought. *If we just look around and make notes, that's not thieving. It might even be good for Neferankhotep. Didn't Stephen say the Egyptians thought being forgotten was the worst thing that could happen?*

They examined the chamber in detail, making sketches of the art and rough copies of some of the texts, but by that evening the lust for new discoveries had taken over.

"Why don't we split our energies?" Stephen suggested over a bowl of mutton stew. "Neville seems to have a talent for figuring out the tombs. Why doesn't he take over in the chamber? I could go on with the texts, and Eddie and Jenny could see if there are other doors. There might be one near this one, or, more likely, by one of the other sculptures."

He suddenly stopped talking and blushed, realizing he'd been overstepping his authority. Sir Neville, not he, was patron of the expedition. Jenny hurriedly looked over at her uncle, but he didn't seem affronted. If anything, he was amused.

"That sounds like a good plan," Neville said. "And I appreciate the compliment to my skills. Eddie, what do you think about checking along the ridge to see if there are any more ventilation shafts?"

"I can do that," Eddie replied, "especially if you can give me a clear idea what to look for. It would give me a chance to hunt as well—unless Jenny wants a go."

Jenny shook her head. "I think there may be an opening over by Isis. I remember noticing when I was copying that the sand sloped oddly along one section of the wall. I didn't give it much thought at the time, but now I'd like to take another look."

"It might be an offering chapel," Stephen said. "Those were usually left open so the living could bring gifts for the deceased. It might hold some interesting sculpture, even a statue of Neferankhotep himself."

"Now that would be something," Neville said. "I know Egyptian art is more symbolic than representational, but there were portrait statues. Wouldn't it be something if we could actually learn what Neferankhotep looked like?"

Jenny was about to agree, trying to find a tactful way to ask her uncle what his intentions were should they find something more portable than wall paintings, when she was interrupted by the sound of movement against the roof of the camel-hair pavilion.

At first she thought the sound was her imagination, but then she realized that the men had gone very still. Mozelle, who had been trying to climb into Jenny's lap—and her stew bowl—was staring upwards with unblinking blue eyes.

Without even realizing she had done so, Jenny drew her revolver from its holster. There was something moving up there, something heavy enough to dimple the fabric downward.

A bird, she thought. *Maybe a hawk, like the one we saw on our way here. No. It's too heavy for that.*

She eased herself out from under the protection of the pavilion in time to see a small and agile shape leap from the roof and down, onto the rocks.

"Just a critter of some sort," she said, her voice shaking as she eased her gun back into its holster. "Probably attracted by the smell of our dinner."

Stephen, however, was picking something white off the ground, where it had slid off the pavilion's peaked roof. Like one mesmerized, he unfolded it.

" 'Flee!' " he read aloud. " 'You have been discovered. Your enemies will strike with the coming of first light.' It's signed, 'Sphinx.' "

Revelation hit Jenny so suddenly she nearly staggered. *So that's who the Sphinx is . . . It must be. What are they doing here?*

She didn't have time to say anything about her revelation. Uncle Neville had rounded on Stephen and Jenny didn't think she'd ever heard him sound so angry.

"Stephen," Sir Neville growled, "this is not the time for one of your jokes!"

"It wasn't me," Stephen protested. "This isn't even like my writing paper . . ."

Eddie came down from one of his watch stands, his manner taut and commanding.

"It wasn't Stephen," he said sharply. "I can't see much detail, but there are campfires down there. Camels picketed along the edge. Whoever's down there has camped close enough to the rock that I can't see them—and I'm not getting myself shot climbing down."

Jenny thought of the note's futile warning. "Flee? We can't flee! All that's out there is desert."

"How about the ruined village?" Neville asked. "Would that offer any cover?"

"None," Eddie said, "and the canyons where I've been hunting are all dead ends where we could easily be trapped. We hold the high ground. If we go down there we'll lose whatever small advantage that gives us. They'll wait until morning. Even knowing what you're doing, getting up here is a bad climb in uncertain light."

"We could hole up in the chamber we found today," Jenny suggested. Her heart was racing, and the stew she'd just eaten sat uncomfortably heavy in her gut. "The walls there would cover our back and flanks, and no one could get a drop on us from above, not without falling into the pit we cleared. It's a shame we've made it so obvious, or we could close the door and hope they'd steal the camels and leave to look for us elsewhere."

"Isn't that chamber just as bad as a dead-end canyon?" Stephen asked. "Why not stay in the open?"

"Because then they could surround us or shoot us," Eddie replied. He was already gathering up key items of gear. "Because the chamber itself offers intangible protection."

"What?" Stephen asked.

"As I see it, our enemies are one of two groups—either those Protectors of the Pharaoh or rival archeologists," Eddie replied, tossing Stephen a handgun and belt. "Put that on."

Jenny, busy filling empty canteens with water, completed Eddie's thought. "And either way they won't want the chamber damaged—archeologists because it's a valuable find, and maybe the way into the tomb, and these Protectors because it belongs to Neferankhotep."

"That's about the size of it," Eddie agreed.

"Closing the door to the chamber once we're inside would be out of the question," Neville said. He'd listened with intense patience, even to the mention of other archeologists—though he must have known to whom these oblique references applied. "All they'd need to do would be to find the ventilation slits and shut them off, and we'd suffocate. A door that let in so little sand isn't going to let in much air—certainly not enough for four people to last very long without passing out."

"Start moving food and water into the chamber," Eddie ordered. "With water, we can hold out longer, maybe negotiate some sort of surrender."

They did this, leaving the pavilion up, and making dummies from their bedrolls to lie alongside the fire. Eddie led a few of the camels to the top of the trail in the hope that they'd decide to wander and provide a distraction, but the animals seemed disinclined to leave.

"Why should they?" he said. "There's water, and we've made sure they didn't exhaust the forage."

Eddie's labors with the camels made Jenny remember Mozelle. It wouldn't do to have the kitten wander, so she stuffed the tiny creature into a drawstring bag, leaving her head outside. Then she put it on top of one of their stacks of gear. Mozelle protested with a surprisingly shrill wail until she forgot why she was unhappy and fell asleep.

The rest of them were not so lucky. Even after the day's hard labors, they could not rest. Sand trickled down from the edge of their pit, its unmetered flow reminding Jenny of a weird hourglass. Dawn's first glimmer was hidden from them by the rim of the valley, but they knew it had come when a shuffling tramp and the falling of rock announced that several people were mounting to the rocky rim.

"They're closing from several different directions," Eddie whispered hoarsely, shifting his rifle and checking the load for the dozenth time. "It's time to make our stand."

The wait seemed unbearably long, but Neville knew it probably lasted no more than a few minutes. Those few minutes were enough to make him acutely aware of their predicament. They were trapped in a dead end—worse than a dead end, in a hole in the ground, their best defense not the guns they handled with varying degrees of confidence, but the nebulous value of some tomb paintings.

If these were the more normal sort of desert bandits, not the Protectors of the Pharaoh or rival archeologists, the art would be scant defense indeed. And even if their "enemies"—as the Sphinx's last note had proclaimed them—were interested in the art work, would they be willing to sacrifice such a nonportable sample to get the gear Neville and his crew had stowed in the chamber with them?

We only have the Sphinx's word that these are enemies, Neville thought frantically. *They could be others, come to use the water here.*

If they knew of the water, his traitor self responded, *then why didn't they come up last night? They would have known the trail. Why are they sneaking up now, and from several directions? Whoever these are, they know we are here and they trust us not at all.*

Neville shifted his grip on his revolver, wishing he'd taken more time to practice on the way out. He'd made certain Stephen learned the basics, but Jenny and Eddie had been the only two of their company to keep in practice.

After what happened last time, after what happened a few weeks ago in Cairo, he thought, *you think I'd have taken this more seriously. Did I really somehow believe that if I ignored the possibility, it wouldn't happen?*

Neville was given no further opportunity for self-recrimination. Voices speaking Arabic were shouting to each other now. They'd found the camp, discovered it empty, and located the pit on the east side of the valley, one discovery following the other so rapidly that the words flowed over each other.

He translated for Jenny and Stephen, neither of whom understood colloquial Arabic well enough to follow the rapid exchange.

"They're coming for us," he ended. "Stephen, you're the weakest shot. Drop back."

The young linguist agreed, Jenny and Eddie had put their rifles aside, preferring handguns in such close quarters, where the angle at which they must shoot—if indeed they must shoot—would be steep.

Sand rained down the edges of the pit as a man came walking to the edge. Initially, all that could be seen was the hem of his long white robe and his booted feet. Then the man squatted, bending slightly forward so he could look into the pit. More sand showered down, not enough to endanger those within the chamber, but enough to remind them all too acutely of their danger. The man who looked down at them wore a curved sword at his hip. He handled a rifle with easy confidence, angling it so that the barrel pointed into the chamber below.

Neville raised his head, looking straight up into the arrogant, hook-nosed face of a desert Bedouin who radiated command as casually as the sun did heat. The Bedouin was clean-shaven, except for a narrow, thready mustache that drooped to either side of his mouth, and a sparse beard at the end of his chin. Neither adornment did anything to enhance his features, which were pocked and scarred, perhaps from measles or smallpox.

I suppose he's adhering to some Moslem regulation, Neville thought, but for the moment he was so flustered he couldn't recall what ruling would apply. *No matter how bad his hair looks, he wouldn't cut it.*

"We meet again," the Bedouin said, in stilted but good English. "Though I think you would not recall me from the first time. It was a night when the fools who followed me thought a mummy walked. I was young, then, a new chieftain, or they would not have dared. I have not forgiven you for that trick, not all these years, all this time. I knew you would return, and I have waited."

"Ah," Neville said, not really knowing what else he could say.

"At last you have come, and you shall go before one greater than I to be punished for your sins," the sheik continued, shifting the rifle slightly so that its barrel was very obviously pointed at Neville.

Up to this point he hadn't seemed to notice the others, but now Jenny angled her own gun at him and spoke:

"Shoot my uncle, mister, and you're going to be wearing the landscape."

The sheik looked neither startled nor surprised, only puzzled. Perhaps, Neville thought, he didn't realize that this was a girl threatening him.

"Wearing the landscape?" the sheik repeated.

"Like in a grave," Jenny said. Her American accents, recently mellowed by contact with English speakers, were harsh. "Don't think I won't do it, either."

The sheik blinked.

"I believe you would try," he said, "but trying and doing are not the same things."

How Jenny might have replied to this, they never knew, for a voice spoke in Arabic from out of sight behind the sheik.

"Are all four of them there? The four of whom we were told?"

"All four," the sheik replied, *"trapped like lice between thumb and forefinger."*

The sheik returned his attention to Neville. "Come out, infidel, and bring your followers with you. You are trapped, and I have many men and many weapons. Come out and we will let you live."

His tone was wheedling and commanding in turn.

"I don't trust him," Jenny said softly, her eyes and weapon never wavering from the sheik.

"He has something in mind," Eddie agreed.

Stephen said nothing, but Neville could hear his breathing, rapid and nervous, echoing from the depths of the chamber.

"Come out, infidels," the sheik repeated. "You have guns, but we have guns, too. We have food, water, and time. You may have food and water, but not so much, and I think not so much time."

Neville refused to answer, and for a long moment the sheik's dark brown eyes met his own lighter orbs, and neither gave.

"If you come out," the sheik said reasonably, "we will let you pay us for escorting you to safety. That would be nice, wouldn't it? You could give us your fine camels and some English gold, and maybe some other presents. If we must shoot you, we will take the camels, of course, and your belongings, but I do not fancy you have much gold with you here in the desert. So you see, we have reason to take you to safety."

"He has a point," Stephen said, his breath rasping beneath the words. "Why don't I believe him?"

"Because you're too smart to believe a liar," Eddie said, keeping his voice low, "and not so much a coward that you want to believe him."

Stephen laughed softly. "I'm so scared, I couldn't spell my own name on a bet."

"You're not running," Eddie said, "or asking us to surrender. That's courage enough."

Neville knew from the sheik's expression that he couldn't make out the quiet exchange, but he guessed that the very levelness of the tones in which it was conducted did more for their position than any expression of bravado. Consequently, he kept his peace, not even responding to the offer of safe conduct.

The sheik settled more comfortably on his heels.

"I can wait all day, English," he said. "I can go sit in the shade of your tent and drink water cooled from the earth. You can go nowhere. I think I shall watch you for a bit, watch your arm grow tired of holding that heavy gun. The good guns are heavy, true?"

Neville bit his lip, forcing himself to maintain what he knew would be an unnerving silence. The others took their cue from him. After the day grew warmer, the sheik did retire. Laughing and singing was heard from the direction of their camp, but the increased trickle of sand told them that someone remained, just out of sight, watching and listening.

It was a long day, harder in that they never dared let down their guard. They rotated posts, though, with Eddie and Stephen standing watch in the front of the chamber so Jenny and Neville could rest, then rotating once more. The water they had carried in kept them from thirst, but could not refresh.

Stephen provided some small distraction for them by translating the inscriptions on the walls. His cultured accents reading off prayers and invocations that had been old millennia ago must have sounded quite peculiar to whomever listened from outside the chamber.

Noon passed and the Bedouin grew quieter, probably taking their afternoon rest. About the time Neville's watch announced that civilized British were taking tea, there was the sound of booted feet crunching on the sand above.

Neville looked up, expecting to see the sheik, but instead confronted the sun-browned, sardonic features of Captain Brentworth.

"I see you decided to go on a dig after all, Sir Neville," Brentworth said. The smile with which he accompanied these words was not a friendly one. "I hope you don't mind our relieving you of your find."

Neville felt his skin grow hot at the implications of that arrogant "our." He spoke before he could think.

"Is Lady Cheshire with you then?"

A new voice, laughing, light, and feminine, gave him his reply. "Of course. Who do you think arranged all of this? My goodness, Sir Neville, but you have led us on a merry chase! You should never have refused to share your information. I should so much rather have been your partner than your opponent."

She purred the word "partner" in a fashion that made Captain Brentworth temporarily shift his glower to her, but she put out her hand and caressed him lightly and the glower faded.

Like a dog, Neville thought, *patted by the master.*

He wondered if he had looked as foolish as Brentworth, and decided he probably had, but forgave himself. No man could look at Audrey Cheshire and not be excused some foolishness.

Voices raised in command came from the direction of the camp. There was a female screech, Sarah Syms saying "Take your hands off of me, you brute!"

Neville felt a momentary wash of confusion. Surely no man would even look at Sarah Syms's horsey features with lust when Audrey Cheshire was near. Then again, didn't the Arabs really like their horses, even let them sleep in their tents?

Cheshire and Brentworth had looked back, almost casually when the fracas arose, but now they were on their feet, every line of their bodies defensive.

"What are you doing?" Lady Cheshire said sharply. "Leave my companion alone! Why are you bringing her here?"

The sheik reappeared. Neville could only see his lower body clearly, but from the spread of his legs, he was defiant.

"Silence, woman! I have had enough of your shrewish words. The time has come for you to know who commands. Drop your weapon."

This last was directed towards Captain Brentworth, who had been in the act of drawing a regulation issue pistol from the holster on his right hip.

Neville saw Brentworth's hand freeze in mid-motion, drop, and hang limp.

An anonymous robed form came forward and removed the gun, patted Brent-worth down and removed a second gun from his boot top.

"What are you doing?" Lady Cheshire demanded, and Neville couldn't help but admire her spirit.

There was an abrupt crack, and a muffled scream. Audrey dropped to her knees, and Neville saw the welt rising on her elegant features. His wide green eyes were wild and terrified. He realized with something like sorrow that she didn't look lovely anymore.

"Now," the sheik said, "all of you other English, in the hole with your countrymen."

Captain Brentworth put himself protectively between Lady Cheshire and the sheik.

"What is this nonsense?" he barked. "We paid you good money to locate these people and this place. We have promised you more on our return. What are you doing?"

"You think that we are your lackeys," the sheik replied, his tones a snide caress. "You are wrong. Neither you nor my friend the headman Riskali, who sent word to me that in his village were English looking for guides to help them pursue other English into the desert, know that my people have ancient knowledge of the secrets this desert cradles in her care."

The sheik's voice rose as he spoke, becoming taut and shrill, a transformation all the more terrifying for his former calm control.

Jenny hissed in Neville's ear, "They're distracted—listening to him rant. Should we make a break for it?"

Neville shook his head. "We'd just be shot."

Eddie growled unhappily, "We may be anyhow, and I'd gladly take someone with me."

Neville glanced at him and saw his friend's features remote and fierce. Jenny looked no kinder.

"I want Lady Cheshire," she said. "If she had kept her nose out of our business, none of this would have happened. You heard the sheik. Cheshire told him we were here!"

Above, Lady Cheshire had raised her tear-streaked face to confront the sheik, "What ancient knowledge? Do you mean these ruins? We will gladly share with you any treasure we find. We could work together. I have contacts in the antiquities markets. You would do far better working with us than selling your finds on the streets of Luxor."

The sheik spat in the sand in front of her, somehow giving the impression that he failed to spit on her because that would somehow profane his spittle.

"Truly, the Prophet knew what he was saying when he decreed that woman is subordinate to man. Your face is fair, your form skinny but not displeasing. Were you not destined for a judgment that far overrules my own, I would take you as a concubine—or, better, sell you in the markets to the South, for truly I believe touching you would shrivel a man's member."

He licked his lips as if reveling in some carnal fantasy only reluctantly relinquished.

"But you have trespassed against an ancient law and an ancient trust. No amount of English gold will free me from my duty."

The shadow of his rifle swept over the pit. "Walk now, down to join the other English. Call your followers to join you. Do this or we will throw you down, and the hole is deep enough that you will feel pain unnecessarily."

"He's serious, Audrey," Captain Brentworth said. "You can't bluff your way through this one."

Slowly, the color draining from her cheeks and leaving the mark of the sheik's blow to show in high contrast, Lady Cheshire held up her hands.

"Lower me down, Robert. Help Sarah and Rashid before you come."

The chamber was cramped now, but Jenny and Neville kept to the fore with guns ready—though if there had ever been a problem that shooting couldn't solve, this was it.

Eddie Bryce pushed past them and stood in the pit, eschewing the shelter so as to look up at the sheik. Scorn shaped every line of his body, and he was terrible in his anger.

"So, you boast of your ancient trust," he said, and he spoke the pure Arabic of the Koranic scholar. "You are the protectors of the Pharaoh Neferankhotep. You are the servants of commands given by heathen gods! To you I say this: There is no god but Allah, and Mohammed is His prophet. Your faith is a lie. You and your men are lower than vipers, for at least a viper wears its own skin. You creep like a thief, wearing the guise of a just man."

For the first time, the sheik faltered. Clearly, he had never before perceived a conflict between his duty to the pharaoh and his duty to Islam. The first was a trust handed down for untold generations from father to son, mother to daughter. The second was not only religion, but social and educational structure. Against this, Eddie had struck a bitter and telling blow.

The sheik paused, and Neville wondered if he was actually going to back down.

Then the sheik laughed. "Fools!" he cried in accents harsher than Eddie's. "There is no god but Allah, and Mohammed is His prophet. That is true. It is also true that a son should be faithful to the commands of his father. My father commanded that I follow this path set by his father, and by his father before him. Such has it been for me and the men of my tribe from a time before Mohammed walked the Earth and spoke the truth that brought light to the world."

Since this exchange had taken place in Arabic, the other Bedouin had followed this argument with ease. Like the sheik, they had initially been unsettled, now they took refuge from that uncomfortable sensation in anger.

If he ordered them to shoot us like fish in a barrel, Neville thought desperately, *they'd do it and laugh. Be quiet, Eddie . . .*

But Eddie Bryce, now wholly Ibrahim ben Josef, couldn't hear Neville's thoughts—nor, had he been able to do so, would he have ceased his righteous indignation.

"So, what do you intend for us, oh faithful one?" Eddie's words were polite, but the sneer in his voice was potent as a slap.

The sheik moved as if he would slide down into the pit and assault Eddie with his bare hands, but he stopped himself in mid-motion. Perhaps he recalled how easily he could become a hostage if he came down. Even a fanatic does not sacrifice himself lightly when there are alternatives.

Good try, Eddie, Neville thought, suddenly understanding.

"What do I intend?" the sheik responded, stepping back from the pit's edge. "You shall know, all too soon, and wish to go back from that knowing. So has it ever been for the hundreds, if not thousands who over the ages have attempted to violate the tomb of the good king. Back now, in with your friends, or I shall have you shot where you stand."

Eddie obeyed, and as he crowded in with them, Neville squeezed his shoulder.

"Clever gambit," he whispered.

"Almost managed it," Eddie said. "Swine's no true son of Islam."

Not hearing this last insult, the sheik strode over to where the carving of Horus had impassively watched events, neither approving or disapproving these actions done in his name.

Neville checked the angle, wondering if he could possibly nail the sheik before he did whatever he was about to do. Apparently, the sheik caught the direction of his gaze.

"Shoot the next one who moves," he said in English, meaning the warning as much for his prisoners as for his men.

Neville could feel all those in the chamber willing themselves into complete immobility. Beside him, Eddie breathed something that might have been a curse. He didn't move his lips, but the tone was unmistakable. One of the women— Cheshire or Syms, certainly—sobbed in an upwelling of panic, but none of the men dared offer comfort.

Before the sculpture of Horus, the sheik made a sweeping bow. In an eerie, sing-song voice he began to chant, his men echoing him in a wailing refrain. His words were Arabic, but there was that in their cadence and shape that hinted at an origin far more ancient.

> *In the beginning, the word was Ptah.*
> *(The word was Ptah.)*
> *Creation sprang forth.*
> *(Creation sprang forth.)*
> *Maat is the balance by which creation abides.*
> *(Maat is the balance.)*
> *Judgment belongs not to man.*
> *(Judgment is not man's.)*
> *For how can the weight also be the scales?*
> *(The weight cannot be the scales.)*
> *Is your soul as light as Maat?*
> *(Is it?)*
> *Discover the judgment of the gods!*
> *(Discover!)*

On the rising note of the final refrain, the sheik pressed the full weight of his body against the flail in Horus's hands. For a terrible, hopeful moment, nothing happened. The air rang with unexpected silence. Then a terrible grating vibration ensued, felt first rather than heard. Something shifted behind the chamber's painted walls.

Behind him, Neville heard someone begin to pray, quickly, and without a great deal of hope.

The sheik leaned over the edge of the pit, laughing maniacally. "Discover the judgment of the gods! Discover the lightness of Maat! Discover the belly of Ammit!"

With the roaring of a wind from nowhere, the spine-chilling shriek of rock against rock, the floor dropped from beneath their feet. Accompanied by a cloud of sand, they fell, screaming in raw terror that overcame the bravest of them.

Above, the floor slid back into place, leaving only darkness, then bone-breaking pain, and finally, mercifully, unconsciousness.

In the Pit

AS FAR as she could tell, Jenny came around first, rasped into consciousness by the rough workings of a sandpaper tongue against her cheek. She'd been dreaming that she'd been thrown by a particularly stubborn bronc that kept laughing as it bucked, and waking wasn't all that unwelcome—at least until she realized how much she ached.

"Mozelle . . ." she murmured, trying to open her eyes. She couldn't. Then she realized that they were open. The darkness was so complete that she had to touch her eyelids to make certain.

A small furry head bumped against her cheek. Jenny struggled upright, oddly disoriented in this total darkness. Mozelle felt her movement and climbed into her lap, up her torso, and settled on her shoulder, buzzing approvingly.

Jenny started to stand, then realized that for all she knew she could be on the edge of a precipice. True, the floor around her felt solid for as far as she could slide, but that didn't mean that one step farther was another drop into nothingness. Her heart beat unnaturally hard at the idea, her gorge rose and for a long moment she fought against being sick.

"Hello?" Jenny called softly. "Anyone here?"

Her voice was swallowed by the surrounding darkness, then someone groaned.

"Uncle Neville? Stephen? Eddie?"

The groan came again, followed by a word.

"Stephen."

"Do you have any matches?" she asked. "I don't, and I'm afraid to move."

"Matches?"

Silence. Jenny imagined Stephen taking inventory of himself, perhaps patting down his pockets.

"I'm sorry," she said, taking comfort in her own voice, "I should have asked if you were all right."

"I hurt like the dickens," Stephen replied, "but nothing seems broken. I'm checking my pockets. If I remember . . . Yes!"

"What?" Jenny asked eagerly.

"I have a full box of matches, and," he paused, triumphant, "a full five inches of candle stub!"

"Light it!"

She heard the scrape of the match even as she spoke. The pale glimmer of candle flame wasn't exactly bright, but it was wonderfully comforting. It showed Stephen's face and hand for a moment before he raised it and held it higher to better illuminate their surroundings.

"Any sign of the others or our lanterns and candles?" Jenny asked. "Uncle Neville made sure Eddie bought a bunch."

"I don't have much hopes for the lanterns," Stephen said, but . . ."

He shuffled to his feet, and the light fell upon a heap of their baggage. It also found Mozelle. The kitten had located a package of dried fish and was tearing into it with intense enjoyment.

"Move, kitty," Stephen said, "we may need those. I've heard dry fish shed light when they burn."

"Yuck!" Jenny said.

"Better than darkness," Stephen said, "but you and Mozelle are in luck. I've found a box of nice, if slightly melted, candles."

"Light a couple," Jenny said. "We need to check on the others."

Stephen paused in the act of obeying. "The air in here . . ."

Jenny had assisted her father after a mining accident.

"I know," she said, "but we have to risk it."

Their talk had disturbed some of those in the gloomy reaches of the cavern.

Groans and muttered questions echoed oddly off the stone, reminding Jenny of a description she'd once read of Hell. Had it been in Dante? The memory seemed impossibly far away.

She accepted the candle Stephen handed her. It was almost as thick as her wrist, and burned with the slightly sweet odor of good beeswax. She stuck several spares under her belt.

"I hear someone over there," she said. "See who it is. If you find my doctor's bag, let me know."

"Yes, Madame General," Stephen said with an attempt at a laugh.

Jenny discovered Uncle Neville near her, hauling himself to a sitting position, hands methodically checking himself for injuries. His eyes blurred and unfocused.

"Are you all right, Uncle?" she asked.

"Think I've wrenched that ankle again," he said, shaking himself to an awareness of her and the light, "and wrenched my shoulder, but I don't think anything's broken."

Jenny lit a candle and set it in the sand beside him.

"I'll be back to look at you in a moment," she promised.

Jenny was already checking the forms nearest to her. Mrs. Syms was face-down in the sand, and for a horrible moment Jenny thought the older woman had smothered. Turning her over and rinsing her mouth with water brought Mrs. Syms sputtering to consciousness.

"My shoulder!" she moaned. "I've broken it. Nathan, why is it so dark?"

Jenny probed the shoulder, feeling the older woman wince.

"Here's a candle," she said. "Let me check that shoulder. Ah . . . the collarbone is broken, I think. I've bandages in my kit, if I can find it."

Stephen had lit a couple more candles, and by their illumination Jenny found her medical gear, glad that Uncle Neville had ordered them to move all but the bulkiest items of their gear into the chamber.

Uncle Neville was helping Eddie, and Stephen was bending over a form indistinct in the flickering light of the half dozen or so candles spotted about the room. Someone else, large, so probably Captain Brentworth, was painfully hauling himself erect.

"Jenny," two voices said almost simultaneously.

They stopped, then Uncle Neville said, "When you're finished there, come take a look at Eddie's elbow. It's swelling pretty badly."

"I think I may need you first," Stephen said. "I've found Rashid, and he won't wake up."

"Be careful how you move him," Jenny said. "See if his throat is free of sand. I'll be right over."

Jenny finished a fast wrap on Mrs. Syms's shoulder.

"Stay quiet and still," she said, catching up her bag. "I'll mix you something for the pain in a moment."

Jenny's own pain was forgotten in the immediate need, but she was aware of how stiffly she was moving. She knelt beside Rashid. The young man's breathing was ragged, but he was breathing. She sniffed his lips and found no telltale odor of either blood or bowel.

"Good," she said. "He may merely have hit his head. Was he unnaturally twisted in any way?"

"Like he'd broken his back?" Stephen replied with immediate understanding. "Not that I saw."

Jenny bent to peel back Rashid's eyelid and felt tiny cold fingers on her arm. Mischief the monkey chattered an anxious question.

"I don't know," she said, "and I won't if you keep bothering me."

The monkey left her and scampered to Rashid's other side, his little old man's face wrinkled with concern. He watched with anxious patience as Jenny bathed Rashid's face and neck with cool water.

"Stephen?" she said. "Can you keep doing this while I go look at Eddie's elbow and give Mrs. Syms something for the pain in her shoulder?"

Stephen nodded. "Captain Brentworth is taking care of Lady Cheshire. Should I ask whether he needs assistance?"

Jenny felt a completely ignoble desire to refuse. After all, Rashid had been only a servant, and Sarah Syms little more. Those two, however, had plotted against Uncle Neville's plans and had brought them to this impasse. She nodded stiffly.

"Do, but don't forget Rashid."

Stephen's expression made quite clear he shared her internal battle. "I won't, but surely we're all in this together now."

Jenny managed an unconvincing smile before she moved away. Eddie's elbow was indeed badly swollen, but she had seen enough similar injuries to know how to wrap it.

"You're in luck," she said. "It's your left arm."

Eddie grinned. "No sick leave for me, doctor?"

"I'm afraid not," she said. "Tell me, do you think Rashid would be angry if I gave him a little brandy? I mean, I know that Mohammedans aren't supposed to drink spirits, but it might help him come around."

"I don't think the provision applies for medical use," Eddie said, "but you can be safe. We have whiskey with us. The rule is against wine and beer. Technically, spirits are all right, though most mullahs say that had Mohammed known about them, he would have outlawed them as well."

Jenny checked his bandage and sling, then mixed Eddie a draught. "It'll help with the pain. Not as much as I'd like, I'm afraid. I don't dare let you get fuddled."

"I saw Mrs. Syms after she finished what you gave her," Eddie agreed. "She's not quite there, is she?"

"That wasn't from what I gave her," Jenny said, worriedly. "She was like that when she came around. She seems to think she's in England."

"Mind snapped," Eddie said. "I've seen it happen before, during battle. Sometimes the mind comes back when the pressure is off."

"I hope so," Jenny said.

She looked around, and spotted Uncle Neville determinedly limping about, inventorying the gear that had fallen with them. It looked like he was dividing it into trash and what might still be useful. Eddie pushed himself upright.

"I'll go help Neville," he said.

Jenny went back to check on Rashid. He hadn't regained consciousness, but his breathing had become more regular. Again she sniffed his lips, found his breath as sweet as that of any young creature. For the first time, she was conscious of him as a young man, and was glad the candlelight hid her blush.

"See if you can get Rashid to swallow a little water," Jenny suggested to Stephen. "Just a little. We don't want to choke him. Later, if he needs a stimulant, we'll give him a bit of whiskey."

By way of reply, Stephen reached for his canteen. Reluctant to go to where Captain Brentworth hovered over Lady Cheshire, Jenny paused.

"Do you need anything, Stephen? I have some powders that will help with stiffness and pains."

"Later," he said. "After all, if we can't find a way out of here, my bruises will hardly matter, will they?"

Jenny had been trying very hard not to think about how trapped they were. She hadn't inspected their prison, but from what she could see, they were at the bottom of a very deep well, its sides cut from the living rock.

"Take it anyhow," she said, offering a dose on a folded slip of paper. "If we do find a way out, those of us who are sound are going to need to give everything we have."

Then, her own words a rebuke in her ears, Jenny crossed over to Brentworth and Cheshire.

"Captain Brentworth, Lady Cheshire," Jenny greeted them, taking refuge in formality that was surely absurd considering the situation. "Are you injured?"

Captain Brentworth shook his head.

"Just banged up a bit, scraped on the sand. Audrey, though . . . She's bleeding terribly."

Lady Cheshire's skin looked very white in the candle light.

"I seem to have a bad cut along my arm," she admitted, "and to have banged my head rather hard. It aches terribly. How is Sarah? And Rashid?"

Jenny reached for the arm Lady Cheshire held so guardedly, feeling the other woman fight the impulse to pull it back.

"Not well," Jenny replied, knowing she was being cruel, but unable to stop herself. "Rashid won't wake, and Mrs. Syms has lost her mind. She also broke her collarbone in the fall. She seems to believe she is in England, and keeps talking to someone named Nathan."

"Her late husband," Lady Cheshire said softly. "Poor woman. Wrap my wrist up, won't you, and I'll see what I can do."

"You'll do her no favors bringing her back to this," Jenny said, indicating their prison with a toss of her head. "Perhaps now that I'm here to hold your hand, Captain Brentworth could help Uncle Neville check our situation."

Captain Brentworth drew himself up, then let out his breath in a great, gusty sigh. Jenny thought he was probably in more pain than he was admitting, but was being strong for Lady Cheshire. That would probably be better than any medicine she could give him.

"Quite right. I ought not need to be told my duty by a slip of a girl. If you will excuse me, Lady Cheshire?"

"Of course, Robert."

Lady Cheshire turned her head to watch him go, or perhaps merely to keep from watching Jenny work on her wounded arm. The skin was badly abraded, and needed to be daubed with water and alcohol before it was wrapped.

"You're lucky not to have a break," Jenny said. Then she forced herself to be kinder. "We're all lucky. The sand isn't soft, but it gave a little when stone would not have done so."

"Rashid is the only one still unconscious?" Lady Cheshire asked. "Good. And everyone can walk?"

"Uncle Neville's ankle is swollen again," Jenny said, "but he can manage with someone to lean on. We may even be able to rig a crutch, if he didn't bring his other one into the chamber."

"Other one?"

"He twisted the ankle earlier," Jenny said, "trying to find water. Stephen nearly died from dehydration. We didn't have your advantages."

Lady Cheshire neither acknowledged, nor ignored the rebuke.

"I am certain that is so," she said.

"Jenny," Stephen called. "Rashid is coming around."

"I'm almost done here," Jenny said. "Don't let him move until I've had a chance to check him over."

She hurried then, her animosity forgotten in this new demand for her skills. "There," she said, finishing the bandage on Lady Cheshire's arm. "I can give you a stronger dose that will deaden the pain, but it will make you sleepy, or I can give you a weaker powder that will blunt the edge of the pain, but not take it away."

"The weaker powder, please," Lady Cheshire said. "I think I should have my wits about me . . . for dealing with Sarah."

Jenny wasn't sure that was what the other woman had meant, but she was will-ing to let the matter go. After all, as Stephen had said, if they couldn't get out of here, what did these aches and pains matter? They might all end up choosing drugged oblivion.

Rashid was indeed awake, but his pupils remained dilated, even when she brought the candle close.

"His brain has been bruised," Jenny said, "but he is young and strong. We must watch him carefully. He must not sleep lest he slip into a coma. Do you un-derstand me, Rashid?"

The Arab youth nodded gravely. He bent his head into his hand.

"Your head hurts?" Jenny said. "I imagine it does. We can't give you anything very strong, though. Drink lots of water, that will help."

Rashid nodded again, moving his head very carefully. Jenny had him shut his eyes and touched his skin at various points, assuring herself that he had not injured his spine, for sensation was often lost when the spine was injured. However, Rashid's spine seemed uninjured. Indeed, barring the concussion, he was in far bet-ter health than many of the others.

"Young flesh," Neville said when he limped over to get Jenny's report. "You children bounced, us old folks broke."

"I thought you told me you weren't that old," Jenny teased, pleased to find her uncle in such good humor when by rights—betrayed, trapped, and injured—he might have despaired.

Maybe it's true that a challenge brings out the best in some people, she thought.

"Right now," Neville said, continuing in his teasing vein, "I feel old as Methuselah, yet as young as springtime."

"What do you mean?" Stephen said. "That sounds like a riddle."

"My body feels old," Neville replied, "but my spirits have lifted. Eddie and I carried one of the candles around the edges of the room and in one place the flame brightened and flickered."

"You mean . . ." Jenny said.

"That's right," Sir Neville confirmed. "We think we've found a door."

Neville had put on a bright face for his young charges, but he was less certain than he pretended that they had found a way out. The door might lead to another shaft. It might be a false door—tombs were replete with these. However, Eddie had been encouraging.

"Neville," he'd said. "There's not nearly enough sand in here to account for several millennia of those villains dropping victims down here. No bones, either, though those could have been covered by the sand from our own fall. Still, I'm willing to bet that there is another, less dramatic, way down here—a maintenance stair—and that this door likely leads to it."

"Stephen," Neville said, shaking himself from memory, "if Jenny no longer needs your assistance, I was wondering if I could borrow you. You have a gift for solving puzzles, and it seems that opening this door offers us one."

Stephen looked at Jenny.

"I'm done," she said. "I'll sit with Rashid, unless you need me, Uncle Neville."

"Sit with him, by all means," Neville replied.

And to think I nearly left her behind, he thought. *My field medicine wouldn't have been up to this—nor would Eddie's.*

Even if you both hadn't, his sardonic inner voice added, *ended up pretty broken up your-selves.*

Neville ignored this. His ankle might feel like fire, the shoulder he'd wrenched was stiffening alarmingly, and his muscles felt as if he'd been kicked by a dozen mules, but he had something that needed doing. He knew that part of the reason for the intensity of his concentration was that he was trying to avoid thinking about Lady Cheshire's duplicitous nature—and the fact that despite this confirmation of their worst suspicions, his admiration for her had not entirely faded. She had been clever, quick-witted, and very brave. How could she know she was hiring men more dishonest than she was?

"When we brought light over to the walls," Neville explained to Stephen, "we realized two things instantly. One, there are sections of the wall that are built from blocks, not cut from bedrock. Two, someone went to the trouble to decorate the walls. That seemed curious, especially if the entire setup was only intended as a trap."

Eddie, now within earshot, added, "That's what made Neville suggest we hold the candle close and see if we found any motion in the air. It was a long shot, but . . ."

He shrugged, holding a candle up in his good hand. "Take a look."

Stephen accepted the candle Eddie handed him. First he held it back, inspecting the entire section of wall, then he brought it close, so he could look at the art in more detail.

Neville cleared his throat and pointed to a section of the wall. "After we started our inspection," he said, "we noticed that at this spot the edges of the blocks were very neatly aligned. You see? Here, and here—the outline of a door. Elsewhere they are stacked interlocked."

"I see it," Stephen said, "and I agree, top and two side of a wide door."

"And look at the art on the door itself," Neville continued, "assuming it is a door."

"Let's," Eddie suggested, sounding a bit exasperated.

"The art on the door," Neville went on deliberately, "is also divided into sections—more like tiles set in place, than sculpture carved directly into the stone—and one tile is missing."

Stephen reached out and tapped the surface of the door with his finger.

"These 'tiles' are stone," he said, "but I see what you mean. The gap is interesting. Did one fall out, or was it left this way deliberately?"

"We didn't try anything," Neville admitted. "I wanted you to inspect it before we monkeyed with it. The door ornamentation is very Egyptian, but somehow it looked—I don't know how else to put it—wrong to me."

Stephen inspected the art for so long that Neville began to fear for their candles. He forced himself to remain patient—reminding himself that they had packed both candles and lantern oil in quantity.

"You were right!" Stephen said suddenly, clearly excited. "Look here. The design is made up of lotus and papyrus flowers—stylized, of course—around a central border. They're interspersed with these round figures—I'll get back to them—but only in the central border is there anything that doesn't fit the overall pattern."

He pointed and continued, "Four figures: a scarab, a mongoose, a snake, and a hawk wearing the uraeus—the cobra crown."

"Is that last Horus again?" Eddie asked.

He sounded genuinely curious. Neville swallowed hard. It could be the information would be useful.

"Maybe," Stephen said, "but I think it's someone else, someone associated with the scarab."

Neville couldn't help himself. "Stephen! This is not the time for a lecture."

"Sorry," Stephen said. He shook his disordered hair out of his face. "The scarab represents the rising sun: Ra in the morning, also known as Khepri. There are various theories why . . ."

He took a look at Neville's face and stopped.

"In that context, the crowned hawk probably represents Ra at mid-day. In later periods, he did get merged with Horus, but in Neferankhotep's day, he wasn't. That's important, because it gives us a clue as to who the mongoose is meant to be."

Neville tried to look encouraging.

"Yes?"

"Ra at evening was called Atum, and Atum was usually depicted as a human wearing the double crown. However, there's evidence that Atum had an animal avatar as well . . ."

"Why not?" Eddie said reasonably. "Everyone else seems to have had at least one."

"And if I recall correctly," Stephen concluded triumphantly, "that avatar was a mongoose—the creature that kills the snake. Ra at night, in the underworld, is threatened by the monster snake, Apophis. If my guess is right, Apophis is represented by the snake tile."

Neville looked at the mural.

"They're not in that order, though," he said. "The hawk comes before the scarab, then the snake, and the mongoose last."

"I think that in order to unlock the door," Stephen replied, "The tiles need to be put in the correct order. I suspect that the empty space was left deliberately— to permit sliding the tiles within the frame."

He put up a hand and pushed down against the tile above the open space. It slid stiffly, grating against sand in the track, into the opening.

"Amazing that it still works after all these years," Eddie murmured. "But then, these are the people who built the Great Pyramid."

Neville leaned forward eagerly. "Then it's just a matter of readjusting the tiles until they are in the correct sequence?"

"That's at least the first step," Stephen said, "and I don't think it's going to be simple. Remember I said I'd come back to the round figured tiles?"

Neville nodded.

"Given the overall context, I'd say that they're meant to represent the sun in the phases of his journey, rather like the phases of the moon, only with the amount of 'colored in' space indicating the sun's position."

Neville bent closer to look at the monochrome stone tiles.

"You mean," he said, "this one that's completely textured—or 'colored in'—indicates noon, while the one with only a little shading on the left edge would be, say, early morning?"

"That's right," Stephen said. "My guess is that the phase tiles need to be set in order with the signifier for the start of a phase dawn, mid-day, evening, and night, set in the appropriate place. It's going to be tedious, but I am sure it can be done. By the way, Sir Neville, you were right that it looked 'off.' The puzzle has two settings—this one and the correct one. In this one, some of the alignments on the flowers and other borders are slightly wrong. I think that's what you saw."

Neville was pleased by the compliment, but he didn't want to make too great a fuss. Instead he slapped the younger man heartily on the shoulder.

"If you're sure you have this figured out," Neville said, "then get to it. We'll bring you water and something to eat, and better light."

"Thank you very kindly," Stephen said. His voice was distant, his hands against the wall. Already, he'd nearly forgotten them in the challenge of the puzzle.

They spent the intervening time collecting the rest of their gear. Neville's crutch had turned up, and he was deeply grateful to be able to take his weight off his injured ankle.

Rashid was more alert now. His pupils, when Jenny tested them, were becoming responsive to light. Sarah Syms remained lost in another world, and Lady Cheshire was reluctant to pull her from it.

"Sarah has faced so much in her life, poor old dear," Lady Cheshire said softly. "Now she's back with her Nathan, at least for now. Why should I force her away?" Her large green eyes met Neville's own, candidly, and full of honest fear. "Reality has so little to offer any of us."

"Stephen is working the door puzzle," Neville said. "We may yet escape this."

"But where do we go?" Lady Cheshire asked. "Those Bedouin are sure to be hanging about. There's water and good hunting, and they've won a summer's worth of loot already. Between your camels and the ones I purchased, they've done quite well for themselves."

Neville heard himself speaking without consciously willing the words.

"Audrey, why did you do it? Why did you follow us?"

Lady Cheshire poked out her chin defiantly, and Neville realized he found the gesture oddly touching.

"Because you lied to me. Because I wanted to take part in archeological dis-coveries once again, and I was certain you were onto something big."

"How could you know?" Neville asked.

"Do you remember when you hosted the Antiquities Society meetings at your house in town?"

Neville nodded.

"One of those times, I left my reticule at your house—purely by accident, I assure you." She smiled a trace sourly, "Not that you have any reason to believe me, but I assure you, it was an accident."

"I believe you," Neville said.

He was aware that Captain Brentworth was looming a short distance away, but he didn't think the implicit threat in the man's massive form was what made him say those words.

"I went back to get it the next day," Lady Cheshire continued. "You were out. Your butler wasn't certain whether the reticule had been found, or where it might have been put. He asked if I would wait, or if I would like it sent on to me.

"I almost had it sent. Then I remembered that your library had seemed quite excellent. I asked if I could wait in the library, and would you mind if I looked at a book or two while I waited. The butler assured me that as long as I left the ones behind the glass untouched, the rest were what he called 'in use.'"

Neville smiled. The staff had always drawn a very distinct line between the ele-gant volumes his late father had collected and his own workaday texts.

"I obeyed the rules," she went on, "I truly did. What had caught my eye the night before was a new atlas of the Upper Nile. I had thought about adding a copy to my own collection, and lifted it down, interested in seeing if the contents were worth the price the printers were asking."

Neville felt his lips curve into a soundless whistle.

"I remember that volume," he said, "and what I was doing with it."

"Then you remember that one of the detail maps had some rather fascinating notation on it," she said, her tone lightening and becoming almost teasing. "'Hawk Rock' with a query mark on it was written in one place. '*The* village' and another query mark at a place along the bank. Then there was 'Miriam's ruin' marked quite definitely. What caught my attention was how many places out in the desert had been circled—areas where, as far as I knew, not only had nothing been found, but nothing had been sought.

"I made some inquiries after I left, and found out that some years before, you had been guide and companion to one Alphonse Liebermann, a rather eccentric

German who had published several papers on the historicity of Moses, and related topics. I found myself wondering what Miriam's ruin might be, and what wonders it might hold."

Neville sighed, "And when you heard I was returning to Egypt, you thought I was going on a dig."

"You were, weren't you?" she retorted fiercely. "You were being so secretive! I decided you were trying to bypass the firman system. I didn't think that was particularly ethical of you, but it gave me an edge. I could follow you, and then, when I caught you with your fist in the biscuit tin, I could demand a part in the project as my payment for not turning you in."

"And you didn't want gold or jewelry?" Neville heard the sneer in his voice.

"I have jewelry," she snapped. "Lots of it, and I can get more easily enough. I wanted the chance to be in on a discovery. My late husband was a fine man in his own way, but he only let me hang around the fringes of his digs. He didn't treat me as you do your niece. For that matter, I'm not like your niece, and I'm too old to change. And who would give me a chance if I did? I tell you, Neville Hawthorne, there are times when a pretty face and form hobble you as much as a broken ankle!"

Neville wasn't sure if he believed her protestations. After all, Audrey played her beauty for everything it was worth. On the other hand, maybe she honestly believed it was her only strength. If so, he pitied her.

He was aware that Audrey had been speaking loudly enough for everyone to hear her story. He might be interested in Audrey Cheshire's personal woes, but his associates would want to know the end of the tale.

"So you followed us to Egypt. Then, when we escaped your observation, you took advantage of what you already knew and followed us upriver."

"That's right," Lady Cheshire said. "We narrowly missed you in Luxor. Then we had to find transport of our own, arrange for camels to meet us, and all the rest. We went directly to the place you had labeled 'Miriam's ruin,' and found nothing but an old, picked-over, rather late-period tomb.

"Robert made inquiries along the bank, and found a village that was still buzzing with tales about the devious English who had recently been there. It wasn't very hard to get the natives to help us find guides who knew the deeper desert. Indeed, I think that if he hadn't been able to contact the Bedouin, Riskali would have guided us himself—you've made an enemy there, Sir Neville."

"I can live with that," Neville replied. "You would have been luckier with Riskali as a guide, never mind that he probably knew nothing about the desert."

"True." Lady Cheshire's indignation collapsed, and she once again looked very tired. "They brought us here after a rather horrid journey through some fright-fully empty desert, and you know the rest."

Neville looked around the candle-lit chamber, at his injured friend, at Jenny gently pouring water between Rashid's lips, at Stephen intent upon the door.

"I do indeed," he said.

Lady Cheshire opened her lips to speak, but whatever she would have said—whether further self-justification or apology—was lost as Stephen suddenly leapt back, nearly extinguishing his candle in his eagerness.

"I've got it!" he cried. "We can open the door!"

20

The Boat of Millions of Years

JENNY JUMPED to her feet when she heard Stephen's announcement, upsetting Mischief, who chattered simian rebuke for her abrupt motion.

"I'm sorry," she said, but she didn't stop. Hurrying over to the door, she found Stephen already launched into an explanation.

"It was just as I thought," he said. "Once I'd worked the tiles into the correct order—a task that required patience more than skill—I heard a distinct thump and click. The door didn't open, though, and I was momentarily baffled."

"Momentarily?" Neville said, and Jenny could hear the hope in his voice.

"Momentarily," Stephen assured him. "I thought about those four tiles: the beetle, the hawk, the mongoose, and the snake. Why were they there? The ornamentation on the circles showed an evident progression. To a scholar of Egyptology, the symbol tiles actually made the puzzle easier. Then revelation struck me. There was a second lock. Clearly the tiles could no longer be slid, so I tried pressing them and . . ."

He demonstrated, pressing them in order: beetle, hawk, mongoose, and, finally, snake. Nothing happened when he pressed the first two, but when he pressed the mongoose, there was a grinding noise. The snake gave the final release and the door moved slightly, not opening, but obviously loose within its frame, where before it had been snug.

"Perhaps that released a counterweight," Neville said, moving forward to push open the door.

"Perhaps so. If you push the tiles in reverse order," Stephen said, raising his hand to do so, "I believe it locks the door."

"Don't," Neville said, gripping his wrist. "It may also reset the tile puzzle, and we don't want you to have to solve it again."

Stephen blinked. "Yes, it might, mightn't it? My apologies, Sir Neville. For a moment I forgot why it was important to solve the puzzle."

"And a good thing, too," Neville assured him, "or anxiety might have slowed you. Let's see what's behind the door."

He glanced around, saw Jenny.

"Grab a couple of candles," he said, "and be ready to light our way."

Jenny took up the candles, but she shook her head in rebuke.

"Let Stephen and Captain Brentworth open the door," she said. "Your ankle is unsound, and we don't know what is on the other side."

She thought her uncle might refuse, but after momentary consideration, he stepped back.

"Brentworth," he said formally, "if you would do the honors?"

The big man moved up without comment, and set both arm and shoulder to the door.

"On my count of three," he said to Stephen, who had taken up his post behind him. "One, two, three!"

At the final count, they pushed. The door resisted, then began to open. Someone, probably Lady Cheshire, cheered excitedly. Captain Brentworth and Stephen pushed with renewed enthusiasm, then, as one, staggered.

Jenny darted forward. "What's wrong?"

Stephen steadied himself, then looked back sheepishly.

"Nothing. The floor is lower here than on the other side. Should have figured it would be uneven, given the amount of sand that has fallen into that shaft. All's well."

They continued pushing. The door opened into a wide corridor, its walls painted with bright scenes of riverbanks and verdant fields. It led forward into darkness.

There was a freshness to the air that promised freedom, but Jenny noted that the candles she held did not flicker any more vigorously.

Wherever the air is coming from, she thought, *must not be close.*

But something else was bothering her more intensely than how far they might need to go to get out of here, or even what they might find on the outside. She turned and looked at Uncle Neville.

"We're going to try to get out of here?" she asked. "All of us?"

He looked at her, frowning in surprise and disapproval.

"Do you think we should do otherwise, Genevieve?"

Jenny shook her head, acutely aware how weary she was, how her eyes were beginning to feel smudged onto her face, of a headache lurking behind her forehead, even of the minor annoyance of her hair escaping from its confining braid.

"I think we should all try to get out of here," she said, "but I'm not sure I want those people . . ." she looked pointedly at Captain Brentworth and Lady Cheshire, "at my back."

Uncle Neville looked at her in shock, but before he could say anything, Lady Cheshire spoke up. "But, Miss Benet, you heard me explain how all of this happened. I admit to being overeager, but . . ."

Jenny interrupted, tired of pretence and politeness. Her diction was slipping, and she knew it and she just didn't care.

"You, ma'am, are a claim jumper, pure and simple. Where I come from, folks don't take kindly to claim jumpers. In fact, they tend to treat 'em just about how they do horse thieves—and that's pretty final, if you catch my drift."

"Claim jumpers?" Lady Cheshire briefly pretended not to understand. "I suppose you could see it that way, but then the Egyptian government might see what Sir Neville was attempting as little different."

"A blackmailing sidewinder of a claim jumper," Jenny said.

Captain Brentworth made an angry move, and Jenny's six-shooter was in her hand. She'd cleaned all her guns while minding Rashid. Rashid had watched her do it, but far from being offended or alarmed, it seemed to her he had approved.

Of course, you can put any darn thought you want onto him, Jenny thought sardonically. *After all, he couldn't exactly call out and warn anyone, could he?*

Jenny kept her revolver leveled on Captain Brentworth.

"That's exactly the kind of thing I'm talking about," she said. "You've got that big man there, and I don't know whether or not he has a gun hidden where the Bedouin didn't take it off him, but I do know he'll do anything you want. That's a weapon in itself. And you've been looking all frail and sheep-eyed, but you're not much more hurt than I am, for all your aching head. Hell, my head aches, and that makes me plain ornery."

"Jenny," Stephen interrupted, his voice even and sensible. "What do you want to do? Shoot them and leave them here?"

"I might want to," Jenny said, "given what they've done to us and to Uncle Neville especially, but I won't. That'd put me on their level. No, I won't do that—but I won't let them walk at my back, possibly armed, just waiting for a chance to get the upper hand. I won't do that, and I think you're all right fools if you'll let it happen."

Stephen glanced at Sir Neville, giving him a chance to speak, but when he said nothing, Stephen said, "That seems sensible, Jenny. I think Lady Cheshire and her associates might even see your point."

Eddie had listened in silence, his expression completely neutral, now he spoke up.

"Neville, I can see you're upset, but I agree with Jenny. We don't know what we'll find when we get outside, but those Bedouin were hired by Lady Cheshire and Captain Brentworth. They're going to be more likely to work with them than with us. If, in fact, they'll work with any of us, and not shoot us down on sight."

"Isn't that last," Lady Cheshire said, her voice very cool, "reason why the captain and I at least should be given weapons? I am a fair shot. He is very good."

Jenny shook her head. "I called you a sidewinder, ma'am, and until you prove otherwise, you're still a sidewinder as I see it. In fact, you're lower than a rattler—at least the snake gives warning."

"What," said Captain Brentworth, his gaze never leaving the revolver leveled at his chest, "do you want?"

"We saw the Arabs search you," she said, "but that doesn't mean you didn't have a holdout, or that you haven't picked up something else since we've been down here. Our gear went all over. It would be easy enough to grab yourself a gun or knife. The Bedouin didn't bother to search Lady Cheshire, not where we could see, but she herself says she's a fair shot."

Eddie was already moving toward Lady Cheshire.

"I'm married," he said, as if that were an explanation, "and I don't think Jenny should let her gun drop just to search you."

Lady Cheshire's lips thinned, but she said nothing as Eddie made a quick but thorough search. His work was assisted in that she had simplified her clothing for travel, and wearing no bustle, and only a few layers of undergarments. He came up with a small, neat gun of the type often called "muff pistols." It wouldn't kill at any distance, but it might up close, and it would certainly maim.

Sarah Syms was unarmed, as was Rashid. Captain Brentworth, however, had picked up Stephen's handgun, dropped in the fall and not remembered until now. Eddie handed it to Stephen. "Captain Brentworth has kindly cleaned off the worst of the sand. Take better care of it in the future."

Sir Neville's expression did not alter from neutral disapproval until the weapons were found. Then the disapproval grew, but it had found a focus.

"I am disappointed in you, Lady Cheshire."

"I had forgotten I had it," she said. "Honestly, I had."

Jenny couldn't tell if her uncle believed the other woman, but he offered no objection to Jenny's plans.

Captain Brentworth said nothing to justify his own armament—not even when Eddie relieved him of a perfectly practical clasp knife, more useful as a tool than as a weapon.

Jenny nodded her thanks.

"Now, as I've said, Captain Brentworth himself is something of a weapon. However, I'd never insult the gentleman by tying him up—not in a dangerous place like this. Instead, he can just do the good thing and keep himself busy helping Rashid along. I don't think Rashid should walk right yet, and rigging a stretcher won't be much of a problem. If the captain takes one end and Lady Cheshire takes the other, they'll get a chance to prove what good-hearted souls they truly are."

As Jenny had hoped, neither raised argument against this. Lady Cheshire had proven herself tough enough to ride through the desert. Her wound wasn't so severe that she could complain that she wasn't up to bearing half of Rashid's stretcher—especially when Captain Brentworth would take most of the weight, and she'd provide mostly balance and steadiness. And if they said they were too good to carry an Arab servant, they'd lose any remaining credit they had with Sir Neville.

"If you handle Rashid at all roughly," Jenny said, keeping her voice level with an effort, trying to infuse a note of humor, "Mischief will certainly have something to say about that . . ."

Again, no one disagreed. A stretcher was rigged. Necessary gear was packed and distributed. Lady Cheshire even suggested that in addition to Rashid, the stretcher could carry some of the dry goods, suspended below.

Eddie took over organization.

"We don't know what we're up against," he said, "so I want an able body up front. Stephen, that'll be you. You can't shoot, but you can read the writing on the walls and any curses or whatever may give us warning."

"Read the writing on the walls," Stephen repeated, chuckling. "That's rather good, Eddie."

Eddie blinked. Clearly, punning had not been his intention.

"I'll go next, since my legs are fine and so's my gun hand. Jenny, I want you to cover the rear. Mrs. Syms will stay with Lady Cheshire and Captain Brentworth near the middle."

Jenny nodded.

Mrs. Syms said cheerfully, "That would be lovely, dear. What a strange gallery this is. I wonder why they haven't laid on the gas. Surely they could afford it. They certainly aren't paying the servants to sweep. Such a lot of sand!"

"And me, Eddie?" Neville asked, sounding more amused than affronted.

"Why you're in charge, *effendi*," Eddie said. "As long as you don't insist on limping in front, you can go wherever you want."

Neville's forced grin made clear who he thought was in charge, but he said nothing.

"Right. Well, I'll dither along in the middle and help along where help is needed. Are we ready?"

Eddie had taken out his compass, and was staring with some confusion at the dial. He shook it.

"Must have gotten jiggered by the fall," he said, dropping it back into his pocket. I was hoping to see which way we'd be heading. Looks as if we'll have to go on guesswork and whatever Stephen can read."

Candles and lantern bases—the mantles had broken in the fall—were distributed. Rashid made clear that he was able to assist at least to the extent of holding one. Jenny patted his hand.

"Don't burn yourself," she warned.

Rashid shook his head—a bit gingerly—to indicate he would take care.

Jenny dropped back to the rear, holstering her revolver, but keeping it ready. Mozelle was twining around her ankles, and she picked the kitten up and set her on her shoulder.

"We're off then," Eddie said. "Lead the way, Stephen, and sing out if you see trouble."

Thumping along on his crutch at the center of the group, assisting Mrs. Syms when she distractedly halted in mid-step to examine some element of her surroundings, Neville struggled with the fact that the achievement of the goal that had occupied him all these years could be so unsatisfactory.

There was no doubt that they had found the tomb of Neferankhotep—or at least some associated part of the mortuary complex. Stephen hazarded that it might be a vast temple, and that they were moving through the public sections, toward a holy of holies. He guessed that eventually their corridor would cross another that led to further public areas. For now the corridor was interrupted only by occasional small side chambers.

The walls surrounding them were covered with frescos depicting the pharaoh going about his daily routine, his figure neatly labeled in hieroglyphs, as if his crowned head might leave some doubt as to which figure was the king's. The art was typically stylized, the colors bold and unsubtle: brown, blue, green, white, red, black, and yellow unblended, set neatly within the lines, like a tidy child's coloring.

Yet the scenes themselves were not at all typical of Egyptian tomb paintings. The king was shown crushing his enemies on the battlefield, but he was also shown mourning the many who had died to make his victory possible. He was shown enjoying lavish banquets, but also visiting the farmers in their fields, and the herders amidst their cattle, dispensing among them a share of the bounty their labor had made possible.

Again and again, Neferankhotep was depicted making offerings to the gods, and those same gods looked back at him—this earthly Horus their brother—and their approval of him was evident in their bearing. Yet the pharaoh did not come across as either self-satisfied or falsely humble, but as a genuinely pious man, a man who knew he was a king and recognized the responsibilities as well as the honors attendant upon his position.

Can it be, Neville thought, *that I have come to believe that what we're doing is desecration rather than discovery?*

No one will force you to carry anything away, his personal demon told him. *Not one of those you brought with you, that is. I'm not sure you can trust the others.*

And Neville knew that this, even more than the chance he had willfully desecrated the tomb of a truly good king, was what was troubling him. Despite numerous warnings, he had chosen to believe in Audrey Cheshire's honesty. He had been unwise to do so. He had not only put his companions at risk, he had stripped away the millennia-old secret that had protected Neferankhotep's peace.

And did I somehow transform Audrey into what she is? he thought. *Is my desire to make a truly distinctive find somehow at fault? Had I been less eager for fame, more in service of historical discovery, might I have accepted her hints that she could be of assistance, and she have remained untempted, unwarped?*

Neville didn't know what answer he wanted—either confirmation that he was at fault, or acceptance that Audrey was nothing more than a scheming fraud. Each brought with it pain. For once the taunting voice of his inner self brought him no insight.

Yet Neville could not remain introspective, surrounded as he was by wonders. The flickering light illuminated not only the elaborate wall frescos, but alcoves holding intricate statues or elegant lamps carved from soapstone or alabaster. Sometimes there were small side-rooms containing caskets of gilded wood, their lids open to reveal scrolls or votive objects. Evenly spaced along the way were vases intricately painted with religious scenes or the texts of prayers, and holding the perfumed dust of flowers.

At intervals along the dark, gently curving corridor through which Neville and his companions made their halting progress were pillars supporting the roof. Some were fashioned to evoke various plants common in the Nile valley, each replete with its own symbolic significance: reed, lotus, palm, papyrus. The shafts of these pillars were heavily carved with hieroglyphs, and Stephen had to be stopped from attempting to translate each text. Other pillars were sculpted in the form of gods and goddesses, serene deific countenances rising above the dim glow of the candlelight so that their features appeared alive and moving in the flickering light.

Neville was concentrating on one of these—the cobra goddess, Wadjet, he thought, in an unusually large depiction—when he realized he was not straining to see as he had before. He drew his gaze down, expecting to find that Eddie, enterprising as usual, had lit more lanterns, and wanting to ask if this was wise. Their supply of oil was, after all, limited, and it might take them a while to find their way to the surface.

Instead Neville discovered that their progress had brought them around a bend, and that the light was coming from ahead of them. It was so clear and brilliant that Neville wondered at its source. Shouldn't the sun have set? The sheik had not set his men on them until after the noontime siesta, and they'd had a long wait in the antechamber.

"Does anyone else see . . ." he pointed, unwilling to ask a specific question lest it make the others think him mad.

Stephen, intent on the wall text nearest to him, seemed startled at being asked to look more than a few feet ahead. Eddie, however, instantly confirmed Neville's impression.

"There's light ahead. Stephen, keep a close eye out for pits or something. That light would make a dandy lure. Anyone trapped down here could be expected to race toward it."

"But," came Lady Cheshire's voice, speaking for the first time since she had attempted to defend retaining the muff pistol, "what could be its source? It must be night by now."

Jenny said coolly, "Time gets funny when you're trapped. You wouldn't believe how slowly it moves. Why, when we were in that chamber up top I thought the sun had stopped moving, time dragged so. It's the waiting that does it."

Neville looked at his pocket watch, but it was no help. "My watch has stopped," he said.

"Mine, too," Stephen said, surprised, "and I know I remembered to wind it."

"I," Captain Brentworth said, "have a watch in my coat pocket, if someone would care to check it."

He was clearly concerned that Jenny might take any motion on his part as an attempt to violate their agreement, and Neville couldn't blame him.

"It's time we took a breather anyway," Neville said. "How are you two doing with the stretcher?"

"Fine," Captain Brentworth said.

Lady Cheshire only nodded and went to lean against one of the pillars, gently chafing her wrists as if they ached.

Canteens were passed around, and when Jenny went to give some water to Rashid, not only did the Arab youth insist on drinking on his own, he made quite clear he felt he could move under his own power.

Jenny reluctantly agreed to let her patient try. She rolled up the stretcher, in case it should be needed. Captain Brentworth offered to carry it.

"Don't worry, Miss Benet," he said very coolly. "I am certain you can shoot me before I cause much harm with it."

Jenny had the grace to look embarrassed.

"Besides," the captain went on, "Rashid *is* my servant. It is only fitting I should look to his welfare."

I wonder if the pictures of Neferankhotep got to him, too? Neville thought. *Probably not. Probably just wanted to get Jenny to see him in a better light. I would if she were holding a gun on me, and her gaze was so cold and unfriendly.*

Curiosity about the light ahead, combined with hope that it would reveal a route to the upper reaches of the valley made them keep their rest stop short. By common consensus, they resumed their burdens, and continued their march.

What they found astonished all of them out of speech.

Jenny came up short when Lady Cheshire suddenly drew to a halt. Her hand dropped to her pistol, then, like a fan opening, the group began moving again, filing into a larger space, and revealing what lay before them.

Jenny forgot her pistol, forgot Lady Cheshire, even forgot the myriad concerns that had dogged her every footstep and blunted her pleasure in the beauty of the surrounding temple. Overwhelmed with shock that melted into wondering awe, she stared.

The area before them was so enormous that it defied categorization. It made any building Jenny had seen in America seem laughably small, made diminutive the cathedrals she had toured in London, even dwarfed the vastness of the Grand Canyon. It was greater than the great outdoors, without horizon, without limit, impossibly, and mind-shatteringly huge.

Jenny felt her foothold on reality trembling, heard Lady Cheshire give a tiny whimper of fear, and felt no scorn, only gratitude for that small, human exclamation. She forced herself to walk a few steps and put a hand on Lady Cheshire's arm, anchoring herself in something comprehensible, and when Lady Cheshire's hand rose and grasped her own Jenny felt a wash of relief.

In front of them, Captain Brentworth had sunk to his knees. Rashid stood staring. Mischief clung to his neck, making nervous hooting sounds. Uncle Neville was frozen in place, his mouth agape. Eddie had bent his head in an attitude of prayer, and Stephen stood, color draining from his sunburned features so rapidly that Jenny feared he might faint.

Only two beings seemed to feel no awe. Mrs. Syms looked about in the same attitude of unfocused interest and curiosity she had shown since awakening from their fall. Mozelle trotted forward, then crouched and began stalking something, the tip of her tail twitching with concentration.

Jenny brought her gaze to focus on the tawny feline form, allowing Mozelle's action to guide her into visual exploration of the vastness that she had shied away from.

What she saw almost forced her into new retreat.

The room was decorated to evoke the banks of the Nile in the lush growth that accompanied the latter stages of inundation. Papyrus reeds grew tall and green, not a single browned or weak stalk among the hardy bunches, their tops bursting into bushy golden-yellow tassels. Lotus and lilies spread round leaves over the water. Their blossoms—white, pale yellow, translucent pink—were open in the sunlight, each petal perfect and distinct. There were buds among the blossoms, elegant in the promise of beauty to come, but not a single withered flower.

Such unwithered beauty was possessed by every flower and grass. It was shared by the birds, insects, and small animals that darted among the verdure, their feathers and wings bright, their fur soft and glistening. The Nile waters shimmered as if stars were submerged in their depth. A perch that leapt out after a darting insect carried flecks of starlight upon its scales.

Jenny heard her own voice, hushed and small, ask, "But dragonflies? Herons? Butterflies? Here? How? I don't understand . . ."

Only Mrs. Syms, unflustered, trailing after Mozelle as if she was walking in some London garden, responded: "I don't know, my dear. Why not ask that nice man in the boat? He doesn't seem to be busy."

Jenny followed the direction the other woman pointed and saw the boat and the man. If, indeed, he could be called a man . . .

The boat was slim with upturned ends rising to tapering points. The hull had been elaborately decorated with brightly colored geometric designs. The boat boasted a single central mast around which an open-sided cabin had been built. In this cabin's shelter, in a chair set before the mast, sat the being Mrs. Syms had so blithely referred to as a man.

He possessed the head of a hawk, but the body of a strong and virile man. His only attire was a kilt of fine linen, a broad jeweled collar, and a variety of arm-bands intricately worked in gold and gemstones. On his head he wore the uraeus crown. The strangest thing about the hawk-headed man was that he glowed. Jenny had the impression that all the diffuse light in this vast chamber somehow em-anated from him.

Later, she would learn she was right.

Mrs. Syms was trotting down to the riverbank, waving her hand to get the boatman's attention.

"Yoo-hoo, boatman!"

The man turned his head and the wide-set bird's eyes stared fixedly at Mrs. Syms. It was impossible to read his expression, and Jenny, stumbling after, Lady Cheshire still gripping her hand, could only hope the masked figure—it must be a mask, mustn't it?—would be kind.

"Yes?" he replied, his tones strong but somehow mournful.

"Boatman, this marvelous garden, how did it get here?"

"It has always been here, since the beginning of time. It will remain here until time itself ends, if it ends."

Mrs. Syms had tilted her head slightly to one side and was studying the man, concern in her every line.

Is she finally seeing all of this? Jenny thought frantically. *It will destroy her . . . drive her mad. Madder? Perhaps she is the only sane one. Certainly, I can't be seeing what I'm seeing, hearing what I'm hearing, and still be sane.*

The others were also coming down to the riverbank. From the look of them, they were seeing the same things she and Mrs. Syms were. Jenny wondered if she should feel relieved at that. She watched as Eddie sidestepped to avoid a particu-larly luxuriant clump of papyrus reeds, and Stephen jumped backward when a pair of ducks, startled by his approach, exploded up out of the water. Uncle Neville prudently tested the soft ground with the tip of his crutch, before he put his weight on it. Captain Brentworth and Rashid walked down slowly side by side, man and master no more, but united by the kinship of familiarity in this strange place.

Like me and Audrey Cheshire, Jenny thought. *I just can't fear her as much, not in this place—and fear is what I felt. Fear is what made me so angry with her, willing even to kill her. I spoke a lot of hot words about right and wrong, but in the end I know my reaction now for fear pure and simple, wearing fancy clothes maybe, but no less fear for all that.*

Mrs. Syms spoke again, "I feel as if I should know you, boatman. Are you He Who Looks Behind? Or are you Charon? I've been thinking I was dead. I saw my Nathan, you know, and spoke with him, yet I know he has been dead for many years. Are you Charon, come to carry me to Nathan?"

"I am not He Who Looks Behind, nor the boatman sometimes called Charon. Nor are you dead." The boatman's voice grew heavy with sorrow. "However, I fear I shall be. My companions have not arrived, and I must take my boat through the hours of night, or fail to depart upon Mandet when I must."

"Mandet?" Stephen's voice sounded very tight, but he was managing to keep some control. "That is the boat on which the god Ra is said to rise into the sky at dawn."

"That is so," the hawk-headed being said, looking now at Stephen, "and I am Ra."

Jenny bit into her lip to keep from screaming, for with those words the boatman had risen to his feet and taken a few steps toward them. With that motion she had seen that the hawk's head was not some clever mask, but as supple and living as that of a real bird. The man's brown skin was unseamed and unscarred. It didn't even bear a line where his collar rested against his skin—and it should have. The ornament was obviously heavy.

Uncle Neville limped forward.

"Ra?" he said. "Why not? That's no more impossible than the rest of this place. Where are your companions? I seem to recall that gods and goddesses, great with power and magic, voyage with you each night, defending your ship from the serpent, Apophis."

"I do not know," Ra said. "All I know is that I must reach the other side of night, for without me day will not come."

Neville took a deep breath.

"May we sail with you, Ra? We could serve as your crew. We are not as powerful as Isis and Thoth and all the rest, but we're better than nothing."

The god studied him, then turned his bright falcon's gaze to the rest of them in turn.

"You may," he said, "and I will thank you for your service, but I perceive something of your thoughts. I may not carry you with me into the world of day. Tuat, the underworld, is the realm of my brother god Osiris. However, if you assist me, I will speak well of you to Osiris."

"We cannot ask more," Neville said. "Bide a moment, and I will speak to my companions."

"I cannot wait long," Ra said. "The sun will not rise without me."

Jenny stepped to her uncle's side.

"Are you serious, Uncle Neville?"

"Serious as the grave," he said. "You see this place. I don't know whether we're suffering under a mass hallucination or what, but this is where we are and we need to get out . . . unless you want to stay on this riverbank after Ra leaves. I have a feeling it's going to get awfully dark."

Captain Brentworth stared at him.

"You're mad. We can just turn around and head back the way we came. We missed a turning or a secret door. The Arabs probably fed us hashish or something. It'll wear off."

Neville's lips twisted in an expression that wasn't quite a grin.

"Have you looked back the way we came?" he said.

Captain Brentworth did. They all did, and Jenny didn't know whether to be surprised or terrified at this latest revelation.

The corridor was gone. What stretched behind them was more of the verdant Nile countryside. Gazelle frolicked in the distance. A lion coughed, and the gazelle scattered. Heron, ibis, ducks, cranes, and countless other water birds foraged. Frogs peeped from damp hollows. Dragonflies caught Ra's light and shattered it into rainbows in the prism of their wings.

"We're here," Neville said, "and I'm no philosopher to say whether this is real or not. I do know my foot is wet where I stepped in a puddle, and that these flowers have scent. That makes it real enough for me."

"So," Jenny interjected, "we can either sit here and hope that we've all been drugged and that it will wear off, or we can go with Ra."

"Ra," Stephen said, his eyes shining in a delicate balance between terror and excitement. "I don't think we'll get a second chance. If Ra fails in his voyage, darkness falls forever."

"You sound like you believe this," Lady Audrey said, not mockingly, more as one who collects information.

"It's odd," Stephen said, "but it's the only game in town."

"I'll go," Brentworth said, "but I must have a rifle. I've read the myths. I know that monsters come after this boat. If the boat's real, well, the monsters might be, too."

Jenny knew the others were waiting on her decision. "All right," she said. "We have a spare or two. Lady Cheshire, do you want your muff pistol or a bigger gun?"

"I'll take the pistol," the lady replied. "But the monsters were kept away by spells, not weapons."

"If you know any spells," Jenny said, realizing that what she had meant as a joke was coming out far too sincerely, "then brush up on them fast."

"And Mrs. Syms?"

Lady Cheshire started to reply, but Sarah Syms turned and gave a beatific smile.

"I think sailing on the river would be lovely, dear. We can talk to that nice man, Ray. He seems to know so much."

Rashid tugged on Captain Brentworth's sleeve, gesturing frantically toward the boat. When they turned to look, Ra was bending to untie the line from the shore.

"I can wait no longer," Ra said almost apologetically. "Already Apophis will have had time to ready his minions. Do you sail with me or remain?"

Jenny looked at her uncle.

"I'll go," she said.

The others nodded. Jenny bent and scooped up Mozelle, who was busily stalking another butterfly. The kitten never seemed to get disheartened at her failure to catch one, and Jenny grinned.

"Come along, little Persistence. We're going for a ride."

Magic

RA LET them put their gear aboard, and Neville was grateful. However real or unreal this was, it seemed wise to keep the water, weapons, and food near at hand.

Once they were aboard, the boat seemed quite a bit larger than it had from the shore. Its slenderness was deceptive. Toward the middle it was wide enough for two ranks of rowers, one on either side, with ample room for someone to walk between the rower's seats and the central cabin.

A steering platform dominated the stern. The rudder was attached to a long pole that angled out of the water to rest on a high frame. The entire structure made a triangle whose base was the platform itself. The steersman stood within that triangle to operate the rudder by means of a pole that extended in front of him. A second platform, this one with high sides, dominated the front of the vessel.

Ra said, "My place is in the center. If I am pulled over the side and so destroyed by my enemies, there is no cause for the voyage to continue, for in that moment all will be lost. Do any of you know how to steer such a vessel?"

Captain Brentworth surprised Neville by promptly volunteering.

"I do. I've sailed the Nile and the Thames both. Will we be using the sail or the oars?"

"The sail," Ra replied, "unless Apophis's magic steals the wind."

"Right," Captain Brentworth said. "I'll just go back and have a look at that rudder."

Ra nodded. "I will direct the sail from the center of the boat, but I could use an assistant. We will also need someone on the front platform to watch for obstacles and probe for the best channels."

Neville wanted to volunteer, but he knew his bad ankle would make his balance chancy. Eddie's arm disqualified him as well, and Rashid could not call out warning. Neville glanced over at Jenny, who looked as if she had reached the same conclusion he had.

"I'll do it," she said, "though I may need a bit of coaching."

"It shall be yours," Ra promised.

Mozelle seemed to approve of this, for she gave a chirping meow and leapt into the god's lap, ignoring the threat implied in the curved beak.

Trust a cat to find the warmest seat in the house, Neville thought.

Rashid grinned at the kitten, and mimed to Ra his own willingness to help with the sails. Mischief leapt from his perch around the youth's neck and climbed the mast.

"The rest of you," Ra said, "must stand ready and alert to repel Apophis and his minions. There will be danger. They are determined, and losing this battle night after night has not made them less assured, only more certain that this time the victory will be theirs."

"I'm willing," Neville said with more confidence than he felt, "and I'm sure the others are, too. Stephen and Eddie, how about you taking the starboard? Lady Cheshire and I shall man port."

"Starboard," Ra commented with a slight, thoughtful smile. "What a lovely word. Now, Rashid, be ready to loose that line and angle the sail to catch the wind. Eddie, Stephen, push us away from the bank."

The wind caught the sails almost instantly, and with unimaginable smoothness, the Boat of Millions of Years was gliding up the sparkling waters of this impossible Nile.

Jenny stood up on the bow platform, holding the long, slender pole with which she was supposed to fend them off obstacles and probe for the channel. What she wanted to be holding was her rifle, but Ra had so thoroughly disapproved of her failure to follow custom that she'd had to settle for propping her weapon against the ornately painted and carved rails that bounded the platform.

After bending over them a couple of times to check the water level, Jenny began to understand that these railings were as functional as her boots. They braced her neatly, keeping her from pitching over the side when the wind-driven boat made one of the many unexpected jerks that left her splashed with spray.

Jenny suspected she was going to be black and blue from bumping into the rails before she got a feel for the boat's motion. She quickly learned to listen for Ra's commands to loosen or tighten the sail, and guess what they would mean to her.

The beautiful shore where they had boarded the boat quickly gave way to a less inviting landscape. Towering cliffs loomed over the boat, making Jenny shrink into herself at the thought that someone up there might drop rocks on them. However, they passed through the cliffs without incident, and found themselves in the midst of a broad, wide stretch of desert. This changed without warning to a swampy canyon.

Jenny had to cry out warnings about a few shoals, shove the boat off a clump of reeds, but so far she had seen nothing sinister or malicious—unless you counted the random and erratic shifts in the surrounding terrain. She was beginning to wonder if Apophis and his minions had gone wherever Ra's usual crew had vanished off to—and was wondering where that might be—when she was jerked back to full attention by a strange sight.

The blue of the Nile's water was suddenly interrupted by scores, then hundreds of tiny v-shaped ripples that caught Ra's light in a truly beautiful fashion. Jenny, however, had ridden white water before, enough to feel instinctive fear alarm at anything interrupting the river's smooth surface.

"Rocks or something ahead," she cried out.

"Reduce sail," Ra commanded instantly.

Jenny had hardly sensed the decrease in their forward motion before the boat was in among the first of the v-shaped ripples. Now she saw what they truly were, and her voice rose, despite her best efforts not to scream.

"Snakes! It's not rocks, it's snakes! Hundreds and hundreds of them. They're trying to slither up the sides . . . Ra, make the boat go faster!"

Ra had already done what he could to increase their speed, but now the Boat of Millions of Years was proving curiously sluggish in its response.

Eddie said, his voice tight with confusion, "They look like horned vipers—but horned vipers don't swim, do they?"

Ra answered, "This place is like and unlike the places you have known. Both differences and similarities may be your doom."

Jenny didn't need to be told this. The vipers looked far too purposeful to be natural. She beat her pole against the sides of the bow, crushing and dislodging the snakes that slithered up the sides in defiance of gravity and nature. She heard Mrs. Syms shriek as a snake flopped onto the deck near her.

Uncle Neville called out, "The rudder's fouled with the blasted things. That's what's slowing us down. There must be hundreds of them. Brentworth, can you haul the rudder out of the water? I'll try to knock them off. The rest of you, grab an oar or something and scrape."

The steering mechanism groaned audibly as Captain Brentworth heaved the rudder—actually dual blades resembling paired long oars—from the water. Jenny glanced back and saw that the rudder blades were lost beneath a writhing mass of shining gray-green serpents. She gagged in horror and revulsion, then went back to pushing the vipers back off the prow.

"Don't anyone get bitten!" Eddie shouted, his unnecessary warning showing how unnerved he was.

Stephen and Lady Cheshire were too busy fending off snakes to respond. Mrs. Syms was reciting what sounded like a panicked prayer. Mischief chattered indignantly from so high up on the mast that he looked like a peculiar pennant.

Prayers won't do much good, Jenny thought in increasing panic. *I wish there were something I could shoot!*

The dull thudding of a stick hitting something soft but solid told her that Uncle Neville was still at work freeing the rudder. Captain Brentworth cursed a few times, doubtless when a snake dropped too close.

Gradually, the boat began picking up speed, leaving the vipers behind. Jenny saw with relief that the snakes clinging to the bow were dropping off as the bow sliced through the waters.

"We're getting clear of them!" she sang out in relief.

"Those were only Apophis's littlest grandchildren," Ra warned. "There will be more and worse."

More and worse came in the form of a flotilla of crocodiles that blocked the river with a fanged, tail-lashing log jam. The boat ran over the first few, but began to bog down as the mass of reptilian bodies grew more and more dense.

Jenny raised her rifle to fire, but lowered it almost immediately. Killing one crocodile would do nothing except add an inert form to the mass. Jarring vibrations came up through the hull, as if the boat were being battered by hundreds of fists. Jenny had a horrid vision of thousands of drowned sailors beating against the boat, pulling themselves arm over rotting, water-logged arm onto the deck. She stifled a cry of dismay.

Ra, as if reading her thoughts, said "The crocodiles batter the hull with the power of their tails. They will break through if we let them. The hours of the night are yet young, but Apophis has power here."

Stephen called out, "Ra, can you heat the water enough that the crocodiles will have to get away or die? I mean, they're reptiles, and reptiles *can't* regulate their own body heat."

Ra considered. "I would be in danger if I went near the side of the boat."

"You'll be in more danger if they sink us!" Stephen retorted, sounding more upset and angry than Jenny had ever heard him before.

And toward a god, too, she thought, a trace hysterically. *How fear makes heroes of us all.*

"You are correct, Stephen," Ra said, setting Mozelle aside as he rose. "Guard me well, and I will do what I can."

"I'll take a turn on the sheets so we can get away as soon as the crocodiles back off," Neville said. "Lady Cheshire, keep a careful eye on our side of the boat."

"I assure you," the lady replied, shifting her grip on the heavy oar she'd been using as a club. "I shall."

Jenny had already decided that beating at the crocodiles with her steering pole would only break the pole. She equipped herself with an oar and watched Ra, ready in case the crocodiles went after him.

"Sobek's children," the god called, leaning dangerously close to the thrashing fanged mass. "I am Ra who strokes you with his arms when you sleep upon the sun-heated river banks. I am Ra who warms the mud in which you bury your eggs. Bite me not, for I will make the waters warm for you, and give you my caress."

The crocodiles seemed to understand—or maybe they were just intimidated by a man who glowed. Certainly, none touched the hand Ra slipped into the waters, though a few came close and sniffed.

Jenny felt her heart flutter with sympathetic fear.

Initially, the crocodiles clustered around the warmth emanating from Ra, but they soon swam back. The water around Ra's hand began to bubble, then boil. Neville set the sail and the vessel picked up speed, the Boat of Millions of Years cutting through a seething cauldron.

Sweat dripped off Jenny's face and soaked her shirt.

What was it that Madame always said? "Women don't sweat, they glow"? Well then, I'm glowing almost as intensely as Ra right now.

Jenny mounted the forward watch platform again. A channel had opened through the mass of crocodiles. She called directions back to Captain Brentworth. Apparently, the crocodiles hadn't damaged the steering oars, for the boat responded smoothly. Behind her she could hear Uncle Neville turning his post back over to Ra. The god thanked him, then said in his penetrating, level tones:

"Very nice work, Robert. If you hadn't kept the rudder blades out of the reach of the crocodiles' teeth and tails, everything I did would not have altered our situation a whit."

It took Jenny a moment to remember that "Robert" was Captain Brentworth's Christian name, and hearing him so addressed by someone other than Lady Cheshire made the man suddenly more human.

She only says his name like it's some sort of caress, a reminder that they're intimate. Ra says it like he's talking to a friend. I guess in his eyes we're all equally worthy.

The thought made Jenny uneasy. It dissolved the remaining barriers between Uncle Neville's companions and Lady Cheshire's party, merging them more deeply into that uncomfortable alliance that had begun on the banks of this impossible Nile.

We're not going to be able to go back to what we were, she thought, *but I don't know if I can trust them. After all, we made up to them, not them to us.*

Aware that she was being unforgiving, Jenny concentrated on watching the waters. She heard Stephen say, happiness and relief evident in his voice: "Well, that solves our problems, doesn't it? Nothing will be able to get near to us with the river so hot."

"The heat will dissipate," Ra said, "nor can I renew it, for if I did, I would be too drained to resist Apophis when he comes."

"Oh," Stephen said, his tone flat with dismay. "Then maybe we shouldn't have tired you out."

"If you had not implored my assistance," Ra said, "we would not have escaped that coil. Yet the next coil is yours to untangle."

"Forgive me, Ra," Jenny asked, her gaze alert for the least ripple on the surface of the river, "but how do your usual guardians manage? I mean, Apophis loses every night, so there must be a way to stop him."

Do I really believe this? she thought, fighting down her fear. *Am I going crazy like Mrs. Syms? I must be if I can talk like this, but I saw those crocodiles. They left teeth marks on my pole. I can still see them. I bashed the snakes when they were trying to come aboard. Should I deny the evidence of my senses, or my sanity?*

Unaware of—or ignoring—her internal struggle, Ra answered Jenny's question.

"My companions count among their number Thoth, Isis, and Hathor, all of whom are knowledgeable in the ways of magic. They use spells to placate, deceive, and drive away those who would stop my voyaging through the night river. Sometimes they summon assistance from our friends."

Mrs. Syms spoke dreamily, "I remember some of those spells. I tried to learn the ones for driving away snakes. I can't stand snakes. I tried it just now, but I can't say for sure it worked. Still, it was amusing to try. My teacher told me that the first thing you had to do was learn the spell that enables you to do magic. *Heka.* That's the Egyptian word, right, Mr. Ray?"

"*Heka* too sails with me," Ra responded, "and he is not least among my protectors."

Lady Cheshire turned to Mrs. Syms. "Sarah, do you remember that spell—the one that enables a person to do magic?"

Jenny recognized the tight urgency in the other woman's voice. Lady Cheshire was also fighting the sense that all of this was unreal, fighting it with the fear that it was—at least somehow—real, and that if this journey were not made on the terms Ra had set forth, they all would die.

Sarah Syms answered happily, "Pretty well. I recited it over and over again, because I wanted to make the magic come to me. Not just for snakes, you understand, but snakes seemed like a good place to start."

"Can you tell us?" Lady Cheshire said, a trace impatiently.

"I suppose," Mrs. Syms looked vague and puzzled. "I don't know why you need to know, though. There aren't any snakes here anymore. We left them all behind."

"They might come back," Lady Cheshire persisted. Glancing back, Jenny saw she was holding her fists very tightly clenched. Fresh blood stained her bandaged arm.

I bet she'd like to slap Mrs. Syms, but doesn't dare. I always thought Audrey Cheshire was a slapper.

"That's true," Mrs. Syms agreed. "Snakes like water, and Egypt has lots of snakes, and there's lots of water here."

"We need to learn the spell that will make it possible for us to do magic," Lady Cheshire said. "You said that came first."

"That's right," Mrs. Syms looked pleased now. Her hobby was being respected. "It helps to have an ankh. The gods always carried those and used them to direct their magic."

"No problem," Stephen said hastily. "Here."

He grabbed a stiff piece of rope from the pile of supplies that had been heaped on the deck, doubled it over, leaving a loop at the top, then tied a second piece of rope over the first to secure the loop and form a cross.

"It isn't very beautiful," Mrs. Syms said dubiously, turning it over in her hand when Stephen handed it to her. "The one my teacher gave me—sold me, really—was carved from cedar and had little bits of gold leaf stuck on it."

Ra spoke. "Rope will do."

Stephen, who had been busily manufacturing an ankh for Lady Cheshire, looked at the god.

"Will it, sir?"

"It will."

Stephen was obviously eager to ask more, but Lady Cheshire shushed him with a meaningful glance at the water. Stephen, reminded that this exercise was not wholly academic, fell silent.

"Now, Sarah," Lady Cheshire said, her tone wheedling rather than commanding. "Tell me this spell."

Extending her arm stiffly downward in an attitude familiar from numerous tomb paintings, Sarah Syms held her rope ankh at her side.

"It goes something like this: *I desire magic, so I have sought things of magic. I have sought them and collected them. I have gathered them unto myself from living and dead, from high places and low, and from all the middle places as well. From all things that creep, fly, and swim over the surface of the Earth, I have taken magic. As I have gathered it, so it is my own.*"

Lady Cheshire nodded. "All right. Say it again a little more slowly and I'll repeat it."

"Me, too," Stephen said, holding up another rope ankh. "That is, if you can spare me, Eddie. I'll only let myself be distracted for a moment, I assure you."

Jenny thought that Uncle Neville looked remarkably controlled, and she admired him for his poise.

It must be part of being British, she thought. *Ra didn't shoot down this crazy idea of Lady Cheshire's. Maybe there's something to it.*

"Of course, Stephen," Uncle Neville responded. "Go ahead. Ra usually has Thoth and Isis both. Doesn't seem quite right we should do without at least two sorcerers."

Jenny glanced at Eddie Bryce, wondering how the Englishman turned Mohammedan was taking this, but Eddie's attention was for the side of the boat.

I'd better watch, too, she reminded herself.

She did, directing her gaze resolutely forward, but listening as Stephen and Lady Cheshire repeated Mrs. Syms's incantation.

Sounds vaguely biblical, Jenny thought. *Especially that part about crawling, flying, and swimming things. I wonder which came first?*

Stephen finished his recitation, then said almost diffidently, "I did manage to pack at least a few books along, Lady Cheshire. Until the next hoard of horrors comes along, perhaps you might want to look at them? Might give us some ideas what to try."

"Wonderful idea, Mr. Holmboe," Lady Cheshire agreed.

The Boat of Millions of Years sailed on in relative peace for a time, though the landscape altered several more times. Jenny was mulling over whether she should ask for an ankh and a chance to recite the spell when Captain Brentworth's deep voice broke the quiet.

"Miss Benet, have we run aground? We seem to be slowing."

"We have not run aground," Ra said before Jenny could reply. "I have been dreading this. Apophis has stolen the wind from our sails."

"Let me guess," Stephen said with false heartiness. "This is one of those problems your associates—Thoth and Isis and the rest—would solve by means of a spell."

"I admit this is so," Ra replied.

"Then we must do the same," Stephen said. "The Boat of the Sun travels west to east at night, right? So we need to summon the West Wind."

"You are certainly full enough of hot air, Mr. Holmboe," Captain Brentworth said mockingly. "Why not just get behind the sail and blow?"

"Robert!" Lady Cheshire snapped, her tone more rebuke than any words would have been. Then it softened. "Captain Brentworth may have a point, Mr. Holmboe, no matter how badly put. Sympathetic magic may work for us."

"Sailors," Eddie offered, "have all sorts of rituals to raise a wind, scratching backstays, I think, and whistling. Or is it not whistling?"

"Does this boat have backstays?" Mrs. Syms asked interestedly. "I suppose these lines holding the sail would do."

She trotted over to one and gave it a good scratch, rather as one might a favorite horse.

Stephen meanwhile had moved to behind the sail and in the fashion of one who is quite aware he looks idiotic was puffing and blowing. Jenny half-expected some mockery from Lady Cheshire, but that elegant creature came to stand beside Stephen and spread her arms, flapping them gently like Leda turning into the swan. As she did so, she repeated over and over again,

"Blow wind, blow! We have places to go! Blow wind, blow!"

Jenny decided a little whistling couldn't exactly hurt, and turning forward as if conscientiously minding her post she whistled a makeshift tune in time with Lady Cheshire's words.

Whether any of this did anything, or whether the wind would have resumed in its own right, no one but Ra could say, and no one quite had the courage to ask him. What was certain is that the wind did resume, and within a few minutes of that resumption, they were once again sailing upriver at a fine clip.

More time passed, and once again it was Captain Brentworth, whose place at the rudder made him sensitive to even minor changes in the boat's motion, who commented on a change.

"Miss Benet, the ship seems a little stiff responding to the rudder. Have we run onto a sandbar or something?"

"No," Jenny called back, leaning over the rails for a better look and probing with her pole. "Not that I tell from here, but you're right, we are slowing."

"We seem to be riding a bit high," Neville added, looking over the port side. "Maybe we hit a sandbar that was too far under to be seen from the surface."

Ra meanwhile was giving orders for the sail to be slackened, so the bottom of the hull would not be torn out against this unseen obstacle.

Uncle Neville picked up one of the oars and leaned over the port side, probing for the bottom.

"Might be that the highest part of whatever we've hit is here where the hull is lowest . . ."

He stopped talking abruptly, probing gently, then with greater force.

"Odd. The oar has hit something, but it doesn't feel like sand or mud. It rather bounces . . ."

A violent shock ran through the hull, and the Boat of Millions of Years began to rise.

Neville reeled back from the rail as the boat lifted up out of the river. Then he heard Jenny scream. He wheeled, trying to recapture his balance as he turned toward the bow.

Jenny was clinging to the rail, staring at something below.

"Hippopotamus!" she cried out. "It's not a sandbank! We've run onto the back of an enormous hippopotamus!"

Neville didn't question the accuracy of her statement. There amidst the clear blue waters of the Nile was a vast shining red bulk that was easily three-quarters the length of the Boat of Millions of Years and far more massive, extending to either side of the hull in an expanse of rubbery hide that bristled here and there with coarse black hair. In contrast to the hippo's bulk, the slender curve of the boat's stern and prow looked fragile and insignificant.

"Jenny! Brentworth! Get down!"

Neville shouted his warning only in time. The irate hippo sank into the water, ridding itself of its burden, then swam ponderously forward to attack the boat's prow. The projecting curve snapped at the impact, the break bisecting Jenny's platform. The darker red flesh of the hippo's mouth, set with huge, square ivory-white teeth, was all too visible before it closed, chewing the dry wood with what Neville thought was more confusion than malice.

"Maybe it thinks we're some peculiar breed of crocodile," Eddie said, his voice taut with excitement. "If it doesn't change it's mind we're dead. A hippo's jaw can crush a croc like we would an egg."

Captain Brentworth was checking the action on his rifle, but Neville could tell he was dubious about its effectiveness against such a foe.

"Even a usual hippopotamus," the captain said, "is armored in fat. Unless we hit this one just right, we're more likely to anger it than kill it."

"We've got to do something," Jenny protested. "You can take out a charging buffalo with a good shot. I'll give it a try. Just tell me where to aim."

Captain Brentworth might have replied, but Lady Cheshire overrode him.

"We can't shoot it, Miss Benet. Even if you made your shot, its death struggles would overturn the boat."

"We have to do something!" Jenny retorted, "or it's going to overturn us anyhow."

Eddie grabbed her arm. "Hush, Jenny. Lady Cheshire's right—and so are you. It's pretty much finished tasting the bow, and is trying to figure out if we might taste better on a second try."

"Taste!" Stephen exclaimed in the tone of one who has had a sudden idea. "Let's distract it with food."

"Where would we get that much fodder?" Neville said, watching the hippopotamus lumber around to begin its return attack. It's all desert here. Even the water's shy of plants."

"Magic!" Stephen said brightly, taking Mrs. Syms by one arm, Lady Cheshire by the other. "Come on, ladies. We have to try."

Neville wasn't at all certain that shooting wasn't the thing to do, but Ra was silent beneath his canopy, so he figured it only made sense to give it a try. There was no harm in waiting. The rifles would have a better chance of penetrating the hippo's fat from close in.

Stephen was talking very quickly, as if to convince himself.

"There are at least a few plants here," he said. "As I see it, all we need to do is make them grow faster and more thickly."

"Won't they tangle the boat?" Lady Cheshire asked.

"Not if we work on the space between us and the hippo," Stephen said. "Lotus and lily were both sacred to Ra, as I recall..."

Neville didn't listen any further. Maybe he could make some sort of spear from one of the oars. If he sharpened the tip...

Eddie guessed what he was about, and pulled out a large knife, and began feverishly shaving away at the oar handle while Neville braced it firm, two one-armed men collaborating at carpentry.

"We're all mad. Aren't we, Sir Neville?" Eddie said with forced cheerfulness. "If we're not, I'm going to have stories to rival the ones Miriam's mother tells of Sinbad and Ali Baba."

Neville grunted. He, for one, didn't want to remember any of this, much less tell tales of it to his—as yet nonexistent—children. He glanced over to the port side where Stephen and Lady Cheshire were trading impromptu verses, enthusiastically echoed by Mrs. Syms and Jenny who were acting as chorus.

There was a note of desperation in their voices—all but that of Mrs. Syms, who seemed to think it all a rather wonderful game. Ra sat silent, his hawk's head stern and dignified.

Is that the dignity of one who wishes to face death well, or the assurance of one who knows he'll pull through? Neville thought.

Eddie signalled that the oar handle was as sharp as he could make it, and Neville carried the makeshift spear over to the side. He stopped in mid-step, astonished at what he saw.

The water, dominated by the angry hippopotamus when last he had looked, was now crammed with greenery. Water lilies and lotus spread their pads side by side, more of the plants emerging from beneath the waters at every moment. Their flowers dotted the water, giving the scene a weirdly festive appearance.

In the midst of this stood the red hippo, shoulder deep in the waters, his massive jaws moving to tear at this unexpected feast. Bits of gilded and painted wood floated near him, testimony to his now forgotten fury.

Ra called out, "Rashid, ready the sail. Captain Brentworth, can you tend the rudder?"

The big man hastened back to his post, still craning his neck to look at the grazing hippopotamus. Neville glanced over at Eddie as they separated to their posts.

"Guess I didn't need a spear after all," he said, ruefully.

Ra—not Eddie—replied, "I wouldn't say that, Neville. You have done well so far, but we have not yet passed Apophis."

———

The minute she succumbed to Mrs. Syms's joyful invitation to "sing along, Miss Benet. It's such fun!" Jenny had given up on logic or reason. She'd sung for all she was worth, not even giggling when a particular verse of the spell recalled a nursery tune or a popular song. She left logic behind her—and with it, strangely, fear.

When the hippo had splintered not only the bow platform, but also the entire prow of the ship, Jenny had been all too aware that the break neatly cut in half her spray-splashed footmarks. It had been that close. If she hadn't listened to Uncle Neville, if she'd paused to do more than to grab her rifle, she'd be in the hippo's belly—along with a huge salad.

When they broke free, Jenny insisted on moving to the prow again.

"I can't stand up high," she said, "but we still need someone to watch."

Though she almost wished someone would, no one protested.

That's the price you pay for acting like you're tough, Jenny Benet, she said to herself. *People feel free to take you at your word.*

The Nile flowed quietly around them, but Jenny became aware that outside the sphere of Ra's immediate surroundings the area was becoming dark.

"We are entering Apophis's strength," Ra said. "Here he will do his worst."

So ready was she for hordes of crocodiles or gigantic monster hippopotami, Jenny nearly missed trouble when it came.

The edge of the waters began to be dotted with rounded interruptions, but as these protruding rocks did not extend into the channel where the Boat of Millions of Years sailed steadily on, she said nothing.

Then Jenny noticed that the rocks were moving. The light was poor, but she watched until she felt almost certain.

"To the rear and sides," she called. "Those rocks. Is it me, or are they moving?"

Stephen said hesitantly, "I think so, but what . . ."

"Turtles!" Eddie interrupted. "Lots of them. Their beaks can take a finger off, even a hand. Keep your hands in the boat!"

Ra was giving orders. The boat picked up speed, but already the turtles were pacing them, in some cases passing them.

"They're so fast!" Jenny said. "Whoever said turtles were slow?"

"On land, they're slow," Lady Cheshire said. "Mr. Holmboe, do you recall the tale of the magician and the courtesan's trinket?"

Stephen laughed aloud.

"I do. Shall we try?"

"I'll feel rather like we will be in imitation of Moses," Lady Cheshire said. "But I don't think it's impiety when for a just cause."

None of this made any sense to Jenny. She readied her rifle, wondering if turtles, like sharks, could be turned away by the scent of blood in the water. She wondered what turtles could do to them anyhow. They couldn't climb, surely, not even as well as a snake, and they couldn't break the boat into pieces. Then she remembered their resemblance to rocks.

They could run us aground, she thought, *pile one on another and then get aboard. Remember that boy who lost two toes to a snapper?*

Lady Cheshire had begun chanting, her voice giving cadence to rather ragged impromptu verse:

"Roll back waters/ roll away/ Roll back waters/ as you did in Snofru's day./ Roll back waters/ reveal the muddy ground/ roll back waters/ in mud is treasure found."

Stephen echoed her, line for line. Each held their makeshift ankh stiffly to one side. With their free hand, they made a pushing gesture, as if shoving the water back.

Winds dying down, then rising again are natural.

Plants growing with incredible swiftness are natural, too. The mind might excuse this in many ways. Perhaps the hippo had stirred up a mat of vegetation that had then floated to the surface. Perhaps Ra's light had caused some natural growth spurt, for both lilies and lotus respond to the sun.

However, there is no way to justify river water peeling back from itself, like an ocean retreating under the pull of a strong tide. There is no way to justify the abrupt appearance of a broad muddy strip, crammed with graceless and floundering turtles, many now revealed to be of extraordinary size. Even more difficult is justifying having one's boat continue to move forward, unaffected by events behind, thudding over the occasional turtle who had not been caught like its brethren. Indeed, the Boat of Millions of Years sailed rather gaily over these few.

Ra laughed with delight. "Usually Thoth and Isis summon the *abdju*-fish and the *dejeseru*-fish, and these make short work of the turtles. Your approach was quite different."

"Why didn't you tell us what to do?" Neville said, rather angrily, Jenny thought, and she didn't blame him. Both Stephen and Lady Cheshire looked exhausted, like they'd been doing something a whole lot harder than sing a few lines of doggerel.

"I feared the fish would not answer," Ra admitted. "What if they have gone wherever the rest of my companions are? I would have mentioned it if the lady had not been so clever. He bowed from the waist, and Lady Cheshire flushed with genuine pleasure.

Jenny thought Lady Cheshire deserved the praise. She herself admired people who thought well on their feet. Perhaps the desire to live up to Lady Cheshire's example was what sustained Jenny when she again turned forward and saw looming before them, not water, not river bank, but what at first seemed a huge tunnel, its reddish pale interior framed by four white curving fangs.

"Ahead," Jenny called, and was pleased to find her voice steady. "Folks, we've reached Apophis."

Apophis

NEVILLE SWUNG around at Jenny's words, and nearly dropped his rifle when he saw the size of the waiting snake.

"Snake" was hardly a fair term for the monster that awaited them. Apophis was so huge that a man could slip down its throat without it even bothering to swallow. The Boat of Millions of Years would give it a bit more trouble, but then the boat wasn't what Apophis wanted. Apophis wanted one passenger. Apophis wanted Ra.

For one moment of pure panicked honesty, Neville considered giving Ra over. After all, the strange being wasn't *really* the sun. Couldn't be. Everyone knew that the sun was some sort of giant furnace in the sky. Hadn't the Egyptians themselves been a bit confused about whether Ra was really the sun or just rode on the same boat?

"Rifles ready," Neville called, speaking quickly, afraid he'd say something else. "Fire on my order."

He was aware of Ra and Rashid reducing sail, letting the boat be pulled away from Apophis's, gaping maw by the current.

"Fire!" he shouted.

Four explosions occurred almost simultaneously. Neville could have sworn that Apophis shuddered slightly from four distinct impacts, but otherwise the enormous snake seemed unaffected. Certainly no blood welled forth within the cavern of its mouth.

Sarah Syms called out, "We're moving backwards. Do you think it will come after us?"

Neville envied Mrs. Syms the composure of her madness, but only said, "I fear so. Ready to fire again . . ."

But Apophis wasn't waiting for them to fire. It worked its mouth slightly, its tongue flickering rapidly as it did so, determined not to lose their scent.

Rehinging its jaw, Neville thought. *It's given up on the idea of swallowing us whole. So why don't I feel better?*

Now Apophis, a powerful coil of black, his head adorned with horns like those of the vipers that had assaulted the boat earlier, could be seen in his might and glory.

The snake reared up and back, the vast extent of its coils still blocking the river. Although not a cobra, Apophis shared the cobra's strength, holding a great length of its body high above the water as it cast about, swaying slightly. Head reared back, tongue flickering, it tasted the air.

"Drop to the deck and cover yourselves!" Ra yelled, the words mingling a man's voice and a falcon's shriek.

Neville obeyed, hearing the thud of the others hitting the deck alongside him, followed by a terrific flapping sound. There was an angry hiss and a sharp, acrid odor. Something wet misted against the thin band of exposed skin at the back of Neville's neck, and where it touched, it burned.

Ra's voice came again. "Rise, quickly now," he commanded. "Apophis cannot try that trick again. He will not have sufficient venom for such a mighty spray."

Neville scrambled to his feet.

"Venom!" Stephen was saying, looking up at the steaming holes in the sail. "Apophis spat his venom at us . . ."

"More like acid than venom," Eddie said, looking down at where his sleeve was perforated with dozens of tiny holes. "If Ra hadn't released the sail . . ."

"Yet I did so, and the cloth intercepted most of the spray," Ra interjected, "though the canvas is ruined. Apophis will not wait long before trying something new. Even now, he must be considering what to do."

Apophis had dropped back, as a man might after firing a shot, uncertain whether he had hit his target, and waiting to assess the damage before trying a new assault.

Jenny cut in. "Is anyone hurt? I have a salve that should ease the burning."

Lady Cheshire answered, "Over here. Rashid is hurt. He left his forearm bare while restraining Mischief."

Neville took a quick glance over to where Rashid knelt on the deck, cradling his arm. The wounded limb bore several large white blisters, looking as if hot ash had stuck to the skin. Rashid bore what must have been terrific pain bravely. In fact, now that Neville paused to consider it, ever since they had entered this strange river valley, the mute youth had been behaving with extraordinary poise and intelligence.

Had coming into this place somehow made him smarter, even as it had robbed Mrs. Syms of her sanity? Or had Rashid's stupidity been an act all along? Neville did not have time to pursue that line of thought, beyond feeling grateful that for whatever reason Rashid was turning out to be an asset rather than a liability.

Ignoring her own small blisters, Jenny hurried to Rashid's side, cleaned the remnants of acid from his skin before smoothing ointment onto the blisters. Mischief sobbed over Rashid's injury, shrilling small notes of sympathy to his master and stroking the youth's face with his slim, black fingers. He paused only to shriek defiance at Apophis.

Neville couldn't help but grin. The little monkey wouldn't even make a tidbit for the enormous snake.

"Thoughts as to what we should do next, anyone?" he said.

Eddie replied immediately. "The way to kill a snake is to cut off its head. Thing is, our rifle shots didn't seem to do much good. Will we do any better with a blade?"

"We don't have much choice but to try, do we?" Captain Brentworth said gruffly. "The boat's drifting back, and I don't fancy getting trapped between the turtles and that snake. I say we lay into it with our rifles, then finish it with the machete I saw in your gear."

"Good thing," Eddie said, a trifle sarcastically, "if we can get it to hold its head politely down for us."

Jenny rose to her feet, cocked her head back, and examined the towering snake with a fair facsimile of fearlessness.

"Eddie, we got any more of that good rope we brought with us? The smooth, strong stuff we were going to use for climbing."

"We have most of it," Eddie replied. "It's with the rest of the gear."

Jenny burrowed through the heap until she came to the rope, then she started fashioning a loop at one end.

"I'll reckon," she said, her American accent becoming thicker by the minute, "that I can lay myself a line right around that varmint's neck. It don't have much in the way of a head, mind, but those scales are so big and coarse I fancy the rope'll find purchase. Think you *hombres* can rassle him down if I do?"

Neville nodded slowly.

"We can try cinching the line around the mast," he said. "That will give us better support. Brentworth, you're by far the strongest of us. Can you serve as anchor?"

Brentworth was already down from the rudder platform. "Strangest game of tug of war I've ever played," he said.

Jenny had prepared her loop and was twirling it slowly, getting a feel for the rope's flexibility and play.

"I've lassoed broncs and bulls," she said. "Even lassoed a buffalo cow once on a dare, but I never caught me any giant snakes."

Ra's voice spoke from beneath the canopy, but his words were addressed to Mozelle.

"No, little hunter, you cannot go and chase that rope," he said, and Neville saw that "rope" the kitten was apparently fascinated with was not the lasso but the gigantic snake. Sitting still on Ra's knee, the kitten arched her back and hissed.

The snake noticed the tiny feline's challenge and emitted a ferocious hiss of its own, sounding like a train's boiler releasing pent-up steam. Then the triangular wedge of its head plunged down in attack, cutting through the air like an arrow released from a bow.

"Yee-haw!" Jenny shouted. Whipping her loop over her head several times, she let it fly. The lasso dropped neatly over the snake's head, falling several yards down the sinuous length of its body before she drew the loop tight.

Apophis felt the strangling coil tighten and drew back, forgetting Mozelle in this new distraction.

Neville had already wrapped the length of the rope around the mast, and now he grabbed hold of the line. He smelled a whiff of flowers and realized Lady Cheshire was behind him. Stephen came behind her. Rashid joined in last, though hauling against the line must have made his blistered skin burn anew.

Mrs. Syms gaped at the writhing mass of giant snake before hurrying to take a place behind Rashid.

"Tug of war! How marvelous! This really is the most fascinating cruise."

Ra had risen and now joined those holding the line. Apophis pulled so hard that the mast creaked, then cracked—a long fissure running end to end, but not snapping the well-seasoned wood. The thrashing of Apophis's lower body smashed the rails along the prow, finishing the destruction the hippopotamus had begun. Only the fact that the snake was straining back, resisting the rope's pull, kept the weight of its body from pulling the front of the boat underwater.

"Neville," Eddie called. "It won't hold for long. Here!"

Feeling the rope holding firmly despite Apophis's struggles, Neville let go of it and took the machete Eddie thrust out to him. Together they hacked at the snake's neck where it narrowed slightly, just behind the swelling of the head. Jenny joined them, wielding the axe they had brought for cutting firewood. The axe was smaller than the machetes, but the heavy wedge of its solid iron head broke the scales and gave the machetes softer ground in which to work.

Thick and viscous, the snake's red blood began to wash the planks. Apophis's lashing motion became erratic as it increased its attempts to break free. Neville slipped on the sodden deck, his weak ankle giving in the uncertain footing. He was struggling to stand up, groping for his machete, when Captain Brentworth shoved in and took his place.

The big man grabbed the machete in both hands, striking down with all his strength, putting the weight of his body behind each blow as neither Neville nor Eddie, hampered by their injuries, had been able to do.

Apophis's body was thicker than the barrel of a big horse, but Captain Brentworth slashed into it with concentrated violence. Bone, tendon, and flesh gave before him, but Apophis continued to thrash, apparently unimpaired. Neville took the axe and rejoined the fray, coordinating his strokes with Brentworth's. Jenny and Eddie moved well out of the way.

There was chanting in the background, Stephen and Lady Cheshire, doubtless, trying one of their spells to defeat the snake. Neville heard the sound as he heard the thudding of his heart, background noise without meaning but with tremendous intensity.

"Back!" Brentworth grunted. "I . . . have . . . it."

The last three words were staccato, one to each outflowing of tormented breath as the captain's blows grew wilder and more powerful. Neville obeyed, exhausted despite his terror, wanting nothing more than to lean against the rail and rest. His ankle throbbed with fresh pain, but he balanced himself and readied his rifle, checking that snake blood and spray hadn't ruined his charge.

Then Brentworth's machete flew up in a final, high arc, a motion that shouted that it contained every ounce of strength remaining to the captain. There was a dull thud as the last bit of thick, scaly hide parted and the machete bit into the wood of the deck.

Apophis's head parted from his body and dropped down onto the deck amid a shower of thick, red blood that tasted foul where it splattered against Neville's lips. Writhing still, but without direction or strength, the serpent's body smashed down onto the deck, then slid off across the broken railings and into the water.

The head continued to spasm, jaws snapping open and shut, tongue lashing out. Everyone scrabbled clear, even Ra, for the head seemed to move with purpose. The curving fangs might not carry enough poison to spray the entire deck, but they surely carried enough to kill a human being.

Yet it was not the fangs, but the tongue that snared Captain Brentworth as he turned away, heading for the rudder platform, the good soldier resuming his post when the battle had ended.

The forked tongue hit him with the force of a battering ram, a fleshy one, but even at its narrowest parts enough to topple a man—even one as big as Captain Brentworth, caught unaware as he was. The captain staggered, trying to regain his balance.

Neville lurched forward to assist him, but he was too far away, and the deck was slick with blood. He slipped and fell forward, catching himself on his hands. Brentworth fell, too—backwards and into Apophis's gaping maw, impaled upon a curving white fang as he toppled. He couldn't even scream before he died.

Blood mingled with venom spurted from the wound, burning as it fell. Then Stephen yelled: "The snake's growing a new body! It can't! A new skin, but not a new body . . ."

Ra started to say something, but, unthinkably, someone interrupted the god.

Mozelle had leapt to the remaining rail when Apophis's head fell on the deck. Now she jumped down, lightly, and with the arrogant grace that even a very small cat can summon at need.

Neville's head swam. Mozelle seemed suddenly very large. Certainly, she did not seem smaller than the snake's head, yet she must be. Its size was not in doubt, not with Robert Brentworth's corpse still impaled on one fang. He knew, despite the evidence of his eyes, that Mozelle was just a tiny kitten.

Yet the snake seemed to feel threatened. It worked the short, fat length of body grown from the bloody stump behind its head, and Brentworth's body was shaken clear. Then, amazingly, it hissed and began to wriggle backwards.

Mozelle stalked forward, her fur standing up along her spine, her back slightly arched. She meowed deep in her throat, a threatening noise, completely unlike her usual shrill mew.

Is the kitten grown large or the snake small? Do either of these terms apply? Neville shook his head again, trying to clear it, and only feeling himself grow dizzy.

Mozelle leaped up onto the roof of Ra's canopied pilot's cabin, and stood poised, one paw raised. Then she sprang, deftly avoiding the slash of Apophis's fangs, the lash of his tongue. *This can't be the same kitten I saw falling over her own feet just last night, can it?* Neville thought, but he knew that somehow it was.

With suddenly leonine jaws, Mozelle grabbed Apophis behind the swell of his head, clamped tightly and shook. The snake wriggled and lashed, but could not break free. Mozelle's tail switched back and forth. Then she sprang up onto the rail, bounded from there to the shore, and vanished into the brush, her prey still wriggling in her jaws.

They had hardly had time to collect their wits when Mozelle returned, looking very satisfied with herself. She leapt onto Jenny's shoulder, purring and rubbing herself against the thick mass of the young woman's hair.

"I wonder if she ate him?" Jenny asked, her voice awed and hushed.

"I don't think so," Stephen said, in a poor imitation of his usual pedantry. "Snakes are symbolic of reincarnation. Apophis will be back."

Lady Cheshire picked her way across the deck to Captain Brentworth's dead and mangled corpse.

"Is he dead?" she asked Ra. "Really and truly dead?"

Ra bent his hawk's head in solemn assent.

"He is dead. Really, truly, and finally dead."

They had sailed past the place where they had battled Apophis. As if to mock them for their grief and shock, the Nile now carried them through surroundings that were as lovely as the place where they had first met Ra. The lush green soothed them, seemed to suggest nothing would be harmed by their taking a rest, but the substitute crew of the Boat of Millions of Years had been through too much to give in to this Lotus Eater lure.

Jenny, reeling with shock and fatigue, was the first to realize that although none of Apophis's minions opposed them, still the boat was not sailing easily up the Nile.

"The sail!" she said, staring upward, aghast. "Look at the sail—and the mast!"

Every pair of eyes, including the gold-rimmed hawk eyes of Ra, looked up. Only the hawk-features, immobile by human standards, did not show shock and dismay.

The broad sail that had carried them so far was in tatters, burnt by the acid of Apophis's venom. Tiny pinpricks spread into gaping holes as they watched, leaving the sail a cobweb that could hardly hold itself together, much less catch the wind. The mast was riven from top to bottom. Even if they could rig a new sail, there was no way the mast could carry it.

"We're drifting backward," Eddie warned. He hopped up onto the rear platform and shifted the rudder so the Boat of Millions of Years drifted sideways, slowing slightly.

"Backward?" Lady Cheshire asked. "To Apophis?"

"To Apophis," Ra agreed. "Even if he remains incapacitated when we reach him, his minions will still be there—and very angry, I fear, for they will have once more suffered the shame of defeat."

"All but the hippo," Stephen said bravely. "He should be glad to see us."

Neville had grabbed one of the remaining oars.

"We've no choice but to row," he said. "Gentlemen, if you each will take an oar . . . Eddie, your arm won't let you row, but you may be able to manage the rudder. Ladies, I hate to ask . . ."

"I can row," Jenny said stoutly, though in truth she didn't know how long she could hold out.

"Are we going sculling now?" Mrs. Syms asked brightly. "What an *interesting* outing this is turning out to be. Don't you think so, Mr. Ray?"

Ra cocked his head to one side, very birdlike, but accepted the oar Neville thrust at him.

"I may honestly say that it is among the oddest voyages I have experienced in very many voyages on this river."

"Let's see if we can get the boat straightened out first," Neville began, but Lady Cheshire cut him off.

"Sir Neville," she said, "take us to the riverbank. We may be able to recruit another crew to row us."

"Lady Cheshire," Neville replied stiffly, "we have seen no sign of human life. Indeed, we have seen little other than reptiles."

"I don't think," Stephen said, "that hippopotami are reptiles."

"Blast your hippopotamus, Stephen Holmboe!" Neville exploded. "Blast your taxonomy, too. The only use I'd have for that water horse is if we could convince it to pull us upstream."

Lady Cheshire persisted. "I don't fancy hippopotami for motive power, Sir Neville, but the ancient Egyptians did provide for laborers."

Jenny saw her own realization touching her uncle's face.

"You mean those shabti things?" he said. "The figurines that were supposed to do the work in the afterlife?"

"Precisely," Lady Cheshire said. "We might be able to create some. Stephen and I have managed a few things so far—we may be granted one more miracle."

"Eddie?" Neville said.

"I'll steer for the riverbank," Eddie replied, "on your command."

"Do it then," Neville said.

Even with all of them pulling on the oars, they more drove the Boat of Millions of Years into the nearest riverbank than landed it. The hippopotamus-mutilated prow cracked a little more as it thumped against the land.

"I hope the sail soaked up most of the venom," Jenny said, "or we're going to need more than rowers."

"I'll take a look for leaks," Neville said, rising. "Eddie, lend me a hand."

"I only have one to lend," Eddie said, "but you're welcome to it."

Rashid motioned that he could help, too, and Neville accepted gladly.

"We may need someone who can climb down the side," he said, "and neither Eddie nor I could handle that."

Jenny was about to offer her assistance when Lady Cheshire touched her arm.

"Please, Jenny," she said, her green eyes intense. "We'll need extra hands to model the figures. I'm sure I can get Sarah to help, but . . ."

"Sure," Jenny said.

Ra had returned to his seat at the center of the vessel, and took Mozelle back into his lap. There was a silent consensus among the humans that they could not ask him to assist in this next step. He'd aided in the defense against Apophis, pulled an oar, managed the sail, and warded off the crocodiles. Jenny had the impression that the god—if god Ra was—was as distressed in his own fashion by all this strangeness as his human crew were.

"I'm better at drawing than modeling," Jenny apologized as she joined Stephen, Lady Cheshire, and Mrs. Syms. "What do we do?"

She stopped and took another look at the two women. "First thing I'm going to do is re-bandage your arm, then take a look at the dressing on Sarah's collarbone."

"Thank you," Lady Cheshire said simply. "Stephen, the book you loaned me contained some sections from the *Book of the Dead*. I thought I saw one for enchanting shabti figures. Can you find that passage and adapt it to our needs?"

"Gladly," Stephen said.

"What are we going to do, Audrey?" Mrs. Syms asked.

"After Miss Benet finishes checking our bandages, we are going on the shore to make mud figures," Lady Cheshire told her. "We can't be too fancy about this," she said when they had all stepped ashore, and a convenient deposit of sticky mud had been located. "How many oarsmen do we need?"

Jenny had counted when they were rowing, wishing then that some of Ra's usual companions would show up and fill the empty benches.

"Six to a side," Jenny said, "if none of us take seats."

"I think we should remain free to do other things, if needed," Lady Cheshire said. "Very well, first we need twelve human figures. They needn't be large."

"They'll be awfully soft," Jenny said, digging out a wet lump with her fingernails.

"I thought," Lady Cheshire said, almost shyly, "that we would ask Ra to bake them for us. If he cannot, we will need to settle for air-drying, but that will take more time."

Sarah Syms was already making a nice little mud doll about six inches tall.

"Good thing they don't need to be life-sized," Jenny asked.

"Indeed." Lady Cheshire glanced at her once well-tended hands with a slight sigh, then dug into the mud with a will, if not with enthusiasm. "The ones in the tombs were not—not usually, at least."

Stephen looked up from his reading and started taking notes. He glanced over at them, and said, "Incise each figure with the ankh for life, the Eye of Horus for protection, and then number each one in order. Lady Cheshire, do you recall Egyptian numbers?"

"The lower ones, yes," she responded, "and the determinative for hundreds and thousands and such."

"Then label each with a hieroglyph between one and twelve," Stephen said. "Might as well be purists. Finish them off with something green—sticking a bit of leaf into the mud should do it. Green's the color of life and strength, as I recall." He briefly flashed an enthusiastic grin, then returned to his scribbling.

The dozen mud figures were soon completed, inscribed, and equipped with oars—more like broad-bladed paddles to Jenny's way of thinking. They wore tidy little loincloths cut from a flexible leaf. Mrs. Syms had insisted in adding hair and facial features, using a stick as a stylus. A couple of broad, thick leaves served as trays to move the completed figures without offering too much damage to the soft clay.

"Ra?" Lady Cheshire said with more hesitation than Jenny had ever heard from her. "Could you . . . uh . . . bake these?"

Ra blinked, then looked at the shabti figures. For a moment, Jenny thought he might refuse. Then he raised his hands and held one over each of the leaf trays. There was a wash of heat, so intense that Jenny's hands rose to cover her eyes of their own volition. When she lowered them, the leaves had been burnt to ash, though the deck beneath them was untouched. The twelve clay figures remained as well, but they hadn't merely been baked; they had been transformed.

Each little man was now shiny reddish-brown, polished and glazed. The leaf ornamentation shown like opaque glass or even emerald. The hieroglyphs were incised into the figures with a fine tracery of gold. The figures' features were more human now—no longer the pinching of a nose, or a mere line to suggest eye or hair, but tidy, realistic sculptures. The paddles they carried, which before had been rough approximations, whittled out by Jenny with her Bowie knife from a portion of splintered planking, were now elegantly curved, with a smoothed haft where the paddler's hand would rest, and a sturdy, leaf-shaped blade.

When Stephen saw the completed shabti figures, his mouth dropped open in surprise.

"My spell isn't going to match your modeling," he said with sincerity. "I've adapted the verse from the *Book of the Dead*, removing references to service in the afterlife. Hopefully, it will do."

Lady Cheshire looked at the figures, then over at Ra, who sat, eyes closed, hand gently stroking Mozelle.

"I think it had better. Ra doesn't look at all well. I think he needs to reach the east."

Stephen cleared his throat. "You may be right. Gather round, all, and take a look at this."

The three women did so, Mrs. Syms with the air of one being invited to take part in a particularly amusing party game.

Jenny read silently the words on the page,

> *Oh Shabti, created by me, joyful in service,*
> *arise at my call, heed my commands,*
> *know full well the task given to you,*
> *even as does the seasoned laborer.*
> *When I call upon you, rise up, take your place.*
> *Say when I call, "Here I am."*

Lady Cheshire nodded, finished her own reading, and said, "Shall we recite it together, each of us holding three of the shabti figures?"

"Holding hands over them, rather," Stephen suggested. "Better not to be touching them, just in case."

Crowding together to use Stephen's crib, they recited the words. Jenny had to fight the urge to look over at Ra—and the increasingly unfathomable Mozelle. If either looked in the least mocking, she knew she'd falter, and a cat could look mocking without even trying.

Then Jenny felt the deck tremble, felt something brush against her fingertips, and forgot about feeling foolish. She moved the hand she held over her three shabti figures, then she jerked it aside as she might have from a burning stove.

The shabti were growing, shifting muscles under reddish-brown skin, moving heads slowly side to side, rolling neck muscles, testing the curl of arms and fingers.

Jenny thought she should be growing accustomed to wonders, but from the way her heart was beating against her ribs, she knew she had not.

She quickly stepped back a pace. She knew that when she said the final lines— *"When I call upon you, rise up, take your place. Say when I call, 'Here I am.'"*—the shabti figures would indeed rise.

The dozen figures stood as one, not mere clay figures any longer, but neither breathing nor truly alive. Their eyes were liquid and moving, but they did not blink. Their hair fell silken to their shoulders, but did not shift in the breeze. When the recitation was concluded, their lips moved and a dozen voices said as one: "Here I am."

Stephen mastered himself first. He'd clearly been thinking about what would be needed if the spell actually worked.

"Take your paddles, men. You know your names, for they are graven into your hearts. Go to the seats in the order of those names: front to back in ascending order, divided with odd number to the port, even to starboard."

And as if these directions were another form of spell, the shabti figures moved to the places indicated. Number One sat in the foremost bench on the left, Number Two on the foremost bench to the right. Their fellows ranked themselves in order behind them.

Uncle Neville spoke, his voice filled with wonder.

"You've found us a crew. I can hardly believe it. Jenny, can you take the late Captain Brentworth's post at the stern? I'll watch from what's left of the bow, and Rashid can take my place here."

Jenny nodded, walking carefully so as not to tread in the still drying marks left by the captain's blood. She grasped the poles that controlled the rudders.

"Ready, Uncle Neville."

"Rowers, forward," came Sir Neville's voice, not quite certain, but willing to try accepting this latest impossibility. "We're going to this river's end. We're taking Ra to where he can ascend again into the sky."

"And the rest of us?" Lady Cheshire said, speaking very carefully, as if she suspected she would not like the answer. "Will the rest of us ascend to the sky?"

Ra answered, "You did not come here seeking the sky, Audrey. You came here seeking the good king, Neferankhotep. It is before him you shall go. I believe he has some questions for you all."

Negative Confessions

RA'S WORDS rung like a pronouncement of doom. Neville had no doubt that even Jenny—the least schooled in Egyptology of them all, unless one counted Rashid, and Neville had no idea what the Arab youth knew or did not know—understood perfectly what the hawk-headed figure had meant. One could not travel up the Nile, touring temple and tomb alike, and not grasp some basic tenets of Egyptian belief.

In the afterlife, if one passed trial before Maat—and Neville had no doubt that Neferankhotep had passed such judgment with ease—the pharaoh became as one with Osiris. Osiris was judge of the dead, though not the only judge, and Neville realized his hand was shaking as he recalled depictions of some of those other judges.

This can't be real! he thought with desperation, but he knew it was. Robert Brentworth was dead, impaled on the fang of a serpent who might otherwise have swallowed the sun. The kitten Jenny had rescued had grown larger than the serpent, and Neville's own boots were stained with the blood of impossible snakes and of crocodiles who had attacked with the determination of men.

If this isn't reality, Neville thought, determinedly silencing the nagging inner voice, *it's a forgery of which God Almighty could be proud. My only other choice is joining Mrs. Syms, and making pretend that we're punting along the Thames or the Severn, doubtless stopping for lunch along the way. I'll settle for unreality, if my only other choice is insanity.*

Stephen seemed to have arrived at some similar conclusion, for he addressed Ra almost conversationally as they followed the hawk-headed man onto the shore.

"I say, Mr. Ra, I don't expect that you'd be able to put in a good word for us, would you? We've done our best by you at least."

"Certainly, the deeds of the end of a life weigh against the crimes done earlier," Ra agreed, "but the final judge is Maat. Is your soul as light as the feather of truth and justice? If so, then you should have no concern about what comes after."

Stephen looked troubled.

"I always thought of truth as a heavy thing indeed," he replied slowly, "since people have so much trouble continuing to carry it. And justice is a slippery concept. I'm not sure that what Eddie's religion considers justice is the same as what mine does. Are such differences in interpretation taken into account, Ra?"

"Ask Osiris," Ra said, "when you reach the halls of judgment."

Ra's next words were spoken in a language Neville did not understand, but in response the shabti figures shipped their oars and the Boat of Millions of Years glided up to the river bank.

"Here is where I change boats," Ra said, almost conversationally, "and we part company. You may stay on this riverbank, but I should warn you—it remains Apophis's country, and he will not think kindly of you after what you have done. Through those doors is the Hall of Judgment. I suggest you pass through them. Even Ammit's jaws would be kinder than what Apophis and his children will do if they catch you."

Neville looked. Two enormous double doors stood where Ra had indicated—and where Neville was absolutely certain nothing had been before. They stood twice as high as a grown man and were intricately inscribed with hieroglyphs. Both the doors and the building into which they led were oddly shaped, the doors having a peculiar curve to their top and the building being quite narrow in comparison to its length.

Didn't I read somewhere that the Hall of Judgment was supposed to be shaped like a gigantic sarcophagus? Neville thought. *That would account for the oddities of that structure—the doors are where the feet would be.*

He tore his gaze from the doors, and offered Ra his best court bow.

"Thank you for permitting us to take passage on your boat, Ra," he said. "It was an interesting trip."

"A bit too interesting," Ra said. "I shall certainly make some stern inquiries after my usual companions."

He bent to pat Mozelle.

"I would ask you to come with me, little one," he said, "but I know you will not leave your friends."

Granting them a regal yet friendly inclination of his head, Ra walked a few steps upstream, then boarded a boat covered stem to stern with delicate gold leaf that glowed like the first pale rays of the rising sun.

As they watched, Ra's hawk head began to transform, growing more compact and ovoid, but the light was very bright now, too bright for Neville to see clearly. In Neville's last glimpse of Ra, the hawk-headed man had become a scarab beetle, and the beetle somehow was both passenger upon the boat, and walking behind it, pushing the vessel's glowing roundness up through the darkness and into the sky.

Neville shook his head, drawing himself back from that vision, for he thought he might stare after the boat of the sun forever, longing besieging his heart as he imagined its celestial voyage. When he looked around, all of his companions except for Mrs. Syms were coming to themselves, longing and wonder naked on their faces. Mrs. Syms merely looked a trace impatient.

"Well," she said, "the temple is here. Are we going to tour it, or not?"

"By all means, Mrs. Syms," Neville said, squaring his shoulders, and stepping forward to open the door. "Let me and Stephen go first. Who knows what might be inside?"

Jenny half expected the door to open before Uncle Neville touched it, creaking open like the portal to a crypt in one of the stories in Stephen's Poe collection, but the door did no such thing. Indeed, it took both of the men working together to shove it ajar, yet once it was set in motion, the door moved smoothly and soundlessly, like any ordinary portal into any fine house.

But this isn't any ordinary portal, nor this any ordinary house, Jenny thought, fighting the impulse to draw one of her revolvers. The weight of the gun might be comforting, but she expected that bullets would prove as useless here as they had against Apophis.

Mozelle rubbed against her ankles, twining around them so that Jenny had to scoop her up or stumble. Once lifted, Mozelle settled herself quite contentedly onto the level platform of Jenny's forearm, sitting upright, like a statue of Bastet.

And what are you, kitten? Jenny thought, glancing down at the fragile ball of tawny fur. *You're so tiny your eyes are still blue and your tail's just a little stick covered with fur, but I saw you when you attacked Apophis, and then you were grander than the grandest lion.*

Mozelle did not answer, even here in this place where words from a cat might have seemed perfectly normal. She only buzzed a warm, vibrating purr that seemed as innocent as Mrs. Syms's pleasure in this newest "tour."

"Uncle Neville, should we get our gear off the boat?" Jenny asked, when her uncle would have stepped into the temple.

Neville Hawthorne quirked half a smile. "I think we may be beyond anything that gear can do for us, but it does seem imprudent to leave it . . ."

Eddie was starting back to board the vessel when a deep voice spoke from beyond the open door.

"Come. There is no need for such here. If you are vindicated, then your soul bird will fly free to where offerings from the upper world await. Come hither without delay."

Jenny opened her mouth, but no words came forth, only a quiet moan.

Eddie only looked at Neville, "Your call, Neville."

"By all means, let us obey our host," Neville replied, a trace too breezily for real confidence. "After all, when in Rome . . ."

"Or rather," Stephen agreed, forcing a laugh, "when in Egypt. Miss Benet?"

He made a sweeping gesture, as if offering to escort her onto a dance floor. Jenny smiled, and set her free hand lightly on the crook of Stephen's arm. Uncle Neville followed suit, offering his own protection to Lady Cheshire. Mrs. Syms accepted Eddie's arm. Rashid, Mischief shrilling anxiously from his shoulder, brought up the rear.

The doors were easily wide enough to admit their little party, even two abreast. They crossed the threshold into a beautiful anteroom accented by an oval pool. Delicate lilies in hues of translucent yellow, pink, and blue floated in the crystalline waters, and tiny fish darted, living flakes of gold and silver beneath the surface.

The walls were adorned with scenes familiar from many tombs, but here, as they had seen elsewhere in the complex, there was a subtle difference from any other depictions of pharaohs living or dead. Once again, the artists' emphasis was as much on Neferankhotep's just use of his great power as on the luxury and grandeur to which that power entitled him.

There was no doubt that their destination was a pair of doors on the other side of the pool, so they walked toward these, keeping stately measure, and taking in the elegance of the chamber as if they were indeed, as Mrs. Syms commented, visiting "the most ideal museum we have seen so far."

"Why," Jenny said, walking around one edge of the pool, and studying a mural depicting Neferankhotep holding court, "doesn't this comfort me?"

"Because," Stephen replied with such immediacy that Jenny knew he had been considering the same matter, "we're human, and the perfection of divine justice is frightening. We want justice to see things *our* way—even when we know deep down inside that our sense of justice is corrupted by our desires, rather than our adherence to perfection."

"And Neferankhotep," Neville added, "seems to have managed divine judgment when still alive and human—I mean, even Jesus lost his temper and despaired and liked to enjoy himself with his friends. Neferankhotep is just too perfect."

"Or rather," Lady Cheshire said, surprising Jenny, for unless speech had been absolutely necessary, Audrey Cheshire had been morosely silent since the death of Captain Brentworth, "Neferankhotep is as perfect as we would like to believe ourselves capable of being—and since he began his life as human as we are, his perfection is a reprimand."

As if an advertisement for what awaited them on the other side, the inner door was adorned with an elaborate painting of the judgment of the soul. An enormous scale dominated the scene, its two pans suspended from a center bar, both holding nothing but air, and so in perfect balance. Jenny had seen the twins of this scale in market places in Alexandria, Cairo, and all the way up the Nile. Its utter mundanity made the beings gathered around it also seem strangely mundane.

Thoth, his tiny ibis head mounted on broad shoulders, should have looked funny, but he did not. There was a scholarly dignity to how he held his stylus, poised in the act of taking some note or consulting some record.

Near one empty pan of the scale crouched the monster Ammit, the merging of crocodile jaws, lion forequarters, and hippopotamus hindquarters not looking at all humorous or peculiar in this context, but rather watchful and terrible.

Anubis, his jackal head making Jenny shiver with remembered terror, knelt near the scales, looking less like a god than like a workman checking his tools and feeling satisfied with their readiness.

In the background of the painting were many other figures. Osiris/Neferankhotep supervised the preparations with detached dignity. Maat, her wings outstretched in deliberate echo of the scales, stood near them, apparently waiting to take her place in one of the empty pans. Dozens of smaller figures, some distorted and horrid, also waited, their gazes fixed on the scales in dreadful anticipation.

"The Forty-Two Judges," Stephen said softly. "Some texts imply that they can be bribed or threatened—if one has magic enough—but I doubt that such tactics will work in Neferankhotep's court."

"No, probably not," Jenny replied. "I wonder . . ."

She forgot what she had been about to ask, forgot for a moment where they were, for the scene before them was coming alive. In the foreground, Thoth and Anubis completed their preparation. The Forty-Two Judges gossiped among themselves, the hissing of their voices making a muted background to the creaking of the scale pans as Anubis tested their motion, and the scratching of Thoth's pen as he finished his notes.

The painted eyes of Neferankhotep were the last things to gain brightness and depth, and as they did so they met Jenny's own eyes—and she knew, impossibly, that his gaze simultaneously met that of each other individual in the anteroom.

"I am Neferankhotep," the mummy-wrapped king said, his tone polite and formal. Then he grinned, white teeth against the green of his skin. "I believe you have been looking for me."

He laughed, and the Forty-Two Judges laughed with him, their voices mingling the cries of birds and the baying of hounds with all ranges of human mirth.

"Here I am," Neferankhotep concluded, "and before me you will be judged."

"Games," Neville replied bluntly when he recovered from his initial shock, "are only amusing when you're not one of the playing pieces. We came here seeking not you, but your tomb. I believe it is only fair that you remember this."

"Remember that you are tomb robbers?" Neferankhotep said. "I had tried to remember otherwise."

"Not tomb robbers," Neville said firmly, "students of history and archeology."

"There is a difference?"

"As we see it, there is." Neville hesitated, then pushed ahead. "Great Neferankhotep, in life you earned a reputation for devotion to justice that was not without human kindness. We find ourselves—against all sane expectation—standing before you for judgment. Well, I ask you, sir, is playing about in this fashion reasonable or in keeping with your reputation?"

Neferankhotep's expression became mildly amused. Neville couldn't help but think how peculiar it was to see living moods on features that still bore more than a slight resemblance to the stylized conventions of Egyptian art.

But no more peculiar, Neville's inner demon taunted him, *than any of the rest of this.*

"You say," Neferankhotep replied, his voice smooth and soothing, "that you had no expectation that you would be brought to judgment. Surely you saw the messages written on the walls in the Valley of Dust. Surely the Protectors warned you what awaited."

Neville blinked.

"Well, yes, but we didn't think those warnings were serious. Old temples are full of curses and the like, and despite the stories the superstitious tell, I've never much believed in the power of dead pharaohs to curse from beyond the grave."

"Yet you believed the tales of my life and burial sufficiently to let them guide you here," Neferankhotep persisted. "How do you resolve this discrepancy?"

"I don't," Neville said firmly. "The one was a possibility—the basis for scientific investigation. The rest of this is an impossibility. I'm more interested in knowing what your intentions are toward myself and my companions."

Neville knew he was being so blunt as to verge on rudeness, knew, even, that he was counting on the reputation for justice of a man with whom he didn't really believe he was speaking. His approach seemed the only way short of groveling to handle this situation, but some part of him kept expecting a renewed burst of laughter followed by the removal of elaborate costumes to reveal the Bedouin sheik and his minions

It didn't happen. Neferankhotep paused, clearly considering Neville's words. The only sound was that of breathing from far more than Neville's six companions—an eerie sound that made the back of his neck prickle.

"You have come here," Neferankhotep said at last, "all but one sound in mind, and all rather battered in body. Some degree of acceptance of your situation must be the end result of this journey."

"Nonsense," Neville replied. "I could argue that those of us who remain sane do so only because we don't believe. Mrs. Syms . . ."

"Yes, Sir Neville?"

"Nothing, ma'am."

"Oh . . ."

"The lady in question," Neville continued, choosing his words more carefully, for he had no desire to jolt her into awareness of their situation, "could be said to be the only one who has believed what she has seen, and that believing has made her mad. However, that is neither here nor there."

"Sanity is not a question?" Neferankhotep asked.

"Not," Neville said, "if you intend to pass judgment on us."

"It is my duty to judge those who come before me," Neferankhotep said, and Thoth nodded solemn agreement.

"Very well," Neville said. "Judge me and me alone. I am the one who led this expedition. I am the one who desired to find you—or rather your resting place. I am the one who hoped to benefit through my discoveries. The others acted only in accord with what I had already set in motion."

Neferankhotep was about to reply when Lady Cheshire interrupted, speaking over half-voiced protests from the others.

"Nonsense, Sir Neville. What you say may be true enough of your niece, Mr. Bryce, and Mr. Holmboe, but I am responsible for my own part in this. Captain Brentworth met his death through his fidelity to me. Sarah and Rashid are little more than servants. If you will be judged for your people, allow me, at least to assume the weight of guilt for my own."

Audrey's words could have been spoken from mere bravado and pride, but nonetheless Neville thought her magnificent, with her green eyes flashing and her shoulders thrown back, straight and valiant as any soldier.

"Guilt, Audrey?" said Neferankhotep. "So you admit to being guilty?"

"I admit to some guilt," Lady Cheshire replied, "though not toward you and your tomb. I agree with Sir Neville. We sought an archeological find, not a holy place. However, I do admit to having deceived Sir Neville, to having been less direct than I might have been, and to having hired dangerous men as a means of gaining my goals. Yes. I admit my guilt in these matters."

"Though only," Neferankhotep said, his dry assessment removing the glory from her defiant speech, "after being discovered and yourself deceived. Judgment will not be deferred, nor blame accepted for the actions of another. None of you who stand here came less than willingly."

"What about Rashid?" Jenny interrupted fiercely. "He's just a servant—almost a slave. He didn't have any choice."

Neville felt a surge of pride for his niece. She made no excuses for herself, but though her pale cheeks testified to her shock, she persisted in defending others.

Neferankhotep was less impressed, "And so you know the hearts and minds of men, even of a youth who cannot speak a word? You seem prepared to set yourself in the place reserved for gods. I speak only the truth, for I am vindicated and stand as and with Osiris. There is not one among your company who did not, for whatever personal reasons, join in this expedition of his own free will."

Stephen stepped forward, bowed to Neferankhotep and spoke, his tones pedantic, "Great king, you say that none can escape judgment. However, on what terms is this judgment to be made? None of us were educated in the religion and mores of ancient Egypt. Judging us on those terms would be entirely unfair."

"That's right," Jenny added. "We're not even all of the same faith. I was raised Catholic like my papa. I think the English are all Anglican, which is the same, but different. Eddie's a convert to Islam, and Rashid . . ."

The Egyptian youth gestured toward Eddie, claiming him as a coreligionist.

"So you see," Jenny finished triumphantly. "We're not even the same as each other."

"Perhaps the laws of ancient Egypt would not be as unfair or unfamiliar as you think," Neferankhotep said. "Consider the Ten Commandments as written in the Bible, a book I believe all of you—for all your other religious differences—consider revelatory of the will of your deity. Compare those commandments to the most basic elements of our own catechism—what your scholars have termed the Negative Confessions."

"The Negative Confessions?" Stephen said. "I believe I am familiar with the text to which you refer. That's the list that begins with 'I have not . . .' followed by specific crimes or faults the deceased swears he has not committed. There are some similarities—though many differences as well."

"Consider first the similarities," Neferankhotep said patiently. "Both contain provisions against killing, stealing, lying, and sexual contact that violates the bonds of marriage. Your commandments show greater concern for refining the rights of property, while ours demonstrate more concern for the personal harmony of the individual soul in relation to society."

"But you admit," Neville said rather desperately, "that there are differences."

"There are," Neferankhotep agreed. "However, when one moves beyond these simple lists to the more detailed rulings contained in other texts in your Bible, even those differences begin to vanish. The one place we are in greatest disagreement is that none of your religions accept the existence of gods other than your strange One in All, All in One."

Dry laughs, quickly muffled, came from the associated gods.

"However," Neferankhotep continued, frowning sternly at his fellow deities, "we are willing to grant that your actions in coming hence are in keeping with fidelity to your monotheist creed, for surely you would not have acted as you did if you truly believed that divine vengeance would be the end result."

"So we're off the hook?" Eddie asked, his words hopeful, but doubt in every line of his face.

"Not in the least," Neferankhotep said. "There remains the question of those commandments you did violate: lying, killing, stealing . . ."

Eddie stepped closer to Neferankhotep, and Neville saw rising in his friend the fire of the convert who followed his religion not through habit nor even through expedience. Eddie might have begun his conversion to Islam out of love for Miriam, but clearly he had worked his way toward devotion to Islam through long intellectual exercise.

Neville felt a momentary flutter of pity for the mullahs who had been forced to deal with the stolid reason of this English farmer's son, yet they must have felt their labors worthwhile in the end. Eddie was a Mohammedan of whom any teacher could be proud.

"Even those commandments that may have been violated," Eddie said to Neferankhotep "are open to interpretation. Consider the case of a man who steals to feed his child. He has without a doubt committed theft. However, if he does not steal and the child dies, then is he guilty of murder through his inaction? Some scholars say that the commandment is against murder, rather than mere killing, but where is the line drawn? Is the soul of a commander who sends soldiers into the field or that of a king who hires an assassin free from complicity? Equally, is the one who kills or steals because so commanded free from guilt because he was only following orders?"

"I cannot argue that there are not subtleties," Neferankhotep replied, his tone without rancor. "Yet equally, you cannot argue that here there is a question of a child needing food, or of a king commanding either army or assassin—unless you are stating such as a means of being excused for your own actions."

"No!" Eddie retorted hotly. "Not in the least. I am merely trying to show that reviewing a list of commandments and deciding which have and have not been violated is not always the best course toward justice."

"Yet," Neferankhotep said, "you must admit it is an equable approach."

"I must do no such thing," Eddie replied.

He was obviously about to launch into another instructive example when a new voice entered the debate. It was a sweet, feminine voice, that for all its sweetness was not without strength and decisiveness.

"Great Osiris living," said the goddess Maat, "you were known both in life and after death as a man who reigned in keeping with maat. These before you appeal to you to continue to rule thusly. Why else would they argue, if they did not believe you were one who would listen? To the end of serving both your reputation and their desire, I beg leave to put a proposal before you."

"Great goddess before whom even gods are judged," Neferankhotep replied, bowing his head, "I listen."

"Let each individual here be judged," Maat said, "only for those deeds that directly relate to their coming before you."

"Interesting," Neferankhotep said. "Why not? I have no desire to be unreasonable."

"Moreover," Maat continued, "judge them by the conventions we share—those you have already explained with such eloquence and grace. However, let all of those judged be given an opportunity to explain themselves, so that no injustice is done. As Edward Bryce has stated, neither truth nor justice are understood in the same fashion, even through the eyes of those who share a code."

"I will agree to these amendments to our usual procedure," Neferankhotep said. "However, each and every member of this company must submit themselves to judgment alone and without assistance. They must accept the penalty if they fail to be found vindicated and in balance with maat."

"This seems reasonable," Maat agreed.

"And what is the penalty?" Neville asked.

The pharaoh indicated the monster Ammit.

"Being thrown to Ammit is traditional."

The monster snapped her jaws in agreement.

"Right," Neville said.

"And our reward when we are judged vindicated?" Jenny asked defiantly, tossing back her hair and thrusting out her chin. "I seem to recall there were rewards for passing judgment. Seems only right we have something good to look forward to for putting up with all this."

"Rewards," Neferankhotep said, "will be discussed if and when you are so judged."

The pharaoh smiled upon them with benign tranquility before waving his crook. A mist descended over them all, wrapping them in stifling folds. Though Neville struggled to reach any of those who he had put under his protection, his limbs would not move, bound by the strength of his own guilt and fear.

When the mist raised, Neville's first thought was that the colors were more brilliant than anything he had ever seen—than anything he had ever even imagined. Compared to the hues with which the assembled gods and goddesses were adorned, the luster of a peacock's tail was as flat as ash, the glory of sunlight a snuffed candlewick, and all the jewels that had ever adorned the wrist or throat of woman were mere unpolished pebbles.

Neville stepped from the mist into this glory, and his words strangled in his throat. Then an odd certainty came to him. If beings who possessed such beauty found him worthy of judging, then he must possess some worth.

"Am I then the first?" he asked.

"Does that matter?" Neferankhotep replied.

"It does to me," Neville said. "If the others have not yet been judged, then I can again appeal to you on their behalf."

"Consider that appeal made," Neferankhotep said, "and leave it behind you. Concern yourself not with the fate of others, but with your own standing. As you yourself must know—for you have repeatedly attempted to take the guilt upon yourself—you are called to defend yourself most especially on the matter of theft. How do you plead?"

"Not guilty," Neville replied firmly. "I have stolen from no one."

"But you cannot say you did not intend theft," Neferankhotep persisted.

Neville squared his shoulders, trying hard not to look where the scales waited to one side, nor at Ammit poised with the patient ferocity of a hunting dog who knows she will be permitted her share of the kill. He felt himself the focus of many pairs of eyes, but addressed himself only to Neferankhotep, and to Maat who stood behind the pharaoh's throne. The good king maintained his aura of kind patience, but the goddess emanated something so overwhelmingly strange that Neville could hardly grasp it. Hers was truth inscrutable and unwavering, yet without any of the malice a human—or a human system of judging truth—might bring to the task.

"I did not intend theft," Neville replied. "For theft to be intended there must be an owner from whom the thief steals. What I intended was no more than a gathering up of something lost—a returning to human memory of something that had been forgotten."

He thought this argument was a good one, for the ancient Egyptians had feared being forgotten more than they had feared death.

Neferankhotep did not appear swayed, for he immediately asked another question.

"Do you then own the land within which my tomb rests? I think not. I think that what you would have done would have been theft, if not from me, then from those who administer treasures from the past for the people of the present."

Neville shook his head, denying the charge.

"I have taken nothing, therefore I cannot be judged as guilty of theft from you or from Egypt."

Neferankhotep's elegant mouth moved in a smile that, while not dismissing the matter, did agree to move to another point.

"Can you say that you have not lied in pursuit of these goals?"

Neville frowned. He honestly could not remember having lied, yet there was something in Neferankhotep's manner that made him believe the pharaoh thought differently.

"What about the lies you told Lady Cheshire?" Neferankhotep prompted. "Certainly you cannot deny you deceived her regarding your intentions."

"I did," Neville agreed. "However, I did so because of the dangers I had met with in the course of my previous attempts."

"You sought to keep her safe from these?" Neferankhotep asked mockingly.

"Not in the least," Neville said. "However, not knowing who had been responsible for the previous attacks, and thinking that the guilty party could well have been a rival within the archeological profession, I did not dare tell Lady Cheshire anything lest the information reach the wrong ears."

"So you did not trust her," Neferankhotep said.

"And is there any commandment that I should?" Neville replied with more bitterness than he had intended.

"No," Neferankhotep replied sadly. "Trust is something earned, never commanded."

Neville saw the sorrow of centuries-past betrayal there, and felt unwilling sympathy for the pharaoh who had striven to give justice to his people, only to be rewarded with theft and violation after his death.

"Try to understand," Neville pleaded. "As I said earlier, this game is only amusing if you're not one of the pieces. I don't doubt you can find instances in the past ten years I've been hunting for this tomb when I've violated the Ten Commandments. For example, I'm not sure how any living soul is supposed to manage not to covet, even if one fights the impulse to act on that desire. If I'm damned, then let me hop up on the scales and get the formalities over."

Neferankhotep shook his head.

"There is nothing in our laws against coveting, as long as one does not act—and you are right, there is no one alive who has not sinned against maat. It is the reason that drove those actions that makes them just or unjust—and I would be verging on violation of maat myself if my questions pressed you to feel fear or anger. Answer but one more question for me."

"What?" Neville knew he sounded belligerent, but as the alternative was trembling as no subject of the queen should do before a foreign king, he resigned himself to rudeness.

"Why have you gone to so much trouble to find this place, Sir Neville Hawthorne, even when you were repeatedly warned against doing so?"

Neville spread his hands.

"Two reasons. One is simple. I hated not succeeding all those years ago when old Alphonse and I first tried to find proof of the truth of the legend. The second is harder to explain, especially since I don't know if your people had anything like archeology."

Neferankhotep shrugged. "Not as a systematic science perhaps, but the monuments of our fathers and father's fathers surrounded us. We were drawn to the past, and sought to connect ourselves to its glories."

"Our people feel that too," Neville said, "but it's more complicated than that. In the time and place where we live, there is so much being discovered daily that constancy is hard to hold onto. Natural science tells us that some rocks are young when judged on the scale of creation, and that living things were not created by a beneficent God, but by the force of a Nature—as Tennyson put it so well, 'red in tooth and claw.' Your people thought themselves living beneath a goddess spangled with stars, that the sun was a god in a boat, the rising and falling of the waters of the Nile a constancy that proved the basic goodness of all things."

"And archeology?" Neferankhotep asked. "How does this alter any of what your natural science has discovered?"

"It doesn't," Neville said, "and for some people, it probably ruins comfortable illusions—maybe for people like Mrs. Syms, who want magic, but not to think about what that magic means."

"Leave Sarah Syms to her own judgment," the pharaoh said. "What is it you seek?"

"The truth behind a legend," Neville said. "The thought that somewhere, somehow there might have been a good king, that heroes might have fought on the plains of Troy, that the past is not all fairy stories and monsters. Alphonse Liebermann looked for evidence of Moses the Lawgiver. He found you. I guess I just kept looking—for you, for Moses, for some evidence that all the great grand things we've been told happened in the past can't be reduced to fossils and mental aberration."

"And if you succeeded?" Neferankhotep asked. "What would you have done?"

"I have succeeded," Neville said. "For I am talking to you, and despite the differences that time and culture have set between us, I have seen and heard enough to know that the legend was true. On that faith in your adherence to maat—to the real truth and justice that is more potent than any code of laws—I rest my case."

Condemned

JENNY TRIED to feel brave when the mist released her, admitting her into the glowing polychrome company of the gods. She was standing about halfway between Neferankhotep's throne and the gleaming set of scales. Thoth stood near the pharaoh, lowering his ledger as if he had just finished showing Neferankhotep and Maat some notes. Anubis stood over by Ammit, thoughtfully scratching the monster between its round, not-quite-hippopotamus, not-quite-lion ears.

Jenny tried to guess if the monster had been recently fed, but she couldn't tell. The grotesque features of the Forty-Two Judges gave nothing away but a certain leering pleasure in her uneasiness. She was glad for Mozelle threading herself around her ankles, and longed to pick the kitten up and hold her, but she figured that this would be less than dignified, maybe even less than respectful—and with so much on the line, not even Jenny Benet was going to flout custom lightly.

Crossing to an intricately carved table with its top painted so it could be used as a senet board, Jenny unbuckled her gun belt and laid it carefully along the edge. Then she took the derringer out of her boot top and set it there as well. She thought about doing the same with her knives, but decided against it. She'd made her point.

"Not that I think they'd do anything to you," she said, her laugh sounding a bit more nervous than she liked, "but where I come from it's just good manners."

"These are weapons?" Neferankhotep asked, and though no one said anything formal, Jenny knew her trial had begun.

"That's right," she said. "Your people had bows and arrows, I seem to recall. Well, these are something like that. They fling a projectile, and can kill from a distance."

"You know how to use these?"

"I do," she said.

"You are very skilled?"

"I am," Jenny said carefully, "a pretty fair hand."

She knew what was coming next, had known it would be coming since Neferankhotep had so carefully explained the parts of the Negative Confessions that matched up with the Ten Commandments. The pharaoh surprised her.

"The Negative Confessions contain injunctions against both lying and slandering. Your Eighth Commandment is usually understood to be against bearing false witness. Tell me, as this was taught to you: was this understood to be restricted to those times when you might be called upon to bear witness—in a court of law, or a circumstance when you would be asked to speak to another's character or actions?"

Jenny considered.

"No, sir. I think as it was taught me it pretty much meant you shouldn't tell a lie, not anywhere or anytime."

"Yet you would have lied to your uncle who has been good to you—who gave you a home when your parents were lost to you. How do you justify this action?"

Jenny wanted to pretend she didn't remember, see if what this Neferankhotep was referring to was the same as what she was thinking, but she figured it wouldn't make much sense acting as if these Egyptian deities didn't have resources she couldn't even imagine. Why, who knew what Thoth had been showing them on that ledger sheet of his? He might have a whole line of photographs set up to record every action, with captions to show what a person said or thought. She'd had a Sunday school teacher who'd said that the Last Judgment before God would be like that, and for months Jenny was shy about using the outhouse or blowing her nose, imagining God watching all that. She'd managed to banish the thought after a while, though it cropped up every so often and made her blush.

She was blushing now, and hoped that they didn't think it was because of the question.

"Well," she said, speaking quickly so they wouldn't think she was hiding anything, "if what you're talking about is how I was going to sneak along on this trip rather than stay back in Cairo, I guess you're sorta right about my willingness to lie. I won't even hedge that I didn't end up having to lie after all, that Uncle Neville took me along. I would have lied if that's what it would have taken."

"And why would you have done this?"

Jenny thought back to her conversations with Papa Antonio.

"My uncle has a friend, Antonio Donati, who told me he was worried about what Uncle Neville was getting into with this trip. He wanted me to go along, keep Uncle careful, since Uncle wouldn't be able to forget I was there and, frail female critter I am, would need looking after."

No one laughed, and Jenny felt her blush deepen.

"So you were guided into willingness to lie by this friend of your uncle's?"

Jenny shook her head.

"I can't blame anyone else. Papa Antonio made it easier to justify what I wanted to do anyhow. I didn't want to sit back in Cairo watching Mary Travers flirt with the soldiers and all that. I wanted to come along and be part of the adventure. I figured I could be useful, too. They didn't have a doctor with them, and I've some skill. Even if we didn't run into violence, there's plenty of bugs and snakes out there. Stephen even nearly got killed by the sun."

"So you would have lied in order to make possible a greater good—the benefits your added skills would grant."

"Sounds good," Jenny agreed. She was feeling reckless, dreading the question that just had to come. "But I'm not going to lie. I'd have done my best to go along even if Uncle Neville had himself a passel of doctors and nurses, too."

"For the adventure."

"That's right."

"And that's all this journey meant to you?"

"Well," Jenny said, slightly puzzled, "isn't that enough? I don't pretend to be a scholar like Stephen, and I don't have Uncle Neville's long-time interest in archeology. Mind, I think I might be catching the bug, but what really had me raring to go was remembering the letters Uncle Neville would send my mama, letters talking about his trips to foreign places and the things he did there. I'd dreamed all my life about being with him on one of those trips—like you dream about being a character in a fairy tale. I wasn't going to give up that dream for a lack of courage."

"Lack of courage?" Neferankhotep pursed his lips thoughtfully. "Is that how you would have seen honesty, and abiding by the ruling set down by one who—in law at least—stood as your father? As a lack of courage?"

Jenny paused long enough to think carefully about this.

"Yes, sir. I think that's about right."

"Yet you had doubts about the justice of this venture."

Jenny nodded. "I did. It probably speaks badly for me, but I think I believed the reality of the stories about you more than the rest of them did. I wasn't sure that what Uncle Neville was after was quite right, but I couldn't stop him, and maybe he'd not find anything. I guess I figured—if I thought about it all that hard—that if we did find something, I could talk to him about how to handle the discovery then."

"And that it wasn't worth discussing before."

"Oh, we did that," Jenny said. "Those Sphinx letters made sure we talked about it at least a bit. Thing was, all I ended up was convinced that there was no talking him out of going until he'd at least given it a try."

She hesitated.

"Sir, do you know who wrote those Sphinx letters?"

"I do."

"And can you tell me?"

"Perhaps later," Neferankhotep said. "This is not the time."

Jenny couldn't bear the waiting any longer.

"Aren't you going to ask me about shooting at that man back at Papa Antonio's?"

Neferankhotep looked at her, his mild eyes stern.

"Does it trouble you because you fear I shall, or for the act itself?"

"The act doesn't bother me none—well, not much," Jenny said. "He was going to kill me, coming into my room that way. I had to do something."

Neferankhotep's expression turned grim.

"Did you know that he died as a result of his wounds?"

"He did?" Jenny felt herself grow pale.

"Later that night."

Jenny said nothing.

"Did you intend to kill him?" Neferankhotep asked.

"Yes. I was scared of what he'd do if I didn't."

"Even though your own commandment warns against killing, and he had not yet harmed you?"

"If I'd given him the chance he would have," Jenny said.

"And you have trained to kill," Neferankhotep pressed, as if certain he must close off every escape—or perhaps provide one.

"I have learned to shoot," Jenny said, "both for hunting and protection. Just because I believe killing another person is wrong doesn't mean everyone else is going to feel that way."

"Do you not believe that publicly displaying your willingness to do violence—as you do when you wear those remarkable weapons—invites violence in return?"

"No, sir, I don't," Jenny replied with intensity. "Many a time I've seen a quarrel in a shop or bar get settled without violence because the reminder of the possibility of violence is there out in the open. Folks know they can walk away from a shouting match, but it isn't so easy to walk away from a bullet."

"Yet you are a healer," Maat said, joining the discussion, her wings rising and falling as if the question made her nervous. "You do not find this a contradiction that violates your personal truth?"

"Ma'am, I'd be happier if no one ever shot another gun for as long as the human race walks this sorry Earth, but as long as they're going to do so, where there's a chance of trouble I'll wear my shooting irons and know how to use them."

"Would you ever use your knowledge of weapons not for defense, but to prevent another from doing harm?"

"I guess I've already done so," Jenny said, "when I stopped that man who came into my room from shooting me. I figure I'd shoot first and ask questions later to stop someone I thought was going to harm Uncle Neville or Stephen or Eddie, or whoever . . . It's hard to know exactly what you'll do until you're there."

Maat frowned, "This readiness to kill is dangerous in you—especially combined with a healer's skills. You claim to feel justified in your action, yet I sense the guilt within you. Guilt combined with the ability to provide justification for killing is very dangerous. How long would it take to cross the boundary between healing and killing—first, perhaps, for mercy but, later . . . ?"

Jenny heard her own death sentence in those words. She wanted to pretend she didn't understand, but she understood all too well. She'd helped her father patch up rough men, bad men, men who would doubtless go out once they were strong, and harm the weak. She'd wondered even then at the wisdom of helping such men, and had asked Papa why he did it, but he'd only said, "The Hippocratic Oath forbids doing harm, Genevieve," and she'd known that for him harm extended even to inaction.

Was she as good a woman as Pierre Benet had been a good man? She doubted it, and knew in her own doubt that she understood why Maat would condemn her, why she would fail in any appeal.

There were no more questions. Neferankhotep looked stern and slightly sad. Maat seemed pale and ill. The Forty-Two Judges muttered to each other, while Thoth took notes and Anubis stood ready. Only Ammit looked pleased, and Jenny could hardly blame her.

"Step onto the scales, Genevieve Benet," Neferankhotep said, "and be weighed against Maat."

Almost blindly, Jenny turned to obey. Either she'd gotten smaller or the scales had gotten larger, because she had no trouble fitting into the polished bronze pan. Maat fluttered across the room, settling into the other pan. Jenny rose slightly, but still the level of her side of the scales remained fair heavier than Maat. "Anubis," Neferankhotep said, "Genevieve Benet has been weighed against Maat and found wanting. Treat her according to our ancient protocols."

Anubis stepped forward, and Jenny pressed her lips together, determined at least not to scream. The jackal-headed god laid a cool, almost leathery hand on her shoulder, pulling Jenny to her feet. Ammit snapped her jaws eagerly, and the Forty-Two Judges crowded forward to better see the execution.

A single mew halted the purposeful progress. Anubis stopped, his hand still resting on Jenny's shoulder. Mozelle leapt up onto Neferankhotep's lap.

The pharaoh lifted the kitten in his wide green hands, and held her before his face. He appeared to be listening to whatever it was the kitten told him with tiny mews and lashings of her small, bristly tail. He listened, and then he set the kitten on the floor where she ran to Jenny and clawed her way into the young woman's lap.

"Oh, sir, will you watch her for me?" Jenny said, finally giving way to tears. "I may be wrong in how I think about things, but I don't want any harm to come to Mozelle."

Neferankhotep rose from his throne and his dark green lips frowned. He stood stiffly, and Jenny noticed that his feet were bound like those of a mummy.

"Maat," he said, turning to address the winged woman, "I have received a plea from this little cat that we spare her human. Mozelle says that the girl is not murderous by nature—only that the challenges Genevieve faces are such that there is no way one can live in the world she has known and not both desire the idea of peaceful coexistence and recognize the reality of violence. Can we act in accord with this appeal?"

Maat bent her lovely face into her hands, folding her wings around her as if making a physical curtain for her thoughts. Jenny held her breath, stroking

Mozelle, and taking comfort in the tremendous force of the tiny kitten's purr. If so little a thing could make so big a rumble . . . If a kitten could also be a lioness who could carry off the head of a sun-swallowing serpent . . . If all of these things were possible, then maybe . . .

Maat unfolded her wings, her features serene, and, just possibly, a touch amused. She addressed her words to the pharaoh.

"I recognize that justice is not unchanging," she said, "nor is truth the same to all peoples. However," and here she turned her gaze solemnly upon Jenny, "I cannot ignore that this girl is capable of creating great harm. We might spare her life, but do the world a great favor by keeping her here with us. Failing that, her death might save others."

Jenny bit back an urge to beg, to promise to be good. Live or die, she wanted to do it with dignity. But what was this mention of keeping her here? They hadn't said anything like this before. Had they?

Neferankhotep replied to Maat, "I acknowledge that you put yourself in the balance in all cases, oh Maat. You feel the lightness of right thinking and the weight of wrong action. Gods and men alike can only try to abide by truth and justice. You are these things. Being so, can you grant this girl her life and her freedom?"

Slowly, as if still not certain she was doing the absolutely correct thing, Maat nodded.

"I will do so, being guided by the wisdom of this small cat who, after all, is an aspect of Sekmet, who is a goddess of both peace and war, and of Bastet, who both battles demons and guards women in their time of greatest vulnerability. May she guide Genevieve to right action."

"Then," Jenny asked, poised on her knees in the scale, "I can go?"

Neferankhotep raised one arm, parting the air to make a doorway into a light and pleasant room.

"Go, and Mozelle with you. Remember always what you have learned here, even when you have forgotten all else."

Jenny bowed. Her knees were shaking too hard for her to even attempt a curtsey. It had been close, so close. She clutched a still purring Mozelle to her, and stepped through the doorway into a room that offered hints of the promise of paradise. There were pools of cool water, palm trees casting dappled shade, and furnishings worthy of a king. Set upon the tables were beaten brass trays piled high with delicacies.

A winsome young woman clad in little more than a jeweled belt was sitting on Stephen's lap, dabbing oil onto the fair-haired young man's sun-ravaged skin. Uncle Neville was seated in an elaborately carved and gilded chair. His trouser leg was pulled up to expose his injured ankle, and a long-jawed, long-nosed physician knelt before him, inspecting the swollen flesh and making tut-tutting sounds.

Had it not been for their rather awkward positions, both men would have leapt to their feet when Jenny arrived. Their first reaction was joy and relief, but that faded when they saw no answering happiness. She knew she looked as if she had barely staggered away intact from some horrible ordeal.

When a handsome, muscular young man—ideal counterpart in every way to Stephen's attendant—came to assist her to a place of honor, she waved him away. She was weary to her bones, and even knowing that Stephen and Uncle Neville were safe gave her only the faintest hint of pleasure.

"Jenny, come and enjoy the rewards of virtue," Stephen said happily. "What's wrong with you? You've passed the judgment of Maat. Come and let the good pharaoh's people treat you like a queen."

Jenny sank down onto a cushion beside the pool, and set Mozelle down. The kitten ignored her black mood, and immediately set about a violent assault on the trailing length of the physician's sash.

"I feel," Jenny said, "like I should be hauled off to some penal colony, not treated like a queen. I didn't pass Maat. I failed. My life was redeemed by the trust of a kitten."

Both Neville and Stephen looked inclined toward disbelief, but neither of them commented. No doubt both of them had seen too much to easily doubt anything. However, Jenny had to admit that Mozelle, now lying on her side and vigorously attacking the tip of her own tail, made an unlikely savior.

The physician turned from his inspection of Neville's ankle.

"Pardon, sweet lady," he said, "but if you are here, you have passed Maat, and are vindicated before the gods. If you have not succeeded solely through your own merits, then this is all the more reason to be grateful. Good Neferankhotep has commanded that you be entertained and soothed from the pain of your wounds. Do not, in your pride, defy him."

The man's eyes were kind, his face lined from many smiles. Even the girl who had been anointing Stephen paused in her labors, but her expression held concern, not the contempt Jenny dreaded.

"I guess I am a mite on the proud side," Jenny admitted, "and I guess that's one of the things I need to learn to put aside."

She rose and stretched. "I'm not too banged up, but I could use a wash."

Her attendant advanced again, clearly pleased. He pointed toward a small pool she hadn't noticed before, discreetly screened from the larger room by flowering papyrus. Jenny looked at the young man and felt a blush climbing straight up to her hairline.

"I don't figure I need someone to bathe me."

Neville and Stephen both shifted uncomfortably. For the first time since Jenny's entrance, Stephen seemed aware of the state of undress of his own attendant. He shrugged, then smiled sheepishly.

"Bath attendants do seem to be the custom of the country," he said at last. "I'm not sure we should violate it."

"What about my much-vaunted reputation?" Jenny sputtered. "I've been guarded and chaperoned since I got to Boston, and now you're telling me to go off with some man?"

"I won't say anything," Stephen promised. "Especially if you promise not to tell my mother about me."

Jenny looked over at Uncle Neville.

"My doctor tells me I need to soak this ankle," he said, "and I'm going to soak all the rest of me while I do it. Jenny, you're old enough that if you're not going to guard your modesty, public and private, there's not much I can do about it short of locking you up, and I'm not doing that. If that handsome shabti there makes you uncomfortable, then I'm sure one of the young ladies would assist."

He indicated a new arrival whose linen gown was, if possible, more revealing than the other girl's jeweled belt.

"Shabti?" Jenny asked.

"So the physician informs me," Neville said. "In paradise, only those who wish to labor need do so. For all other things, there are shabti."

Jenny rubbed her temples, then began to laugh. At first her laughter bore an edge of hysteria, but gradually it transformed into something healthy and healing.

"Why not accept what's given?" she said, and followed her shabti to the indicated pool. It was filled with perfumed waters, neither too hot nor too cold, and did wonderful things for her aching muscles—so did the probing fingers of the shabti.

In truth, Neville wasn't much worried about Jenny. Ever since he had left the judgment hall, he'd been shrouded in a feeling of perfect contentment, a contentment the ministrations of the shabti did nothing to interrupt.

Clean and gowned in something vaguely Egyptian, though far less revealing than what was worn by the shabti girls, Jenny rejoined them. The tensions had washed from her along with the grime, and she sat tickling a length of reed along the edge of the pool for the delighted Mozelle to chase.

A gust of wind carried Rashid to them, and he smiled warm greeting before he was taken off to be ministered to by his own lovely attendants—one of whom carried the happily chattering Mischief. The Arab youth could not, of course, comment about his ordeal, but the peace on his face seemed to argue that everything had gone well.

As more time passed, Neville's own thoughts destroyed his tranquility. Where were the others? He had thought that Neferankhotep was dealing with the rival groups separately. However, if that were so, Eddie would have joined them by now. Rashid's arrival seemed to argue that Neville's assumption was incorrect. Or was it? Jenny had nearly failed. What about Eddie?

"I wonder," he said to the general air, trying to keep a note of concern out of his voice, "what criteria Neferankhotep uses to select the order of his interviews?"

"You mean alphabetical order, or by age or, perhaps, like a seating arrangement at a dinner party," Stephen said, getting into the idea, "alternating male and female. Or perhaps by social rank or level of education . . ."

"Or maybe," Jenny interrupted, much more serious, "by how hard it's going to be to pass. I understand Stephen was here first, then you, Uncle, then me, then Rashid."

"None of the orders I've suggested work then," Stephen said. "I'm older than you, Jenny, but both of your names come before mine in the alphabet. Socially, all of you but Rashid outrank me . . ."

"Rashid might be an Arab prince for all we know," Jenny said.

"Right. In any case," Stephen said, "if they were working from the bottom of the social ladder then I would certainly be toward the bottom. Where would Eddie fit in? In England he's not ranked very high, but by religious standing in an Islamic country he outranks all of us nonbelievers."

"It's Eddie I'm worried about," Neville said bluntly. "Maat seems fairly absolute. How would those beings who interviewed us view a religious convert?"

"Eddie's wonderful!" Jenny said passionately. "He's stood by you even when you've been difficult, warning you even when he knew you wouldn't listen."

Neville nodded. "However, what if his conversion to Islam was less sincere than he believed? What if there is a gap between his innermost beliefs and what he is living? Maat might not be very understanding then."

A gust of wind disturbed the tranquil surfaces of the bathing pools and Mrs. Syms emerged apparently from nowhere. She walked with her head high, her lips slightly parted. Her eyes were dreamy and unfocused, and she seemed completely unaware of the rather decadent pleasures surrounding her.

Two burly male shabti came to assist her, and she addressed them as Tom and Ralph, asking after their families, and the success of a church choir outing. The physician rose from where he had been listening to their conversation, and directed the shabti to escort Mrs. Syms to a newly created oasis. He followed, and as from a great distance they could hear Mrs. Syms addressing him as "Doctor" and thanking him for making a house call at such an inconvenient hour.

"She's still crazy," Jenny said with gentle pity. "I wonder why? Couldn't the gods—or whatever they are—couldn't they fix the damage?"

"One would think so," Stephen said. "Thoth is a god of both knowledge and healing. Curing delusions should be easy for him."

"Maybe," Neville said slowly, feeling his way to the answer, "curing her would bring her into violation of Maat. As deeply as it pains me to admit it, Lady Cheshire did intend to sabotage our expedition, and Mrs. Syms was her ally in a way Rashid was not. Perhaps as long as she remains insane, and thus ignorant of what she agreed to do, she is innocent."

"But if she remembers," Stephen said, "she is not."

The pity in Jenny's eyes was for Neville now, and he found it hard to bear.

"So you have little hope for Lady Cheshire," she said.

"None."

"And yet Audrey did show good qualities at the end," Jenny admitted. "She was courageous and creative in her magical innovations, nor did she try to pretend she had been pushed into her course by another—say by Captain Brentworth. He would not have been able to gainsay her. I don't like what she did, but I was beginning to respect her . . . at least a little."

"I cannot pretend that my initial admiration for the lady," Neville said, "did not have more to do with the color of her eyes and the luster of her hair, but I, too, began to see her other qualities. Unhappily, I also began to see that some of them were less than what I desired."

"But you wouldn't wish her damned," Stephen said. "None of us would. It simply isn't Christian."

Neville's response was cut short when a fresh gust of wind announced the arrival of Eddie Bryce. The other man looked thoughtful, but not particularly somber. He broke into a wide grin at the noisy welcome that greeted him.

The physician claimed Eddie first, replying to their questions with reassurances that Mrs. Syms was resting well, but should not be disturbed. Then Eddie accepted the ministrations of several shabti handmaidens, noting that it might be best if Miriam didn't hear of this part of their adventure.

"Six of us through then," he said, "and perhaps that is all. I suspect we will not see Lady Cheshire again."

"You speak as from a certainty," Neville said.

"I understood that I had been kept for last," Eddie explained, "since Nefer-ankhotep knew I was a religious convert, and wanted to do his best to understand the faiths that have come into the world since his leaving it. I must admit that proving the depth and sincerity of my conversion was a bit of a sticky wicket, but once that was done, there were lots of questions, especially from Neferankhotep and Thoth."

"We were worried," Jenny admitted.

"So was I," Eddie said. "It was not an easy examination—in fact, I'm lucky that the mullahs gave me the benefit of a doubt. I think they liked that I was will-ing to take Miriam's faith rather than forcing her to adopt mine. Thoth and Ne-ferankhotep had no such bias."

"So we have lost Lady Cheshire," Jenny said softly. "Audrey did us a great wrong, but I'm wondering—shouldn't we try to plead mercy for her?"

"She deserves what she got," Eddie Bryce said firmly. "She intended robbery and perhaps even murder. If Rashid could speak, I'm certain he could confirm what I say."

Rashid, who had rejoined them while the physician was looking at Eddie's arm, looked deliberately blank.

"I don't think he'll testify against those who were, to at least some extent, kind to him," Neville guessed. "Jenny, I was thinking much the same thing. Stephen said it isn't Christian to wish such a fate on someone, and he's right—for-give me, Eddie."

"I was raised Christian," Eddie said, "and maybe I can see your point. Still, Audrey Cheshire's not going to become an angel just for your wishing it."

"Even so," Neville persisted, "even if I knew the lady would never speak to me again, I would like to try."

"What if it's too late?" Jenny said dubiously. "Isn't the sinner supposed to be instantly thrown to Ammit?"

"We can only ask," Neville said, "and hope."

"And pray," Stephen added. Then a wicked grin asserted itself, almost despite himself, "Though we'd better be careful to whom we pray if we don't want to be tried all over again for violating monotheism!"

A gong struck, and the physician gave them a tight, thin-lipped smile.

"I believe your request will be granted," he said. "Neferankhotep will hear your plea. Take care what you say, for even my skills cannot heal one who has met the wrath of angry gods."

The air parted as though a curtain on a stage. Before them was the Hall of Judgment. Neferankhotep again sat on his throne, his advisors arrayed alongside him. The Forty-Two Judges muttered from their long benches, and other fantastic figures had joined the throng. Neville recognized Isis, Horus, Geb, Ptah, Shu, and, perhaps hopefully, Ra.

There were others whose names he did not easily recall, beings with the heads of scorpions, snakes, hippopotami, rams, and baboons. There were those who resembled humans but for horns or animal ears or oddly tinted skins.

Yet despite this outlandish and rather horrid assembly, Neville found he had eyes for only one figure. Audrey Cheshire, still in her soiled and sandy riding costume, her black hair tumbled loose, tangled, and filthy, knelt in the brass pan of the scales. These touched the stone floor, mutely testifying that she had been far heavier than the bird-winged goddess who sat so lightly on the other side.

Ammit waited with confused patience for her rightful meat, but Anubis laid his hand on the monster's head as if commanding she wait just a little longer.

"We have heard your appeal," Neferankhotep said, his tones stern and for once without the faintest trace of kindness. "We have been generous with all of you, have adapted our laws, and have let go free those whose goodness we doubted. Yet still you ask for more. State clearly what you wish, and what you are willing to do to gain it."

Neville threw back his shoulders and stepped forward, noting as he did so that there was not the faintest hint of pain from his ankle.

"Good pharaoh," he said, "we do not question the justice of your ruling regarding the woman Audrey Cheshire, yet we beg to be given opportunity to redeem her. One of the basic tenets of Christianity is forgiveness of those who have done wrong."

"So forgive her if you would," Neferankhotep replied. "How does this affect what I will decree?"

"We ask you to let us have her," Neville said, "to bring her back into the world, for if we were simply to forgive her while permitting what fate awaits, our forgiveness would be hollow."

Stephen spoke into the uncomprehending silence that followed this noble statement.

"From a purely legal point of view," he said, "there is reason to let her go as well. You agreed to judge her based on our codes. Well, by the legal codes of our land, execution is considered a very severe punishment for attempted theft."

He laid a slight stress on the word "attempted," obviously as a reminder that, like the rest of them, Lady Cheshire had not had much success in her ventures. Neville loved him for this generosity of spirit.

Neferankhotep's expression remained impassive.

"I had intended to speak with you about what is due to you since you have passed judgment, for as Miss Benet reminded me, the soul who is vindicated is granted many rewards. Would you forgo these in return for the opportunity to re-deem one who has done you such great wrongs? Before you speak, let me remind you that the hospitality I have offered you thus far is to the delights of the afterlife what a grain of sand is to a sprawling desert."

Neville shrugged. "I could not enjoy even paradise if I thought I had acted against what was right."

Eddie gave a gusty sigh. "Neither could I. Besides, what I really want is to go home to my wife and family. Are you telling us that is impossible?"

Neferankhotep shook his head. "It can be made possible. If you insist on at-tempting to redeem this woman, it may be impossible."

"Still," Eddie said, "Neville's right. I'd have to live knowing what I let happen. Count me in."

The others agreed, and Neferankhotep shook his head.

"So Thoth told me it would be. Very well. We have a task for you. If you suc-ceed, you will win Audrey Cheshire's life, and also keep the rewards we would have given you. If you fail, you will find yourself longing for the jaws of Ammit, for that devouring pain will be nothing to the torments devised for you."

Tomb Robbers

"I T SEEMS only right," Neferankhotep said, "that in order to redeem Audrey Cheshire you must reverse the crime of which you yourselves were so nearly guilty. You yourselves might have desecrated my tomb had this not been a place uniquely blessed by the gods. Your charge will be to prevent the desecration of another tomb, one belonging to a pharaoh towards whom we have special reason to feel gratitude."

There was a pause, and Jenny thought that Neferankhotep would explain just what this anonymous king had done to earn the gratitude of deities, instead the good king indicated Ra.

"You have done Ra a kindness, and so he has chosen to honor you with his counsel."

As the hawk-headed sun god stepped forward from among the ranked gods a wash of brilliance came from him, curtaining the humans from the other gods—or perhaps removing them to some other place entirely. The privacy, or at least the illusion thereof, was comforting after having been under the inspection of so many sets of eyes. Jenny felt herself relaxing as she had not even under the sybaritic ministrations of the shabti.

"In your own day," Ra said, "the place to which I shall conduct you is called The Valley of the Kings. The pharaoh whose tomb you must secure from violation is among these."

"We were in the Valley," Stephen said. "I wonder if we saw this tomb?"

"No," Ra said. "Even in your own day it remains undiscovered, its very existence held in doubt."

"We must have done a good job then," Stephen said cheerfully.

"I fear this does not follow," Ra said. "It may not have been discovered because it has been looted beyond recognition as a tomb. It may have been stripped and reused for the interment of another. All these are possible within the great fan of time."

Stephen's cheerfulness faded, and he nodded.

"I think I understand," he said. "Forgive my interruption."

Ra inclined his head in graceful acknowledgment of the apology.

"In order to succeed in your task, you must do two things. One, you must secure the tomb against the theft that will otherwise occur on the night of your coming. Two, you must somehow assure that no other theft will take place. It will not be easy. Once already the tomb has been violated, but at that time the priests were more vigilant, and the thieves were stopped before they could violate the king's body. They did succeed sufficiently that tales of the treasure that remains within the tomb have been told down the years within their families."

"So," Neville said, "we need to manage something that will counteract years of storytelling—tales that doubtless have grown in the telling."

"They did not need to grow very far," Ra said, and there was a hint of dry laughter in his tones. "The wealth with which this pharaoh was entombed was considerable. As Neferankhotep said, the gods had great reason to honor this king for actions done under his reign."

Jenny shivered. "Then is this another tomb created by the gods themselves, like Neferankhotep's?"

"No. We have only bestowed that honor once," Ra said. "The offerings made here were mortal ones, but made with an awareness that this king would be well-beloved by the gods, and that his burial should not be skimped, lest the same gods ask why when those responsible for making the offerings came to judgment."

Eddie asked, "This tomb has been robbed once before? Certainly arrangements were made to protect it afterwards."

"Such arrangements were made," Ra agreed. "However, time has passed. Corrupt priests and guards have been bribed. More honest men are serving elsewhere this night. The thieves will have time to remove sufficient impediments for them to be able to steal at least the more portable items. They may even have time to break larger items so that they can be stripped of gilding and other ornamentation."

Stephen looked very worried.

"That pretty much means the pharaoh's mummy will be desecrated," he said. "If the thieves want portable items, they're not going to overlook the charms and amulets in the wrappings."

"That is how it will be," Ra agreed, "if you cannot stop the thieves."

"Can you tell us something about the layout?" Neville asked. "That might help us position ourselves most effectively."

Ra crouched, a very natural and human motion, and sketched a plan in the sand at their feet.

Where did the sand come from? Jenny thought. *I'm sure we were standing on stone.*

"The tomb has but one entrance," Ra said, "by a long stair that leads into a sloping corridor. There are two doors, one at the base of the stair, one at the entry to the tomb. After the first theft, the length of the corridor was filled with rubble, much of it quite massive. Depending on when you choose to arrive, the thieves will remove enough of this rubble to enable them to penetrate the interior of the tomb. However, they will not clear the entire corridor."

Neville held up one hand.

"Wait, Mr. Ra. Are you saying that we can arrive at any time we wish?"

Ra tilted his head in a very birdlike fashion.

"Of course. Either I will choose the time, or you will. The same goes for the place you will appear. The one thing I will not do is bring you in at a variety of times. That would be too much like taking part in a task that must be yours alone."

Neville nodded. "I can see that, rather like delivering reinforcements or creating a new queen on the chess board when all you have is a pawn."

Her uncle's reference to a queen made Jenny think of something. "Ra, will we be able to reclaim our weapons? I left my revolvers and derringer in the Hall of Judgment. I'm pretty sure the rest of the firearms are with our gear."

"You will not want those," Ra said firmly. "The damage they would cause would be worse than what the tomb robbers would create."

"Oh," Jenny said. She didn't quite agree, but she knew enough to know when argument would not be welcome.

"Knives are all right?" Eddie asked, partially unsheathing his own long blade as if offering to put it aside at Ra's command.

"Perfectly," Ra assured him. "We do not care if the thieves are damaged, but we would prefer not aiding in damage to the tomb."

"But the mummy's the important thing, isn't it?" Stephen asked.

"It is the most important thing," Ra agreed.

Neville held up a hand for silence, a gesture that almost—but not quite—included the hawk-headed god.

"We've learned some valuable things," he said. "However, before we start refining our plan, let's learn what we can about the layout."

Ra placed his fingertip in the sand again.

"Beyond the second door is a room longer than it is wide." He drew a narrow rectangle, marked it in two places. "There are two doors from this room, here and here. The room itself is filled with burial goods, so that only a narrow strip down the center remains."

Stephen leaned forward. "And the marks you made—which one leads to the burial chamber?"

Neville frowned at the young linguist, but Ra did not seem offended. Indeed, he went on as if he had not heard Stephen's question.

"This mark, nearly across from the door in which you would enter the chamber, indicates the door into a small room meant to hold offerings to sustain the king in the afterlife. It is cluttered with a wide variety of goods. Indeed, there is hardly enough room for one person to stand. This mark on this narrow wall farther from the door indicates the entrance to the burial chamber."

Ra drew a fatter rectangle, almost a square, and indicated another door at one end.

"The burial chamber is lined with several shrines. The coffin is within these. The door leads to a room containing even more treasure, including the canopic shrine. It would be very good if this could be saved from violation as well."

Jenny sighed. "I guess it would be best if we saved everything, but how much can we mess up and still be said to succeed?"

Ra looked at her, his avian gaze unforgiving.

"The pharaoh must remain undisturbed in his tomb, secured from further violation. Those are the most important things, but the burial goods are not mere treasures set as a vain boast of earthly power. They are meant to sustain the deceased in the afterlife, and as such are important to his well-being."

"I'm sorry," Jenny said. "I guess I just got overwhelmed for a moment. I'm not quitting."

"That is very wise," Ra said, and something in his tone made Jenny's heart skip a beat.

Uncle Neville looked up from studying the diagram.

"Mr. Ra, how large are these rooms?"

"Their dimensions matter little," Ra said, "for they are crowded with furnishings. I would say that one, maybe two of you could stand within and still have space to move."

"The robbers must be small men," Neville said.

"Some are," Ra agreed, "but not all. However, people of your own day are generally larger than people of that time. Even Miss Benet would be considered quite a tall woman when compared to the average."

"One, maybe two inside," Neville said, glancing around their company. "Stephen's out then. He's the largest of us by far. Rashid and Eddie . . ."

Jenny cut in.

"Uncle, I'm smaller than Eddie or Rashid, and I know how to handle myself in close quarters. Papa made sure of that."

Neville looked worried, but he nodded.

"You're right. I would not be doing any of us a favor if I crowded us in so that the thieves had all the advantages. Besides, if those of us on the outside do our part, there won't be much to do inside."

That seemed to cheer him considerably, and Jenny permitted herself a small feeling of relief. She was learning a lot about the consequences of volunteering for dangerous positions, but what she was learning wasn't just that danger scared her stiff. It was learning that the one thing that scared her more was standing by and leaving others to take the risks.

"Timing is going to be everything in this," Neville said, thinking aloud. "Eddie, any thoughts?"

Eddie frowned. "Much as I hate the idea, we'd better let them have penetrated to the inside. Part of making sure the priests and guards take better care in the future is making sure they realize how close they came to losing everything. Another thought—let's not kill anyone if we don't have to. Let the thieves rat on their accomplices. That'll do more good than a heap of dead bodies."

"I like that," Neville agreed. Then he looked worried. "How can we make them understand? I doubt they speak any language we do."

Stephen said hesitantly, "There is some reason to believe that modern Coptic is a survival of the ancient Egyptian tongue. I have studied it, but I don't suppose . . ."

"No," Ra said, shaking his head. "The language you know is not enough alike."

"I didn't think so," Stephen said, obviously disappointed, "any more than we'd understand Old English if we heard it spoken—or even Middle English. When you think about Shakespeare's plays, even Elizabethan sounds fairly odd, and that's only a couple of hundred years diverged from our own language."

"Exactly," Ra said. "However, if you feel that speaking to these people will make it possible for you to better do your task, I believe I can grant you that. It will not be a lasting gift, but only a part of acclimating you to that other time. The gods have agreed I may do that."

But Jenny thought he looked rather uncomfortable nonetheless, and was warmed to think of this strange being bending the rules for them.

They seem to do a lot of that, she thought. *I guess it's up to us not to disappoint them.*

"However," Ra said in the tones of a teacher proving how strict he is after a moment of indulgence, "I shall keep the kitten and the monkey with me. They are not to be included in this task."

Jenny didn't know whether to be relieved or disappointed. Mischief was certain to be nothing but trouble, but Mozelle had proven herself oddly useful. If she showed herself as a lion again that would give the thieves pause. That gave Jenny an idea.

"Ra, will this acclimatizing us to another time mean we'll look like the Egyptians?"

Ra blinked. "I suppose you could."

"But what if we didn't want to look like them?" Jenny quickly clarified her thoughts. "I think one look at us would be pretty terrifying. The Egyptian empire might have had trade with neighboring nations, but I doubt the average thief would have done so—especially as far up river as Luxor."

Uncle Neville laughed.

"I like that, Jenny. How about it, Mr. Ra? Can we stay looking like ourselves?"

"If that is what you wish," Ra said, "then it will be so."

They all considered the rough map in silence, then Ra added, "The tomb is cut out of the cliffside. There is a level, open area above. Usually guards would pass by it on their patrols. Tonight they will not. It is like this . . ."

He sketched out the area, marking a few large obstacles.

"These are rocks, left from cutting away the stone when the tomb was made."

"They may provide some cover," Eddie said, but his tone expressed doubt.

Ra drew a few more marks.

"These are where the rubble cleared from the tunnels was placed. The mounds are about waist high on a man—an Egyptian man, not one of you English giants."

"Very good," Neville said.

Neville gestured toward the map.

"If we have Jenny and Rashid go inside, that leaves three of us to handle the men outside. I suggest we space ourselves out. Behind those rocks," he pointed to three, "should be best. At a prearranged signal, we make some sort of noise, try to spook them."

He glanced over at Ra.

"What's the lighting situation?"

"Lighting?" Ra looked amused. "The thieves may have paid off the guards, but there is still reason for them to take care. The only lights are for those working in the tomb itself. These are small lamps burning fat. They give some light, but the robbers work more by touch."

"I expect so," Neville agreed. "Time enough to inspect their loot when they're safely away. What is the phase of the moon?"

"Khons is a waning crescent," Ra answered, "but the night is clear and at the time you will arrive he will give some light."

"Enough to let them get a good look at us," Neville said. "That's just fine. You told Jenny we can't bring firearms, but can we bring anything else?"

"What you are wearing," Ra said, "and perhaps a few other small things, within reason."

"You already said we could have our knives," Neville said, "but we're hoping not to kill anyone. How about a stout short club for each of us, some lengths of rope, writing paper, ink, and pens?"

Ra looked amused.

"These are not unreasonable."

Jenny admired how her uncle was acting, treating the matter as it was part of his normal day's work to plan operations into the past—or was it future?—at the behest of a variety of theriomorphic creatures who just might possibly be gods. She decided to imitate him.

"I'd also like my doctor's bag," she said. "We're going to do our best not to harm anyone, but that doesn't mean the robbers will feel the same way—or we might hurt one of them. Is that reasonable?"

Ra inclined his hawk head, gestured, and Jenny's familiar bag appeared on the sand next to the map. He made a second gesture, producing this time the rope and the clubs. Wordlessly, Eddie handed these out.

Jenny noted that her supply of rope had already been cut into lengths just about perfect to use to tie someone up. The clubs were about the size of a policeman's billy—to which they bore more than a passing resemblance. She wondered if Ra had somehow drawn an image out of Uncle Neville's mind and reproduced it.

She tucked the lengths of rope into her bag, then slid the bag's straps over her shoulders so that her hands would be free—a neat adaptation designed by a mountain man who had stayed with her family while his broken ankle was mending. Swinging the club to accustom herself to its weight and heft, she tried to look as if she coshed people on a regular basis.

Neville glanced around the circle.

"Everyone comfortable with their part in this?"

Stephen cleared his throat.

"We haven't asked just how many men we'll be dealing with."

"Ten or so," Ra replied, cooperative as ever. "Several will be within the tomb, several positioned along the tunnel to hand out items as they are secured, and the rest are above ground, packing away those things that have been stolen, and watching just in case their bribes were not enough to keep away guards who might find a profit in turning them in—after taking a bribe in advance."

"We'll worry about the ones in the tunnel later," Neville decided. "Above and below first."

He turned and looked squarely at Jenny.

"Are you sure you're up to this, Jenny? We might be better off keeping you and your medical kit above—in fact, the more I think about it, the better I like that idea."

Jenny shook her head.

"I'm going down. I have a feeling any of the rest of you would be crowded."

Rashid laid his hand lightly on her arm.

"Except for Rashid, of course," she said.

The Egyptian youth beamed, then handed Mischief to Ra. Club in hand, he stood ready for whatever was to come.

Jenny attempted to mirror Rashid's attitude, but she knew she didn't seem nearly so confident.

Neville tried hard not to think about the task he was about to undertake. It was so much easier to plan if he thought of this as just another military action, leaving out where, when, and against whom this action was going to occur.

To his surprise, he found this selective amnesia worked. After his attempt to convince Jenny to take a different post had failed—an effort he had suspected was futile, but one he had to make—he looked around his group.

"All right, you two who are staying with me, pick your positions."

Predictably, Eddie chose the post closest to the opening of the tomb, Stephen the one farthest back. Neville thought it showed wisdom on both of their parts. Whatever Neferankhotep's physician had done for him had mended Neville's newer injuries, but the ones he had sustained all those years before remained, limiting his mobility.

Eddie's post placed him behind one of the rubble heaps, and he looked over at Ra.

"Will we be visible from the moment we appear?"

"That is so," Ra said.

Eddie hunkered down in a crouch.

"You said the rubble heaps were about waist high, so this should give me a moment to reconnoiter."

Stephen licked his lips, obviously nervous, but still game.

"The rock I've chosen," he asked, "how high is it?"

Ra made a gesture about four feet off the ground.

"This is where they have picketed their donkeys," he said. "Does that change your mind?"

"Not as long as I don't land right on a donkey," Stephen said. "I might be useful there."

Neville mentally kicked himself for not asking such an obvious question. The tomb robbers would not have gone to such trouble only to settle for what they could carry off in their pockets.

"Can you tell us where the robbers themselves will be?"

Ra considered, "I think that would be too much. Even though they desecrate this tomb, they are, after their own fashion, my worshippers as well—many of them more so than the king whose tomb we move to defend."

With this cryptic comment, Ra turned to Jenny and Rashid.

"Into which room do you wish to be placed?"

Jenny glanced at Rashid, then indicated the larger, central room.

"This one okay? I figure everyone has to go through there. If we go further back, they may just wall us up."

The Egyptian youth nodded.

"They may try that anyhow," Eddie said. "You're going to be on the wrong side of that tunnel."

Jenny gave him a grin.

"We're counting on you to make sure that tunnel stays open."

"Are you prepared?" Ra asked.

Neville watched as four heads nodded, then he turned to Ra.

"We're ready."

Ra nodded stiffly, and raised his hands as in benediction. A glow of golden light as of the rising sun wrapped them each around, then almost instantly began to fade. Neville felt the surface under his boot soles change from smooth sand to sand interspersed with broken chunks of rock.

Better watch my footing, he thought. Then the time for thought had ended.

Despite the brilliance of Ra's translation, Neville found he could see perfectly—or at least as well as the natural light permitted. Within a moment he had located four men.

One was standing at the entrance to the tomb, accepting an irregularly shaped bundle a second man was handing out to him. A third man was crossing the open area between the entrance to the tomb and the slightly higher ground where the donkeys were tied. As he passed Neville's hiding place, Neville caught the odor of a strong, musky perfume from the objects he carried slung back to front over his broad shoulders. A fourth man, only partially visible, was busy packing bundles onto the mules. All four men were stripped to the waist, though the night was not oppressively hot. Indeed, Neville guessed the season to be sometime in the winter.

There was a rhythm to their labors, to the way the man in the entrance to the tomb handed out his bundles, to the way the second man secured them about his person, to the steady tread of the man crossing to the donkeys, that suggested they had been about their labors for some time now, and expected to continue working a good deal longer.

There was no excitement, no eagerness, though they must be handling fortunes in every load—especially when compared to their daily earnings. Nor was there any fear, neither of gods or of men. The tomb robbers were doing a job, a job at which they were very good, and that was all.

Then the man nearest to the donkeys let out a scream of raw wordless terror. Its high shrill notes falling to guttural moans cut through the nighttime silence like lightning through a storm-darkened sky.

Neville had been worried that sound might bring attentive guards, but no one would come into a graveyard after hearing that horror-stricken cry. Even the most devout would believe that the gods were taking a hand in daily affairs.

The man crossing toward the donkeys froze, uncertain what to do. Neville didn't give him a chance to decide. Moving as stealthily as possible, he swung his club, catching the man hard behind the knees and dropping him onto his loincloth-covered backside. The thief fell with a thud, releasing so strong an odor of flowers and exotic spices that Neville nearly stepped back in revulsion.

Instead he stepped forward, letting the man see his pale features, his un-Egyptian beard and slightly curling hair. The man's eyes widened in terror. He tried to surge to his feet, though whether to run or to fight, Neville would never know, for his feet slipped in the costly oils spilled on the ground around him. He fell onto his knees, and remained there, trembling.

Eddie was not having as easy a time of it. He had gone for the men in the doorway of the tomb. Perhaps there was courage in numbers, perhaps the surrounding stone had deadened the sound of their fellow's cry, perhaps these two were made of stronger stuff, but the man on the outside wheeled, dodging Eddie's cudgel with lithe, muscular grace. He swung at Eddie, a bare-fisted punch that argued he was a brawler. Eddie dodged, but now the other man was crawling out of the tomb entrance, eager to join the fray.

Neville looked down at his oil-soaked and trembling victim, and made a quick decision. He could hear Stephen saying something back among the donkeys. If Neville waited to tie up his man, Eddie might be badly hurt. Who knew how many others would emerge from below? For a fleeting moment, Neville wished desperately to know how things were going for Jenny, then he knew he could not spare the concentration.

"Stephen! I've one here, hurry!"

Stephen's glad-sounding response came instantly, and Neville limped as fast as he could to where Eddie had backed up against a rubble mound and was whaling away with his cudgel. One of his opponents had a mace-like weapon and was swinging at Eddie with this. The other had a simpler club. Neither appeared to have knives or swords.

But then worked metal would be expensive, Neville thought, *and I doubt their authorities like armed peasantry any more than ours do.*

"I'm coming, Eddie!" he called, hoping that the sound of his voice would prove a distraction.

The man with the mace checked his blow, turning to face this new intruder. Although he handled his weapon with confidence, his eyes were wild. He might not have broken at the sound of his fellow's scream, but clearly he was shaken by the appearance of these peculiar guardians.

"Who paid you, barbarian? Who paid you? Was it Pawara? I knew he'd cross us!"

All of this was gasped out between ferocious swings of his mace.

"Pawara didn't send us," Neville replied, blocking some blows with his mace, dodging others. "Ra did. We have ridden the Boat of Millions of Years with Ra, and have looked on the face of Anubis, protector of the dead."

The mace wielder looked properly terrified, but he didn't stop fighting.

No wonder, Neville thought. *He knows he's damned if he dies now and goes to Osiris with this on his soul. Tomb robbing violates the Negative Confessions—and I bet he's violated a few others, too. Better, as he sees it, to fight and hope to escape, and make amends later.*

Eddie's opponent had been disheartened by his fellow's shift in focus, but he continued working at Eddie, taking full advantage of the uneven footing nearer to the rubble heap. But Eddie was not only a soldier trained in the rough service of Her Majesty's Army. He had spent the last ten years living between the worlds in an Egypt that didn't know what to make of him—and that tested that uncertainty with violence.

Eddie countered his man's blows with evident ease, then after the first panicked frenzy had let up, began beating him back. His attitude was so matter-of-fact and methodical that it, rather than any single swing, broke his opponent's morale.

The tomb robber savagely blocked one of Eddie's blows, almost knocking Eddie's club from his hand. Taking advantage of the momentary interruption, he turned to flee, his own club extended half behind him as he ran. Eddie reached out and caught hold of it, jerking hard. The man lost his balance and reeled a few steps before Eddie hit him and he went down.

Neville had caught glimpses of this while blocking his own opponent's increasingly erratic attacks. The man's intensifying fear didn't make Neville's fight any easier. The blows might have less concentrated force behind them, but Neville began to feel that they might land anywhere. One wild swing did graze Neville across the back of his left hand, the sharpened edge of the bit of stone or metal set in the heavy wood slicing the skin open as neatly as a razor.

It was a messy cut, but when Neville flexed his fingers they moved unhindered. He swore, and the man actually cringed back a step—apparently more afraid than triumphant at wounding this self-proclaimed champion of the gods.

Momentarily spurred to anger by the surge of pain, Neville swung down hard. He heard the thief's collarbone crack beneath the impact and instantly regretted his own violence. The man went down on his knees, dropped the mace and cowered. Neville closed on him, kicking the mace out of the way, and resisting a rather absurd impulse to apologize. He knew perfectly well that the man wouldn't have felt the least regret if he'd gotten the upper hand.

Panting slightly, Stephen came trotting over, two lengths of rope dangling from his hand.

"You'd better wrap that hand, Neville," he said. "I'll tie this one up."

The thief, looking up in sudden hope when Neville didn't kill him, cringed in horror at his first sight of Stephen's pale blonde hair and sunburned face.

"I keep having this effect on people," Stephen said cheerfully. "Well, I'm blond and determined to be fair."

Neville grinned.

"Your man under control, Eddie?"

"Yes," Eddie replied, but his voice sounded distracted.

"Did he hurt you?"

"No," Eddie paused long enough to jerk his man over to one side, clear of the entrance to the tunnel. "But I don't like the sound of what's coming out of the tunnel."

He had hardly finished speaking when one thief, followed closely by another, burst onto the surface. Eddie readied his club and closed the first. Neville headed for the second, yelling to Stephen to secure the prisoners and keep a close eye for anyone attracted by the noise.

The emerging men seemed infuriated, terrified, or both, but there was no time to determine whether their discovery of what had happened to their above ground colleagues or something else had triggered the mood.

Jenny, what's going on down there? Neville thought desperately. Then his man was swinging at him and another man was emerging from the tunnel, and once again, he had no time to spare for the luxury of thought.

Sweet Balm

JENNY EMERGED from the glow of Ra's brilliance into a flickering flame-lit dimness that reflected from the warm hue of pure gold. The sources of the light were three or four clay lamps perched on various pieces of furnishing so elaborately carved and painted, she grasped only details, not items as a whole.

There was the head of a hippopotamus, strangely elongated. Another of a lion. There was a statue of man, his skin as black as ebony, but with Egyptian, rather than Nubian, features. There was a hand with gently curved fingers, part of a larger painting, hidden by odds and ends heaped in front of it. The corner of a painted box showed a man in a chariot. A heap of wickerwork lay tumbled on the floor.

As soon as her mind had registered this, Jenny was aware that not all the chaos in these initial impressions was due to the flickering light. The room in which she stood had been well and thoroughly ransacked. Incredibly embroidered garments were spilled out on the floor, the boxes that had held them turned on their sides. A beaded sandal lay on its edge, looking oddly pathetic. A small jar had spilled some dark powder onto the stone floor. Its mate stood upright, but with its lid poorly set, as if it had been opened, the contents inspected, and dismissed as being with-out value.

Jenny was aware of Rashid's warmth where he stood at her shoulder, of the closeness of air little circulated for long years, and then, so overwhelmingly that it was hard to separate from its surroundings, the odor of perfume, the essence of flowers, musk, and rare spices, so concentrated that she wondered if her lungs could find air to breathe.

She took a few panting breaths, just to assure herself that she could indeed breathe, then Rashid had touched her lightly on the arm and pointed down.

A man—or rather the backside of a man—protruded into the room from be-neath what Jenny now realized was one of the long couches so prevalent in depic-tions of Egyptian domesticity. The couch was shaped like an animal of some sort, a cross between a hippo and a crocodile. Reminded of Ammit, Jenny wondered that the man had the courage to crawl beneath it.

But then he hasn't met Ammit. He doesn't know that she is real.

The top of the couch was loaded down with treasures, but apparently these were nothing compared to whatever was in the room beyond, for the thief's atten-tion was concentrated on what was below. They could hear his voice, muffled by the thickness of the walls.

Rashid held up his hand, two fingers raised.

Jenny nodded. It did seem likely there were two of them—one within the chamber on the other side of the wall, and this one half in and half out, doubtless relaying things to where they could be ferried to the surface.

That reminded her that Ra had indicated there were three doors into this room. Jenny quickly located the hole in the door that must lead to the tunnel to the surface. It was dark, but when she stepped closer, remaining to one side so that she would not silhouette herself against the comparative brightness of the room, she thought she could hear movement on the other side.

There was a small stack of what looked like wine or water bottles stacked on the floor near the hole, and a thin line of drops leading back to the hole beneath the Ammit couch.

Got it, Jenny thought. *They're removing something liquid from that inner room. Perfume I guess or scented unguents. Ungulates, as Stephen would say.*

She was aware of a desire to giggle, to share her joke with Rashid, and knew it for nerves.

Smart of the thieves, she thought, forcing herself to think clearly. *Gold or carvings marked with the pharaoh's name might be harder to sell—at least if you didn't want people to know right off you'd been robbing burials—but perfume might come from anywhere, and there'd be a good market for it right here in Thebes, with all the temples and tombs.*

Rashid touched her arm again and indicated the third door. It was right where Ra had told them it would be, but harder to find since it wasn't so much a door as a small hole cut in the wall where the door would be. The space was flanked by two matching statues, magnificent depictions of pharaoh as a warrior holding spear and some other weapon. His skin was shining black, his trappings all of gold.

They must have been intended to defend the king, Jenny thought. *Well, they haven't done much of a job, but they needn't worry. We're here now.*

She put her lips near Rashid's ear.

"Can you find out if anyone is through that hole now?"

He nodded.

Jenny kept her attention on the man beneath the Ammit couch. His hindquarters were wriggling slightly, as if he was beginning to work his way backwards. A small cascade of pebbles announced that someone was coming back down the tunnel. She felt her heart beat wildly.

Rashid touched her arm, pointed to the hole behind, nodded and tapped his ear.

Someone in there. Rashid could hear him. He doesn't seem worried, though, so whoever it is must seem busy.

Rashid had moved to the side of the tunnel entrance. He picked up one of the wineskins, sniffed it, and wrinkled his nose. Then a mischievous expression crossed his face. He pointed to the tunnel, then to himself, then to Jenny, then to the man under the couch. This one was clearly extracting himself.

Lastly, Rashid handed Jenny one of the waterskins. It was filled almost to bursting with some oily substance. He mimed opening the top, then squeezing.

Jenny grinned at him.

"I like it," she mouthed, and stepped back to let her intended victim get free.

He did so, revealing in the flickering lamp light a hooked-nose face, pock-marked from some disease.

"This is the last of it," he said, obviously not realizing that the indistinct figure standing to one side was not one of his associates come to help bear away the loot. "Taneni's looking to see what else . . ."

He stopped, realizing that not only was Jenny not one of his gang, but that she was like no one he had ever seen before. He drew in breath to shout, and Jenny hit him full in the face with a jet of perfumed oil from the waterskin in her hands. It simultaneously choked and gagged him, leaving him sputtering, rubbing his eyes to clear away the stinging oil.

Jenny grabbed the tomb robber by the shoulders, her hands slipping slightly until she got purchase on the back of his loin wrap. She dragged him forward fairly easily. She had never been particularly weak, and the rigors of the journey had toughened her further. Moreover, her captive was small and light, clearly chosen for this post—as she and Rashid had been—because of his build.

The man started to struggle, but as soon as he blinked the worst of the oil from his eyes, Jenny had made sure her very un-Egyptian features were visible to him. Whether these or the sight of Rashid standing poised and ready were what subdued him, Jenny had no trouble getting him to lie on his stomach while she bound his hands and ankles. She gagged him with a bit of linen from one of the spilled coffers.

Rashid had returned his attention to the tunnel, and Jenny kept a ready eye on the hole beneath the Ammit couch from which Taneni might emerge at any time.

"Hem? Taneni?" came a voice from the tunnel. "Something's wrong up top. You might want . . ."

A man's head and shoulders emerged from the top of the door. He was streaked with grime, and scored with numerous small cuts and scratches, doubtless garnered through repeated trips up and down the tunnel in the rubble.

What Hem and Taneni might want to do was interrupted when the thief caught sight of Rashid. As with Jenny's thief—now identified probably as Hem—a gout of scented oil in his face eliminated his ability to struggle effectively.

Jenny didn't see the entirety of this, for Taneni called out, "Hem? What was that? I've set a small stack of interesting stuff by the hole. Get moving with it."

Jenny was readying her club, wondering if she should say something to try to lure Taneni out, when she glimpsed motion from the corner of her eye. A man so thin yet so tall that he reminded her of a serpent was emerging from the hole in the far wall. Unlike the other two who had been caught unaware, this thief had clearly been spying on them for some time. A knife was caught in his teeth, and even as Jenny noticed him, he wriggled through the hole with the hipless dexterity of a snake, regained his feet, and came at her, knife in hand.

She had no oil ready, and couldn't delay for the small moment it would take to grab one of those bags Hem had been bringing out. Her club was ready, though, and she blocked the first downthrust of the knife with ease, noticing as she did so that it was a beautiful thing, worked with gold.

Probably a grave good, she thought. *Doesn't mean he won't know how to use it.*

Her club was awkward to use in the confined space, especially as she didn't want to break anything if she could possibly avoid doing so. A nick along her forearm from her opponent's knife reduced her concern for antiquities considerably. However, her opponent was also limited. His long arms and legs did not move easily in the confined space, and he caught his elbow a solid rap against one of the statues of the king.

I guess they are doing their job, Jenny thought, seeing from the look on the man's face that he'd hit his funny bone, and was in more pain than such a blow would usually occasion.

Taking advantage of his momentary inaction, she drew her club back and down close to her side. Then she brought it up again with all the force she could put behind it, landing hard between his legs.

The dangling fabric of his loincloth absorbed some of the force, but he'd wrapped it tightly, doubtless to make squirming through holes easier. Snake screamed as the club caught his privates, doubling over and dropping his knife.

Jenny was amazed and slightly appalled at the pain she had caused, but she didn't let this stop her from knocking the tall man down. There was a muffled chinking sound as items stuffed into the fabric of his loincloth dropped to the floor, but Jenny had more to worry about than treasure.

Taneni was climbing out from the hole under the Ammit couch, clearly prepared for trouble. He appeared little more than a boy, but carried a knife as if quite ready to use it.

Rashid's back was turned, as he kept watch on the tunnel entrance. Jenny didn't know if she could reach Taneni and keep control of her human snake, who even now was beginning to recover from the shock, murder in his eyes.

"Rashid!" she called out. "Behind you."

The Egyptian youth wheeled and struck Taneni full in the face with oil from a bottle he had ready.

Taneni screamed at him, "Idiot! Do you know what that's worth?"

I wonder if he thought Rashid was one of their own, Jenny thought, giving in to a strange sense of humor.

She'd taken her cue from the pharaohs and stepped on the back of her captive. Using her weight to hold Snake down, she reminded him with a tap of her club on his inner thigh that she was in position to cause him a great deal more pain. The human snake stopped struggling at once.

Rashid dealt with Taneni, and as they were making sure their captives had been secured, Sir Neville's voice came hollow sounding and distant down the tunnel.

"Jenny? Rashid? Are you all right?"

Jenny glanced at Rashid, who grinned at her, tapping his throat in an unnecessary reminder that he couldn't speak. She stepped over to the hole in the door.

"We're fine," she called. "Only a few scrapes."

In truth, the nick from Snake's knife hurt quite a bit, but she'd already seen it wasn't dangerous.

"We've collected six," Neville called. "How about you?"

"Four here. Three were working the chambers, a fourth came out of the tunnel."

"And the sarcophagus? Is the pharaoh's body intact?"

Jenny glanced at Rashid who shrugged, then indicated he would check. A moment later he returned, his eyes shining with wonder, a quiet smile on his face. He almost seemed to have forgotten his own mission, then he shook himself and gave a thumbs up gesture.

"All intact," Jenny called. "What do we do with our prisoners?"

"It would be best if we had them up here," Neville said. "Air's going to get pretty thick."

"Air's already pretty thick," Jenny replied. "They were stealing perfumed oils along with the other stuff. Some of it got spilled."

"See if you can convince them to climb up, one at a time. We'll secure them as they emerge. Stephen's drafting a note that may buy their lives—if they'll turn Queen's Evidence, that is."

Jenny heard Stephen's voice say faintly, "Pharaoh's evidence."

"Right," Jenny called.

The thieves, beaten, bound, and thoroughly demoralized now that they realized that their captors were very strange strangers indeed, offered no trouble at all when given the opportunity to climb up. Snake made a grab for the cloth-wrapped packet he had dropped, but Jenny knocked his hand away.

"That belongs to the pharaoh," she said. "If it didn't before, it does now. Consider it an offering for your life."

That cowed him, and from that moment forward he was the most cooperative of the captives.

As the thieves made their climb one by one, Jenny took the time to clean her cut. The blade had been honed so sharp the wound probably wouldn't even scar, and she took a moment to inspect the weapon. The blade was chipped from obsidian and glittered beautifully in contrast to the duller glow of the gold in the haft.

She and Rashid took turns inspecting the other chambers. When Jenny crawled through the hole that led back to the burial chamber, she instantly understood the awed look in Rashid's eyes. The entirety of it was sheathed in gold, apparently from portable walls that had been carried down. These were closed, and she didn't need to be an Egyptologist to guess that the pharaoh's coffin rested on the other side.

Let him stay there undisturbed, she thought. *Not only would that please his gods, it's nice to think that something has been left untouched.*

The room adjoining the burial chamber proved to be full of beautiful items, these oriented more toward the sacred than secular care of the pharaoh. Dominating it all was a tall shrine, guarded by four goddesses whose expressions were heartbreakingly wistful, as if they knew their task was for all eternity, and somehow futile.

Taneni had completely wrecked the other room. The jars from which he had looted the oils stood open. Others, smelling of soured wine and beer, stood with their seals broken open. Furniture and items of clothing were up-ended this way and that, yet with a sense of method, as if the boy had searched carefully, but with no care for damage to what he could not remove.

Yet, despite the beauty, the glow of gold, the elegant treasures demanding further inspection, Jenny was glad when her turn came to climb out. The place was somehow sad. Remembering how Neferankhotep had requested he be buried simply, so that his people could be taken care of rather than his kingdom's wealth being buried away, Jenny thought it was rather a pity they had been forced to stop the thieves. As the marks of illness on Hem's face attested, the gauntness and look of underfeeding that marked each thief, their lives were far from easy.

Neville was unaccountably relieved when Jenny's tired and dirt-smeared face appeared at the top of the tunnel, happy when Rashid, slightly less battered looking, appeared after.

"Stephen's working on a note," he said, explaining to cover his relief. "We're leaving it along with these fellows, and the open tomb—a reminder that the attendants should be watching more carefully."

"How do we know someone won't come looting before honest guards arrive?" Jenny asked worriedly.

"We thought of that," Neville assured her. "We didn't have much trouble getting one of the thieves to talk. In fact, after he got a look at Stephen, it was all we could do to get him to stop talking."

Stephen looked up from where he was laboring over a piece of paper.

"Handsome is as handsome does," he said complacently, "and here it seems my fair-haired beauty does nicely indeed."

"For scaring the . . ." Neville swallowed and started again. "For thoroughly frightening people, your appearance certainly does something."

He returned his attention to Jenny. The young woman was grinning at him, probably because of his rapid self-censorship.

"Our talkative friend told us where we could find an honest priest," Neville went on. "Eddie has gone to drop a few significant hints."

"Won't the priest find him rather odd-looking?" Jenny asked. "I mean, Eddie's darker than Stephen, but he still doesn't look like an Egyptian."

"All the better," Neville said, with more confidence than he felt. He'd raised the same objection. "As Eddie said, if the priest sees an odd-looking fellow, his curiosity will be aroused—but Eddie doesn't plan on being seen. It's dark, and there will be plenty of shadows."

"How does this sound?" Stephen interrupted. He cleared his throat and read rather self-consciously. "'Amon-Ra watches over the young king. Behold! These men were seized while attempting to loot the pharaoh's tomb. Make their trial public so that all may know the terrible fate that awaits those who violate these sacred premises, yet show mercy to those who, though sworn to guard and honor, were easily bribed to blindness. Justice must be mitigated by mercy. Remember! Your soul will be weighed against Maat.'"

Neville leaned over to inspect the neat hieroglyphs.

"That's pretty elegant work for such a fast job," he said, wondering once again if Stephen was the Sphinx. The handwriting didn't look the same, but . . .

"I hope I didn't spell anything too terribly wrong," Stephen confessed. "I wish I had my grammars."

"Why did you say Amon-Ra, rather than just Ra?" Jenny asked curiously.

Stephen relaxed, comfortable in his pedantry.

"I saw that several of the items the thieves had carried out referred to either Amon alone, or Amon-Ra, and recalled that in the New Kingdom Amon became one of the most important gods. I thought I might as well invoke him, and since Ra was our escort here, I didn't want to leave him out."

"How kind of you," a familiar even voice said. Ra had appeared, standing just out of sight of where the prisoners sat bound among their donkeys. "Is all complete?"

"As complete as we can make it," Neville said, resisting the impulse to snap "sir," as he might have to a superior officer. "We only need for Eddie to return."

"I shall gather him to me," Ra said. "He has delivered his message successfully, and already the faithful one is summoning his litter and a legion of torchbearers."

Stephen studied his note and rapidly wrote a few more characters.

"What are you doing?" Neville asked.

"Adding a postscript that they should tidy up the tomb before resealing it. From what we've seen, it's probably a mess."

He finished, and used a looted statuette to anchor his note in a visible spot in front of the huddle of bound prisoners.

"It is," Jenny agreed, "and it smells like a brothel."

Neville cocked an eyebrow at her, "And how would you know what a brothel smells like, young lady?"

"Easy," she said. "Who do you think Papa sent in when he had a patient in one? You don't think Mama would let *him* go in, do you?"

Somewhere in the laughter that followed this statement, Ra gathered them into the light of his presence, and when the glow dimmed to gentle gold they were again standing before Neferankhotep.

They were no longer in the Hall of Judgment, but in a beautiful chamber that combined the best of the indoors and outdoors. There were pools of water and banks of flowers, but also elegant furnishings, and ornamented pillars that appeared to hold the sky upon their fluted tops. Music was supplied both by chorusing birds, and by the harps and sistrums of perfectly beautiful young women.

Although still attired as Osiris, Neferankhotep seemed more relaxed. His feet were no longer bound, and he sat in casual comfort on a gilded stool, playing senet with the physician. A pretty woman leaned over his shoulder, offering her opinions on the best strategies. Everyone was laughing.

"My wife, Menwi," Neferankhotep said, introducing the beautiful woman. Then, "You have been successful?"

"We have been," Neville said. "The pharaoh's tomb is saved from those who would have looted it, and his future safety secured to the best of our ability."

Ra nodded, "I can confirm this, and that it was done without the taking of life."

"Very good," Neferankhotep said. He was about to say something more when Jenny broke in.

"Your Majesty, the tomb we saved, is it safe forever?"

"Forever is a very long time," Neferankhotep said. "However, I can say that in your own day and time, it remains secure."

Jenny nodded. Mozelle emerged from where she had been sleeping on a heap of pillows and padded across to Jenny, pausing to meow imperiously at the pharaoh before pawing at the hem of Jenny's robe in a command that she be picked up. The musicians gathered their instruments and departed, as did the physician and Menwi. Ra remained, silent as the painted decorations on the walls.

I wonder if we keep the cat, Neville thought, *or if she is indeed some sort of goddess, and so will remain.*

He wondered other things as well, and Neferankhotep's next words anticipated the questions he was trying to find a polite way to ask.

"You have done well," Neferankhotep said, "and will win freedom from punishment for Audrey Cheshire. She and Sarah Syms will be brought to you shortly. However, before you meet with them, you must understand that you have won something else as well."

No one said anything, but the question was almost a physical presence in the silence. Even the birds fell silent as if waiting for the pharaoh's next words.

Neferankhotep continued, "You have won the right to eternal paradise. You have been judged and vindicated. There is no need for you to return to your world and its difficulties. Everything you could desire is here."

Certainly that seemed possible. The tranquility and beauty of Neferankhotep's garden was tantalizing, as was the hint that beyond the delicately carved stonework gateway lay other gardens, other fields, beautiful rivers, towering mountains—in short, anything one could desire.

Neville felt a tug at his heart. It would be very nice to stay. He wondered if the remaining stiffness from his old injuries would vanish. He was feeling the first touch of age's long fingers. Here he would never grow old, and if Audrey stayed with him, paradise might hold new delights as well as preservation of old.

Eddie was shaking his head.

"I hope you don't intend to try and keep us, sir," he said. "I have a wife and children I need to get home to."

"You will not be kept from them," Neferankhotep assured him. "Nor do all of you need to make the same decision. Those who remain will simply have died on this venture into the unexplored desert. It does happen."

"Too frequently," Eddie agreed. "However, I'll take my risks with living."

Stephen looked around rather forlornly. Neville didn't doubt that he was comparing this luxury with his straitened circumstances back in London. But Stephen, too, shook his head.

"I need to go back," he said. "My mother and sisters depend on me—and there's still so much research to do, so much to learn. I suspect I won't be talking about these discoveries . . ."

"No," Neferankhotep said. "No evidence will remain to support your claims. You would ruin rather than enhance your reputation."

Stephen looked momentarily sad, then he brightened.

"But no one can take what I've learned. That will certainly help."

"Without a doubt," the pharaoh agreed.

Neville sighed. He had no family but Jenny, but there were others who depended on him, friends who would mourn him. He'd be selfish to abandon them.

"I'll go back, too," he said.

Jenny reached out and squeezed his hand, "And I'll go with you, just so you have a new problem to keep your mind occupied."

She looked at Neferankhotep.

"Do I get to keep Mozelle?"

"That is up to her," the pharaoh said.

Mozelle purred, but she also jumped down from Jenny's hold. Maybe it was to get a drink of water. Maybe not. Now the only one left was Rashid.

He bowed deeply to the pharaoh, then made a gesture that encompassed the others, and pointed up.

"He, too, wishes to go."

Neville looked at the youth. "If you want to return to England with us, you would be welcome. If you wish to remain in Egypt, I will be happy to speak to various people on your behalf."

Rashid then did something curious. He turned to Stephen and made a gesture as if scribbling.

"You want pen and paper?" Stephen said. "I thought you couldn't write."

Rashid repeated the writing gesture, and Stephen handed him the necessary articles, still contained in the box in which he had carried them through time.

Rashid sat cross-legged on the floor, a fresh sheet of paper on the box braced against his knee. He wrote perhaps a dozen words, then showed them to Neville.

"Before you offer me your kindness," they said, *"you must know. I am the Sphinx."*

Jenny felt her head swim as reality adjusted itself far more strikingly than it had done when Ra carried them back in time. She had long thought Rashid was more intelligent than Captain Brentworth believed, a belief Rashid had validated by his actions once they had all been taken into Tuat. However, Jenny had never dreamed Rashid was well-educated enough to be the Sphinx.

"What?" she said, her question echoed by all the others, and Rashid began again to write, positioning himself so that the others could read over his shoulders.

"I was born in Cairo, and when I was very small a fever came. It killed all my family but for me, and me it left mute. I was fortunate, however. My parents had loyal friends, and these secured for me a place in an orphanage.

"It was a good orphanage, run by English who were interested in providing an educated population for Egypt, one that would be free from the usual clan and family ties. They thought that such might be the answer to some of Egypt's factional problems."

"I think I know that place," Neville said, sounding mildly surprised. "I gave some money to it when I came into my inheritance. Sent some books for the library when I merged my library with my father's."

Rashid gestured so eloquently to be permitted to continue his tale that Jenny felt a wash of pity. How horrible for an intelligent young man to be forced to act like an idiot. Her pity transformed into anger as she thought of the daily misery of that life. Maybe it wasn't so sad after all that Captain Brentworth had ended his life impaled on Apophis's fang.

Rashid continued writing:

"Those who ran this orphanage were determined that even a mute boy should be able to make his way in the world. There I learned to read and write, to tend a gentleman as a personal servant, and many other useful things. They were kind to me, and I learned English as easily as I learned the myriad street dialects of Cairo.

"Captain Brentworth took me from this place. Hired me, is the accurate way to state it, but I rapidly learned that my pay would be irregular or devoured in the expenses of my keep. I also learned that he had no interest in my intellectual attainments. Gradually he either forgot I could read and write, or he thought the orphanage had lied to him. In any case, soon he came to believe his own slighting dismissal of my capacities. I also realized that he was less cruel to me when he thought of me as a sort of two-legged dog or horse, not responsible for my own thinking.

"This was not as terrible a life as it might have been. True, I was reduced to menial servitude when I had hoped for better. On the other hand, I never went hungry or without clothing. Captain Brentworth never attempted to keep me from following Islam, nor did he belittle me for doing so. I saw too many starving and sick, too many paying lip service to a religion in which they did not believe, to think my situation the worst it could be.

"Moreover, Captain Brentworth took me to many interesting countries with him, and permitted me to keep Mischief as a pet. I tell you all of this, so you will understand my confusion when I overheard my master speaking with Lady Cheshire as that lady explained her plans to learn what one Sir Neville Hawthorne intended to discover in Egypt, and to take over that project for herself if he would not confide in her.

"I knew the name Neville Hawthorne. When I was in the orphanage, we prayed daily for our benefactors, each by name. More importantly, in the library many of the books I had most enjoyed were inscribed with the Hawthorne name. I listened carefully, and did some research until I confirmed that this Sir Neville and the Neville Hawthorne who had been the benefactor of my childhood were one and the same.

"I was in a terrible dilemma. I had no desire to betray one who had, after all, given me food, clothing, and shelter for many years. Yet I had no desire to be party to a fraud to one who had also done me—and many other bereft children—a kindness. I resolved to warn the one without doing so in such a direct a fashion that it would betray the other. Later, I met all of you, and your courtesy and consideration of myself, one who was only a native servant, encouraged me to continue in my efforts."

Rashid looked a bit sheepish: *"From overhearing what you have said since, I believe I was too clever for my own purpose. I also admit that I was enjoying the game. It was delightful to play at puzzles with those who rose to the challenge."*

Stephen beamed. "I did enjoy them, Rashid. Deuced clever. You'll have to try some others on me now that we've no need to hide your abilities. Tell me, how did you learn hieroglyphs?"

"Lady Cheshire studied them most assiduously. Captain Brentworth did so also. Their books and notes were often left for me to tidy away. It was easy to borrow one or two for my own use during those times they were not in use. I had many years to learn, and I was interested since Lord Cheshire, for whom my master worked for many years, lived and breathed Egyptology."

"How old are you?" Neville asked.

"I don't know precisely, but I believe I am twenty-one or twenty-two. I worked for Captain Brentworth for seven years."

"You look younger," Neville said dubiously.

"You can check the orphanage records," Rashid wrote, and Jenny thought he looked a trace defensive.

"It's just the lack of a beard," Neville said soothingly, "but then many Egyptians are not hairy. So, you're the Sphinx who gave us so many sleepless hours. I think I can forgive you that. Are you interested in a job, or shall I ask around for you in Cairo?"

Jenny realized she was holding her breath. She suddenly knew she didn't want this enigmatic young man to vanish from her life.

"I would be very happy," Rashid wrote, beaming, *"to enter your employ."*

Jenny clapped as if at the conclusion of a play.

Neferankhotep, also looking pleased, cleared his throat.

"The time has come for you to leave us. Audrey Cheshire will be released to you as promised. However, do not expect her to be grateful. You may have won her freedom, but Audrey will not have forgotten that she was judged and found wanting."

"I understand," Neville murmured.

Jenny thought he looked rather nervous. She hurried to distract him.

"And Mrs. Syms," she asked. "Will her mind be healed?"

"She has chosen a reality in which she is more content," Neferankhotep said. "Indeed, we could keep her here, and she might not even know the difference, but I think it best she return to your homeland. Clearly, it is where she wishes to be."

"Lady Cheshire certainly won't abandon her now," Neville said. "Whatever her other flaws, she has always shown kindness to Mrs. Syms."

"That," Neferankhotep agreed, "is true."

He stood, and the crook and flail that were his emblems as both Osiris and pharaoh were in his hands.

"There are many types of kindness," he said, "and many types of law, but in the end truth and justice are the bedrock upon which good lives are built. May you be content with your choice to continue the struggle to build such lives."

He motioned with the flail.

"Walk along the corridor you see before you, and it will return you to the world you have left. Once you leave, do not seek to return, for the way will be forever closed. Your companions will join you."

"Let's go, then," Jenny said. She made a gesture somewhere between a bow and a curtsey, wondering how they would explain their odd attire. "Thank you, Pharaoh Neferankhotep, for everything you have taught me."

Eddie grinned, offering a salaam after the Arab fashion.

"It has been interesting, sir, very. Perhaps someday I'll tell my children tales of this place—but only perhaps."

Neferankhotep's lips moved in one last smile.

"A wise provision. Go now, all of you. I know your hearts and am warmed by the kindness within them. Stay within maat, and perhaps someday we shall meet again."

They passed between a pair of obelisks down the corridor Neferankhotep had indicated—another corridor that had not seemed to be there until needed.

I'm actually getting used to miracles, Jenny thought.

After they had taken a few steps, Jenny glanced back.

The garden courtyard had taken on a two-dimensional quality, becoming like a fresh, bright painting. The musicians had reappeared, but the music they played was lost to her ears. Neferankhotep was playing senet with Ra. Menwi and the physician were re-entering, their hands filled with flowers.

Turning away, Jenny hurried to join the others, and found Mozelle coiling around her ankles. She scooped her up, tears of joy blinding her last view of the colorful scene.

"Corridor gets dark after this turn," Eddie called back, even as Jenny struggled to wipe her eyes clear. "Link hands to shoulders so we'll not lose each other."

They did this, shuffling forward, testing their footing with every step.

"Sand underfoot now," Eddie said. "Step carefully. It slides."

"Are we playing blind man's bluff?" Mrs. Syms asked querulously.

Jenny was opening her mouth to answer when Lady Cheshire's voice spoke, "More like Follow the Leader, Sarah. Don't worry. I think I see light ahead."

She was not mistaken. A single starlike glow grew, blooming into a flower, then clearly into a door. There was the sound of many voices raised in conversation.

"I think I've seen this place," Eddie said, puzzled. "It's the Ramesseum. Somehow, we're back in Luxor!"

"Luxor," Neville said, "but Luxor when?"

Jenny was to the rear of the party, and so she noticed what the men had not—what they were wearing. She was dressed in a walking dress, comfortable shoes, and wide-brimmed hat. One hand held a parasol, the other a guide book. Mozelle bumped against the edges of her skirt, clearly delighted.

The others were also dressed in perfect accord with how they would have been attired for a day of touring. Stephen even had his slightly out-of-date coat and hat, Eddie his flowing Arab robes. They all looked mostly clean and fairly fresh—not as if they had been traveling in the desert for weeks, followed by a sojourn in a subterranean tomb. The reason for this became apparent when they exited the structure they had been "touring" and were met by Reis Awad, the captain of their own dahabeeyah.

"So nearly done with the voyage," he said, "and still you must stop to see the Ramesseum first. You will return to the *Mallard* now. The cook's heart will be broken into shards as fine as sand if you do not dine upon the banquet he has prepared in your honor. The men will sing, and some will dance, though their spirits will be heavy at the thought of losing our favorite passengers."

Jenny wondered how Uncle Neville was going to explain the presence of Lady Cheshire, Mrs. Syms, and Rashid, but Reis Awad continued before anyone could offer an explanation.

"And you have found the English ladies, and the Egyptian scholar. How very fine! Their luggage has been transferred aboard the *Mallard* and we shall take it with your own to the hotel in Luxor but tomorrow, after dinner. Tonight you are our guests."

He beamed at them, and began to usher them along, bustling like a quail hen trailing her brood—though he was as often behind as in front.

Lady Cheshire cleared her throat, and Jenny found her breath coming tight. What would this woman do? And how would Uncle Neville take her rejection?

"Sir Neville," came the precise, lovely voice, "I really must thank you for taking us in. You are too kind."

Jenny listened hard for a note of sarcasm in the beautiful voice, but heard nothing of the sort. She breathed easier, allowing herself to hope, promising herself to watch. She saw something of the same mixed response in Rashid's dark eyes, and they shared a conspiratorial smile.

Stephen and Eddie walked quickly ahead, Eddie pointing out the sights as might any experienced tour guide, Stephen gaping in wonder and delight.